RETHINKING GOOD GOVERNANCE

Praise for the Book

Here is a hugely important book for India and Indians, especially those who should be the guardians of the nation and rulers delivering good governance. Vinod Rai has been at the centre of the structure which counts as the State. He has now exposed the various faults and failures from which the structure suffers.

—Lord Meghnad Desai,
Life Peer at the House of Lords

Anyone seeking to understand the workings of the Indian government should read *Rethinking Good Governance*. This lucid and observant volume offers detailed and scholarly analyses of the country's key accountability agencies—from the Parliament to temple administration—whose functions underpin and affect all facets of life in India. Written with the incisive insights of an insider, Vinod Rai provides a balanced and honest assessment of the public institutions that constitute the pillars of the Indian State and explains how their functioning or failures have come to define the state of parliamentary democracy and governance in India.

—Professor Tan Tai Yong,
President, Yale-NUS College

Unlike China, India has taken the more difficult path of building a democracy along with economic growth. Its democratic institutions are challenged by loosening animal spirits of both its businesses and its politicians. Reining them in is often necessary. Vinod Rai's candid book presents challenges and solutions.

—Arun Maira, business leader; Chairman,
HelpAge International; and
former member of India's Planning Commission

RETHINKING GOOD GOVERNANCE

Holding to Account India's Public Institutions

VINOD RAI

Foreword by
PRANAB MUKHERJEE

Published by
Rupa Publications India Pvt. Ltd 2019
7/16, Ansari Road, Daryaganj
New Delhi 110002

Sales Centres:

Allahabad Bengaluru Chennai
Hyderabad Jaipur Kathmandu
Kolkata Mumbai

Copyright © Vinod Rai 2019

The views and opinions expressed in this book are the author's own and the facts are as reported by him which have been verified to the extent possible, and the publishers are not in any way liable for the same.

While every effort has been made to trace copyright holders and obtain permission, this has not been possible in all cases. References of the works consulted by the author has been provided, but it is possible that it may contain unintentional omissions. Any error brought to our attention will be remedied in future editions.

All rights reserved.
No part of this publication may be reproduced, transmitted, or stored in a retrieval system, in any form or by any means, electronic, mechanical, photocopying, recording or otherwise, without the prior permission of the publisher.

ISBN: 978-93-5333-631-8

Second impression 2019

10 9 8 7 6 5 4 3 2

The moral right of the author has been asserted.

Printed at Nutech Print Services, Faridabad

This book is sold subject to the condition that it shall not, by way of trade or otherwise, be lent, resold, hired out, or otherwise circulated, without the publisher's prior consent, in any form of binding or cover other than that in which it is published.

CONTENTS

Foreword   *vii*

Introduction: Holding to Account   *xi*

1. The Parliament of India: Will It Emerge as the Main Pillar of Democracy?   1
2. The Supreme Court: Providing the Bedrock for Good Governance   24
3. The Election Commission: Empowering Citizens to Determine Their Destiny   51
4. The Reserve Bank of India: Protecting the Economy from the Executive   75
5. The Comptroller and Auditor General: The Fifth Pillar of Democracy   96
6. The Central Bureau of Investigation: Is the Citadel Crumbling?   120
7. The Civil Services: Has the Steel Frame Sagged?   139
8. The Central Vigilance Commission: Teeth Must Replace Dentures   162
9. Right to Information: Balancing Power and Accountability   179

10.	Sports Administration: The Priest Becomes More Important than the Deity	200
11.	Temple Administration: More than Divine Intervention	222
12.	Case Study: Adarsh Cooperative Housing Society—A Case of the Fence Eating the Crop	244

Epilogue: Towards Robust and Participative Governance   266

Acknowledgements   270

Index   273

FOREWORD

By Pranab Mukherjee

Global history is replete with examples where economic-development effort in countries could not be sustained over time due to the lack of a good governance platform that could incubate and nurture developmental efforts. India's experience of a vibrant parliamentary democracy is targeted at ensuring an inclusive development agenda that seeks to empower people and promote transparency in administration.

Policy formulation is certainly the prerogative of any elected government. However, what are the responsibilities and duties factored into this power? Is there total discretion, with no accountability imposed upon the persons exercising this power? Do the people who elect them not have the right to expect a certain ethical standard from those who exercise this fiduciary trust? The time has come that these questions need to be asked and have to be answered by those in positions of power. This is fundamental for the preservation of our nation and a truly democratic society. Democracy will be the loser if those in power cease to hear voices other than their own.

Our governance systems have been strengthened by democratic decentralization and the active participation of people in the process of administration. The introduction of local self-government at the grass-roots level has empowered people to ensure transparency and accountability at all levels of administration. It has introduced the element of vigilante in the devolution of public funds and projects, thereby ensuring minimum leakage.

Despite these remarkable achievements, critical gaps in the public decision-making process remain. There is a pressing need, on the one hand to improve organizational capabilities to cater to the increasing demand for services and improvement in the quality of service delivery, and on the other, to improve transparency and accountability. We, therefore, urgently need innovative solutions that will ensure a quantum leap in governance standards.

Considering his long and distinguished innings in public life, Vinod Rai is an eminently suited person to lead this discourse, which holds India's public institutions to account and paves the way for a more active, responsive, sustainable and efficient administration for the country at all levels of the government. *Rethinking Good Governance* is an incisive and objective analysis of India's public institutions, which mirror our national character.

In the last seven decades, the country has established a successful parliamentary democracy, an independent judiciary and strong institutions such as the Election Commission of India, the Comptroller and Auditor General, the Central Vigilance Commission and the Central Information Commission, which sustain and support our democratic structure. However, in the recent past, these institutions have come under severe strain and their credibility has been questioned. There is widespread cynicism and disillusionment with their governance and functioning. This book helps understand the correctives that can restore credibility and win back people's trust to save India's democracy.

Rai presents a scholarly analysis of each of these institutions. He traces their history, highlights their inherent strengths and flaws, offers suggestions to counter their deficiencies and explains how the credibility of these institutions get eroded and how it can be restored.

I have always maintained that disruption in the Parliament is a betrayal of the commitment made to the people. It also provides a helping hand to the government by scuttling the Opposition space. The country needs a parliament that debates, discusses and decides, and not disrupt. The temple of democracy must also provide better oversight over the government.

As an upholder of the rule of law and an enforcer of the right to liberty, the role of the judiciary is sacrosanct. The faith and confidence people have in the judiciary must always be maintained. We need a judiciary that gives justice without delay. It is for this reason that the Constitution invests our independent judiciary, especially the Supreme Court, with extensive jurisdiction over the acts of the legislature and the executive. It is the judiciary that ensures the effectiveness of judicial review. However, judicial activism should not lead to the dilution of the separation of powers, which is a constitutional scheme.

A few months ago, I expressed concern over the alleged tampering and suspicious movement of Electronic Voting Machines (EVMs). The onus of ensuring institutional integrity lies with the Election Commission, and I insisted that the institution put all speculation to rest. After all, only the 'workmen' decide how the institutional 'tools' perform. Fortunately, the position was clarified by a competent authority and the public was assured of the safety and security of the machines that recorded the votes in the last Lok Sabha elections.

The introduction of the Right to Information has been a major positive development in the pursuit of a transparent and accountable government. Similarly, autonomy to institutions such as the Reserve Bank of India, the Election Commission and the Central Vigilance Commission has only made our parliamentary democracy stronger. However, our Constitution provides a delicate balance of power between various institutions of the State. This balance has to be maintained. Each organ of our democracy must function within its own sphere and must not take over what is assigned to others. Any attempt by any organ of the State to overreach will unnecessarily lead to dissonance within the system. It is, therefore, necessary that all constitutional authorities introspect on their respective roles and adhere to the calibrated system of checks and balances, which forms the bedrock of our governance structures.

Any democratic system survives and becomes effective only on the strength of its public institutions. Therefore, good governance must be our unwavering goal. We should improve implementation of the rule of law and a consensual approach. I am of the firm opinion that as long as we have faith in our basic democratic values and the supremacy of our people and the parliamentary processes, we shall be able to tide over any crisis that we may face.

In the final analysis, *Rethinking Good Governance* will go a long way in creating public awareness for robust and participative governance, so important in a parliamentary democracy. I am confident that this book will encourage much discussion and debate on the direction that the country's public institutions must take in the years ahead.

I, therefore, commend and dedicate *Rethinking Good Governance* to every citizen concerned about India's democratic future.

Pranab Mukherjee
(Former President of India)

INTRODUCTION
Holding to Account

Accountability institutions script the destiny of nations. They support good governance, which in turn promotes sustainable economic development and thereby nurtures the welfare of people. The most vital bond between a people and its government is that of trust, and it is these accountability institutions that help maintain that trust. The transparency and openness seen in any society, the readiness with which it can indulge in creative disruption, and the ease with which the rule of law is permitted to prevail are important indicators of an able administration. It is on the strength of these institutions that the distance between 'the ruler and the ruled' gets reduced and the 'ruler' is made accountable to the 'ruled'. These institutions serve as the pillars supporting the foundation of any robust and vibrant democracy. Weakening the strength of any of the pillars leads to the democratic edifice being shaken.

Institutions born from the country's Constitution, or from statutes passed by the Parliament, are commonly referred to as horizontal accountability institutions. They are also known as formal institutions as they are part of the formal State apparatus whose rules and regulations are codified. They comprise the Parliament, Supreme Court, Election Commission of India (ECI) and the Central Vigilance Commission (CVC), among others.

They are mandated, either by the Constitution itself or by an act of the Parliament, to check abuses by public institutions and departments of government.

However, more recently, institutions of vertical accountability, or informal institutions, such as the media, citizens' groups or non-governmental organizations (NGOs), have emerged as the keepers of the people's conscience and provide very effective vigilance in government-functioning. Thus, vertical accountability is the means through which citizens, the media and civil society seek to enforce standards of good performance on public institutions. These informal institutions are energized by people's participation and have been instrumental in holding those in authority to account. Their efficacy is borne out by the vigilantism displayed by the people. This vigilantism could be enforced at the ground level where government schemes are under implementation, and citizen groups are analysing government policies or even legally challenging decisions taken by the government.

The capacity of the State to check corruption and ensure probity in administration, post-Independence, has not met with much success. Norms, rules and institutions to ensure transparency and a clean administration abound. The widely perceived inadequacy is in the agents and agencies implementing them. The need of the hour is institutional capability to enforce laws and regulations. Institutional capability should be architectured to incentivize action, which contributes to nation-building, rather than personal aggrandizement. Good governance should encourage correct behaviour and demonstrate the risk of errant behaviour.

The Parliament is the most representative and visible institution upholding democratic values, and accounts for its legitimacy. The challenges facing the Indian Parliament have been immense. Analysis that follows in these chapters points to a distinct decline in recent years in the effectiveness of the

Parliament as an institution of accountability and oversight. Instruments that the Parliament can use for accountability, such as motions on the floor of the House, the quality of debate and the committee system, are increasingly being rendered ineffective and dysfunctional. The Parliament has passed critical legislation such as the Right to Information (RTI) Act, Goods and Services Tax (GST) Act, Insolvency and Bankruptcy Code, and Fiscal Responsibility and Budget Management Act, 2003, as a means of bringing the government under greater fiscal discipline and public oversight. Yet, parliamentary scrutiny of the executive in financial matters remains weak. This is largely due to the tools of oversight not being effectively utilized. The Parliament also faces a daunting challenge as modern legislation places a responsibility upon the capacity and political inclination of Members of Parliament (MPs), who appear to be least inclined to shoulder such responsibility, to attend to legislation. Analysis also reveals that the profusion of political parties in the Parliament, most of which are institutionally weak, has substantially increased the barriers to collective action.

It can be safely surmised that the Parliament's inability to come to terms with these challenges is as much of its own making as it is a consequence of any structural changes in Indian politics. The Parliament is losing efficacy in fiscal management, the economy, social policy and the terms on which India is integrating into the global economy, because of self-abdication and not because of uncontrollable exogenous factors. This is a direct consequence of the calibre of those who enter the Parliament. Considering the number of cases pending against elected members, the greater fear is that those mandated to undertake lawmaking may be lawbreakers themselves. Nothing could be more illustrative of the declining respect for decorum in the Parliament than the then Speaker admonishing the members of the Lok Sabha by making the following observation in the House: 'The whole country is ashamed of its parliamentarians. The Parliament may still be a great institution but its members are no longer great men. How long can a great institution remain great in the hands of small men.'[1] This decline in the image of the Parliament requires immediate corrective action if it has to rejuvenate itself and establish trust between itself and the people it represents.

A survey of institutional autonomy around the world would reveal that prevalence of evidence of accountability and transparency has supported reform and hence sustainable economic development. In India, a strong judicial and constitutional culture supports good governance. The judiciary supports fundamental rights and thereby enhances citizens' personal security and ability to pursue developmental goals. A proactive Supreme Court, unmindful of the mindset of the executive, has been instrumental in striking down government legislation that interferes with constitutional provisions and transgresses into the liberties of the common man. The Court, in seven decades of Independent India, has shown remarkable dynamism in interpreting the Constitution and ensuring that the welfare of the common man remains paramount. In a country where disregard for the law is more commonplace than regard for it, and where governments often err in their responsibilities towards public welfare and sustainable goals, the Court has, time and again, stepped in to be the course corrector. It is looked upon as a bulwark, which protects the common man from arbitrary use of power by the State and its functionaries. This has provided the citizen the confidence that their liberties and constitutional rights are well protected and in safe hands.

Electoral systems are yet another critical pillar of the formal institutional environment that affects commitment to enlightened governance and sustainability of the reform process. The errant

---

[1]Somnath Chatterjee; *Keeping the Faith: Memoirs of a Parliamentarian*; HarperCollins (2014)

among those seeking election and hence political office have had to bow before the indefatigable capacity of the ECI to ensure fair play in the election process. There is evidence to show that alacrity and objectivity in decision-making in the ECI ensure that the wily politician is not able to have his way. The attempts of political parties to circumvent election rigour have also been repeatedly brought to naught by the vigilantism displayed by the ECI. It is this remarkable feature of the ECI which has earned it worldwide credibility and been instrumental in establishing the culture of a robust and 'no-nonsense' electoral system. We examine how, time and again, the ECI has stymied attempts to derail the electoral process and thereby maintained the trust of the citizen in the democratic process of the country.

At the close of elections to the Parliament in May 2019, cash, drugs/narcotics, liquor and precious metal (gold, silver, etc.) worth ₹3,456.22 crore (₹34.56 billion) were seized. It was assessed that this amount was pretty much 90 per cent of the expenditure incurred by the government in conducting the 2014 Lok Sabha election.[2] The Vellore parliamentary constituency in Tamil Nadu made history: it was the first time that the Election Commission countermanded a poll due to abuse of money power in the election process. The dominant feature supporting the autonomy of the ECI is the fact that it is a creation of the Constitution and hence not beholden to any political dispensation, thereby facilitating decision-making purely on merit. This pillar of the Indian democracy has been a stellar feature in ensuring good governance.

Good governance also requires accountability, which necessitates effective monitoring and answerability. The use

---

[2] Mukesh Rawat; 'Seizure worth Rs 34,56,22,00,000 during 2019 LS polls: How drugs, cash, gold & booze kept netas busy'; India Today; 16 April 2019; https://www.indiatoday.in/elections/lok-sabha-2019/story/campaign-cash-drugs-alcohol-gold-seizures-election-commission-updates-1501954-2019-04-16 (accessed on 10 July 2019)

of Supreme Audit Institutions (SAIs) has been an important factor in tracking the devolution of funds and ensuring efficient use of resources across all levels of the government. Globally, democracies are expanding the remit of the national auditor to reflect a transformational shift from the conventional audit of public expenditure to public accountability. Accountability is now the citizen's demand and hence the need to reposition the traditional audit body as an agency that will provide the nation, and the common man, assurance that the government is indeed spending wisely to ensure welfare and economic development. To the extent that these institutions have been given independence from the executive, they have built trust and credibility by ensuring that they hold the executive financially accountable to the legislature. The national auditor has been instrumental in providing objective assessments of the economy, efficiency and effectiveness of government-spending.

Studies of the functioning of religious institutions as well as sports bodies point to the inadequacies of these institutions to cater to their mandate, if they are administratively not well structured. Administration of a religious body has to be premised on an edifice, which not only provides functional efficiency but ensures unfettered facility of worship to devotees. Religious institutions are no different from corporate bodies in ensuring that their administration is founded on probity, efficiency and transparency. The trust and religious fervour among devotees for the deity that inspires them cannot be made a casualty of poor administrative management. The same structural environment is of utmost importance in a sports body. It is commonly said that cricket in India is not a passion, it is a religion. If so, it is all the more necessary that the ethical content in the administration of these institutions is not allowed to diminish.

Transformational and dynamic political leadership, seeking to provide assurance to citizens of being responsive to their needs and aspirations, can nurture good governance by building a capable, professional and independent civil service. This enhances the credibility of the executive for sustainable development, efficient delivery of services and transformation of national plans and development strategies for the welfare of the citizen. The need of the hour is to professionalize the civil service and recruit young people who can be moulded into capable, honest and apolitical officials. This can be done by ensuring requisite mid-career training in a chosen professional sector after the general administrative foundation has been built in each official to ensure that they can manage the complex administration and development agenda that has to be addressed by them at higher levels in the government. The move to laterally induct experienced and professional experts into the public administration setup has been a welcome one. The government must weed out non-performers, provide an incentive for dynamic performance and institute a legal framework which insulates and indemnifies bona fide decisions taken in good faith. A civil service can be effective only when it is allowed to perform on its own merit, strength and capability without any extraneous influences. The present system leaves much to be desired. There is need for a radical overhaul of the civil service to ensure elements of independence, professional capability and the capacity to ignore malevolent external influence. The RTI facility provided to the citizen has made administration more transparent and this should inject strength into the civil service. Self-seeking behaviour among its own, as well as among those who are politically above it, needs to be curbed. These qualities were the hallmark of the service in the past. They need to come to the fore again for the institution to regain its lost lustre.

Transparency requires free and open flow of information. It requires the citizenry to zealously guard its right to hold the government to account. It is only an informed citizenry, the ultimate stakeholder in any democracy, that can ensure an effective and responsive governance structure that creates institutional capability to build an administration premised on an edifice of probity, accountability and transparency.

Such an informed citizenry can be supported by an alert and independent media. The media should have the freedom to investigate and question, yet display maturity and eschew sensationalism. As institutions of vertical accountability, the media and NGOs need to ensure objectivity and independence to build practices of good governance. This is not too tall an order, as has been demonstrated by the Mazdoor Kisan Shakti Sangathan (MKSS)—an association for the empowerment of labourers and farmers—a grass-roots organization in Rajasthan. They were pioneers in seeking transparency in administration, the right to information and corruption-free implementation of government schemes and lobbying for legal and constitutional provisions to improve governance and monitor the conduct of officials implementing government schemes. The MKSS used its Jan Sunwai (people's hearing) programme effectively to expose wrongdoing in public works and other government schemes at the grass-roots level.

The effort towards nation-building through good governance has to be embedded in the agenda for the building of institutions empowered to question and monitor every action of governmental organizations and persons in authority. Such a movement will have to ensure the independence and autonomy of these institutions. It will require training and equipping the personnel who populate these institutions to work without fear or favour. Media and civil society organizations must show alacrity and ensure vigilance in the performance of these institutions.

We now proceed to examine the working of some select institutions in India. We also visit a couple of organizations where the lack of good governance has rendered the trust of a people in its administrators, misplaced.

1

THE PARLIAMENT OF INDIA

Will It Emerge as the Main Pillar of Democracy?

It was May 2014, replete with the dust of summer in India. After a gruelling election campaign, a new government had just been voted to power. The image that impressed itself indelibly on the minds of the people was of the incoming prime minister, Narendra Modi, driving up to the Parliament House and, on alighting from the car, kneeling and in true Indian tradition, touching his forehead to the steps leading to the hallowed building. The gesture was illustrative of the importance attached in a parliamentary democracy to the legislature, often regarded as the temple of democracy.

It goes to the credit of the founding fathers of the Indian Constitution that we adopted the parliamentary form of government right from its inception, premised on direct elections to the Lok Sabha, or the House of the People. India was among the pioneers in granting universal adult suffrage to itself, a facility that the United States (US) approved only in 1920 (after 144 years) and the United Kingdom (UK) in 1918 (after 100 years). This bold decision was taken despite the fact that barely 14 per cent of the population was literate then. India had just recovered from a painful partition. The social, geographical and religious diversities in the country were huge and complex. It was probably to exorcise the shackles of social, religious and economic discrimination that people were empowered to directly choose their representatives in the Parliament and the legislative assemblies.

THE MOST DEFINING INSTITUTION OF A DEMOCRATIC REPUBLIC

The process leading to Independence and the adoption of parliamentary democracy in India took many years to fructify. The Government of India Act of 1919 had introduced a system of 'provincial diarchy', wherein some subjects were transferred, under self-rule, to elected provincial governments. This system had led to dissatisfaction and raised a persistent demand for reforms, culminating in the Government of India Act of 1935. This Act sought to have a federal system with provincial autonomy and for the first time provided for a division of the legislative functions between the provincial and the central legislature. The Act mandated the formation of an all-India federation based on a union of the British India provinces and the princely states. It provided for a bicameral union legislature to include representation to the princely states too. The Act, however, could not gain much traction as it was rejected by the Congress on the grounds that the Indian people had not been consulted on the process leading to its promulgation. A significant feature of the Act, however, was the introduction of direct elections, which increased the size of the electorate from seven million to thirty-five million.

After much negotiation, on 9 December 1946, the Constituent Assembly met for the first time in New Delhi to determine the Constitution that the country should adopt. Dr Sachidananda Sinha, the oldest parliamentarian in India, was in the chair.

It is very illuminating to recall the lofty ideals with which all the members approached the task of Constitution formulation.

Speaking during the debate in the Constituent Assembly, Dr B.R. Ambedkar made the following fervent appeal:

> So far as the ultimate goal is concerned, I think none of us need have any apprehensions. ...Our difficulty is not about the ultimate future. Our difficulty is how to make the heterogeneous mass that we have today take a decision in common and march on the way, which leads us to unity. Our difficulty is not with regard to the ultimate, our difficulty is with regard to the beginning... therefore, I should have thought that in order to make us willing friends, in order to induce every party, every section in this country to take to the road it would be an act of greatest statesmanship for the majority party even to make a concession to the prejudices of people who are not prepared to march together and it is for that, that I propose to make this appeal. Let us leave aside slogans, let us leave aside words, which frighten people. Let us even make a concession to the prejudices of our opponents, bring them in, so that they may willingly join with us on marching upon that road, which as I said, if we walk long enough, must necessarily lead us to unity.[1]

Significantly, he had the foresight to talk about issues that still bedevil the country today. Dr Ambedkar was making a fervent appeal to abandon slogans which 'frighten people' and have the 'majority party even to make concessions to the prejudices of people', so that the nation could march on the path of unity. These are much desired ideals that have relevance in binding together the social fabric of cohesiveness in the country.

---

[1] Republic Day quotes: Leading lights of the Constituent Assembly and their thoughts on Republic; *The Indian Express*; 26 January 2018; https://indianexpress.com/article/india/republic-day-quotes-leading-lights-of-the-constituent-assembly-and-their-thoughts-on-republic/ Accessed on 9 June 2019.

The Constitution of India was finally adopted on 26 November 1949. It was signed by Rajendra Prasad as the president of the Constituent Assembly, with the final session of the august body being held on 24 January 1950. The Constitution transformed India into a sovereign, democratic republic with a federal structure and parliamentary form of government. The Constituent Assembly was converted into the provisional Parliament of India and functioned as such until after the first general election based on adult franchise. The first general election, under the new Constitution, was held over 1951–52 and the first elected bicameral parliament came into being in May 1952.

DUAL ACCOUNTABILITY

The Parliament is an important pillar of democracy as it is aimed at the fulfilment of the aspirations of citizens through their elected representatives in the House. It exercises control over the executive, and hence ensures achievement of the objectives listed in the manifesto of a political party that seeks to form the government after elections. It is thus an institution mandated to ensure a responsible government, in the process ensuring its own accountability to the electorate. It has a twofold accountability: first, as an accountability institution—which is supreme in a parliamentary democracy and expected to ensure good governance by the executive (the government); and second, as a repository of the people's trust, which the people can hold accountable at election time if the government fails to ensure their welfare and well-being.

As the highest lawmaking body of the country, the primary role of the Parliament is to enact legislation. It is, however, not only a lawmaking body but has to ensure that the government executes all public policies according to the legislative intent behind those policies. It empowers the government to impose taxes to mobilize resources by approving the Budget, the collection of revenue and the incurring expenditure. The Constitution has vested the Parliament with sufficient instruments through which it can enforce accountability in the government.

However, the efficacy of these instruments can only be as good as the parliamentarians and the political parties who deploy them. Fragmentation among political parties in the past two decades has undermined the capacity of the Opposition to cobble together a unified forum of parties to hold the government to account. As a consequence, and due to its inability to make the ruling party accommodate its interpellations on legislation and other policy proposals, the Opposition has often been seen to be resorting to disrupting proceedings in the House. It becomes important to understand the reasons for this deviant posturing and the limited manner in which the Parliament has been able to hold the government to account.

A NEW LOW IN PARLIAMENTARY DECORUM

The Parliament has a majesty and sanctity of its own. It has a written and unwritten code for its members and others to conduct themselves. Any infraction of such prescribed behaviour can attract breach of privilege of the Parliament and hence result in serious consequences for a non-member. There are also repeated directions coming from the government for officials to show due deference to parliamentarians. There is a long list of 'dos and don'ts': for example, how an MP should be received and dealt with if he were to visit the office of a bureaucrat. It requires that the officer attend to him or his calls with priority, stand up and receive him as well as see him off, and ensure that the issue he desires to discuss is promptly addressed. Similar priority treatment has to be accorded to parliamentarians at airports by airlines, railways and such other agencies.

There is also a reciprocal side to the privilege claimed by parliamentarians, which imposes certain obligations on them. They, however, appear to be rather disdainful of any such shackles on them. They need to realize that today's citizenry has begun to question actions, motives and attitudes of parliamentarians not just in the House but also in their dealings with the common man. Instances of MPs or MLAs taking the law into their own hands at toll booths, or their kin indulging in high-handedness, are regularly reported. It is widely believed that once elected, they become dismissive of their obligations and display complete lack of empathy for the common man, knowing full well that they will be held accountable only five years later. Thus, even though there is the provision of an option, 'None of the above' (NOTA), on the ballot today, the electorate lacks viable alternatives. Political parties have begun to choose candidates not for their education, debating acumen, experience or capability, but based on their 'winnability' factor after taking into consideration religious and caste concentration in the constituency.

Of late, there have been many reports of parliamentarians themselves not adhering to the decorum expected of lawmakers in the House. In 2008 we saw the rather 'jaw-dropping' video clips of esteemed members of the House displaying wads of currency notes that were ostensibly offered to them by the United Progressive Alliance (UPA) supporters to have them abstain from voting in a no-confidence motion in connection with the Indo-US nuclear deal (popularly known as the 123 Agreement). Members wresting out microphones and hurling projectiles, and indeed footwear, at one another and even the Chair, has become commonplace. There is the reprehensible episode during the Budget session of the Tamil Nadu Assembly in 1989 when J. Jayalalithaa, as an Opposition leader, merely remarked in the House that the chief minister had no moral right to continue. The remark led to pandemonium, with Dravida Munnetra Kazhagam

(DMK) members protesting violently. She was manhandled, with some DMK members allegedly trying to pull away her sari.

However, the one incident which, in the words of the Lok Sabha Speaker, 'shamed the country and the Parliament' witnessed ugly forms of protest and display of unparliamentary behaviour in the Lower House on 13 February 2014. Three MPs had to be hospitalized after they were attacked with pepper spray amid the ruckus that ensued over the introduction of the Telangana Bill. It was a new low in India's parliamentary history when a Congress member, L. Rajagopal, who was opposed to Andhra Pradesh's division, allegedly used pepper spray on members supporting the Bill. A computer screen was broken when members from both sides came to blows just as the home minister stood up to introduce the Bill.

In December 2010, the winter session of the Parliament ended without transacting any substantial business. This is probably the only occasion in parliamentary history when an entire session was virtually washed out due to a stand-off between the government and the Opposition over the findings by the Comptroller and Auditor General (CAG) on the allocation of the 2G spectrum. In the entire session, normal proceedings were witnessed only on the first day, when members in the Rajya Sabha assembled and then dispersed after condoning the death of a member. Of the twenty-three days in the session that the Houses met, they had to be adjourned within minutes of convening, as each time Opposition members trooped into the well, shouting slogans demanding a joint parliamentary committee (JPC) probe into the 2G spectrum allocation and causing pandemonium. This became a daily routine in both Houses.

In the 11th Lok Sabha (1996–97) barely 5.2 per cent of time was lost due to disruptions. However, the trend in the recent past has been depressing. In the 13th Lok Sabha (1999–2004), the time lost was 18.9 per cent, while this figure became 19.6 per cent in the 14th Lok Sabha (2004–09). In the 15th Lok Sabha (2009–2014), the time lost to disruption was a distressing 39 per cent.

Last year witnessed another first in the history of our parliament. The Annual Financial Statement or Budget is among the most important Bills discussed in Parliament. Thousands of man hours go into the formulation of the Budget document. It is a task of utmost priority, with all preparatory deliberations being conducted in utmost secrecy. The Budget is discussed in the Cabinet, committed before the president and then placed in the Parliament for debate and passage. In March 2018, however, the Lok Sabha passed the Budget without discussion amid continuing protests from the Opposition. It was passed using the guillotine process—a procedure by which all outstanding demands are put to vote at once, irrespective of whether they have been discussed. The Budget for 2018–19 was passed by a voice vote—a formality being completed.

Against the background of these events, which portray the Parliament and its members in poor light, the caution administered by the newly re-elected Prime Minister (PM), Narendra Modi, was apt. Speaking in the Central Hall of the Parliament on his re-election as the leader of the ruling National Democratic Alliance (NDA), he observed that members must shun the VIP culture and ensure that they do not display arrogance of power. He talked of the quality of humility and exhorted them to work for the nation and not confine their activities or perspective to their respective constituencies. Providing some very earthy and commonplace advice, the PM-elect cautioned them against befriending the wrong people and asked them to rise above the narrow confines of caste and religion which tend to divide society.[2] These are the

---

[2]Gyan Varma; 'After Sabka Saath, Sabka Vikas, win Sabka Vishwas: Modi to NDA parliamentarians'; Livemint; 25 May 2019; https://www.livemint.com/politics/news/after-sabka-saath-sabka-vikas-win-sabka-vishwas-modi-to-nda-parliamentarians-1558795939436.html

very qualities that parliamentarians need to inculcate.

ETHICS AND POLITICAL MORALITY

On 2 May 2002, the Supreme Court directed the ECI to call for disclosure by each candidate seeking election to the Parliament, or an assembly, of the assets owned by them, their spouses and dependent children. Consequently, by an order dated 28 June, the ECI made it mandatory for candidates contesting elections to declare their assets and net worth. This declaration brings into the public domain assets that the candidate has accumulated over the past five-year period, thereby exerting some moral pressure on the contestants. The same order mandates all candidates to furnish information on whether they have been convicted/acquitted/discharged of any criminal offence in the past and have undergone punishment or fine.

An analysis by the Association for Democratic Reforms (ADR) of the 16th Lok Sabha, constituted after the general election of 2014, had concluded that the largest number of politicians with criminal records was elected to the Parliament in that election. The analysis, which covers 541 of the 543 winning candidates, shows that 186 members (one-third of the MPs) declared that they had criminal cases pending against them (in the 2009 election the number of such MPs was 158).[3] Of these, 112 had declared that the cases pertained to murder, attempt to murder, kidnapping and crimes against women.

In the general election of 2019, it is reported that as against 34 per cent of the parliamentarians having a criminal record in the 2014 poll, this time the figure was 43 per cent. There is a mind-

---

Accessed on 9 June 2019.
[3]'Lok Sabha Election Watch 2014'; https://adrindia.org/sites/default/files/Lok_Sabha_Report_2014_compressed.pdf
Accessed on 9 June 2019.

boggling case of an elected MP from the Ghosi constituency in Uttar Pradesh (UP). He is accused of rape and has been on the run after an FIR was registered against him on 1 May 2019. He was denied interim bail by the Supreme Court on 17 May. He approached the Court again on 27 May after being elected, for protection from arrest. When the vacation bench presided over by the Chief Justice of India (CJI) asked his counsel how many criminal cases he had pending against him, the reply was 'sixteen'. And he is out on bail in all of them.[4]

It is surprising that the number of graduates elected in 2019 has declined from 78 per cent to 72 per cent, with the average assets owned by the successful contestant being ₹209 million as against ₹147 million earlier.[5] Thus, the average wealth of the persons elected has increased by ₹70 million in comparison with 2014.

A distressing observation made in the ADR report is that the chances of such candidates winning were higher than of those with a clean record. It has been argued that the hardcore politician, who is in the business of politics, is hardly deterred by the fact that such details about him are public knowledge. However, conventional opinion would have it that since a candidate's declared assets, as affirmed by him, are in the public domain, any benami wealth/property traceable to him becomes easy to track down. This happened in the case of Lalu Prasad Yadav, who continues to languish in prison. Thus, the deterrent factor is indeed of consequence.

---

[4]'Supreme Court denies BSP MP protection from arrest in rape case'; *Hindustan Times*; 28 May 2019; https://www.hindustantimes.com/india-news/supreme-court-denies-bsp-mp-protection-from-arrest-in-rape-case/story-N4SUT594nrZF3TqkyDHLRK.html
Accessed on 9 June 2019.
[5]Ajit Kumar Jha; 'Changing face of the legislature'; *India Today*; 7 June 2019; https://www.indiatoday.in/magazine/the-big-story/story/20190617-changing-face-of-the-legislature-1543576-2019-06-07
Accessed on 5 July 2019.

The trend is, however, indicative that firstly, parties are increasingly choosing local musclemen as their candidates for their 'winnability' factor. Secondly, whereas these elements used to be the power behind the parliamentarian earlier, they have now decided to come up front, and have received encouragement to be the 'front' in the Parliament itself. Thirdly, the fact that courts take inordinately long to decide cases gives these elements a free run for most of their tenure in the House. Owing to these factors, the deterrence aspect has been blunted.

This trend needs to be curbed if the people are to be given the confidence that the leaders they elect are indeed trustworthy and fit to be their representatives. For a person to be nominated on the board of directors of a bank, the individual has to fulfil a well-defined 'fit and proper' set of criteria laid down by the government and the Reserve Bank of India (RBI). There are no reasons why similar norms should not be applicable to lawmakers, who constitute the most important pillar of Indian democracy. Hence, it is essential to ensure that persons charge-sheeted for major offences by a court, attracting imprisonment exceeding three years, should be debarred. Of course, to ensure that there is no misuse by political parties to disqualify one another's candidates, it should be specified that the case should have been registered at least six months ahead of the election.

On the other hand, MPs are known to protect their parliamentary privileges very zealously. At the slightest hint of any behavioural or administrative lapse by officialdom, they have the concerned person pulled up before the privileges committee. It thus follows as a natural corollary that since parliamentarians are looked up to by people they represent, it is only proper that they conduct themselves with rectitude and propriety to serve as models for citizens. The Parliament does not have a code of conduct for its members. Since charity begins at home, it is appropriate that parliamentarians prepare a code of conduct for themselves to evidence concern for public opinion.

WOMEN IN PARLIAMENT

In a list compiled by the Inter-Parliamentary Union, India ranks 153 out of 190 nations in the proportion of women in the popularly elected House of the Parliament. In the 17th Lok Sabha, we have seventy-eight women members (14 per cent) out of a total strength of 542, which includes a twenty-five-year-old lady engineering graduate, who is the youngest MP in Indian history. This is marginally better than the earlier number of sixty-two women in the 16th Lok Sabha, but is way behind even Pakistan, which has women's representation of about 20 per cent of the total.

While we reserve and rotate sarpanches and gram pradhans necessarily between men and women, there is no reason for such proportional representation not to be provided in the Parliament. It is also a fact that women at the gram panchayat level have performed exceedingly well, despite many archaic customs and a predominantly patriarchal mindset in rural areas. There is thus no reason to believe that a larger proportion of women in the Parliament would not bring in a socio-economic phenomenon which would better prioritize the people's aspirations. The Women's Reservation Bill has been introduced many times and been allowed to lapse. If we can have a woman president, prime minister, speakers, chief ministers and political party heads, there is every reason to introduce more balanced gender representation in Parliament. If the 73rd and 74th Amendments providing for reservation for women in local bodies were passed by Parliament, why does it not adopt the same standards for itself? I daresay that issues such as Swachh Bharat, rural health, midday meal schemes, and a myriad other proposals emanating from the Parliament would have more practical content were they to be scrutinized by a larger proportion of women members. The 17th Lok Sabha, which has just been constituted, should take this path-breaking decision. It would certainly help the Parliament reinvent itself with more progressive and superior legislative content.

INSTRUMENTS OF GOOD GOVERNANCE

Besides its legislative function, the Parliament also provides legitimacy to the government through the degree of accountability it exercises over the executive. The Constitution makers had the larger national objective of ensuring that a polity which was, in some ways, deprived and divided was provided a stake in the process of development and hence bestowed on it the right to participate in the parliamentary democratic process. It was to ensure that the people's representatives work for their welfare and erase the socio-economic ills that plagued the country before Independence. It was towards the attainment of these objectives that the Parliament was given sweeping powers and parliamentarians placed on a pedestal.

The Constitution placed upon the MPs a very onerous responsibility—to ensure orderly functioning, to conduct themselves with a rare decorum so as to set a model before the nation and thereby fulfil the pledge that the nation took. To ensure the Parliament's effectiveness in discharging its duties, various instruments have been devised, which can hold the administration responsible to it. However, the efficacy of the Parliament as an instrument for ensuring good governance is not dependent merely on the architecture provided by the Constitution, it is ultimately reliant on the sincerity and skill of the MPs in discharging their responsibilities, whether it be through the mechanism of Question Hour, Zero Hour, committees or debates in the House.

The inquisition to which the ministers can be subjected

during Question Hour is instrumental in establishing the accountability of the executive to the Parliament. Experienced and consummate parliamentarians utilize this opportunity to put the government under the scanner and, at times, can embarrass the government departments by raising penetrating questions and highlighting incompetence, neglect, malfeasance or wastage. Questions that MPs can ask the government in the House are classified as 'Starred' or 'Unstarred'. The former require written replies and also a discussion on the subject, thereby ensuring that the minister is thoroughly prepared. In preparing answers to starred questions, the departments spend hours collecting and collating material and briefing the minister on every aspect of the issue. There is zero tolerance for error in these answers and hence a great deal of effort is devoted to preparing them.

Despite all these provisions, effective scrutiny of the government has, in the recent past, been diluted by the very fact that Parliament sessions get disrupted, Question Hour is drowned in sloganeering by MPs, and the new phenomenon of members trooping into the well of the House and not permitting the Speaker to conduct the proceedings. This trend reflects adversely on the maturity of our parliamentarians in using the medium granted to them by the Constitution makers for ensuring that the government is truly 'of the people, by the people and for the people'.

Debates and repartees in Parliament, however, have their own share of entertainment. In the context of preparing ministers to answer starred questions in Parliament, there is a practice of arming the minister with answers to questions that are likely to be raised supplementary to the main question. There was a lady minister, a long-standing parliamentarian, who was not very proficient in English, yet took pride in speaking it. On question day for her ministry, when answering supplementary questions, she was prompt in her replies. Question one was asked. Her response was immediate, as she read it out from the papers before her. Question two was asked. Bang, the reply was read out. Question three was asked by the member, somewhat exasperatedly. Again, she read out the reply with alacrity. The MP asking the questions threw up his hands. The Speaker could not contain himself. He burst out laughing, as did the rest of the House—except the minister. She wondered why people around her were laughing. Then the speaker explained: 'Madam, your answers are very prompt. Thank you. There is no flaw except for the minor issue that there is no link between the questions asked of you and the replies given by you.' It transpired that, regardless of the question being asked, the minister was reading out any one answer from the briefs provided to her by her officials!

Parliamentarians must recognize that the House is meant for debating issues and resolving matters in the best interest of the nation. It is within the precincts of the House that issues need to be debated. The trend has been to boycott sittings of the House, or troop to the Speaker's table and raise slogans and thus waste precious Parliament time. The very same MPs then wax eloquent before television cameras or at street gatherings outside. Such behaviour is detrimental to the efficient functioning of democracy and is a big let-down of the trust reposed in them by the people.

COMMITTEES OF THE HOUSE

In the first report to the 10th Lok Sabha, the Rules Committee had, inter alia, recommended: 'To make parliamentary activity more effective, to make the executive more accountable, and to avail of expert and public opinion wherever necessary', standing committees should be convened. The Rules Committee recommended that these committees should, inter alia, consider:

i. Requests for grants from the ministries concerned and report them to the Lok Sabha;
ii. Such bills pertaining to the ministries concerned, as are

referred to by the speaker, and report thereon to the house;
iii. The papers on basic, major and important policies referred to them by the speaker and report thereon to the house;
iv. The annual reports and the reports on implementation of the policies thereon to the house; and
v. Other matters referred to them by the speaker.[6]

The legislative and other business that the Parliament is called upon to attend, being considerable in volume, does not leave the members with time to devote attention to detail while discussing issues in the House. This is due to the fact that the Parliament has only three sittings in a year and the total meeting time is barely a hundred days. It is to facilitate in-depth examination and ensure better focus of the discussion in Parliament, as also to keep the concerned department on alert, that committees have been mandated as instruments to address accountability. The creation of seventeen department-related standing committees in 1993 was an endeavour to ensure parliamentary oversight of administration. The emphasis was on concentrating on long-term plans, policies and the philosophies guiding the working of the executive. These committees were meant to provide necessary direction, guidance and input for broad policy formulations and were functionally categorized as those which were to enquire or to scrutinize and control.

However, the efficacy of these committees has also been very limited as their recommendations have lost relevance in the overall functioning of the departments to which they are

---

[6]Devesh Kapur and Pratap Bhanu Mehta; 'The Indian Parliament as an Institution of Accountability'; Democracy, Governance and Human Rights Programme Paper Number 23 January 2006 https://pdfs.semanticscholar.org/2afd/3b8b66df3d25594cdcd7d18dcc5c74f13f35.pdf
Accessed on 9 June 2019.

attached. This is largely due to the fact that the members rarely come prepared, the meetings are few and far between in terms of time, and there is no accountability of a department in case it fails to heed the recommendations.

The more important committees are the financial committees, such as the Public Accounts Committee (PAC, probably the most important and feared committee), the Committee on Public Undertakings (COPU) and the Estimates Committee. When there is a requirement, ad hoc committees are set up from time to time to address specific issues, but they cease to exist after submitting their reports.

All reports tabled by the CAG are automatically referred to the PAC. If the PAC were to objectively and judiciously take up audit reports for detailed examination, it would serve as a very fearsome watchdog over government departments. However, despite the fact that from 1965 a leading member of the Opposition chairs the PAC, over time, the efficacy of the committee regarding its avowed objectives has been considerably diluted. One very major inadequacy noticed in recent times has been the frequency of the meetings of this committee. For example, the CAG places about forty reports in the Parliament every year. No doubt that all these reports cannot be examined by the PAC, but it can certainly prioritize them, depending on materiality, sensitivity and importance of the programme audited, for in-depth examination. However, data collected from the PRS Legislative Research secretariat indicates that in the current millennium, in the period up to 2006, the committee met an average of nineteen times a year and after that, upto 2014, only eleven times a year.[7] Such sporadic meetings can hardly lead to any kind of meaningful examination that could hold the departments even remotely accountable to the

---

[7]PRS Blog; December 2010; https://www.prsindia.org/theprsblog/?archive_date=201012
Accessed on 9 June 2019.

Parliament. This has been a very debilitating factor in parliamentary control over the executive or exchequer.

Sub-committees of the PAC and COPU help provide an effective and in-depth examination of the CAG reports. However, poor attendance (barely 60 per cent) and inadequate application of the members to the reports dilutes the experiment. The CAG reports thus get routinely referred to the concerned departments for reporting the action taken by them. As a consequence of this routine action, neither can the delinquents be held accountable nor are any major remedial measures taken in the functioning of the departmental schemes.

An alert PAC holding frequent meetings would be a very effective instrument to keep the executive under constant scrutiny and bring it to book when there are signs of laxity, wastage or malfeasance. In fact, there was an incident wherein the home secretary did not attend a sub-committee meeting of the PAC. He was effectively pulled up by the committee and had to not only explain his absence but express regret for his non-attendance.[8] Such sharp responses from MPs are very effective in ensuring that the executive is held accountable to the legislature through the parliamentary committees.

A very good example of a vigilant PAC attempting to hold the government to account in a totally non-partisan approach was seen in 2010 when the PAC began a *suo motu* examination of the 2G spectrum allocation procedure (*suo motu* in the sense that the CAG audit report had not been placed in the Parliament as yet). The PAC is always chaired by a prominent Opposition leader. It

---

[8] C.L. Manoj; 'Home secretary Rajiv Mehrishi expresses regret for skipping Public Accounts Committee meet'; *The Economic Times*; 8 April 2017; https://economictimes.indiatimes.com/news/politics-and-nation/home-secretary-rajiv-mehrish-expresses-regret-for-skipping-public-accounts-committee-meet/articleshow/58073838.cms
Accessed on 9 June 2019.

is thus usually the Opposition MPs who ask all the searching questions that keep the department on its toes. However, it was a ruling-party MP who sought clarification from the then finance secretary about the quantum of loss that could have been incurred by the manner in which the 2G licences had been allocated. The finance secretary insisted that the ministry was not equipped to make such computations.

The MP then set about making the computation himself. He based his calculation on the premium obtained by a particular company which had offloaded its shares in the market after having been allocated the spectrum. He arrived at a back-of-the envelope figure of ₹70,000 crore at only 40–50 per cent of the shares being sold! He concluded by saying that it was obvious how much the government of India could have gained by transparent bidding of the licences.

Where committees have been vigilant and regular in their functioning, they have been able to effectively provide parliamentary oversight of governmental functioning. However, instances of failure to provide oversight are increasing. A case in point is again that of the PAC examining the 2G imbroglio. Due to a totally partisan approach, the committee could not submit its report in that session as issues degenerated around narrow partisan lines. Even the JPC set up for an in-depth examination of the same issue became ineffective.

OPPOSITION: PUTTING THE GOVERNMENT UNDER THE SCANNER

The role of the Opposition in the Parliament is to keep the government on its toes, and is very critical. An alert Opposition not only ensures that the executive does not become lax and take liberties with norms and regulations, but also that the delinquent among the government functionaries are brought to book. A weak or disparate Opposition loses efficacy in imposing any kind of deterrence on the government. In the recent past, Opposition parties have become fragmented and many in number with reduced count of members in each party, thereby not being able to form a united and combined Opposition. The attempt has become to malign one another and show the other in poor light, rather than bring out the administrative and policy weaknesses of the government.

From the time that parliamentary debates have begun to be televised, the attempt by Opposition members is more to score short-term political points than labour to deliver good-quality speeches to enable policy or legislative improvements. Thus, political scandals, financial scams, instances of alleged corruption, religious innuendos and Dalit-related issues have gained greater prominence. The very fact that parliamentarians have been chosen by political parties not for their perceived debating or legislative acumen leads to a consequential decline in quality and tenor of debates. More often than not, the Opposition stance is more for the sake of opposing than for improving the proposal being introduced by the treasury benches.

A common instrument of any effective Opposition disagreeing with the government's policies and hence wanting to bring it to its knees is the attempt to introduce a no-confidence motion. This, however, has lost its efficacy, as a fragmented Opposition in the House is incapable of mustering unified support from the large number of parties that constitute the Opposition now. As against a maximum number of twenty-eight parties that constituted the 11th Lok Sabha (1996), the number of parties in the House post-1998 is thirty-seven to thirty-eight parties. The present Lok Sabha (17th) comprises thirty-six political parties and four independents. It is easy for the party in power to break up an attempt to create an alliance leading to a no-confidence by allurements in such a fragmented opposition. The different methodologies that have been adopted for breaking Opposition unity, such as persuading Opposition parties/members to absent themselves or conduct 'walkouts' and not vote in favour of the no-confidence motion, have reduced the entire exercise to a farce, thus losing out on a very potent instrument in the Parliament to seek accountability from the government.

So why is such a trend gaining ground? One reason, of course, is a consequence of the 24x7 media, often in overdrive, wanting to put out 'breaking news' or 'exclusive coverage' all the time, thereby seeking to sensationalize events. Keeping the visibility factor in mind, the 'get popular quick' type of politician has realized that a learned, mature or statesman-like performance in the Parliament does not win brownie points with the electorate. They have thus perfected the craft of using national or vernacular television or televised the Parliament proceedings to their advantage in driving a popular image of their own for their followers. The centre of action is no longer perceived to be in the House, where they can score valid and effective debating points over the government, but outside it, where they get better media coverage to display to the public their alacrity and willingness to rise to the defence of the people they represent.

On the other hand, if there is a requirement for them to be active and vocal on the floor of the House, they would rather resort to theatrics to stall the proceedings and thereby 'play to the gallery', which, in this case, would be their followers. As a consequence, the conventional and more staid role that a parliamentarian is required to perform gets relegated to a low order, with other 'eye-catching' activities taking precedence. This is the singular, most important, factor that has led to the degeneration of parliamentary proceedings. The theatre of action has thus shifted from quality debate in the Parliament to action on the streets or even debating on TV channels.

REDEFINING THE QUALITY AND VIBRANCY OF OUR DEMOCRACY

The Parliament is avowedly one of the most defining institutions of a democratic republic. The quality and vibrancy of a democracy is clearly manifest in the quality of accountability and oversight that the Parliament can provide over the executive to ensure good governance. The architecture of the Indian parliamentary structure has been elegantly and appropriately crafted, so as to give all the functionaries who work in the system enough tools to make it a pillar for providing the people all the elements of good governance, welfare, benefits of economic development, and the safety and security of existence as a nation. It is undeniable that it is a vibrant parliamentary democracy that has landed India knocking at double-digit economic growth and among the top five economic powers in the world today.

However, the Parliament's efficacy as an agent for introducing far-reaching reforms and a qualitative uplift for the common man as his representative in the national capital, leaves much to be desired. To make economic growth sustainable in the long run, it will have to be premised on an edifice created by a responsible parliament and an even more responsible Opposition willing to carry the burden of ensuring that the government functions for the long-term well-being of the people. It is commonly believed that important legislation, such as setting up the institution of a constitutional Lokpal, having political parties declare the source of their funding, holding judges accountable, reserving constituencies for women, ending reservation on mere caste considerations in government jobs and so on, could have been passed had the Parliament risen above the narrow confines of party, caste, region and religion. On the other hand, repeated passing of resolutions to feather their own nests, such as allowances, pensions, Members of the Parliament Local Area

Development Scheme (MPLADS) amount enhancements and so-called parliamentary privileges, have only served to create a poor image of their intent.

As a consequence of the drawbacks highlighted above, the Parliament is becoming an increasingly ineffective instrument for timely legislative intervention or as a check on the functioning of the government, thereby ceding space to the judiciary or other non-elected institutions. Financial management, social-sector scheme monitoring, maintaining supervision of government spending and thereby ensuring that funds are actually spent for the purpose for which they were approved, are elements of policy oversight fast receding from parliamentary control. What could be a sadder commentary on the functioning of the Parliament than the fact that an entire session gets washed out by disruptions or that a whole year's Budget gets passed without any debate?

I still believe it is not too late for the Parliament to rise like the phoenix and begin to reinvigorate itself. It hardly requires a gargantuan effort. It merely requires every party to throw up a leader or two who will encourage parliamentarians to set aside their personal agenda and commit themselves to the welfare of the people. They only need to create an incubating atmosphere for the economy to rejuvenate itself in, despite the many ills that confront it. Parliament, in any democracy, is too critical an institution not to be functioning to the expectations of the people.

2

THE SUPREME COURT

Providing the Bedrock for Good Governance

…[We] owe a responsibility to the institution and the nation. Our efforts have failed in convincing CJI [Chief Justice of India] to take steps to protect the institution… This is an extraordinary event in the history of any nation, more particularly this nation and an extraordinary event in the institution of judiciary… It is with no pleasure that we are compelled to call this press conference. But sometimes administration of the Supreme Court is not in order and many things which are less than desirable have happened in the last few months… About a couple of months back, four of us gave a signed letter to the Chief Justice of India. We wanted a particular thing to be done in a particular manner. But the way it was done, it raised further questions about the integrity of the institution…[1]

Justice Jasti Chelameswar, 12 January 2018

---

[1]'Supreme Court crisis: All not okay, democracy at stake, say four seniormost judges'; *The Hindu BusinessLine*; 12 January 2018; https://www.thehindubusinessline.com/news/supreme-court-crisis-all-not-okay-democracy-at-stake-say-four-seniormost-judges/article10028921.ece Accessed on 3 July 2019.

This was the statement of the second-most senior judge of the Supreme Court, about the most senior, indeed, the CJI. By any standard, a most alarming and ominous reference to an institution which, over the seven decades since Independence, has kept itself from the public gaze. On that winter morning, sitting in Justice Chelameswar's residence, the four most senior judges, looking exceedingly distressed, did the unthinkable by addressing the press, faulting their own, in front of a battery of cameras.

This event constitutes a landmark in the history of the Supreme Court. The Court has seen much dissension among its own, but none has been aired so publicly. This is all the more reason to examine how such a situation emerged. Let us see the issue in its proper perspective, over the years.

The Constitution of India designates the Supreme Court as the highest judicial forum and the final court of appeal. It empowers the Supreme Court to conduct judicial review as the highest constitutional court. The Court has original, appellate and advisory jurisdiction. Being the highest court of judicial appeal, all appeals against verdicts of the high courts of different states lie with the Supreme Court. The CJI presides over the Supreme Court, and there is a provision to appoint thirty other judges.

STEEPED IN HISTORY

The Supreme Court of India, in its present form, came into being with the country adopting the Constitution in 1950, with the first sitting of the Court being held on 28 January 1950. The inaugural sitting was in the Chamber of Princes in the Parliament building, which provides for bicameral chambers, viz., the Council of States and the House of the People. The erstwhile Federal Court sat in this building from its inception and the Supreme Court continued to function from this chamber until it moved into its present premises.

The architecture of the building that now houses the Supreme Court is of interest. The design of the building is in the shape of a traditional balanced weighing scale, symbolizing the scales of justice. There is a central beam with two halls on either side, depicting the pans of the weighing scale. The central beam comprises the court halls, including the court of the CJI, which is in the centre. The Supreme Court moved into this building in 1958.

The Court, by virtue of being the highest court in the land, has the power to punish a person who has committed contempt of any court in the country, including itself. Articles 129 and 142 of the Constitution vest the Supreme Court with this power. On 10 May 2006, the Court took an unprecedented decision when it directed a minister of the Maharashtra government, Swaroop Singh Naik, to be jailed for a month on a charge of contempt of court for violating an order protecting forests.[2]

JUDICIAL APPOINTMENTS: COLLEGIUM VS COMMISSION

The Constitution has laid down the method of appointment of the CJI, and judges of the Supreme Court and the high courts. The president shall make these appointments after consulting the CJI and the judges of the Supreme Court. This process of appointment has been examined and reinterpreted by the Supreme Court many times between 1982 and 1999. Since 1993, in a process mandated by the Court, a collegium of judges, comprising the CJI and four of the most senior judges of the Supreme Court, make the recommendations for the appointment of judges to the president. The recommendations are more or

---

[2]'Maha minister, officer sent to jail'; *Hindustan Times*; 11 May 2006; https://www.hindustantimes.com/india/maha-minister-officer-sent-to-jail/story-SI1SU8sOGHdTgTWfpaxmOK.html Accessed on 3 July 2019.

less binding on the government. All that the government can do is merely seek reconsideration of the recommendations by the collegium, and if the latter unanimously reiterates the earlier recommendations, the appointment has to be made.

Justice J.S. Verma, who was the CJI pronouncing the 1993 verdict,[3] has observed that the judgement was meant to be a participatory process (involving the Court and the government) so that the suitability of a judge in respect of legal acumen could be adjudged by the judiciary while with regard to his antecedents, the opinion of the executive would be predominant. However, it does not seem to have worked that way—leading to mistrust between the two.

Many commissions and bodies have faulted the collegium system of appointing judges. Some of the appointments that have been made through this process have drawn adverse attention. In this context, the NDA government had sought to alter the process of appointment and introduced a constitutional amendment Bill in August 2014—The National Judicial Appointments Commission (NJAC) Bill 2014. It sought to amend the Constitution to replace the collegium system with an independent commission called the NJAC. The NJAC would comprise (i) the CJI (ii) the two most senior judges of the Supreme Court (iii) the Union law minister and (iv) two eminent persons to be nominated by the prime minister, the CJI and the leader of the Opposition in the Lok Sabha. This amendment was passed in 2014 by both Houses of Parliament and received the assent of the president.[4] Twenty state legislatures also passed it.

---

[3] *Supreme Court Vs Union of India*; https://indiankanoon.org/doc/753224/ Accessed on 5 July 2019.

[4] 'Parliament approves historic bill to overturn collegium system'; *The Indian Express*; 14 August 2014; https://indianexpress.com/article/india/politics/rajya-sabha-passes-judicial-appointments-bill/ Accessed on 3 July 2019.

No sooner was the president's assent granted, than a spate of Public Interest Petitions (PILs) were filed in the Supreme Court, challenging the amendment. The PILs on the setting up of the NJAC were heard by a five-judge bench of the Court. It delivered a 1,000-page judgement holding that any involvement of the executive in the appointment of judges impinges on the independence of the judiciary.[5]

The NJAC was viewed by the Court as violative of the principle of separation of powers between the executive and the judiciary, which is a basic feature of the Constitution. The verdict further observed that the presence of the law minister on the panel would impinge on the principle of independence of the judiciary. His role, along with that of the PM in the selection of two other eminent persons, who could veto any decision, would be a retrograde step. The Court also observed that it would be 'disastrous' to include lay persons with undefined qualifications on the selection panel. The judgement stated that the collegium, accused of lacking transparency and promoting nepotism, would be 'fine-tuned' to obviate such criticism in future.[6]

The verdict unleashed a barrage of opinions, arguing for both sides. There are, of course, some very committed viewpoints. Unfortunately, some senior political functionaries have perceived this verdict as 'a setback to parliamentary sovereignty'.[7] Eminent

---

[5] Utkarsh Anand; 'Supreme Court strikes down NJAC, revives collegium system'; *The Indian Express*; 17 October 2015; https://indianexpress.com/article/india/india-news-india/sc-strikes-down-njac-revives-collegium-system-of-appointing-judges/
Accessed on 3 July 2019.

[6] 'Full text: The Supreme Court judgment on the NJAC controversy'; *Firstpost*; 16 October 2015; https://www.firstpost.com/india/full-text-the-supreme-court-judgement-on-the-njac-controversy-2471300.html
Accessed on 3 July 2019.

[7] 'NJAC verdict: Setback to parliamentary sovereignty, says Govt'; *Business Standard*; 16 October 2015; https://www.business-standard.com/article/

jurists have also faulted it. Justice A.P. Shah, former chairman of the Law Commission and a former chief justice of the Delhi High Court, commented: 'The Supreme Court judgement that struck down the NJAC for appointment of judges is grossly flawed and deserving of harsh criticism.' He felt the NJAC was 'a very good idea'. 'There were some deficiencies which could have been read down. It is disturbing that the apex court was comfortable that judicial independence would be safe in the collegium system.'[8]

In fact, India is the only country where judges get to select judges. Our system is very different from that which prevails in other democracies, such as the UK, the US and Canada. In each of these countries, the legislature or eminent persons outside the judiciary undertake the selection. That system seems to have worked to the satisfaction of the judiciary, the executive and the public at large in those jurisdictions.

COLLEGIUM SYSTEM: AN OLD BOYS' CLUB?

Much can be said about the merits and demerits of each system. In an ideal system, where there is trust and faith of each pillar of democracy in the other, there would be no scope for disagreement. The executive is invariably a major litigant in quite a few cases coming up before the Court. There have also been open allegations of the government attempting to appoint on the bench judges who have been commonly seen to be 'pliable'.

On the other hand, the collegium is seen as opaque and a

---

current-affairs/njac-verdict-setback-to-parliamentary-sovereignty-says-govt-115101600971_1.html
Accessed on 3 July 2019.
[8]Pradeep Thakur; 'SC order striking down NJAC was greatly flawed: Justice Shah'; *The Times of India*; 16 September 2017; https://timesofindia.indiatimes.com/india/sc-order-striking-down-njac-was-greatly-flawed-justice-shah/articleshow/60705622.cms
Accessed on 3 July 2019.

bit of an 'old boys' club'. It has also thrown up appointments whose credibility has been questioned. Such appointments have indeed undermined the people's faith in the judiciary. In fact, among the five-judge bench itself, one judge argued for the NJAC's acceptance. He faulted the collegium system as being the exclusive domain of the judiciary, adding that the executive and civil society must have a say in the selection process. This judge went on to observe that the Court could not claim to be the sole protector of people's rights, and referred to instances where the Court had failed to live up to citizens' expectations in preserving liberties. The judge specifically drew attention to the awkward situation resulting from the appointment of Justice P.D. Dinakaran, a Madras High Court judge, to the Supreme Court, who was later appointed as the chief justice of the Sikkim High Court.[9] The dissenting judge ended by quoting Macaulay's dictum: 'Reform that you may preserve'.

Another judge on this bench had earlier made observations on the functioning of the collegium and stated that 'deserving persons had been ignored wholly for subjective reasons, social and other national realities were overlooked, certain appointments purposely delayed so as to benefit or to deny such benefits to the less patronised'.[10] These comments constitute grave indictment of the Court from its own.

The judgement sparked serious, as well as essential, debate. The issue is not so much the independence of the judiciary

---

[9] J. Venkatesan; 'Justice Dinakaran resigns'; *The Hindu*; 29 July 2011; https://www.thehindu.com/news/national/Justice-Dinakaran-resigns/article13799237.ece
Accessed on 5 July 2019.

[10]*Institute of South Asian Studies; 'Judicial Appointments Debate In India: Need For Integrity And Transparency – Analysis'; Eurasia Review;* 27 October 2015; https://www.eurasiareview.com/27102015-judicial-appointments-debate-in-india-need-for-integrity-and-transparency-analysis/
Accessed on 11 July 2019.

or the setback to the supremacy of the Parliament. In fact, if either of these institutions had been functioning along the lines expected of them, the need for either to seek protection of its 'independence' or 'supremacy' would never have arisen. Credibility gets established by deeds and performance, not by self-proclamation. Institutions craft their own credibility, which lies in their accountability, transparent functioning and trust evoked from the public. Neither will the NJAC system redeem people's faith in the Parliament or the executive, nor will the collegium system absolve the judiciary of the kind of observation it has been subject to. This can happen only by sheer display of 'above the board' performance. The people are the true and ultimate judges of the performance of democratic institutions. Hence, whilst 'independence' and 'supremacy' will be the basis of arguments advanced by the respective institutions, it is only they themselves who can redeem people's faith by their performance.

VERDICTS THAT SHOOK THE NATION

Protection of Fundamental Rights Guaranteed in the Constitution

The framers of the Constitution provided for the guarantee of fundamental rights. In 1951, for the first time, the question of whether the fundamental rights could also be amended under Article 368 came up for consideration before the Supreme Court. The issue arose largely due to the apparent contradiction between Articles 368 and 13. Article 13 in the original Constitution maintained that the State shall not make any law that takes away or abridges the rights given to the citizens in Part III and any such law made in contravention of this Article shall be deemed void. It thus prevented the Parliament from amending the Constitution in such a way as to take away the citizens' fundamental rights.

The validity of the first constitutional amendment (1951), which curtailed the right to property, was challenged in *Shankari Prasad Vs Union of India*. This case brought out the apparent disharmony between Articles 368 and 13.

The Supreme Court ruled that the power to amend the Constitution under Article 368 included the power to amend the fundamental rights and that the word 'law' in Article 13(8) connoted only an ordinary law made in exercise of the legislative powers and did not include a constitutional amendment made in exercise of constituent power. Therefore, a constitutional amendment would be valid even if it abridged or took away any of the fundamental rights. The Court applied the principle of harmonic construction, as there was a conflict between Articles 368 and 13. It ruled that the provisions of the Constitution should be interpreted such that they did not conflict with one another and there was harmony among them.

The political executive witnessed an initial stage of judicial activism in *Golaknath Vs State of Punjab* in 1967. In this case, the Supreme Court first maintained the inviolability of the fundamental rights as guaranteed in the Constitution. A bench of eleven judges (such a large bench was constituted for the first time) deliberated whether any part of the fundamental rights provisions could be revoked or limited by amending the Constitution. In a momentous judgement, it declared that the fundamental rights were transcendental and inviolable and the Parliament had no power to take away or abridge any of them through constitutional amendment. It held that the fundamental rights included in Part III of the Constitution had been granted a 'transcendental position' and were beyond the reach of the Parliament. It also declared unconstitutional any amendment that 'takes away or abridges' a fundamental right conferred by Part III.

This ruling created a kind of constitutional deadlock between the Parliament and the judiciary. To reiterate its supremacy, the

Parliament passed the 24th Amendment in 1971 to abrogate the Supreme Court judgement. It amended the Constitution to provide expressly that the Parliament had the power to amend any part of the Constitution, including the provisions related to the fundamental rights. This was done by amending Articles 13 and 368 to exclude amendments made under Article 368 from Article 13's prohibition of any law abridging or taking away any of the fundamental rights.

This amendment came up for review before the Court in 1973 in the landmark case of *Kesavananda Bharati Vs State of Kerala*. The issue under contention was that the Kerala government, under its Land Reforms Act, imposed certain restrictions on the owners of land, drawing from its powers under Article 21 of the Constitution. However, this restriction on the management of its property was contested by Kesavananda Bharati, a seer of an ashram in the Kasaragod district of Kerala in 1970. The ashram contested the government's order under Article 26, concerning the right to manage religiously owned property without government interference. The case was heard by the largest ever constitution bench of thirteen judges over five months, as it was expected to profoundly affect the basic features of democracy.

The thirteen-judge bench deliberated on the limitations, if any, of the powers of the elected representatives of the people and the nature of the fundamental rights of an individual. In a sharply divided verdict (7–6), the Court held that while the Parliament had 'wide' powers, it did not have the power to destroy or emasculate the basic elements or fundamental features of the Constitution. The Court thus upheld the 'basic structure doctrine' by only the narrowest of margins. However, over the years, this verdict has gained widespread acceptance and legitimacy due to subsequent cases and judgements.

Declaration of Emergency

Probably the most significant among these was the imposition of a state of emergency by then PM Indira Gandhi in 1975, and the subsequent attempt to suppress her prosecution through the 39th Amendment.

In this case, a watershed in Indian political and judicial history, a constitution bench comprising the five most senior judges of the Court handed out a verdict (during the Emergency imposed by PM Indira Gandhi in 1975–77) in what is popularly known as the Habeas Corpus case *(ADM Jabalpur Vs S.S. Shukla)*, where detenus under the restrictive Maintenance of Internal Security Act (MISA) argued that the right to life and personal liberty (Article 21) could not be suspended even during periods of national emergency.

The Constitution at the time had provided that all fundamental rights, including the right to life under Article 21, could be suspended during a state of emergency. The Habeas Corpus majority decision, therefore, deferred to the original intent of the framers of the Constitution and ordered: '…in view of the Presidential Order dated 27 June 1975, no person has any locus to move any writ petition under Article 226 before a High Court for habeas corpus or any other writ or order or direction to challenge the legality of an order of detention.'[11]

This judgement was passed with a four-to-one majority. The dissenting judge, Justice H.R. Khanna, stated in his judgement: '…[Detention] without trial is an anathema to all those who love personal liberty'. It is widely believed that this dissenting opinion

---

[11]Ashok H. Desai; 'How the Judiciary Defied the Government to Uphold Constitutional Values During the Emergency'; *The Wire*; 25 June 2017; https://thewire.in/society/how-the-judiciary-defied-the-government-to-uphold-constitutional-values-during-the-emergency
Accessed on 3 July 2019.

cost the judge the position of CJI as he was superseded for that appointment, in a break from the convention of appointing the most senior judge (which he was). This judgement is seen as abject surrender of the Court to the then political executive. Three decades later, Justice P.N. Bhagwati, one of the four judges, regretted his decision.[12]

While deciding the Kesavananda Bharati case, the underlying apprehension of the majority bench that elected representatives could not be trusted to act responsibly was perceived to be unprecedented. However, after the Parliament approved the 39th Amendment, it was widely believed that this apprehension was indeed well founded.

Raj Narain, a socialist leader, had contested and lost the election against Indira Gandhi in the Rae Bareli parliamentary constituency in 1971. He filed a petition in the Allahabad High Court challenging her election on the grounds that she had misused the state machinery while electioneering. On 12 June 1975,[13] the High Court found her guilty, declared the election null and void, and barred her from holding elected office for six years. The Court gave the Congress party twenty days to make arrangements to replace Indira Gandhi in her official post as PM.

However, she managed to get a conditional stay from the Supreme Court, allowing her to continue in the Lok Sabha but neither vote nor speak there, thus making her dysfunctional. On 26 June 1975, she persuaded the president to declare a state of

---

[12]'Former CJI Bhagwati, who regretted verdict during Emergency, no more'; *The Indian Express*; 16 June 2017; https://indianexpress.com/article/india/ex-cji-prafullachandra-natwarlal-bhagwati-who-regretted-verdict-during-emergency-no-more/ Accessed on 3 July 2019.

[13]Case study—Indira Gandhi v Raj Narain, AIR 1975; *Law News and Network*; 21 October 2014; https://lawnn.com/case-study-indira-nehru-gandhi-v-raj-narain-air-1975/ Accessed on 3 July 2019.

emergency under Article 352, citing a grave situation wherein the security of India was being threatened by internal disturbances. She also pushed for the 39th Amendment to secure her position and prevent her removal from politics.

The 39th Amendment Bill of 10 August 1975 placed the election of the president, vice-president and speaker of the Lok Sabha beyond the scrutiny of the courts. It was moved by the government to pre-empt a hearing by the Supreme Court in the appeal against the Allahabad High Court verdict setting aside the PM's election on the grounds of electoral malpractice. A constitution bench of the Supreme Court, however, used the 'basic structure doctrine' to strike down the 39th Amendment. This verdict, it is commonly held, paved the way for restoration of democracy in India.

During the Emergency, the Parliament also passed the 42nd Amendment, inserting Clause (4) in Article 368. It prevented any court from reviewing any amendment to the Constitution on any ground. It also added Clause (5), which mandated that there would be no limit on the constitutional power of the Parliament to amend, vary, add or repeal the provisions of the Constitution.

A few years after the Emergency, however, the Supreme Court rejected the absoluteness of the 42nd Amendment and reaffirmed its power of judicial review in what is known as the Minerva Mills case (1980).[14] This verdict established the superiority of the Constitution over any other institution, including the Parliament. It maintained that the Parliament could not have unlimited power of amendment, resulting in damage or destruction of the Constitution to which it owed its existence, and from which it derived its power.

---

[14]Supreme Court of India; *Minerva Mills Ltd. & Ors Vs Union Of India & Ors* on 31 July 1980; https://indiankanoon.org/doc/1939993/ Accessed on 3 July 2019.

PIL: THE RISE OF NEW JURISPRUDENCE

The Supreme Court's creative and expansive interpretations of Article 21 (dealing with the right to life and personal liberty), primarily after the Emergency period, have given rise to new jurisprudence of the PIL, which has vigorously promoted many crucial economic and social rights (constitutionally protected but not enforceable), including, but not restricted to, the rights to free education, livelihood, a clean environment, food and many others. Civil and political rights (traditionally safeguarded in the Fundamental Rights chapter of the Constitution) have also been expanded and more fiercely protected. The PIL has brought the enjoyment of fundamental rights by a citizen well within their reach and has indeed made it a reality for them.

On the one hand, it has ensured that hapless individuals in asylums and prisons can seek redressal of their genuine grievances; on the other, it has ensured the obligation of those in power to exercise that power judiciously and be accountable. Whilst much can be said about abuse of rights drawn from the Constitution, on balance, the introduction of the PIL has brought great succour to the hapless and deprived sections of society. These new interpretations have opened up the avenue for litigation on a number of important issues.

SERVING AS THE LAST REFUGE

There have been some more verdicts emanating from the Court following PILs which certain groups believe are instances of 'judicial activism or overreach' and by which the Court is transgressing into the domain of the executive. Judicial activism commonly refers to court rulings that are partially or fully based on the judge's political or personal consideration rather than existing law. Talk about judicial activism has gained currency all over the globe. It is probably because excessive democratic liberty needs a countervailing balance, which Constitution framers in many democracies have provided by way of judicial review. This provision gives the judiciary the mandate to nullify decisions taken by popularly elected representatives in the legislature.

It is possible that courts have indeed begun to use this mechanism too often. It could also be because other instruments of the State are becoming less alert in their response to people-related issues. Judicial intervention in policymaking can either be an activity in support of legislative and executive policy choices, or in opposition to them. The latter intervention raises cries of judicial activism. The essence of true judicial activism is the rendering of a decision which is in tune with the temper and tempo of the times. Activism in judicial policymaking furthers the cause of social change or articulates concepts such as liberty, equality or justice. It has to be an arm of social revolution. An activist judge is more in sync with the developing social environment and merely activates the legal process to make it play a vital role to bring forth a decision in tune with the need of the hour.

It is, therefore, important to examine two of these cases to evaluate the role of the Court, the circumstances under which it interfered and the rationale/validity of that 'transgression'.

Spectrum Allocation for 2G Services

The government allots spectrums to different mobile telephony companies to provide wireless services. The procedure for allotment has differed from time to time. In 2008, the Department of Telecommunications (DoT) in the Government of India decided to allot the spectrum in conformity with a policy commonly referred to as first-come-first-served (FCFS). However, when the allotment of licences was made to 120 companies on a single day, it drew the attention of the media, Parliament and civil society, as the procedure adopted was neither transparent nor fair and it was felt that particular companies had been favoured by the department by discriminately applying the norms.

The CAG, who audited the procedure of allotment, concluded in November 2010 that the allotment procedure had been irregular, benefiting the allottee companies and leading to huge loss to the national exchequer. Soon, several NGOs and individual citizens filed a PIL against the Union of India and various private companies, contesting the allocation of the 2G spectrum. After very detailed hearings, the Supreme Court, on 2 February 2012, declared the allotment of the spectrum 'unconstitutional and arbitrary', cancelling the 122 licences issued in 2008.[15] According to the Court, the minister 'wanted to favour some companies at the cost of the public exchequer' and 'virtually gifted away important national assets. Although the policy for awarding licences was FCFS, the minister changed the rules'. With this order, the Court not only sent out a very clear message that when a government policy is not transparent or fair, it is liable to be struck down, but also went ahead and quashed the very licences which the government had issued under the policy.

Government Allotment of Coal Blocks

From July 1992, the allotment of coal mines was done by a process of screening applications through an interministerial screening committee. Until around 2003, there was not much pressure from those who sought coal mines for power generation, as the price of imported coal was very attractive. However, from 2004 the international prices of coal turned buoyant and applications for coal mines started piling up. Since there

---

[15] 'Verdict of Supreme Court on 2G Spectrum Allocations—Pre Consultation Comments (Preliminary) of CUTS to TRAI'; https://main.trai.gov.in/sites/default/files/CUTS_plimanry.pdf Accessed on 3 July 2019.

were only a limited number of mines to be allotted, there was considerable lobbying by the applicants as the difference in the price of coal supplied by the public-sector Coal India Limited (CIL), or imported coal, and the coal mined from captive mines was substantial.

The then secretary in the department of coal felt that the allocation process being followed for these coal mines was not transparent. Since allottees received 'windfall gains' (his words) from captive coal blocks, he sensed intense lobbying. He recommended a transparent and fair auction for further allotment of coal mines. This recommendation was accepted by the minister of coal, who, by chance, at the time happened to be the PM, who was holding the portfolio in the absence of a regular minister. Though the PM had approved the change in allocation procedure, the auction process never got implemented until 2012, on grounds of requiring an amendment in legislation and so on. Meanwhile, since applications had already been received for further allotment of coal blocks and amendment to legislation was taking time, the government decided to consider the pending applications for allotment in 2005, under the earlier screening committee procedure.

In a routine audit done by the CAG, it was found that allocation through an auction process had been inordinately delayed by the government on grounds which did not stand the test of public scrutiny. Such delay in the introduction of the process for competitive bidding had rendered the existing process rather beneficial for the private companies that received allotment in 2005, though the decision to adopt the auction method had been taken in 2004. The essence of the CAG's argument was that the government had the authority to allocate coal blocks by a process of competitive bidding but chose not to. As a result, both public-sector enterprises and private firms paid less than they might have.

The issue roused massive media reaction and public outrage. A PIL was filed in the Supreme Court seeking to cancel the allotment of 194 coal blocks on grounds of arbitrariness, illegality, unconstitutionality and public interest. The Court ordered the government to inform it of reasons for not following the 2004 decision of 'competitive bidding'. On 24 September 2014, the Court cancelled the allocations of 214 licences issued by the government.[16]

These two cases point to a very significant feature of a democratic society. Democracy is founded on three pillars—the legislature, executive and judiciary. They provide checks and balances in relation to one another to ensure good governance for the development and welfare of the people. Good governance is a kind of zero-sum game, where each of these pillars has to play its part. In case any one does not perform its role with alacrity, it runs the risk of ceding space to the other. Thus, when the executive did not move quickly to sort out the issue of environmental pollution in the early 2000s, it was the Court that banned diesel vehicles and insisted on their conversion to compressed natural gas (CNG). Similarly, when the administration of cricket in the country became the preserve of a few who were exploiting it to fulfil their own agenda, the Court stepped in to regulate and develop cricket in India.

In the case of allotment of spectrum and coal mine blocks, all relevant stakeholders, such as the Parliament, the media, citizens and the national auditor, apprised the executive of the irregularities being committed. However, no corrective steps appeared to be forthcoming from the government, despite the

---

[16]Krishnadas Rajagopal; 'Supreme Court quashes allocation of 214 coal blocks'; *The Hindu*; 24 September 2014; https://www.thehindu.com/news/national/supreme-court-quashes-allocation-of-all-but-four-of-218-coal-blocks/article6441855.ece
Accessed on 3 July 2019.

issue being repeatedly raised even in Parliament. It was then that the PILs were filed. The Court had to step in to assure the citizenry of its being the guardian of the interests of the common man and protector of the nation's natural resources. Under these circumstances, the Court served as the last refuge and can hardly be accused of overreach. It was only goading a lackadaisical executive setup to deliver on the oath its members had taken under the Constitution.

There have been opinions voiced very prominently that, in recent times, the Court has indulged in 'judicial activism' and has stepped beyond its mandate. Such observations have arisen owing to verdicts in cases involving fundamental rights, review of parliamentary legislation and executive orders, or rulings taking on the role of the legislature or executive by regulating public order. Thus, in the Court cancelling the allotment of spectrum licences or coal mines, it was merely ensuring that a transparent and objective process is undertaken that can stand the test of public scrutiny and thereby build confidence between a people and their government.

ACTIVISM AND ASSERTIVENESS

Coupled with the so-called judicial activism is the factor of the Court becoming more assertive. It is a natural corollary. The Court intervenes only when other agencies have not fulfilled their responsibility. Invariably, issues affecting the public where the Court has had to intervene are those concerning air pollution, felling of trees, environmental damage to the Yamuna riverbed, switchover to CNG-driven vehicles, solid waste disposal, etc. These are all public concerns, where action by the concerned executive bodies has been woefully lacking. Mere directives and gentle nudges have not provided any perceptible change in the attitude or functioning of these agencies. That is when the Court has had to take a strident attitude.

To some extent this is justifiable; if, even after the Court issues directives, agencies are loathe to act, it smacks of a breakdown in the system. Reviving it definitely requires a jolt. And public perception has been that unless the Court comes down heavily, things do not move. To that extent, courts have been seen to provide succour for the common man's daily inconveniences, thereby having his support for its assertiveness.

Take the Board of Control for Cricket in India (BCCI) case: the Court had to step in and make elected office-bearers, who had been involved with the cricket body for decades, quit. There is no justification for anyone to believe that they are the only capable cricket administrators in the country or state, and despite having been on the job for forty years, be unwilling to let others take over. Had it not been for the Court, younger and possibly more capable persons would never have got an opportunity. This action alone of the Court has come in for much appreciation, as it will serve as a template for all sports bodies.

CITADEL FALLS FROM WITHIN

There have been whispers and indeed open talk too, of instances of misconduct among judges of the Supreme Court. The past few years have seen the Court embroiled in several controversies. There have been serious allegations of corruption at the highest level of the judiciary, expensive private holidays on taxpayers' money, a refusal to divulge details of judges' assets to the public, secrecy in the appointment of judges, refusal to make information public under the RTI Act, and so on.

Recommendations for appointment by the judiciary have come in for serious criticism from a former president of India, Dr A.P.J. Abdul Kalam. In November 2006, President Kalam had serious reservations about approving the recommendation of the Supreme Court collegium for the appointment of the chief justice of the Punjab and Haryana High Court. He returned the file in the first instance on the grounds that the collegium was expanded from the prescribed three to four, to overcome dissent within it, and also some 'deprecatory' written remarks by three Supreme Court judges. When the recommendation came back to the president after following the correct procedure, he approved it as per convention.[17] Former PM Manmohan Singh has also publicly stated that corruption is one of the major challenges facing the judiciary, and suggested that there is an urgent need to eradicate this menace.[18]

Now, to return to the press conference of 12 January 2018: this unprecedented act evoked varied reactions. People, including legal eagles, have taken potshots at the event with divergent views, depending on which side of the political divide they sit on. The executive always reacts with glee at dissension in courts—they have their own agenda. It will be very difficult to sit in judgement of whether the act was wise or not. It is, however, an undeniable fact that the press conference hit at the institutional integrity of the Supreme Court. The judges are personages of experience. They could not have been acting out of naiveté, innocently hoping that the rot could be stemmed by bringing it out in the public domain. Even if a grand moral stand had been contemplated, they should have recalled the past precedence of the three judges who had been bypassed by the Indira Gandhi government and resigned.

It was business as usual in the Court. So what were they seeking to achieve by their 'democracy in danger' talk? The factor

---

[17]'A controversial judicial appointment: The Hindu'; *Zee News*; 1 December 2006; https://zeenews.india.com/home/a-controversial-judicial-appointment-the-hindu_339221.html
Accessed on 3 July 2019.
[18]'Have more courts to tackle graft cases: Manmohan'; *The Economic Times*; 20 April 2008; https://m.economictimes.com/dateline-india/have-more-courts-to-tackle-graft-cases-manmohan/articleshow/2964588.cms
Accessed on 3 July 2019.

of collegiality demands that dissension in such high constitutional bodies is best kept within the four walls. It has been famously observed, and repeatedly too, that a citadel never falls but from within. In this case, by sharing the rot with the world outside, they could not have expected that the CJI, against whose ways their ire was directed, would mend his ways. They merely served to erode the edifice of an institution which had, at one time, given the nation a verdict as historic and noble as the Kesavananda Bharati verdict.

The reverberations of the press conference had barely died down when there was a startling allegation by a Supreme Court female staffer of sexual harassment against the CJI. This prompted the CJI to take the unprecedented step of calling a hearing, presided over by him, in Court No. 1 on a Saturday, at which he claimed it was a conspiracy to 'deactivate the CJI's office'. The lady alleged she had been removed from office when she had rebuffed his advances and that the services of her relatives had also been terminated.

A three-judge internal committee was set up to inquire into the allegations. It comprised two female judges. At its initial sitting, the committee disallowed the complainant the assistance of a lawyer. She soon withdrew from the inquiry, stating she had 'serious concerns and reservations about the committee'. The panel decided to proceed with the inquiry *ex parte* and gave the CJI a clean chit, finding 'no substance in the allegations'.

Prominent citizens and legal experts have faulted the handling of the complaint from the initial hearing that the CJI conducted himself. Ideally, the probe should have been by an external committee. Secondly, the basic request to be assisted by a lawyer was denied when 'she was pitted against three powerful judges of a powerful institution'.[19] The complainant has been denied not only

---

[19]Kaunain Sheriff M. and Seema Chishti; 'This episode is going to haunt SC in years to come. Justice AP Shah'; *The Indian Express*; 7 May 2019; https://indianexpress.com/article/india/justice-ap-shah-sexual-harassment-

the report but her own testimony as the inquiry is confidential. She has been denied due process and this may well go against the Supreme Court itself. With all the conspiracy theories and claims of baseless allegations, the Court may have acquitted itself better by following a transparent process, entrusting the inquiry to an external committee, and permitting the complainant the assistance of a lawyer. Since the CJI had said the allegation was baseless, he could well have been given a clean chit and the report then put in the public domain.

NEXT-GENERATION REFORMS TO ADDRESS HIGH PENDENCY

There is truth in the dictum that justice delayed is justice denied. Thus the most urgent reform action needed is around elimination of judicial delay and ensuring judicial efficiency. Pendency of cases in courts across the country is a huge cause for concern. Whilst the problem is recognized by all and concern expressed, definitive steps taken to resolve the issue are totally lacking. Recently, Minister of Law and Justice Ravi Shankar Prasad urged the chief justices of the twenty-four high courts to expedite recruitment of judicial officers. High courts need to hold timely examinations to recruit judges for lower courts.

He stated the pendency in district and subordinate courts to be 2,76,74,499 cases.[20] Such high pendency implies that a huge number of undertrials are languishing in jails. In fact, 67 per cent of the prison population consists of undertrials and

---

case-against-cji-ranjan-gogoi-this-episode-is-going-to-haunt-sc-in-years-to-come-5713956/
Accessed on 3 July 2019.

[20]'India has 19 judges per 10 lakh people: Data'; *The Economic Times*; 24 September 2018; https://economictimes.indiatimes.com/news/politics-and-nation/india-has-19-judges-per-10-lakh-people-data/printarticle/65935214.cms
Accessed on 3 July 2019.

47 per cent of them are in the age group of eighteen to thirty years.[21] They are also largely from the underprivileged classes and probably unfairly lodged in jails for petty offences. For them, time spent as undertrials may be more than the sentence itself. This leads to overcrowding in jails, besides the avoidable expense to the exchequer.

Justice R.M. Lodha, a former CJI, had proposed to make the judiciary work throughout the year (instead of the present system of having long vacations, especially in the higher courts) in order to reduce pendency of cases. This proposal would not have resulted in an increase in the number of working days or working hours of any judges. It was only to ensure a system of rotation so that judges would be taking their breaks at different times so as to ensure that some benches were working round the year. The Bar Council of India, however, rejected the proposal mainly because it would have inconvenienced the advocates who would have had to work throughout the year. A typical case of too much democracy!

Among other proposals, though not effectively acted upon, is one by the CJI to the state governments to consider plea bargaining in an endeavour to reduce pendency.[22] Considering that 46 per cent of the pending litigation involves the government, an innovative approach is essential if the judicial system has to be of any succour to the common man. The government needs

---

[21]'3.3 crore cases pending in Indian courts, pendency figure at its highest: CJI Dipak Misra'; *Business Today*; 28 June 2018; https://www.businesstoday.in/current/economy-politics/3-3-crore-cases-pending-indian-courts-pendency-figure-highest-cji-dipak-misra/story/279664.html Accessed on 3 July 2019.

[22]'SC asks states to consider plea bargaining to reduce pendency of cases'; *Business Standard*; 23 July 2018; https://www.business-standard.com/article/news-ani/sc-asks-states-to-consider-plea-bargaining-to-reduce-pendency-of-cases-118072301104_1.html Accessed on 3 July 2019.

to be proactive in reducing the number of vacancies in courts at all levels. It will continue to be a sad commentary on the judicial system in a democracy when a Salman Khan can ensure that his bail application is heard and bail granted to him overnight, whereas others cannot get a hearing for months.[23]

To ensure timely delivery of justice, reforms in the judicial system need to be fast-tracked. As per the Ministry of Law and Justice, India has only nineteen judges per million people. This is against the 110 per million in the US. The actual strength of the judiciary is 16,726 as against a sanctioned strength of 22,474. There is also the urgent need to improve the court management and infrastructure available, especially in the lower courts. The adoption of 'online filing and management', as has been done for application of passports, needs to be introduced. The imposition of penalty for repeated adjournments is long overdue.

THE COURSE CORRECTOR

In the final analysis, the Supreme Court's evolution in Independent India has been such that it has largely retained its stature and been lauded for pushing the country in a liberal direction, ensuring that societal reforms and the socio-economic ethos remain progressive. In recent times, it has handed out progressive judgements by abolishing instant divorce in the Muslim community, declaring privacy a fundamental right and defending freedom of expression by ordering state governments to lift a ban on a film that hardline Hindu groups found objectionable.

Its direction to the states to upload First Information

---

[23]'Blackbuck poaching case: Salman Khan granted bail by Jodhpur court'; *The Times of India*; 7 April 2018; https://timesofindia.indiatimes.com/entertainment/hindi/bollywood/news/blackbuck-poaching-case-salman-khan-granted-bail-by-jodhpur-court/articleshow/63651934.cms Accessed on 3 July 2019.

Reports (FIRs) online within twenty-four hours of their filing has introduced transparency and reduced discretion of police officers. The introduction of the alternative disputes redressal system put in place by the courts is commendable, as even criminal cases are being resolved through this mechanism. The Court decriminalized the law on consensual gay sex and in the LGBT fraternity. It has separately tried to clean up politics, ordering that trials against politicians be completed within a year. The Court has ordered that in case there is a delay, judges will have to explain the reasons for it. This is a major step, as more than one-third of the members elected to Parliament seem to have criminal cases pending against them. It had earlier barred lawmakers from elections if found guilty of offences carrying a jail term of at least two years.

The Court had the conviction as a defender of the Constitution to protect the various freedoms in the dark days of the Emergency. Expounding on the 'basic structure doctrine', it put the interests of the common man above everything else. The Court has displayed heartwarming dynamism in interpreting the law in sync with the times. A Constitution is a living document. Its efficacy lies in its interpretation. A remarkable achievement of the apex court has been its use of the Constitution as a tool to provide a bedrock for good governance. When all else was crumbling, the Court, time and again, came to the rescue of the nation, thereby being the course corrector. It is this function that has brought forth societal trust and gratitude.

All institutions that take on a progressive role have to introspect on when and how they have to dismount the tiger. The ideal would be when the other pillars perform to the expectations that the people have of them. Trust cannot be commanded. It has to be earned. Earning trust can come about only when Caesar's wife is seen to remain above suspicion.

It is fitting to recall the words of the then CJI-designate, Justice Ranjan Gogoi, at the Ramnath Goenka Memorial Lecture 2018:

'If the judiciary wishes to preserve its moral and institutional leverage, it must remain uncontaminated.'[24] The Supreme Court is too crucial a pillar for its institutional credibility to be eroded. Press conferences by judges, allegations from within and opacity in its decision-making process will only chip away at this hard-earned credibility. The Court can maintain its credibility only if it acts on the now-famous aphorism of Justice J.S. Verma: 'Be you ever so high, you are not above the law.'

---

[24]'Full Text: Justice Ranjan Gogoi delivers the third Ramnath Goenka Memorial Lecture — The Vision of Justice'; *The Indian Express*; 14 July 2018; https://indianexpress.com/article/india/justice-ranjan-gogoi-at-rng-lecture-independent-judges-and-noisy-journalists-are-democracys-first-line-of-defence-5257119/
Accessed on 18 July 2019.

3

THE ELECTION COMMISSION

Empowering Citizens to Determine Their Destiny

On 15 May 2019, around 6 p.m., in a nationally televised press conference, the ECI, using its powers, for the first time, under Article 324 of the Constitution, declared that canvassing in West Bengal for the seventh and the last phase of the general election, scheduled to end at 5 p.m. on 17 May, would end at 10 p.m. on 16 May–nineteen hours ahead. This was due to the unprecedented violence in the state. It also directed Rajiv Kumar, the former police commissioner of Kolkata, who was under investigation by the Central Bureau of Investigation (CBI), to demit charge forthwith and report to the Ministry of Home Affairs (MHA) at 10 a.m. the next day. This was a very resolute ECI, asserting its authority to ensure fair and trouble-free elections.

Only four weeks earlier (on 15 April), the ECI had argued before the Supreme Court that its powers to rein in politicians who sought votes on the basis of caste or religion were 'very limited'. The Court had to goad the ECI into taking decisions on complaints against high-ranking functionaries of the Bharatiya Janata Party (BJP), which had been pending for about five weeks, before 6 May. Nudged into action, it promptly suspended Azam Khan, Yogi Adityanath and Mayawati from campaigning for forty-eight to seventy-two hours, while at the same time letting off PM Narendra Modi and BJP President Amit Shah. Are the ECI's powers actually limited? Did it exercise its residual power judiciously and objectively or does it have a great deal of explaining to do to re-establish its formidable reputation?

While we need to examine the entire gamut of powers vested in the ECI by the Constitution and its impeccable credibility, let us first wade through the daunting challenge every general election proffers.

A MODERN MARVEL

India's general elections have often been described as the 'greatest show on earth', 'a jumbo exercise' or 'the largest mobilization of administrative resources'. Such a description is apposite; the exercise involves providing for roughly 15 per cent of the global population to cast its votes. To derive an idea of its magnitude, we need to study the following statistics:

In 2019, the size of the electorate was 900 million. Of these, 150 million were first-time voters. The ECI has 2,354 registered political parties. However, only about 500 fielded candidates. In 2014, a total of 8,251 candidates had contested 543 seats for the Lok Sabha. As against 930,000 polling stations with 1,495,430 electronic voting machines (EVMs) and 989 counting centres in 2014, the 2019 election provided about 2.3 million EVMs and voter verifiable paper audit trail (VVPAT) machines installed in 1,035,000 polling stations.

- The smallest constituency in 2019 comprised 47,972 voters (Lakshadweep), as against 2,950,000 voters in Malkajgiri (Telangana).
- In this mammoth exercise, elephants, camels, boats, cycles, helicopters, trains and planes were used to transport officials, security personnel and voters.

- In Ladakh, Jammu & Kashmir (J&K), in 2014, a dozen polling personnel trekked 45 km in knee-deep snow to enable thirty-seven citizens to vote.[1] In 2019, in Banej village in Gir forest of Junagadh constituency, the ECI set up a booth for a single voter.
- In Kerala, in 2014, a plantation called Kakkayam Estate had become defunct. As a consequence, 350 people, who had been living and working on the estate, migrated to another area. However, one person stayed behind. The ECI had to retain one booth with six officials for him to cast his vote. When this person died, his death was reported by the media as the 'death of a polling booth'.[2]
- In 2014, for the first time in the electoral history of India, the None of the Above (NOTA) option was introduced for voters.

The conduct of elections in India has certainly been a modern marvel. The exercise is undertaken just about every year as a consequence of some state going to the polls or a general election being held. The ECI accomplishes flawless execution which has hitherto never seen a glitch of any kind. It is pertinent to understand the evolution of the ECI and the manner in which the machinery, along with its mandate, has matured over the seventy years that India has been Independent.

CONSTITUTIONAL STATUS: A VISIONARY DECISION

The founding fathers of India's Constitution had the wisdom and vision to devote a separate chapter to elections. This was

---

[1] Anjana Pasricha; 'India's election involves daunting logistical challenges'; VOA; 25 March 2014; https://www.voanews.com/east-asia/indias-election-involves-daunting-logistical-challenges
Accessed on 2 July 2019.
[2] S.Y. Quraishi; *An Undocumented Wonder: The Making of the Great Indian Election*; Rupa Publications (2014)

provided in Part XV of the Constitution. The framers adopted the Westminster model of parliamentary government with modifications to suit the Indian democracy. A major modification was the setting up of the ECI in a form that has ensured a free and fair democratic process for electing a truly representative government. During the deliberations of the Constituent Assembly, the House unanimously affirmed that to ensure the credibility and freedom of elections to the legislative bodies, the ECI must be free of any kind of interference from the executive of the day.[3]

The drafting committee then put in a separate part containing Articles 289, 290 and so on. They inserted Article 289, which transferred the superintendence, direction and control of preparation of the electoral rolls and of all elections to Parliament and legislatures of the states to a body outside the executive, to be called the Election Commission of India. That is the provision contained in sub-clause (1), which established the fundamental principle that the election machinery should be outside the control of the executive (the government). Sub-clause (2) says that there shall be a chief election commissioner (CEC) and such other election commissioners (ECs) as the president may, from time to time, appoint.

The rather visionary decision taken then was to centralize the election machinery in the hands of one central commission and not consider separate commissions for states. This decision was taken under the guidance of Dr Ambedkar, recognizing that franchise is a fundamental right in a democracy and that no person who is entitled to be brought into the electoral rolls on the grounds of being an adult of twenty-one years of age, should be excluded merely as a result of the prejudice of a local government.

The fear seemed genuine, as a divide had begun to appear

---

[3]S.K. Mendiratta: Election laws, practices and procedures. Constituent Assembly debates. 15 June 1948

between the original inhabitants of any particular region and others who were living there but happened to be racially, linguistically or culturally different from them. It was observed that the regional governments were attempting to keep this category of people out of the electoral rolls. Such alienation would have struck at the very root of democratic government. Thus, it was decided that the entire election machinery should be in the hands of a central election commission, which alone would be entitled to issue directives to returning officers, polling officers and others engaged in the preparation and revision of electoral rolls so that no injustice was done to any citizen, who, under the Constitution, was entitled to inclusion in the electoral rolls.

This objective was achieved by the setting up of a central election commission, a permanent body, under Article 324(1) of the Constitution. The Constituent Assembly of J&K also reposed faith in the ECI and entrusted to it the task of holding elections to its legislature. This far-sighted decision has been a major contributor to the independence and continued credibility of the ECI and hence the entire election process in the country.

A NATION VOTES

The Constituent Assembly, which adopted the Constitution on 26 November 1949, was converted into a provisional parliament until the regular parliament was voted in. It was this assembly which decided on universal adult suffrage in the very first year of the nation's birth when other, far more mature and older democracies have taken years, nay, centuries to provide their people this facility. It goes to the credit of the members of the assembly that they had the foresight and courage of conviction to entrust the year-old democracy with a mandate that others had feared to enforce. It also goes to the credit of the Indian bureaucratic setup that, despite the upheaval of the Partition bringing about widespread lawlessness and migration, the newly born nation commenced the election process on 10 September 1951.

In his book, *An Undocumented Wonder*, former CEC Dr S.Y. Quraishi records that polling started on 25 October and was held in sixty-eight phases, ending on 21 February 1952. A total of 196,084 polling stations were set up, among which 27,527 were exclusively for women, for an electorate of 173,212,343, of whom 105,950,083 actually cast their votes. It also goes to the credit of the voters that when literacy was barely 16 per cent in the country and the secrecy of the balloting process had to be maintained, they exercised their franchise and gave themselves a truly democratically elected government. To overcome the literacy constraint, each contesting candidate was allotted a separate box labelled with his name and election symbol.[4]

COMPOSITION: THE CAPTAIN AND HIS TEAM

Article 324(2) lays down that the ECI shall comprise the CEC and such number of other ECs, if any, as the president may from time to time fix. When any other EC is appointed, the CEC shall act as the chairman of the ECI [Article 324(3)]. However, all ECs have equal say in decision-making. When there's a difference of opinion, the majority will prevail. The first election commission was set up as a permanent constitutional body on 25 January 1950, and the first CEC was appointed on 21 March that year.

The fact that the president decides on the composition of the ECI essentially means that the government of the day decides it. This provision in the Constitution has led to a great deal of churning in governments deliberating on whether the ECI should be a single-member body or a multimember one. At the time of inception, it

---

[4]S.Y. Quraishi; *An Undocumented Wonder: The Making of the Great Indian Election*; Rupa Publications (2014)

was decided to have only one EC. Thus, until 1989, there was only one CEC. However, on 7 October 1989, the president, in exercise of powers under Article 324(2), decided to make the ECI a multimember body and, by a notification issued on that day, fixed, until further orders, the number of ECs at two (besides the CEC). By a further notification, on 16 October, the president appointed S.S. Dhanoa and V.S. Seigell as ECs.

However, on 1 January 1990, the president converted the ECI into a single-member body again and rescinded the two earlier notifications. Dhanoa challenged this before the Supreme Court, contending, inter alia, that, once appointed, an EC continued in office for his full term as determined under Article 324(5) and the president had no power to cut short the tenure. It was also urged that the ECI being an independent body, its independent functioning could not be eroded in any manner by removing the two ECs.

A division bench of the Supreme Court rejected Dhanoa's contentions and dismissed his petition on 24 July 1991. It held that there was no need for the ECs' posts:

> ...[At] the time the appointments were made, and that in the absence of a clear definition of their role in the Commission, particularly, vis-a-vis the Chief Election Commissioner, the abolition of the posts, far from striking at the independence of the Commission, paved the way for its smooth and effective functioning.[5]

The Court further observed that the creation and abolition of posts is the prerogative of the executive, and Article 324(2) leaves it to the president to fix and appoint such number of ECs as he may, from time to time, determine. It maintained that the power

---

[5]Supreme Court of India; S.S. Dhanoa Vs Union of India and Ors on 24 July 1991; https://indiankanoon.org/doc/852842/?type=print Accessed on 2 July 2019.

of the president to create the posts is unfettered, so is his power to reduce or abolish them.

Pursuant to these observations of the Supreme Court, the Parliament enacted the Chief Election Commissioner and other Election Commissioners (Conditions of Service) Act, 1991. It fixed the tenure of the CEC and ECs, when appointed, as six years. The CEC was to retire at sixty-five years and would receive the same salary and other perquisites as a Supreme Court judge. The ECs were to also retire at sixty-five years and derive the salary and other benefits available to a high court judge.

Meanwhile, T.N. Seshan, the then CEC, challenged before the Supreme Court the president's decision to make the ECI a multimember body and the appointment of the two ECs as mala fide. His grievance was that the motive behind the government appointing two more ECs was to dilute his authority, since the two new appointees would do the bidding of the ruling party. Dismissing the petitions, the Court held that under Article 324 the ECI could be single-member or multimember.

Since 1 October 1993, the ECI functions as a three-member body, with the CEC and ECs being appointed by the president. No specific qualifications have been prescribed for the three officials. Their tenure is six years, subject to a maximum age of sixty-five years. The CEC can be removed only by impeachment in the Parliament and by a two-third majority. However, the ECs can be removed on the recommendation of the CEC. Hence, they enjoy limited protection. The budget of the ECI is voted, not charged (in the sense that it does not become an automatic liability on the consolidated fund).

The ECI is represented in a state, for the conduct of parliamentary and assembly elections, by the chief electoral officer. For the conduct of elections to lower bodies such as the municipal corporations, municipalities, district councils and village councils, state election commissions have been set up by the 73rd and 74th Amendments (1992), which came into effect on 1 June 1993.

PLENARY POWER

The ECI's functions can be demarcated between its core or primary function and the other functions that devolve upon it by virtue of its constitutional status. The core function, as mandated by the Constitution, is the superintendence, direction and control of elections to various bodies such as the Parliament, the legislative assemblies, and the offices of the president and the vice-president of the country. It is also vested with the powers to prepare the electoral rolls for the conduct of the elections to these bodies/offices. The powers of the ECI have been repeatedly questioned in courts but the Supreme Court has held that where a specific law is silent, the reservoir of powers under Article 324(1) gives it the right to issue all directions necessary for the conduct of smooth, free and fair elections. In a verdict delivered by a constitution bench of the Supreme Court in an election petition in 1977, it maintained that Article 324 is a plenary provision vesting the comprehensive responsibility of national and state elections in the ECI. It went on to observe that the words 'superintendence, direction and control' stipulate, in the Article, powers in the broadest terms. Thus, this Article vests in the ECI powers that are quasi-judicial and, indeed, also administrative. This was the power that it exercised when it announced the truncation of campaigning in West Bengal in the course of the 2019 general election.

In May 2002, the Supreme Court held in another case (*Union of India Vs Association for Democratic Reforms*): '...[The] jurisdiction of the election commission was wide enough to include all powers which were necessary for the smooth conduct of elections and the word "elections" is used in a wide sense to include the entire process of election which consists of several stages and embraces many steps."[6]

SCRAMBLE FOR SYMBOLS

All associations or bodies of individual citizens desiring to be categorized as political parties and contesting elections under the name and banner of a political party have to get themselves registered with the ECI. The Supreme Court has held that this is a quasi-judicial function performed by the ECI. These registered political parties are then designated as national or state parties, depending on their performance in elections and fulfilment of certain laid-down criteria. In the event of a split in any of these parties, the ECI has the power to decide on the allocation of the original symbol of the party. In cases of a re-merger or a merger with other political parties, it is for the ECI to decide on the nature of the split/merger and the allocation of the symbol. In the course of exercising this power, it was mandated by the Supreme Court that the ECI exercises the judicial power of the State and is deemed to be a quasi-judicial tribunal against whose decision the appeal lies only to the apex court under its appellate jurisdiction.

A very interesting recent case is the dispute around the allotment of the original symbol of the Samajwadi Party (SP) upon its splitting. This party in UP had serious internal dissension, leading to the creation of two factions, one led by the founder and supremo of the party, Mulayam Singh Yadav, and the other by his son and the then chief minister, Akhilesh Yadav. The issue came to a head when both factions claimed the bicycle symbol of the party. They staked their claim before

---

[6]Election Commission of India; 27 March 2003; http://www.adrindia.org/sites/default/files/Order_Assests_Affidavits.pdf Accessed on 2 July 2019.

the ECI barely a week before the date of filing of nominations for assembly elections.

After due inquiry and hearing both factions, the ECI decided to allot the symbol to the Akhilesh faction on the basis of its filing affidavits of 205 out of 228 MLAs, 56 out of 68 MLCs, 15 out of 24 MPs, and 28 out of 45 national executive members. Besides, 2,440 national convention delegates out of 5,731 had also filed affidavits. The situation was very piquant as Mulayam was the founder-president of the party and was the party president at that point of time, until the Akhilesh faction anointed the latter the president. Nevertheless, the ECI took the decision to allot the symbol to the Akhilesh faction on the affirmations made by the elected members of the party under the Election Symbols (Reservation and Allotment) Order, 1968.[7]

ENSURING A LEVEL PLAYING FIELD

It is important to analyse a fairly potent weapon that has subsequently been bestowed on the ECI under Article 324 itself. The ECI issues the Model Code of Conduct (MCC), a set of guidelines for the general conduct of political parties and candidates during elections mainly with respect to speeches, polling booths, election manifestos, processions and general conduct after announcement of elections. This set of guidelines has been evolved with the consensus of political parties, which have consented to abide by the principles embodied in the code, in letter and in spirit.

The MCC comes into force immediately on announcement of

---

[7]'Akhilesh has majority support of legislators, party delegates: EC'; *Business Standard*; 16 January 2017; https://www.business-standard.com/article/politics/akhilesh-has-majority-support-of-legislators-party-delegates-ec-117011601268_1.html
Accessed on 5 July 2019.

the election schedule by the ECI to ensure free and fair elections. Much of it is designed to avert communal clashes and corrupt practices. There have recently been instances of politicians making hate speeches, pitching one community against another or making promises of new projects that may influence voters. The code ensures that such unethical practices do not take place. It prohibits the distribution of liquor to voters, and bars the ruling party from making announcements that may sway voters or from taking policy decisions that would favour the interests of the party in power. The code is basically designed to ensure a level playing field for all political parties.

The code has been effective in regulating the conduct of political parties largely because it is self-regulatory in nature and is not backed or created by an Act. Despite the fact that it does not arm the ECI with any penal powers other than a reprimand or censure, any castigation by it for violation of the code has very adverse repercussions for a politician or party among the citizenry, inviting ridicule and condemnation. A widely reported case of a minister violating the MCC and falling foul of the ECI was of then Union Minister of Law and Justice Salman Khurshid, who, while canvassing for his wife's candidature in the legislative assembly election, promised in his speech that if elected to power in the state, the Congress would give religious minorities 9 per cent out of the 27.5 per cent OBC quota for government jobs.[8] This was seen as violative of the code and the minister was censured by the ECI. However, he was defiant and went on to state that he would reiterate his stance even if 'they hang

---

[8]'Petition filed against Khurshid over Muslim sub-quota remark'; *The Times of India*; 14 February 2012; https://timesofindia.indiatimes.com/india/Petition-filed-against-Khurshid-over-Muslim-sub-quotaremark/articleshow/11885214.cms
Accessed on 2 July 2019.

me'. Though the Congress initially defended him,[9] realizing the seriousness of the delinquency, it later sought to distance itself by stating that 'people occupying posts of responsibility should speak responsibly'.

The ECI was compelled to write to the president about the violation by the minister and his subsequent 'improper and unlawful' defiance of its censure. The president forwarded the letter to the PM, who sought an explanation from the minister. At this point, Khurshid was compelled to express regret, saying that it was never his intention to transgress the law and undermine the code of conduct.[10] This apology ended the row, clearly indicating the superiority of the constitutional body and its principled stand, irrespective of parties, personalities or the government.

EVMs VS THE BALLOT

Certain political parties had raised doubts that the EVMs could be tampered with in such a way that, irrespective of the button pressed, the vote would go to a particular candidate. Such a claim obviously suffered from a typical loser's syndrome. The parties had not pointed fingers at the credibility of the EVM when they were in the winning position. Nevertheless, the allegation did raise doubts in the mind of the common man and hence it became the responsibility of the ECI to assure the public about the machines being tamper-proof. In fact, the Aam Aadmi Party (AAP) went to the extent of demonstrating in the Delhi legislative

---

[9]'EC complains to President against "defiant" Khurshid'; *Rediff News*; 11 February 2012; https://m.rediff.com/news/slide-show/slide-show-1-ec-complains-to-president-against-defiant-khurshid/20120211.htm Accessed on 2 July 2019.

[10]'EC may put lid on row with Khurshid'; *The Deccan Herald*; 14 February 2012; https://www.deccanherald.com/content/227072/ec-may-put-lid-row.html Accessed on 2 July 2019.

assembly the manner in which the machine could be tampered with.

This compelled the ECI to issue a letter stating:

> …[It] is possible for anyone to make any electronic gadget which 'looks like' an ECI EVM and demonstrate any magic or tampering. Very simply put, any 'look-alike' machine is just a different gadget, which is manifestly designed and made to function in a 'tampered' manner and has no relevance, incidence or bearing on the Commission's EVMs. Any person with reasonable common sense can understand that gadgets other than ECI EVMs can be programmed to perform in a pre-determined way, but it simply cannot be implied that ECI EVMs will behave in the same manner because the ECI EVMs are technically secured and function under an elaborate administrative and security protocol. Such so-called demonstration on extraneous and duplicate gadgets, which are not owned by the ECI, cannot be exploited to influence our intelligent citizens and electorate to assail or vilify the EVMs used by the Commission in its electoral process.[11]

In response to another report by the British Broadcasting Corporation (BBC) that an American had managed to hack the EVM, the ECI further clarified that the report was false. It was stated that the American opened an EVM, changed some parts, and hacked the new parts he had put in the machine. He did not hack the original Indian machine.[12] It has to be recognized that

---

[11] 'ECI EVMs are Non-Tamperable'; Press Information Bureau; Government of India; Election Commission; 9 May 2017; http://pib.nic.in/newsite/PrintRelease.aspx?relid=161677 Accessed on 2 July 2019.

[12] 'EVMs Cannot Be Hacked Or Tampered With: 5-Fact Explanation'; *NDTV* 16 March 2017; https://www.ndtv.com/opinion/no-ballot-papers-are-not-

to tamper with EVMs that are kept under the safe custody of the district magistrates, one has to access these EVMs (hundreds of thousands of machines), break the seals and replace parts on a mass scale needed for rigging elections. This is well nigh impossible as all the machines are securely stored in strong rooms of the district collectorate.

To ensure that the process is completely beyond reproach, the ECI, in consultation with representatives of seven national and thirty-five recognized state parties, further clarified that all future elections would be held with voting machines that have a paper trail attached. The VVPAT system records the candidate and the symbol that every person votes for but the voter cannot take the receipt home.

In *An Undocumented Wonder*, Quraishi narrates the election contested by C.P. Joshi, president of the Rajasthan Pradesh Congress Committee in 2008. While his party won a majority in the election, he himself lost his contest by one vote. He sought a recount of the postal ballots as, usually, there is neither any scope nor possibility of a mistake in the EVM. There was no change after the recount. He then sought a re-tabulation of the total votes of each EVM, since this is done manually, and he suspected that a mistake in the counting could have crept in. There was still no change in the vote count even after this exercise. He had *still* lost by one vote and was compelled to accept the poll verdict. Ironically, it was later discovered that two members of his family had not voted, preferring to go to the temple instead, thereby depriving him of victory and possibly the chief ministership! However, in a personal discussion that I had with Joshi on 11 May 2019, while watching the final cricket match of the women's IPL in Jaipur, he maintained that his wife had voted along with him.

---

better-than-evms-5-facts-1669926
Accessed on 2 July 2019.

CURBING MONEY POWER IN ELECTIONS

It is commonly believed that a major malady plaguing Indian democracy has been the use of money power in elections and the amassing of wealth by those elected. The government or the income tax authorities has not been able to do much to check this. Lok Prahari, an NGO, filed a PIL, drawing attention to the exponential rise in the assets of a politician in a span of five years between two successive elections.

Delivering its verdict in what is now a landmark move in electoral reforms, the Supreme Court directed that politicians, their spouses and associates must declare their sources of income, along with their assets, in order to qualify for contesting elections.[13] The Court directed that their assets and sources of income be continuously monitored to maintain the purity of the electoral process and the integrity of the democratic structure of this country. The Court also observed that 'manifold and undue accretion of assets' by legislators or their associates in itself becomes a ground for disqualification.

This direction by the Court is a very welcome development as it will serve to introduce greater transparency in the electoral process and, in the bargain, develop trust between the elected and the electorate. This is so, as now the person seeking election is required to file an affidavit on behalf of himself, his spouse and all dependants, specifying their PAN numbers, incomes declared in tax returns, moveable assets like bank accounts, shares and jewellery, immoveable assets and financial liabilities. This renders them subject to scrutiny by civil society.

---

[13]Krishnadas Rajagopal; 'Show source of income to contest elections, Supreme Court tells politicians'; *The Hindu*. 16 February 2018; https://www.thehindu.com/news/national/reveal-source-of-income-sc-orders-politicians/article22771987.ece
Accessed on 2 July 2019.

The reasoning behind the Court directive is that the voter enjoys a fundamental right in making an informed choice among those seeking his vote and needs to know the full details of the person he is going to vote for. The Court has also suggested that a law be passed disqualifying those with disproportionate income. The passing of such a statute will definitely be indicative of a desire by the Parliament to introduce transparency among politicians as well. This will ensure that insidious means of amassing wealth, or the ambition to join politics to amass wealth, are curbed.

In an attempt to limit the spending of political parties on election campaigns, the ECI has been attempting certain reforms. It has proposed to limit a party's election spending to a maximum of 50 per cent of the combined maximum spend for all its candidates. The ECI has placed a cap between ₹2 million and ₹2.8 million for an assembly candidate's spending and between ₹5 million and ₹7 million for a parliamentary candidate. The ECI has also sought to limit anonymous donations to political parties to 20 per cent of a party's total collections.

In the 2019 general election, donations to political parties were also permitted through election bonds sold by the State Bank of India (SBI). These bonds were introduced to maintain the anonymity of the donor, as only the bank has a record of the identity of the entity/person purchasing the bond. The ECI has also stipulated a ceiling of ₹2,000 for online or cash donations. However, some parties, such as the Bahujan Samaj Party (BSP), never declare any donors as they maintain that all their individual donations are less than ₹2,000! There are about forty reform measures that have been suggested by the ECI and other related bodies that are still to be considered. It would be a noble gesture on the part of the government if, during its current tenure, these are widely discussed and the more practicable and effective suggestions implemented.

ONE NATION, ONE ELECTION

There has been much talk of holding simultaneous elections to the legislative assemblies and the Parliament. The advantages ascribed to such a move include economizing on the massive expenditure that is currently incurred for the conduct of separate elections, the so-called 'policy paralysis' that results from the imposition of the MCC during election time, delay in delivery of essential services as the administrative machinery gets diverted, and repeated withdrawal from routine duties of crucial manpower that is deployed during election time. In 2016, the code was notified in Maharashtra for 307 days—in different areas—due to elections to the Parliament, the assembly or local bodies.[14]

Though India did begin by conducting simultaneous polls in 1961, however, with reorganization in some states and tenures of some assemblies cut short, the practice could not be continued. The Standing Committee of Parliament on Personnel, Public Grievances, Law and Justice, in an analysis of the feasibility of conducting simultaneous elections, noted that, of the sixteen Lok Sabhas that were constituted prior to the 2019 election, seven were dissolved prematurely due to coalition governments.[15]

---

[14]Liz Mathew; 'BJP chief Amit Shah to Law Commission: Simultaneous polls can be implemented'; *The Indian Express*; 14 August 2018; https://indianexpress.com/article/india/one-nation-one-poll-amit-shah-law-commission-simultaneous-polls-5305372/
Accessed on 2 July 2019.

[15]Standing Committee Report Summary: Feasibility of holding simultaneous elections to Lok Sabha and State Legislative Assemblies; PRS Legislative Research; 4 January 2016
https://www.prsindia.org/sites/default/files/parliament_or_policy_pdfs/1451885664_SCR%20Summary-%20feasibility%20of%20holding%20simultaneous%20central%20and%20state%20elections_0.pdf
Accessed on 3 July 2019.

However, it observed that, lately, the legislatures have been completing their terms and the Anti-Defection Act, 1985, has curbed defection, which has had a direct bearing on governments completing their terms.

The BJP, in the ruling NDA combine, is keen on holding simultaneous elections and its then president, Amit Shah, had written to the Law Commission in this regard. However, in a media interaction, the then CEC, O.P. Rawat, had stated: 'If the term of some State Assemblies needs to be curtailed or extended, then a constitutional amendment will be required.[16] ...Logistics arrangements with regard to 100 per cent availability of VVPATs will be a constraint.'[17] The government continues to pursue this objective and if a practical and legal method is evolved, it will certainly save on avoidable expenditure and 'downtime' in government-functioning to keep providing staff for elections to different bodies.

FIRM, OBJECTIVE AND TRANSPARENT

The contribution of Seshan in enhancing the prestige and efficacy of the ECI needs be acknowledged. It was he who reaffirmed the majestic supremacy of the institution in the entire election process. If the politician fears any agency, it is only the ECI.

In 1996, as the election observer in Lucknow constituency,

---

[16]'Simultaneous polls need legal framework'; *The Hindu*; 14 August 2018; https://www.thehindu.com/news/national/simultaneous-polls-need-legal-framework/article24691855.ece
Accessed on 3 July 2019.

[17]Smriti Kak Ramachandran; 'EC to use EVMs with paper trail in future polls, Kejriwal "sad" about hackathon'; *Hindustan Times*; 13 May 2017; https://www.hindustantimes.com/india-news/evm-tampering-all-future-elections-to-be-held-with-voting-machines-with-paper-trail-says-election-commission/story-NoOWRS77lJ5VbqZNbrn8xL.html
Accessed on 3 July 2019.

I chanced upon an interesting episode. A colleague of mine was the election observer in a neighbouring constituency and we were both staying in the state guest house. While he was on election duty in the office of the returning officer, a candidate came to file his nomination. It has become the trend for candidates to arrive in a procession with a band and cheering party workers. Also in attendance are the private security personnel of the candidate (if he is an important local citizen). The local police inspector on duty at the door of the office of the returning officer barred the others and permitted only five persons to accompany the candidate into the room. A minor argument ensued, as members of the private security posse of the candidate wanted to accompany him. The police inspector explained to them that instructions allowed for only five persons to accompany the candidate inside the room and that the security of the candidate, in the returning officer's room, would be ensured by the police.

This apparently infuriated a private bodyguard. Once the candidate had filed his nomination and stepped out of the office, the bodyguard pulled out his weapon and shot the inspector at point-blank range. Yet, such is the influence of local leaders that the incident was not reported by the district administration. But the episode had left the election observer aghast. In the guest house, we discussed the matter and decided that he must report it to the ECI. He did so.

A query from the ECI revealed that no action had been taken by the police over the killing (the candidate was from an influential family and it had managed to hush it up). It was then that the fury of Seshan and the might of the ECI came to the fore. The entire state government was hauled up, the candidate penalized, the election deferred and the chief secretary of the state had to explain the inaction. This incident is demonstrative of the considerable power that the ECI wields in the election process—a very welcome development.

There is enough historical evidence to show that the courts are no deterrent for the wily politician, as cases can drag on for years. For instance, Lalu Prasad Yadav was convicted in December 2017 for misdeeds in 1990–94. Sukh Ram was convicted in 2016 for bribes allegedly taken in 1996. The CBI also takes years for successful prosecution and at times politicians have been known to switch parties in the hope that being part of the ruling combine will help their case with the agency. It is thus ultimately only the objectivity and alacrity of decision-making in the ECI that serves as a deterrent for the politician.

Being a constitutional body enjoying autonomy and a guaranteed tenure provides the confidence to the commissioners to neither be beholden to any party nor need to play footsie with any politician. They are able to take decisions purely on merit and thus ensure that the process is not vitiated.

The ECI's credibility and reputation for independence and objectivity were also amply demonstrated in the election to the Rajya Sabha from Gujarat in 2017. Ahmed Patel, the political secretary to the then Congress president and four-time winner, was contesting against a former Congress member who had recently defected to the BJP. Two dissident MLAs of the Congress, who had apparently committed to vote for the BJP candidate, decided to demonstrate that they had fulfilled their commitment. After marking the ballot paper, they displayed it to the BJP president, who was present in the hall, before dropping it into the ballot box.

Since these elections are held by secret ballot, the rules permit the ballot to be shown only to the authorized party representative, which the party president was not. Thus there appeared to be a potential case for rejecting these two votes. The incident led to high drama, with the Congress holding up the counting process, seeking rejection of these two votes, and the BJP seeking commencement of counting on the grounds that the validity of ballots, once cast, cannot be questioned.

Party bigwigs from both sides made a beeline for the ECI headquarters in Delhi to argue their respective cases. The political grapevine maintained that video footage of the polling process showed that the two MLAs had indeed displayed their ballots to an unauthorized representative but, since the CEC was from the Gujarat cadre of the IAS and an appointee of the present government, he would be prevailed upon to decide the case in favour of the BJP. The ECI then watched the video and, upholding the credibility of the institution, passed an order rejecting the votes of the two legislators—maintaining that they had 'violated the voting procedure and secrecy of ballots'.[18]

This was a landmark verdict, reaffirming that independent constitutional bodies deliver on merit. It is such incidents that strengthen the edifice of accountability institutions, which are so critical for the efficient functioning of a vibrant democracy.

Earlier in this chapter, a reference has been made to decisions taken by the ECI on certain complaints of violation of the MCC against the PM and the BJP president. Media reports have been drawing attention to dissension among the ECs on some of these issues. It appears that one of the three commissioners was not in favour of a 'clean chit' to the PM. While a majority decision is perfectly in order, no decision, not even of the Supreme Court, can always be unanimous. It is contended that the dissenting commissioner desired his views be appropriately recorded. It is understood that the legal cell of the ECI is not in favour of recording these dissensions, as Model Code violations are not part of quasi-judicial hearings.

The issue seems to have snowballed, with the dissenting

---

[18]'Gujarat Rajya Sabha polls: EC rejects ballots of Cong MLAs who voted for BJP'; *The Hindu BusinessLine*; 9 August 2017; https://www.thehindubusinessline.com/news/national/gujarat-rajya-sabha-polls-ec-rejects-ballots-of-cong-mlas-who-voted-for-bjp/article9807756.ece Accessed on 2 July 2019.

commissioner desiring to recuse himself from future meetings if his views were not recorded. The entire controversy appears to have been avoidable. Admittedly, while the ECI aspires for unanimous decisions, its rules provide for a majority ruling in the absence of unanimity. Institutions such as the ECI have very robust and well-considered processes for its functioning. These have evolved over the years and have withstood scrutiny over multiple elections. These conventions need to be respected. Notings exchanged within the ECI, and among commissioners, are well documented. Having such a record maintains the credibility of the institution. In any democracy, the role of the election commission is far too critical for any dent in its reputation by such avoidable controversy.

WITHOUT FEAR OR FAVOUR

The ECI has been credited with delivering flawless elections, year after year, with zero tolerance for error. How has this been possible, especially since it is manned by those very officials who comprise the Indian bureaucracy, which has otherwise been labelled as lethargic, laid-back and non-innovative? It is amazing that the same bureaucracy that becomes the handmaiden of politicians, is alleged to kowtow to all their political whims and is purported to be lacking in probity and professional integrity, manages to overcome its own obvious inadequacies to deliver such immaculate elections. The very same bureaucracy manages to contain unruly and wanton politicians, create a level playing field, ensure that there is no booth capturing, as was the practice in the past, and constrains money and muscle power. It is indeed a remarkable commentary on the bureaucracy, which, after all the perceived inadequacies, is able to get its act together and function as a well-oiled machine.

The ECI has gone through turbulent times. Its credibility

has been repeatedly tested in courts. Its functioning and, lately, its reliance on EVMs have withstood the test of scrutiny. It has weathered all this stoically. This has been its strength. It has received support and often acclaim from citizens, the media, courts and even political parties, who, more often than not, love to hate it. All this has been possible only because the ECI has been firm, objective and transparent in its conduct. It is truly a beacon of hope, empowering the citizenry to determine a nation's destiny and thereby strengthen the foundation of Indian democracy. It needs to maintain the immaculate reputation it has built over the years and endeavour to ensure that it can withstand the repeated attempts by political groups to weaken it. The Constitution framers endowed it with ample powers and it needs to fulfil its constitutional duty without fear or favour.

4

THE RESERVE BANK OF INDIA

Protecting the Economy from the Executive

'I promise to pay the bearer the sum of one hundred rupees.'
This is the affirmation made by the governor of the RBI on the face of every currency note above the value of one rupee (in this case one hundred rupees). The affirmation is made in accordance with Section 26 of the RBI Act, under which the issuer of the banknote (the RBI) accepts the liability to pay the value of the note. It is a declaration of the banknote being legal tender for the specified amount.

On the other hand, governments fix the valuation of the currency. A classic example of the government announcing a devaluation of its currency is that of Chancellor James Callaghan in the UK stating in 1967 that the government had decided to lower the exchange rate of the pound sterling by 14 per cent. In an effort to reassure the public, Prime Minister Harold Wilson famously said, 'that doesn't mean, of course, that the pound here in Britain, in your pocket or purse or in your bank, has been devalued.'[1]

---

[1] Daniel Harari; '"Pound in your pocket" devaluation: 50 years on'; House of Commons Library; 17 November 2017; https://commonslibrary.parliament.uk/economy-business/economy-economy/pound-in-your-pocket-devaluation-50-years-on/
Accessed on 12 July 2019.

These two statements illustrate the relationship of any central bank and its government. What precisely is the import of these two examples and how does it play out in India?

The war with Pakistan in 1965, followed by two successive years of drought, put severe pressure on the economy, such that the government was compelled to consider devaluing the Indian rupee. It was a difficult decision for the government to take, as it would be widely criticized and be seen as a weakening of the economy. It would also be perceived as the government bowing to the pressures of external agencies such as the World Bank and the International Monetary Fund (IMF). It is said that the decision was so momentous and expected to have such far-reaching consequences that, having taken the decision to devalue the rupee on 5 June 1966, Indira Gandhi, the then PM, watched *Dr Zhivago* to overcome her nervousness ahead of the announcement the next day.[2] The devaluation was substantial since the value of the rupee declined from ₹4.76 to ₹7.5, to the dollar. This decline in its value by a whopping 57 per cent meant that every purchase on the international market for Indians would be costlier by about 60 per cent. The rupee then was pegged to the pound, which in turn was pegged to the dollar.

What, then, is the credibility of the pledge made by the governor and how does the government take a decision to devalue the currency, which in some ways erodes the external value of the money in my hand? This pertains to the rather interesting relationship between the central bank and the government, and the extent of accountability that the bank can establish in the financial markets as a regulator.

The RBI came into existence on 1 April 1935. It was originally

---

[2]Jayanta Roy Chowdhury; 'Lessons from a tale of two rupee devaluations'; *The Telegraph*; 24 June 2013; https://www.telegraphindia.com/business/lessons-from-a-tale-of-two-rupee-devaluations/cid/286954 Accessed on 10 June 2019.

set up as a private shareholders' bank, but was subsequently nationalized in 1949. At the time of its creation, macro policies being pursued by the government were those of fiscal control and monetary deflation, balanced budgets and minimizing sterling costs of its commitments abroad. Until the time of its creation, the central government was performing all the functions of the central bank.

The preamble to the RBI Act states: '... [To] constitute a Reserve Bank for India to regulate the issue of Bank notes and the keeping of reserves with a view to securing monetary stability in [India] and generally to operate the currency and credit system of the country to its advantage.' The same Act mandates the creation of the bank for the purposes of taking over the management of the currency from the central government and of carrying on the business of banking in accordance with the provisions of the Act. Thus, the bank is the monetary authority of the country and has been entrusted with the power to regulate commercial banking and its supervision in the country.

LANDMARK IN INDIA'S ECONOMIC HISTORY

In the early part of 1991, there was a great deal of uncertainty surrounding the stability of the then government led by PM Chandra Shekhar, as his relationship with the Congress, which rendered outside support, was becoming tenuous. He had taken over after the government led by V.P. Singh had fallen. That was the time when India was facing a massive balance of payments crisis and it was felt that the country had barely enough foreign exchange to pay for a fortnight's imports. The RBI had recommended import compression to restrict the use of scarce foreign exchange. The IMF had agreed to release a tranche of foreign exchange, but this was not enough to tackle the situation. It was widely felt that India had enough gold, which could be utilized to bring in funds. The full Budget could not be passed as the government had lost majority in Parliament, with the Congress having withdrawn support. The country was staring at a severe foreign exchange crisis and, with time running out, the prospects of a sovereign default by India looked imminent.

Journalist Shaji Vikraman, in a series of articles in *The Indian Express* on the evolution of issues in the RBI, writes that multilateral institutions such as the IMF and the World Bank put their funding on hold during this period.[3] The spring meeting of these institutions that year could not yield any commitment to provide the much-needed funds. Meanwhile, the assassination of Rajiv Gandhi in May 1991 led to political uncertainty in the country. It was under these conditions that officials drew up a plan to pledge gold. Gold was shipped out a few days after polling had taken place in the last week of May. UBS bought Indian gold and India managed to raise much-needed foreign exchange to the order of $200 million. The Bank of England and Bank of Japan were unwilling to lend unless India provided collateral for borrowing from them. The fact that India was a depository of gold at the IMF did not cut much ice with them and both the central banks insisted on the physical delivery of gold. So, between 4 July and 18 July, the RBI pledged 46.91 tonnes of gold with the Bank of England and the Bank of Japan to raise $400 million.

This landmark event in the economic history of India, and of the RBI, has been narrated by Dr C. Rangarajan, former governor of the RBI, who was then the deputy governor in the thick of the action, in an article written by him in *The Indian*

---

[3] Shaji Vikraman; 'In fact: How govts pledged gold to pull economy back from the brink'; *The Indian Express*; 5 April 2017; https://indianexpress.com/article/explained/in-fact-how-govts-pledged-gold-to-pull-economy-back-from-the-brink/
Accessed on 10 June 2019.

Express.[4] He mentions that the entire episode was not without its drama: one complication that arose was in the requirement of a declaration prescribed by the government to disclose the nature of any commodity being exported. It was suspected that such a declaration about gold being shipped out would have its own sensibilities in the Indian context. After much deliberation, the Ministry of Finance decided to issue a special authorization to send the consignment without the declaration. He also mentions how the convoy transporting the gold to the airport had to stop midway for an apparent tyre burst of one of the vehicles—and the tension that such a stoppage of the convoy created!

Dr Rangarajan goes on to record:

> The total loan raised against the pledge of gold was $405 million. Today, it may look small, but this amount was crucial to prevent a default at the time. There was no intention on the part of the RBI or the government to hide the transaction from the public. It is only that the RBI wanted to make it public once the operation was over. The shipment of gold made everyone aware of the enormity of the crisis facing India and paved the way for economic reforms.[5]

WHEN POLITICS TROUNCED ECONOMICS

There have been examples around the globe of differences between the government and the central bank. Quite early

---

[4]C. Rangarajan; '1991's golden transaction'; *The Indian Express*; 28 March 2016; https://indianexpress.com/article/opinion/columns/1991s-golden-transaction/
Accessed on 10 June 2019.

[5]C. Rangarajan; '1991's golden transaction'; *The Indian Express*; 28 March 2016; https://indianexpress.com/article/opinion/columns/1991s-golden-transaction/
Accessed on 10 June 2019.

in the history of the RBI, the institution witnessed certain fundamental issues concerning its independence vis-à-vis the government. The resignation of the first governor, Sir Osborne Smith, was over a difference between him and the then finance minister over the lowering of the bank rate as also the exchange rate of the rupee.[6] The RBI then felt, and this feeling has persisted over the years and among governors who have been at the helm of the bank, that the government attempted to interfere, if not dominate, with its views on issues that are rightfully the mandate of the central bank. In the 1950s, these differences prevailed between the then finance minister, T.T. Krishnamachari (TTK), and the governor, Sir Benegal Rama Rau. TTK seemed to pay scant respect to the autonomy of the RBI and made no bones about calling it a department of the government. The governor even complained to the PM that the finance minister had behaved in an intemperate manner with him. The last straw on the camel's back was when the finance minister announced the monetary policy in Parliament, which the governor thought was his prerogative, and in any case differed from what the RBI was to announce. Seeing no other viable option for himself, the governor resigned, despite attempts made by the PM and the then home minister, G.B. Pant, to resolve the differences between him and the finance minister.[7]

An important milestone in the development of banking in the country was the move to nationalize private-sector banks. The Left parties and some radical Congressmen (known as the Syndicate) had persistently demanded the nationalization of banks to prevent concentration of wealth in private hands and to mobilize more resources for economic development. They had argued that, in the period from 1947 to 1955, 361 private

---

[6] *History of the RBI 1935-51.* Vol. 1 Reprinted in 1970
[7] Ibid

banks had 'failed' across the country, translating to an average of over forty banks per year. This resulted in depositors losing all their money as they were not offered any guarantee by their respective banks. It was also felt that commercial banks were seen as catering only to large industries and business houses. Agriculture as a sector was largely ignored by these banks. In 1950, only 2.3 per cent of the bank loans were channelled to farmers. The situation worsened, with the figure declining to 2.2 per cent by 1967.

The government did not favour outright nationalization as it would involve payment of large-scale compensation to shareholders of banks, and would create other complications due to the lack of adequate and competent technical personnel; it therefore decided to introduce social control over them in 1968 without actually owning these institutions. L.K. Jha, the then governor of the RBI, supported the concept of social control but was not in favour of nationalization. Soon, politics trounced economics and the then PM, Indira Gandhi, despite protests from her finance minister, Morarji Desai, announced the decision to nationalize fourteen banks on 29 July 1969.

Mrs Gandhi herself took over the finance portfolio, thereby making it difficult for Desai to remain in the cabinet. When he expressed his strong resentment at her action, she told him he could continue in the Cabinet as deputy PM and hold charge of some other portfolio. Desai described it as 'an amazing proposal and a very clever move', and conveyed his inability to continue in the Cabinet. He wrote to her:

> If you wanted a change in the finance ministry, you could have discussed it with me. You know very well that I never discussed any matter with you in an improper manner. Even when I have differed from you on some matters, I have never been guilty of impropriety or discourtesy. But now you have

behaved towards me in a manner in which no one would behave even with a clerk.[8]

Meanwhile, Jha, who had been appointed governor on 1 July 1967, was appointed India's ambassador to the US in May 1970, prior to the completion of his term as governor.

These differences in perception of various issues between the RBI and the government have continued. In some ways, it is but natural that such differences will arise because the monetary authority will invariably be concerned about managing inflation, whereas the fiscal authority or government will be seeking to manage and accelerate growth.

Dr Y.V. Reddy, who served as governor from 2003 to 2008, maintains that a notable disagreement during his tenure was on the question of permitting foreign direct investment (FDI) in private-sector banks. This issue had been discussed with the NDA government, with Jaswant Singh as finance minister, and was later taken up by the UPA government, which came to power in 2004. Reddy felt that the time was not yet ripe to allow FDI in banking.

P. Chidambaram, the then finance minister, however, maintained that the government could not go back on its commitment made to the global community and that decisions could not be altered based on the personal convictions of successive governors. He reportedly told Reddy,

> Governor, this is a national commitment made to the global financial community. How do we justify a reversal of such a policy? Is it because there is a change in the incumbency of the governor? Do we review our commitments every time a

---

[8]R.J. Venkateswaran; 'Indira Gandhi versus Morarji Desai—The real reason for bank nationalization'; *The Hindu BusinessLine*; 7 February 2000; https://www.thehindubusinessline.com/2000/02/07/stories/040708m4.htm Accessed on 10 June 2019.

governor of the RBI changes? On what basis do we change these decisions?[9]

Not being in agreement with the introduction of such a policy, Reddy called up the then secretary, Department of Economic Affairs (DEA), Dr Rakesh Mohan, and offered to get himself admitted to a hospital under the pretext of ill health and subsequently quit the post to facilitate the appointment of a new governor by the government. Finally, a compromise was worked out and a roadmap formulated permitting FDI in banking, which was announced in the 2005 Budget. The roadmap was planned by Reddy in such a way that by the time it would be implemented, he would have retired from the post of governor!

In his book *Who Moved My Interest Rate?*,[10] Dr D. Subbarao, RBI governor from 2008 to 2013, talks of attempts by the government, in other indirect ways, to influence the central bank. He refers to an occasion when the RBI, in its mid-term policy review, was expected to make an announcement on its policy rate. In the routine pre-policy meeting, he informed the finance minister of his decision to not cut the policy rate in view of the inflationary trends and continued concern about the fiscal situation.

The finance minister clearly wanted a rate cut and was unhappy with the governor's decision to leave it untouched. In a hurriedly convened press conference ahead of the mid-term policy review announcement by the RBI to reveal the government's fiscal roadmap, the finance minister declared, 'I am making the statement so that everybody in India acknowledges the steps we are taking and also acknowledges that the government is

---

[9]R.J. Venkateswaran; 'Indira Gandhi versus Morarji Desai—The real reason for bank nationalization'; *The Hindu BusinessLine*; 7 February 2000; https://www.thehindubusinessline.com/2000/02/07/stories/040708m4.htm Accessed on 10 June 2019.
[10]Duvvuri Subbarao; *Who Moved My Interest Rate?: Leading the Reserve Bank of India through Five Turbulent Years*; Penguin Books (2016)

determined to bring about fiscal consolidation.' Clarifying further in response to a question on whether the RBI would cut rates based on his announcement, he said, 'I sincerely hope everybody will read the statement and take note of that.' This was a clear message to the RBI to toe the government's line. However, the RBI did not cut rates, expressing concern over inflation. Post the policy announcement, when the finance minister's reaction was sought on the RBI's policy rate stance, he stated, 'Growth is as much a concern as inflation. If the government has to walk alone to face the challenge of growth, we will walk alone.' This is representative of the differing perceptions between the central bank and the finance minister or the government.

There have been veiled attempts by many governments to either gain a foothold in the policy-formulation space and not leave it to the RBI or in subtle ways to try to influence decisions being taken by the bank. A manifestation of this emerged when, in his Budget speech of 2011–12, the finance minister announced the formation of a Financial Sector Legislative Reforms Commission (FSLRC) to rewrite and harmonize financial sector legislation, rules and regulations. The FSLRC was formed on the premise that most legal and institutional structures of the financial sector in India had been created over a century ago. There are more than sixty-one Acts and multiple rules and regulations that govern the sector, many of which date back several decades, when the financial landscape was very different. For example, the RBI Act and the Insurance Act are from 1934 and 1938, respectively. The FSLRC was formed to review and recast these old laws in tune with the modern requirements of the financial sector.

However, when the report of the FSLRC was presented in 2013, it was found that a common theme across the FSLRC recommendations was to propose some fundamental changes to the regulatory architecture. The report sought to systemically transfer the powers of the RBI to the government or to a newly proposed unified financial regulator. In the case of the monetary policy committee, public debt office, capital controls and the systemic risk and resolution corporation, the suggestions pertaining to the manner of appointments implied that the Ministry of Finance would get to wield sufficient influence to enforce its writ. This went against the basic canon of having regulators with autonomy and accountability.

Similarly, in the regulation of non-banking financial companies (NBFCs) and financial institutions, money and government securities markets, the Securities and Exchange Board of India (SEBI) was recommended to be the regulator. The RBI was thus reduced to a monetary authority and banking regulator. Even the oversight and regulation of the payments system was to be withdrawn from it.

RBI observers viewed this as an attempt by the government to arrogate powers to itself. This may not augur well for the autonomy of regulators in the financial markets as an independent and objective approach to policy formulation and management of the monetary policy is definitely desirable. While the FSLRC has given its report, issues such as the monetary policy committee have been functioning smoothly. The monetary policy committee, which has six members, now seems to be functioning on the principle of majority decision-making. In the meeting held in April 2019, the committee voted for a rate cut on a 4–2 majority decision. Such decisions on setting the interest rate were earlier entirely in the domain of the RBI.

BRAVING THE DEMON

No analysis of the functioning of the RBI would be complete unless we focus closely on its role in the management of currency supply after the announcement on 8 November 2016 declaring

₹500 and ₹1,000 denomination notes invalid as legal tender. It is not known when and to what extent the RBI was privy to the announcement. The only information available in the public domain is the statement subsequently made by the governor before the PAC that the RBI and the government had been in dialogue about scrapping high-denomination currency notes. Dr Raghuram Rajan, former governor of the RBI, talks about the issue in his book, *I Do What I Do*, in the following words:

> I was asked by the government in February 2016 for my views on demonetisation, which I gave orally. Although there might be long-term benefits, I felt the likely short-term economic costs would outweigh them, and felt there were potentially better alternatives to achieve the main goals. I made these views known in no uncertain terms. I was then asked to prepare a note, which the RBI put together and handed to the government. It outlined the potential costs and benefits of demonetisation, as well as alternatives that could achieve similar aims. If the government, on weighing the pros and cons, still decided to go ahead with demonetisation, the note outlined the preparation that would be needed, and the time that preparation would take. The RBI flagged what would happen if preparation was inadequate.[11]

There is a great deal of speculation about how things progressed on the day the announcement was actually made. A fact available in the public domain is that earlier on the evening of the announcement by the PM, the RBI Board met and approved an agenda item, which was tabled only in the meeting, proposing to recommend to the government to declare the ₹500 and ₹1,000 denomination notes no longer legal tender. Anecdotal evidence

---

[11]Raghuram G. Rajan; *I Do What I Do*; HarperCollins (2017)

suggests that once the Board took the decision, the members were persuaded to stay 'confined' (captive) in the boardroom of the RBI until such time as the announcement was made by the PM on national television!

There have been varied opinions emerging from different quarters about the erosion in the autonomy of the RBI in this decision. What can hardly be contested is that the final call for demonetization was definitely the prerogative of the government. However, since currency management is not only an important responsibility of the RBI, but one which it has very zealously protected, it was essential for the government to take the bank into confidence since the distribution of currency and other attendant logistical issues would necessarily have to be managed by it. Thus, whilst it could be argued that the policy decision was taken by the government, and this was despite the advice of the governor, the fact remains that preparedness for the eventuality and speedier currency printing, and more efficient distribution, could certainly have been managed better by the RBI.

In the aftermath of this decision, the non-availability of replacement currency notes at bank branches and ATMs showed the RBI in poor light. It can hardly be denied that, if 86 per cent of the currency in circulation is sucked out, replacement and that too in a high-cash-transaction economy, will, by all proportions, be a gigantic task requiring weeks. So one would not like to judge the RBI harshly, but the capability of an institution to deliver is best tested in difficult times. The fact that currency notes that were newly introduced were of a size different from any that were in circulation necessitated a recalibration of the cassettes in each ATM. Pan-India, there are about 200,000 ATMs. It is learnt that it takes about an hour to recalibrate each ATM. This explains the nature and extent of the inconvenience that was subsequently faced by the public. These factors, and inadequate media management, left the public feeling that the failing was of the central bank.

TACKLING THE NPA CRISIS

Banking is all about trust. Trust between the people and the institution from where they either borrow money or into which they deposit their savings for safekeeping and returns. It is in this context that the role of the regulator came up for questioning when the banks started showing stressed assets on their balance sheets. Senior officers of the RBI are on the boards of directors of all public-sector banks. They are experts and experienced in bank regulation and detecting early warning signs of distress. Besides, teams of professionals from the RBI inspect banks and their branches on a regular basis, and it is quite strange that even they did not see signs of imminent distress in bank accounts. Explaining to the PAC, the then RBI governor Rajan mentioned the following as the principal reasons for the burgeoning stressed assets:

- Domestic and global economic slowdown.
- Delays in statutory and other approvals, especially for projects under implementation.
- Aggressive lending practices during upturn, as evidenced from high corporate leverage.
- Laxity in credit risk appraisal and loan monitoring in banks.
- Lack of appraisal of skills for projects that need specialized skills, resulting in acceptance of inflated cost and aggressive projections.
- Wilful default, loan fraud and corruption.

Barring the first two of these six causes, there was every opportunity for the RBI officers to have shown greater alacrity in the oversight they provided to the banks under their inspection. The then governor also highlighted the rather lax credit discipline in banks. The quality of appraisal of proposals and the discipline in the follow-up of recovery is one of the main factors in the build-up of stressed assets. In this context, what has come up for adverse attention is the failure of the risk-based supervisory process followed by the RBI since the build-up did not occur overnight.

It is a recognized fact that infrastructure projects assumed a major priority around 2006. Several companies which either did not have domain experience or the financial capability, by virtue of their political connections, managed to get major contracts. Soon, quite a few of the projects ran into delays for statutory clearances, largely from environment-related angles. This led to time and thus cost overruns. Being financially heavily over-leveraged, these companies began to face an unsustainable debt burden, thereby leading to a crisis situation.

It is also a fact that quite a few of these major cases were being ever-greened by the banks to suppress the massive non-performing asset (NPA) bubble looming on the horizon. It speaks volumes of the capability of the RBI inspectors and efficacy of the representatives on the boards of public-sector banks that they did not see these signals. The rapid-growing nature of the NPA problem necessitated prompt and early concomitant measures from the RBI to signal intent but this was not forthcoming well in time. Action in only a few cases early in the build-up would have provided effective deterrence and served to enforce a strengthening of the overall credit culture. The endeavour should have been to strengthen the supervisory and regulatory framework to ensure timely recognition and disclosure of incipient stress and to facilitate effective and meaningful resolution.

In public-sector banks, RBI nominees are on the board as well as on the management committee, which approves large loans and write-offs. Within its considerable statutory powers, the RBI could have insisted upon better lending practices even where the government's priorities were being pursued to ensure sufficient credit availability. Also, many bad loans were in sectors where there was no policy push.

ACCOUNTABILITY TO THE GOVERNMENT AND THE PUBLIC

The RBI is a principal organ of governance in a parliamentary democracy with a well-defined mandate which is differentiated from other organs of state administration. It is a public institution which has a role much larger than merely being a banking regulator or managing the supply of money or controlling inflation.

Banking is a service, extended as much to the man on the street as to the government. If the common man is being overcharged for transferring money from his workplace in the city to his family in the village, or if I am being overcharged for the amount outstanding on my credit card, or being charged to draw from the ATM of one bank while my account is in another bank, it is the responsibility of the central bank to ensure that services rendered to me by commercial banks are efficient and reasonable. Hence, the role, efficacy and alertness of the central bank impinge very much on the common man too.

The bank, thus, is as close to the common man as it is to the government or the Bank for International Settlements (BIS) in Basel, Switzerland. It is an institution, the efficient running of which is essential to the country. It has to be governed well and, in turn, has to effectuate the efficient running of the financial sector. To that extent, the common man is a stakeholder in the good governance of the RBI.

Like all central banks around the globe, the RBI has been established to perform a very critical function. It is essential that in terms of statute and practice it be given the space to perform its role efficiently. While discharging its role, it is dependent on the efficient functioning of many institutions in the financial sector. In the case of the RBI, its efficacy gets stymied to a certain extent by the fact that about 70 per cent of the banking setup is owned by the government.

Besides this, the RBI Act does leave certain grey areas in interpreting the relationship of the bank with the government. There is, in fact, a provision in Act for written directives being given by the government in public interest to the bank. This provision in the Act came up for much debate during the tenure of Dr Urjit Patel as governor. Thus, whilst the supremacy of the sovereign cannot be contested, it is imperative to provide operational control to the RBI. That would be in line with the raison d'être of an autonomous body to regulate the sector. Whilst the jurisdiction of the RBI over public-sector banks, as contra-distinct from private-sector banks, is restricted in the statute itself, directives from the bank to public-sector banks are indeed honoured, and that is the only way a regulator can be effective.

On the other hand, it is incumbent on the RBI to be in close consultation with the government on issues of wider policy ramifications. Consultation does not in any way compromise the independence or autonomy of the institution. It only helps to build trust and thereby enhance the confidence of a people in their public institutions.

In the recent past, the RBI has seen a fairly fast turnover of governors. Rajan did a term of merely three years and opted to return to academia. His successor, Patel, did not even complete his three-year term, resigning after two years. Such early exits are not beneficial to the economy as the consistency of policy formulation takes on a short-term approach. High turnover reflects as much on the incumbent as on those in the government involved in monetary policy formulation, and hence requires a great deal of maturity in engagement. A balanced approach, with at least five-year tenures, has in the past seen long-term approaches beneficial to the financial sector.

ACHIEVING A FINE BALANCE

There has been a substantial change in the role of the central bank before and after 1970. The post-1991 era brought in further complexities in the bank, keeping pace with the new economic-reforms architecture that the executive was putting in place. It was a whole new financial environment that was being envisioned. The RBI had to play not only a supportive but a very proactive role in this transformation. One of the secrets of successful emerging economies has been that the central banks responded and transformed their ideology and regulatory culture to meet the need of the hour.

From this perspective, the RBI cannot be made completely autonomous from the executive. But it is necessary to clarify in the same breath that the RBI need not be subservient to the executive. Thus, the cohesiveness of policy formulation pertaining to the financial sector demands close consultation and coordination between the two institutions. However, the central bank of any country will have to be viewed differently from any other executive body, as the entire monetary and financial system, which forms the backbone of any economy, is shaped by the policies and regulations of the central bank. Although the central bank is the creation of a statute by the legislature, and its top appointments, namely the governor and the deputy governors, are appointed by the executive and can be removed by it, it does not imply that the writ of the executive overrides all other functional considerations.

We have seen situations of very substantial differences of opinion between the two institutions, both so very critical to the economy in any parliamentary democracy; but with appropriate tact and respect for professional advice, issues have been settled to the satisfaction of all concerned and to the benefit of the country.

Critics have argued that the RBI is not and cannot be completely independent of the State, nor can it be an indistinguishable part of it. Some have argued that it is a separation of authority rather than separation of powers, as both the government and the central bank can exercise jurisdiction over the monetary function.[12] It is this fine distinction that both the government and the central bank authorities will have to recognize. Governors recognize that complete autonomy of the central bank within India's democratic system is not possible, given the complexity of the economic system. What the governors have felt is that within the limits of parliamentary democracy, where the government is ultimately answerable to the Parliament, there is a strong case for the central bank to be given some autonomy to pursue monetary policy (which ultimately is the responsibility of the RBI) and hold it accountable for the same.

Financial regulation attempts to balance two competing administrative goals. On the one hand, as with much of administrative law, accountability is a core goal. Accountability undergirds the democratic legitimacy of administrative agencies. On the other hand, unlike with much of administrative law, independence plays a critical role. Independence helps to protect financial regulatory agencies from political interference and—with some important caveats—arguably helps guard against some forms of industry capture. In addition, with respect to the RBI, independence serves to improve the credibility of its price stability mandate by insulating its decision-making from politics and, in particular, from political pressure in favour of easy money during election cycles. 'Too much' accountability—at least in some forms—may reduce independence. And 'too much' independence—at least in some forms—may reduce

---

[12]Deena Khatkhate; 'Reserve Bank of India: A Study in the Separation and Attrition of Powers', *Public Institutions in India: Performance and Design*, edited by Devesh Kapur and Pratap Bhanu Mehta, Oxford University Press, (2005)

accountability. Moreover, steps to meet one or the other of these goals may also affect the efficacy of the organization. Having a financial regulatory system that properly balances accountability and independence but fails to protect households from abuse and the real economy from the catastrophic failure of the financial sector cannot be any country's goal.

Instances of friction that have sometimes surfaced are bound to happen, given the political and economic compulsions of the RBI and the central government. A lot, however, depends on the individuals at the centre of the action, particularly the governor of the central bank, the finance minister and perhaps the PM. It is essentially these three individuals who have to smoothen the rough edges, if any, in the coordination process. The friction that has occurred is essentially due to the lack of uniformity in perception of the situation, mostly by two of the three important personae, namely the governor of the central bank and the finance minister, resulting in policies that may not reflect unanimity.

In the final analysis, how autonomous the institution is and how independent the governor of the central bank feels, depends, to a large extent, on the individual acumen of the person at the top. We have seen that governors have expressed their concern to the government on issues that they have not felt comfortable with and yet have remained effective in their posts. Our democratic system is sufficiently vibrant to accept such divergent views and the top leadership has been found to be receptive to such concerns, except on a few occasions when political considerations might have overridden such advice.

Ultimately, the prevailing checks and balances in our democratic system have come to the rescue of institutions and their top leadership. It is for them to understand the system in which they work, and the experience at the RBI has shown that each of the governors, who have all been very experienced either as administrators or as practising economists, has displayed an understanding of the limitation of their functional areas as defined by their mandate. It is this understanding that ultimately is the litmus test of their performance. If they have brought in innovative measures in strengthening the autonomy of the institution, it has been well within the mandate, and if they have travelled an extra mile to strengthen the autonomy, they have managed to convince the government regarding their measures by extending the envelope of their mandate. To what lengths this extension can go depends entirely on the person at the helm of affairs at the central bank and their ability to carry the government along. This capability in the incumbent would determine the benefit that the country at large would derive.

5

THE COMPTROLLER AND AUGUST AUDITOR GENERAL

The Fifth Pillar of Democracy

Never in the past has the CAG decided to comment on a policy issue. It should limit the office to the role defined in the Constitution.[1]

—Former Prime Minister Dr Manmohan Singh

If the PM of the country had this perception of the mandate of the CAG, what precisely is the mandate? What is the expectation from the institution of the CAG and how was the mandate conceptualized by the Constitution makers? In proceeding to analyse the mandate and the contribution of the institution of the auditor-general, we need to trace its origin.

TRACING THE ORIGIN

The institution of the CAG traces its history back to over 150 years during the colonial era. The post of accountant-general

---

[1] Transcript of Prime Minister Manmohan Singh's Question and Answer session with Editors; *NDTV*; 29 June 2011; https://www.ndtv.com/india-news/transcript-of-prime-minister-manmohan-singhs-question-and-answer-session-with-editors-459896
Accessed on 5 June 2019.

to the government of India was created in May 1858; subsequent expansion of its mandate vested in it a combined authority for both audit and accounting functions of the central government and provinces. The Government of India Acts of 1919 and 1935 provided the CAG the independence that remains at the core of its role. The 1935 Act provided for his appointment by the Crown and not by the secretary of state; he could be removed from office 'in like manner and on the like grounds as a judge of the federal court'. He was also debarred from holding any office under the Crown in India after demitting office. These provisions, aimed at his independence, were very similar to the constitutional provisions of free India. The detailed audit and accounting functions of the auditor-general were laid down in the Audit and Accounts Order, 1936. Interestingly, these provisions were in use until the Comptroller and Auditor General's (Duties, Powers and Conditions of Service) Act, or the DPC Act, was enacted in 1971 (referred to as the Audit Act or DPC Act in this chapter).

The Constitution built on the above edifice to strengthen the post. Recognizing that 'this dignitary or officer, is probably the most important officer in the constitution of India'[2], it envisioned the CAG as a constitutional authority[3] through Articles 148 to 151.

The DPC Act formally vested in the CAG the authority of audit of the accounts of the Union government, the state governments as well as their commercial organizations (government companies and corporations) and such bodies as received grants/loans from the governments (autonomous bodies). The enactment of the DPC Act[4] came at a time when the institution found itself

---

[2]In the words of Dr B.R. Ambedkar, the chairman of the drafting committee for the Constitution.
[3]As differentiated from a statutory authority, that is, established under a statute. This casts an iron grid around the provisions that govern the CAG.
[4]Till such time, the CAG's duties and powers were regulated as per the Audit and Accounts Order, 1936.

emasculated due to cuts in budgets,[5] while the canvas had been broadened with the federal financial integration, without significant additional manpower. But the CAG found support for strengthening the institution from the economic committee set up by the government, which agreed with the auditor-general that a strong and efficient audit department was the best ally of the finance ministry.

Governments are facing a growing demand from citizens to be more accountable, transparent and effective. The media, including social media, has allowed this growing assertion. In this context, the CAG stands out as an institution that is not swayed by political allegiances or alliances, and is hence perceived as an institution that has remained impartial and objective, ergo, trusted.

PILLARS OF GOOD GOVERNANCE

In a democracy, the people entrust the management of the nation's resources to their elected representatives, who, in turn, entrust the function to the executive arm of the government. Therefore, an effective system of accountability of the executive to the legislature is fundamental. The Parliament relies on the CAG to provide independent assurance that governmental activities are carried out and accounted for, consistent with the Parliament's expressed intentions. One way to help restore citizens' confidence in public institutions is to ensure that scarce resources are used in ways that maximize value for money and deliver results, i.e., to have information about whether the implementation of policies and projects, approved and budgeted by the Parliament, has been

---

[5]Due to the economy measures introduced during the Great Depression followed by World War II, when large-scale transfer of officers to priority departments took place. The Partition made matters worse.

economic, efficient and effective.[6]

It is the Supreme Audit Institutions, or SAIs (the generic nomenclature for auditors-general worldwide), that bring into focus improprieties committed by persons holding high offices and safeguard the interests of various stakeholders. It is against this background that the auditor-general acquires prominence and is provided with a constitutional safeguard. The institution provides an assurance to the Parliament, and through it to the public, that money approved by the Parliament has been spent for the intended purpose.

Over the years, this mandate has evolved and different geographies have assigned the SAIs a far more overarching role to give confidence to the legislature by infusing transparency in government spending. Among other countries, the repositioning of the SAI of the US deserves mention. The SAI was known as the Government Accounting Office (GAO). In 2004, several proposals were introduced in the 110th Congress to augment its mandate. One of these proposals was to re-designate the institution as the Government Accountability Office (the acronym continues to be GAO) to better reflect the agency's evolution and the revised mandate. The underlying belief was that the public deserves to know all aspects of government-functioning—from policymaking to expenditure—and that the auditor-general's mandate is to hold the government financially accountable to the legislature.

In India, the role of the national auditor was not accorded any less importance. In fact, as early as 2 June 1954, Dr S. Radhakrishnan, the then vice-president of India, while speaking at a function in the office of the accountant-general, Madras (now Tamil Nadu), drew the attention of the officers

---

[6]Definitions sourced from the Performance Auditing Guidelines 2014; Comptroller and Auditor-General of India; https://cag.gov.in/sites/default/files/guidelines/PA_Guidelines2014.pdf
Accessed on 5 June 2019.

to their duty towards the nation in the following words:

> The Comptroller and Auditor General is responsible not to the government. He must serve as the check on the government. The government may make mistakes. It is wrong to assume that the government can do no wrong. The Auditor General is independent of the executive. It is the duty of the Audit and Accounts Department to carry out the financial policies of the government and maintain the authority to Parliament. If I have to give one advice and if I am presumptuous enough to give any advice to the officers of the Audit and Accounts Department, it is this: 'Do not shrink from the truth for fear of offending men in high places.'[7]

This reflects the high expectations of the office in India, and in all such democracies: seeking good and sustainable development for the people.

SAIs typically undertake three types of audit. First is the compliance audit, which tests compliance with rules, laws and regulations. Next is the financial audit, which certifies financial statements of various departments, corporations or autonomous bodies rendering 'true and fair accounts', viz. whether they are properly prepared and with adequate disclosures. The third is the performance audit, wherein an attempt is made to establish whether policies, programmes and projects of the government are working in a cost-effective and efficient manner. This type of audit goes a step further to ascertain the qualitative aspects of government programmes.

If one were to carry out an audit of, say, the midday meal programme of the government in a compliance audit, the auditor

---

[7] Era Sezhiyan; 'Checks and balances'; *Frontline*; December 2007–January 2008; https://frontline.thehindu.com/static/html/fl2425/stories/20080104 242508500. htm;
Accessed on 5 June 2019.

would verify whether the funds have been expended and accounted for, with a utilization certificate being provided. Once he is satisfied that the expenditure has been made as per the norms and entries in the relevant books of account, he would validate the expense. However, in a performance audit, the auditor would go a step further to verify whether the programme objectives—such as the improvement in the nutritional status of the children, additional enrolment of children of disadvantaged groups such as Adivasis, Dalits and girls, and the positive impact on attendance and decline in school dropout rate—have been fulfilled. Thus, in addition to all the financial audit checks, the performance audit seeks to assess whether a programme, scheme or activity also deploys sound means to achieve its intended socio-economic objectives.

The performance audit is of more recent origin and has been introduced in keeping with the greater role that transparency has come to occupy in governance and the validating function that only a constitutional body like the auditor-general can provide to the general public, legislature, government and the entities that are audited. The democratic principle is based on the public's right to hold the government accountable for its actions through general elections. In order for this principle to have significance, the public needs information on how public resources are being spent and public services performed. By providing objective and reliable information on these issues, the performance audit contributes to transparency and accountability. It evaluates policies and advises on the sub-optimality of governmental policies. An important requirement of this model of auditing is that it has to quantify the revenues forgone by the exchequer in the execution of its various programmes.

Owing to this function of the performance audit, it does comment on the sub-optimality of the actions/policies followed by governments. In fact, in the JPC set up by the UPA government in March 2011 to discuss the issues pertaining to the allocation of the 2G spectrum by the government, one of the members felt that the CAG did not have a mandate to conduct a performance audit. He had to be enlightened that, besides Article 149 of the Constitution, the DPC Act of 1971 and the Regulations of Audit & Accounts, framed in 2007 and notified in the official gazette, there was an order issued by the UPA government on 13 June 2006, stating, inter alia: 'It is hereby clarified that performance audit, which is concerned with the audit of economy, efficiency and effectiveness in the receipt and application of public funds, is deemed to be within the scope of audit by the CAG....'[8] The mandate of the CAG for conducting performance audits was also upheld in 2013 by the Supreme Court in *Arvind Gupta Vs Union of India (UOI) and Ors*, where it held that such power was in-built in the DPC Act, 1971.[9]

In a landmark verdict in *Association of Unified Telecom Service Providers of India and Ors. Vs UOI and Ors.* and *Cellular Operators Association of India and Ors. Vs Department of Telecommunication & Ors*,[10] the Supreme Court decreed that the accounts of private telecom companies operating under licence from the government were subject to audit by the CAG. The Court's approach was nuanced to restrict the audit to that of accounts alone (and not the wider performance audit), while

---

[8]Instructions of Government of India; Ministry of Finance; Department of Economic Affairs; Budget Division; New Delhi, 13 June 2006; https://cag.gov.in/content/instructions-government-india
Accessed on 5 June 2019.

[9]Arvind Gupta Vs Union of India, (2013) 1 SCC 393; https://www.supremecourtcases.com/index2.php?option=com_content&itemid=99999999&do_pdf=1&id=25333
Accessed on 5 June 2019.

[10]Assn. of Unified Tele Services Providers Vs Union of India, (2014) 6 SCC 110; https://www.supremecourtcases.com/index2.php?option=com_content&itemid=99999999&do_pdf=1&id=45824
Accessed on 5 June 2019.

observing that 'a synergy between the two would be not only for the benefit of the industry, the economy of the country, the society at large but would go a long way in establishing public confidence in good corporate governance'.

The Supreme Court upheld the decision of the Delhi High Court that the wave 'spectrum', which was the subject of the licence, was a natural resource. It also held that the Parliament had an obligation to ascertain whether the entire receipts by way of licence fee and spectrum charges had been realized by the Union of India and credited to the government coffers. In another petition filed in the Supreme Court urging it to declare performance audits conducted by the CAG as *ultra vires* of the Constitution, the Court observed:

> The CAG is not a *munim* (accountant) to go into balance sheets. The CAG is a constitutional authority entitled to review and conduct performance audit on revenue allocations relating to the centre, the states and the union territories [and examine matters relating to the economy and how the government uses its resources [...] Don't undermine the office of the CAG.[11]

Thus, the provisions in the Constitution, the gazette notification of June 2006 and the aforementioned verdict of the Supreme Court conclusively establish the mandate of the CAG.

SOCIAL ACCOUNTABILITY GAINS GROUND

Sixty-five per cent of India's population is under thirty-five years of age. This is a generation that has embraced technology and

---

[11]'Don't undermine office of CAG, says Supreme Court'; *The Hindu*; 1 October 2012; https://www.thehindu.com/news/national/Don't-undermine-office-of-CAG-says-Supreme-Court/article12541316.ece Accessed on 5 June 2019.

social media to inform itself; its modes of intervention also leverage these tools. In the context of greater citizen assertiveness to be informed, the term 'social accountability' has gained ground, defined as 'an approach towards building accountability that relies on civic engagement i.e., in which it is ordinary citizens and civil society organisations, who participate directly in exacting accountability.'[12]

As citizens seek greater influence on governance, the CAG needs to find innovative ways to engage with the public. To this end, the CAG has fashioned its outreach to the public in many ways, including tools of audit like beneficiary surveys, seeking citizens' views through workshops as well as social media at the stage of audit planning, and reimagining its own website as well as its public relations (media).

The CAG brought out multiple versions of the same report, including 'Noddy books'—a concise report shorn of technicalities or data overload meant for use by ordinary citizens. These books comprised fifteen pages of bold, printed material with photographs explaining the inadequacies that had been observed during the course of the audit. The books also enclosed compact discs containing the full report for those interested in the detailed audit findings.

These books were designed to sensitize public opinion on audit reports on social-sector schemes such as rural health, primary education and rural employment. They were distributed to legislators, citizen groups, college students and other informed persons who had interest in the agencies at work. It was the first time that good practices observed by the audit teams were noted and included in reports for wider dissemination in other states. The attempt was to sensitize public opinion about the effective

---

[12]*Strategic Environmental Assessment in Policy and Sector Reform: Conceptual Model and Operational Guidance*; The World Bank; World Bank Publications, 11 November 2010

operation of these government schemes and thereby add to a kind of 'social audit' of the efficiency of their implementation.

NOT A 'WE' AND 'THEY' RELATIONSHIP

It has to be recognized that the working of the CAG is, in some ways, contrarian to the functioning of the government. However, this does not imply that the audit reports impede government-functioning or are intended to portray it in poor light. Audit reports are meant to upgrade the quality of government administration and need to be accepted as guidance for future operations. There is no 'we' and 'they' relationship between auditor and executive. Both are partners in improving governance and sit on the same side of the table, engaged in the common task of providing good governance.

If the entity that has been audited accepts the observations in a positive manner and acts accordingly, the administration improves qualitatively and society benefits. On the other hand, if departments stonewall audit observations, the government loses and society suffers. The auditor is merely a messenger, bringing to light any inadequacies or ills in government-functioning. It is unfortunate that, at times, government functionaries have not taken these reports in the right spirit and, instead of taking corrective steps, have begun to criticize the functioning of the CAG itself.

Indeed, such piquant situations have arisen several times. The quoted comment by Dr Manmohan Singh at the editors' conference was not premised on a factually accurate observation. Thus it was felt that since the PM had obviously been incorrectly briefed, he should be made aware of the ground realities. However, as it was not really appropriate for two constitutional authorities to enter into a dialogue via the media, a letter was written to the PM explaining that the CAG had, in fact, at no stage exceeded its mandate or transgressed into policy space. The PM's attention was drawn to the report dealing with the allocation of the 2G spectrum, wherein the very first page had the following statement: 'While accepting the government's prerogative to formulate the policy of Unified Access Services Licences (UASL), it was felt that an in-depth examination of implementation of such policy needed to be done.'[13] Nowhere does the report make any reference to or comment on the formulation of policy by the Cabinet.

If not directly, in a large number of indirect ways, pressure is brought to bear on the national auditor through statements made in the media. It is rather disheartening when such statements come from senior and experienced public functionaries.

One was from a tall leader like Sharad Pawar, who said,

> CAG has taken certain decisions that have created a different atmosphere in the country. I have a serious objection—when we see half reports being leaked, when CAG officials are addressing press conferences and talking about sensational things. [...] I haven't seen something like this in the forty-five years of my career as a politician [...] We have to think ourselves whether we have selected a proper person.[14]

M. Veerappa Moily, the then Union minister of law, justice and company affairs, and more importantly, the Chairman of the Second Administrative Commission (which produced a stellar report), said,

---

[13]Report of Joint Parliamentary Committee (JPC) to Examine Matters Relating to Allocation and Pricing of Telecom Licences and Spectrum; http://164.100.47.194/Loksabha/writereaddata/InvestigativeJPC/InvestigativeJPC_635612535475047737.pdf
Accessed on 5 June 2019.

[14]Rohini Singh and Soma Banerjee; 'I haven't seen CAG function like this in 45 years of my career: Sharad Pawar'; *The Economic Times*; 14 June 2012; https://www.pressreader.com/india/the-economic-times/20120614/textview
Accessed on 5 July 2019.

The spirit of inquiry so central to democracy, has to be accepted and institutionalised. In this context a word about audit in India would be appropriate. The institution of the comptroller and auditor general of India, a constitutional body itself, is designed to be a bulwark against omissions and commissions of the executive, under the supervision of the legislature. But the way the institution of audit has functioned has not exactly fulfilled what the Indian constitution had in mind while creating the institution. [...] Scandals and scams are known even while they are being planned and executed. If audit draws attention to them forthwith in a well published manner such scandal can be halted in mid-stride. Post-mortems are useful but can only be conducted when the patient is dead.[15]

It is most unfortunate that such exalted personalities do not understand that the CAG's audit is an external audit, which, by mandate and definition, is done only post the event. It is the internal audit, which is within the government setup itself, which is to draw attention to scandals forthwith and halt them mid-stride!

In a diametrically different appreciation of the role of the CAG, the then finance minister, Pranab Mukherjee, speaking at an economic editors' conference on 19 October 2011, had a very contrary opinion. He said that the CAG had not exceeded its limitations by pointing out lapses in government activities. It was the auditor's constitutional responsibility and it must do it. He further said,

---

[15]Jayant Das; 'Do your bit to arrest the downhill trend in public life'; *The Pioneer*; 29 October 2014; https://www.dailypioneer.com/2014/state-editions/do-your-bit-to-arrest-the-downhill-trend-in-public-life.html Accessed on 5 July 2019.
http://editorialsamarth.blogspot.com/2010/09/editorial-230910.html Accessed on 5 July 2019.

Out of 100, if the government has done 98 correct things they will ignore it. They will just pick up the two things where irregularities have taken place. I am making it clear that I do not think the CAG is exceeding its jurisdiction, because the basic responsibility of the CAG is to identify if there is a lapse.[16]

In fact, in a written reply to the Parliament, he emphasized, 'As custodian of the public purse, CAG has played the role of a vanguard in reporting on financial irregularities, irrespective of the government in power.'[17]

These instances have been cited only to demonstrate how easily the intent and observations of the auditor can be misinterpreted.

CREATING TRUST, NOT FEAR

Much has also been made of the fear of the CAG's audit that slows decision-making and in fact creates policy paralysis. I emphatically maintain that this notion is a bogey or an alibi for non-performance. If it were a stumbling block, why would 192 countries opt to have the institution of auditor-general and even accord it lofty constitutional status? The fact that every country has provided for a national auditor evidences that world leaders

---

[16]'Pranab backs CAG, says not exceeding its limitations'; *Hindustan Times*; 19 October 2011; https://www.hindustantimes.com/delhi-news/pranab-backs-cag-says-not-exceeding-its-limitations/story-MrgWuDzVMc9qARKlMzr8dN.html
Accessed on 5 June 2019.

[17]Saubhadra Chatterji; 'Finance ministry gives clean chit to CAG'; *Hindustan Times*; 24 December 2012;
https://www.hindustantimes.com/delhi-news/finance-ministry-gives-clean-chit-to-cag/story-mejsnu177diRB3YjYlkxGM.html
Accessed on 5 July 2019.

have seen wisdom in establishing these institutions.

In any parliamentary democracy, the people have given to themselves an elaborate devolution of powers between institutions. The Parliament and the judiciary are accountability institutions, which derive a constitutional mandate to legislate and ensure that the rule of law prevails. However, quite often, since the executive or the legislature cannot discharge all the powers granted to it directly by the Constitution, they create institutions such as independent regulators, public auditors, election commissions and public service commissions, with an arm's-length approach for transparent and effective functioning. Embedded in the creation of these institutions is the core belief that they will be allowed independence and freedom of functioning. Permitting them such freedom only enhances trust between the government and its people.

IMPORTANT INADEQUACIES

The 73rd and 74th Amendments to the Constitution in 1993 have been hailed as epoch-making and vital pieces of legislation that resulted in the creation of 'institutions of self-governance'. These institutions have become the main channels (especially Panchayati Raj Institutions, or PRIs) for implementing state and centrally sponsored schemes. While enormous powers were conferred on the PRIs, a suitable and effective auditing mechanism was lacking. In fact, their accounting capability was very rudimentary and needed to be bolstered. Since the DPC Act is from 1971, viz. prior to these two constitutional amendments, it did not provide for an automatic audit mandate for the CAG over these bodies. Similarly, public-private partnership (PPP) projects, which were conceptualized in the late 1980s, were also not covered by the audit mandate of the Audit Act of 1971.

The Audit Act of 1971, as it stands today, also suffers from three serious inadequacies. First, a frequently levelled criticism against audit reports is that they are released months after the event has taken place; as a consequence, neither is the issue relevant nor can effective accountability against the wrongdoers be established. The reason for such delay in preparation of audit reports is lack of timely response from the entity being audited. When the first audit queries are raised, the entity being audited is requested to give its response 'at the earliest'. Neither is a time frame prescribed, nor is it adhered to. In the event of a delay in response, the auditor has no option but to keep sending reminders. He can take no other precipitate action. Contrast this with the RTI Act. Under the RTI Act, there is a compulsion for the public body to respond within thirty days of the query. Under the Audit Act, there is no such stipulation or penalty, even if an audited entity fails to respond. If a time limit, as prescribed under the RTI Act, is provided under the DPC Act, audit reports would be substantially sped up.

Second, a sizeable chunk of government spending on schemes is channelled through local bodies and 'special societies' set up to implement these schemes. The then Planning Commission was taken aback when, in a presentation made to it in 2009, it was revealed that under the 1971 Act, about two-thirds of the central plan expenditure did not fall within the automatic audit mandate of the CAG since the spending was through such bodies.

The third inadequacy is that once the audit report is handed over to the government by the CAG for being placed in the Parliament/legislature, there is no time limit prescribed within which it has to be tabled in the House. Consequently, reports perceived as inconvenient or damaging to the government are kept from timely placement in the House, thereby thwarting the possibility of speedy corrective action.

To draw attention to these inadequacies and seek a remedy, a presentation was made to the then finance minister and, after obtaining his consent, three amendments to the DPC Act were proposed by the CAG in November 2009. The first proposal was to stipulate a time limit of one month, within which responses to audit queries should be provided. Second, it was proposed to bring local bodies and PPP projects also under the purview of the Audit Act. Third, it was proposed that audit reports be placed in the legislature within seven days of being presented to the government. If the legislature was not in session, they should be placed within seven days of its reconvening. These proposed amendments, submitted to the government in November 2009, still await action.

EFFICACY OF THE PAC SYSTEM

Article 151 of the Constitution requires that the CAG's audit reports pertaining to the Union government be submitted to the president, 'who shall cause them to be laid before each House of Parliament'. Similarly, in the case of the states, the reports are submitted to the governor. The reports are then automatically referred to the PAC for examination. Reports pertaining to public-sector enterprises go to the Committee on Public Undertakings (COPU).

On an average, the CAG submits about forty reports to the Parliament every year. About thirty of these go to the PAC, and are expected to be examined in detail by it. As has been the experience of the past two decades, even if PAC meetings are held regularly, it does not meet more than once a month. Thus, the PAC does not get to examine more than half a dozen reports in a year (most reports involve at least two sittings).

A PRS[18] study reveals that the committee met an average of

---

[18]PRS Legislative Research, commonly referred to as PRS, is an Indian non-profit organization that was established in September 2005 as an independent research institute to make the Indian legislative process better informed, more transparent and participatory.

nineteen times in a year for the decade up to 2006. Thereafter, it had met only eleven times in a year up to 2014.

This is an indication of the cursory examination that these reports undergo. As a consequence, issues of a very serious nature go unattended and are routinely referred to the concerned departments, seeking '"action taken" statements', from them, which again, get routinely filed. Thus, the very efficacy of the PAC system needs to be revaluated. A method that was devised was to constitute sub-committees within the PAC and have them conduct in-depth examination of audit reports. However, this has also not kept pace and the frequency of meetings continues to be very low. It is essential that corrective action be taken regarding the issues highlighted in the reports.

NOT JUST AN ACCOUNTANT

The traditional role of public auditors is to conduct financial attest audits. However, today's citizen has become far more demanding and discerning, as highlighted by the several instances when members of the public wrote to us alleging that we were biased in not conducting audits of certain irregularities that appeared in the public domain. One such issue was the publicly perceived 'waste of government resources' in the construction of parks with stone statues of elephants by the then chief minister of UP, Mayawati. The state accountant-general's office (the state arm of the CAG) checked on the budgetary position for such parks. It was found that there was indeed a budgetary provision for parks and that since this provision had been approved by the legislature, the CAG could not fault the government for spending on these parks. This was a typical case where the CAG showed that budget formulation and devolution was the sole prerogative of the government and that the CAG merely audited the implementation of that budgetary provision. The prerogative of deciding on what to defray budgetary resources was that of the legislature.

On the other hand, this act of the chief minister of erecting statues of herself and of elephants (her party symbol) was challenged by a PIL in the Supreme Court, contending that public money could not be utilized for building statues of oneself and for promoting a political party. It was reported that the tentative view of the Court was that Mayawati, chief of the BSP, would have to deposit the public money utilized for building statues of her. These remarks were made in the courtroom while posting the case for final hearing and disposal.[19]

In such a scenario, the question that arises is: does the public auditor fulfil his mandate by merely placing audit reports in the Parliament? If the outcome of good governance is improvement in the life of its citizenry, should the same not be the outcome of the public audit? Audit of the government has the positive impact of creating the trust of society in its government. Such awareness supports desirable values and underpins accountability, thereby leading to efficient decision-making. Once citizens are sensitized about these findings, they are emboldened to hold their representatives accountable. Simultaneously, it motivates custodians of the public purse to use public resources effectively.

Additionally, stakeholder expectations have undergone an enormous change in recent years. They encompass SAIs as the fifth pillar of any democracy, acting as a check on government-functioning. SAIs are seen as institutions for combating corruption and a counter-measure to the excesses or inadequacies of government-functioning. They are expected to not merely act

---

[19]"Mayawati has to deposit "public money" used for erecting her statues, says SC'; *The Hindu BusinessLine*; 8 February 2019; https://www.thehindubusinessline.com/news/national/mayawati-has-to-deposit-public-money-used-for-erecting-her-statues-says-sc/article26214937.ece Accessed on 5 June 2019.

by the letter of their mandate, but more by the spirit of that mandate. These stakeholders are not necessarily the Parliament, government or citizens, but also foreign investors interested in the robustness of the country's regulatory systems. It is thus increasingly important that SAIs be responsive to changes in perception and priority of society and, through their reports, empower citizens to hold the government to be financially responsible for its actions.

The manner in which the role of the SAI has evolved in democracies around the world makes it clear that the public feels the CAG's constitutionally mandated responsibility does not end with placing its report in the Parliament or that it is confined to this mechanical function.

The fact that the framers of constitutions worldwide appointed exalted dignitaries as auditors-general and accorded them independence from the executive and constitutional status is indicative of the expectations of the Parliament and the public at large that the CAG is more than a mere accountant tabulating government expenditure.

The time has come when governments and government entities will have to be constantly aware of the need to ensure transparency and accountability in their functioning. Traditional accountability relationships rely on top-down or external donor-driven monitoring of service providers. They often fail. As a complementary strategy, social accountability strengthens citizen-clients to monitor and extract accountability. Two sets of obstacles must be overcome for this to happen: citizens must have reliable information about their entitlements and the performance of services, and they must be able to take actions based on that information to demand accountability, something which often requires collective action. In this way, social accountability can improve service delivery, especially for the poor. It is in this role that the CAG must seek to educate public opinion on the performance of the government that they have chosen to represent them.

PARADIGM SHIFT IN THE AUDIT MANDATE

The right of the federal auditor to carry out performance audits of government entities in our country is now established beyond question. The right to examine the underlying transactions of even private concerns to provide assurance about the State receiving its legitimate share of revenues arising out of the use of public resources has been judicially reinforced, even without specific mention of this in the audit mandate. This paradigm shift in the audit mandate also calls for development of appropriate policies and procedures, the need for bringing in expert knowledge and for substantial capacity development within the department.

At the same time, it has to be recognized that there ought to be a built-in arrangement within the department for ensuring its own accountability. No organization can insulate itself to well-meaning criticism from within. The institution should create the appropriate institutional mechanisms for introspection and generation of new ideas through continual self-appraisal and accumulation of relevant knowledge. Regular training programmes in the most developed institutes are accessed for officers to periodically keep themselves updated on the latest developments in skilling of the auditing community. In fact, it is in recognition of these capabilities that for the first time, the audit for such specialized international agencies as the World Intellectual Property Organization (WIPO) and the International Atomic Energy Agency (IAEA) was entrusted to the CAG of India in 2011 and 2012. It was the first time that a SAI outside Europe was entrusted with this responsibility.

An oft-asked question has been: who audits the CAG? In effect, how does the public at large derive assurance that the institution of the CAG of India is professionally competent and capable of auditing the most technical of institutions? It is also essential for the organization to benchmark itself with the best in the world and get validation of its capabilities. Thus, to ensure that the institution has adequate oversight of its own procedures and practices, a peer review of the CAG was undertaken by an expert team of fourteen auditors drawn from the SAIs of Australia, New Zealand, the UK and Canada, under the supervision of the auditor-general of Australia, in 2011, to benchmark our capabilities with the best global practices. The report prepared by the international team of auditors has been put out in the public domain.

UPHOLDING THE CARDINAL PRINCIPLES

Accountability and transparency, the two cardinal principles of good governance in a democratic setup, depend for their observance to a large extent on how well the public audit function is discharged. It is for this reason that the legislatures of many countries have ensured independence and security of the tenure of SAIs. The avowed objective of the creation of such lofty institutions is to enable them to hold the executive accountable to the legislature.

India's Constitution makers have provided adequate safeguards to ensure the independence and autonomy of the incumbent, as also to ensure that they do not show leanings towards the government in power towards the end of his tenure to seek further benefits of office. To ensure autonomy in functioning, the CAG has a guaranteed tenure of six years. He can be removed from office only by impeachment in the Parliament. Similarly, his budget is an automatic charge to the consolidated fund of India, like that of the Supreme Court, and hence not subject to a vote in the Parliament. To ensure his independent functioning at all times, he is eligible neither for a second term nor for any assignment with the government or the public sector after demitting office. These are remarkable provisions, binding on the government and the incumbent.

Accountability is the obligation of those holding power to take responsibility for their behaviour and actions. It becomes an even more important obligation when the management of public funds is involved. The government spends a huge amount of money in creating infrastructure, providing services and running various schemes for the welfare of its people. A large chunk of the government's money comes from taxes compulsorily collected from its citizens. The government is, therefore, obligated to work in the interest of its citizens and deliver accountable governance. It is answerable to the public for its policies, decisions and performance. It is in this direction that the public auditor provides assurance on the correctness of government spending and thereby ensures comfort to the Parliament and the public at large.

All over the world, SAIs have expanded their remit beyond the traditional compliance and financial auditing, and included performance auditing in recent times. It reflects a change of focus from the traditional audit of public expenditure to public accountability, with an emphasis on delivery. The earlier transactional model of audit examined only the regularity and legality of financial transactions, but the expanding role of the government necessitated reforms in the way it functioned, requiring professionalization of bureaucracy, emphasis on outcomes rather than on inputs and expenditure, and establishment of internal control mechanisms within government organizations. Accountability now being the focal point, new accountability models and institutions had to be created, often by expanding the powers of the existing institutions and by redefining their roles.

As the number of government transactions multiply into

millions, the traditional compliance and financial audit has to be restructured through a system-based approach. The CAG has been a pioneer in the use of information technology (IT) in audit and has been helping other countries, through its international centre for information systems and audit, in upgrading their systems to ensure that bias and subjectivity do not colour the audit approach.

The final shift from financial controls and compliance to the evaluation of performance of government entities and outcomes of programmes is only a logical consequence of this process. Audit now provides, to the benefit of the government, objective assessments of the economy, and the efficiency and effectiveness of its programmes and activities.

The faith vested in the institution of the CAG of India, guaranteed primarily by its constitutional status and provisions that protect it from overreach of the government and the legislature, remains fundamental to good governance in the country. An enhanced ability of the CAG to leverage the constitutional status with outreach to the citizens, using new technological tools and by building relevant competencies, will ensure that it delivers on the trust and faith that the citizens repose in it.

Good governance is the exercise of power and authority by the institutions of the State as mandated by the Constitution for channelling our resources towards the socio-economic development of the people. Accountability of public functionaries is an integral part of any good governance framework, but it extends far beyond mere compliance with legal obligations and maintenance of probity on their part. The test of accountability is the efficient delivery of public service and its outreach to the citizen at the end of the queue. Accountability, in its broadest sense, is recognized today as inclusive of equity and justice, fairness and transparency, participation and empowerment. Worldwide, SAIs provide that comfort to the public and legislatures. Their autonomy and independence need to be maintained and respected for establishment of probity and public accountability in government-functioning.

6

THE CENTRAL BUREAU OF INVESTIGATION

Is the Citadel Crumbling?

Court number one in the Supreme Court traditionally houses the bench presided over by the CJI. On 8 May 2013, a packed court heard, in pin-drop silence, the chief justice ask the director of the CBI: 'What business did they (officials in PMO and coal ministry) have to come and peruse the report? They ask you and you allow it? Even if you allowed it, how did you accept the suggestion (to alter the report)? Prima facie, it is very difficult to comprehend a situation in which outsiders are taking part in the investigation.'

He said: 'The status report was meant for the court and not the officers whose departments are involved. The heart of the report is changed? What is the job of the investigator? Is this collaborative investigation? It is a sordid saga that there are many masters and one parrot.'[1] The bench was castigating the CBI director for allowing brazen interference by the government

---

[1]'CBI a "caged parrot", "heart" of Coalgate report changed: Supreme Court'; *The Times of India*; 8 May 2013; https://timesofindia.indiatimes.com/india/CBI-a-caged-parrot-heart-of-Coalgate-report-changed-Supreme-Court/articleshow/19952260.cms
Accessed on 8 June 2019.

in the preparation of the affidavit the CBI had to file before the Court.

Was this the new nadir that the credibility of the premier investigative agency of the country had hit? Perhaps not. Worse has transpired since, which I have made an attempt to examine.

The CBI derives its investigative powers from the Delhi Special Police Establishment (DSPE) Act, 1946. This Act empowers it only for specific offences notified by the central government under Section 3 of the Act. These offences are: corruption, murder, kidnapping, abduction and certain economic offences. In the recent past, while the most high-profile cases entrusted to it have been related to corruption, there have also been cases of murder and homicide—the most significant being the investigation into the death of former PM Rajiv Gandhi. This was a case in which the CBI acquitted itself very well, bringing the investigation to a very satisfactory conclusion.

The CBI being in the news is not something new. The agency first came up for adverse attention for its lax investigative skills when the Supreme Court was deliberating on the Jain Hawala case (also known as the Vineet Narain case) in 1997. The Court ruled that while the government would be answerable for the CBI's functioning, to introduce objectivity, the CVC was entrusted with the superintendence of the CBI's functioning. In the same judgement, the Court decreed a statutory status for the CVC, thereby ensuring its independence.

Over the years, the CBI has often been described as the 'handmaiden' of the government in power. During the Supreme Court-supervised investigation of the coal mine allocations, referred to above, the Court expressed displeasure at the government's interference in the probe report, famously saying: 'The heart of the report was changed on the suggestions of the government officials. It (CBI) is a caged parrot speaking in its master's voice.' This was a severe indictment of the agency.

However, the recent imbroglio involving two of its most senior functionaries as the dramatis personae, drew adverse public attention it could very well have done without. It is apparent today that there is a serious deficit of the qualities underlined by its motto—'Industry, Impartiality, Integrity'.

Insiders who have been associated with the agency in its heyday swear by the competence and professionalism of the organization, terming the work culture and environment highly professional, particularly in the 1990s. They maintain that the investigators mostly work independently; but, in stray instances, pressures emanate from different quarters. Most officers withstand such pressures—documentation in the CBI is very meticulous, and since views are clearly documented and hence difficult to overrule, non-interference is ensured.

The CBI is also credited with hosting officers of unmatched professional capability and impeccable integrity. They are handpicked from different cadres for their exceptional skills and apolitical nature. It is only a recent trend wherein politically aligned officers have tried to bypass such scrutiny by taking recourse to legal interpretations. The internal vigilance mechanism appears to have been made partisan and the selection of officers of either mediocre calibre or recognized allegiances has impacted the credibility and professionalism of the agency. This has given rise to the belief that the citadel of an impeccably honest and professional workforce with a credible work culture is crumbling.

The manner in which two of its past directors[2] were embroiled in allegedly questionable dealings with businessmen who were

---

[2] Ranjit Sinha, the director in 2013, alluded to political interference by Government of India ministers before the Supreme Court. This created a storm within the government. Though the government denied any such interference, the Court prevailed, and ministers had to resign. It is ironical that the very same director is now facing a Court-ordered investigation in the coal block allocation case.

being investigated for serious infringements has brought the agency into disrepute.[3] It is also of serious concern that despite its directors being chosen by a high-profile panel comprising the PM, leader of the Opposition in the Lower House and the CJI, the selected functionaries were found woefully inadequate for the assignment.[4]

EVENTS LEADING TO THE PRESENT NADIR IN REPUTATION

In October 2017, Rakesh Asthana, a Gujarat-cadre police officer, was appointed to the number two position in the organization by a panel headed by the central vigilance commissioner. During the selection process itself, Alok Verma, the director, raised doubts about the integrity of the officer as he was being probed for his role in a case against a Gujarat-based company. However, Verma was prevailed upon to appoint Asthana. This appointment was subsequently questioned in court by an NGO. The court decided not to interfere. Verma was not convinced of Asthana's suitability for the assignment and hence did not repose trust in his deputy.

Asthana did not take kindly to this, and cast aspersions on Verma for thwarting investigations in important cases. He reported this to the CVC, who sought details from the CBI about Verma. But these details were not forwarded by the CBI, which claimed that this was an attempt by Asthana to intimidate officers investigating those cases.

This led to multiple allegations being levelled by these functionaries against each other and the matter escalated to

---

[3] A.P. Singh, another director, is being investigated for having connived with Moin Qureshi, a meat exporter who is alleged to have run hawala operations.
[4] Pranab Dhal Samanta; 'Frenemies inside the gate'; *The Economic Times*; 5 November 2018; https://www.pressreader.com/india/the-economic-times/20181105/281951723826453
Accessed on 8 June 2019.

the level of the cabinet secretary. The allegations against Verma were that he had accepted a consideration of ₹20 million while investigating one Satish Sana, a Hyderabad-based businessman, in a case involving meat exporter Moin Qureshi, who is being probed for tax evasion and money laundering.

Asthana further alleged that Verma had even scuttled the attempt to arrest Sana and that Verma had removed him (Asthana) from the team probing high-profile cases, including that against former Finance Minister P. Chidambaram. The CBI soon filed an FIR against Asthana and consequently a deputy superintendent of police (DSP), who was working with him, was arrested. In the complaint leading to the FIR, the allegation was that Asthana had extorted money from Sana.

Soon, both officials approached courts to safeguard themselves against coercive steps. At this point, the government intervened and sent both officers on leave while divesting them of their powers. It is also believed that their offices were sealed and searched.

The CBI director has a fixed tenure of two years, as mandated by the Supreme Court in the Vineet Narain case of 1997. He can be removed only by the committee that appoints him. It has been contended that sending the director on leave is tantamount to flouting the directions of the Court in the Vineet Narain case.[5] Verma contested his removal on this ground in the Supreme Court. The Court asked the CVC to investigate the allegations against Verma. The investigation was supervised by a retired Supreme Court judge.

After perusing the report of the CVC, on 8 January 2019 the Court passed orders reinstating Verma and asserting that transfer of the director without the consent of the selection committee negated the legislative intent to ensure the independence of the

---

[5]Was CBI director Alok Verma removed illegally?; *India Today* TV; 24 October 2018

CBI. The Court directed the PM-led committee to meet and examine whether Verma needed to be removed. As for Verma, it directed that he would 'cease and desist' from taking policy decisions and would take only routine administrative decisions.

The PM-led committee then met on 10 January 2019 to consider the CVC report against Verma. While the leader of the Opposition, a member of the committee, felt that the charges had not been proven and that he should be reinstated with full powers and allowed to complete his tenure, the other two members (the PM and the judge representing the CJI) decided he should be removed.

He was thus removed and posted as the director general of the fire services. Verma did not take up the new post and resigned (his scheduled date of completion of tenure was 31 January 2019). What adds a comical twist to the entire episode is that the officer temporarily vested with interim charge to manage the agency also has aspersions being cast on his background!

Such adverse media attention for an agency that comes to the mind of any person whenever there is a sensational case has impacted the credibility of the institution. The taint will take a long time to erase. How did this come to pass?

First, the seeds of discord were sown when, despite there being a full-time director, another person was appointed as a special director. The CBI is a police organization and, like all uniformed services, follows hierarchy very closely and is bound by it. Posting a special director and entrusting him with all high-profile cases sowed the seed of dissonance in this hierarchical structure. The problem was compounded by the fact that the director had red-flagged the incoming person's integrity. That aspect should have been investigated, and only after clearing the incoming person of all doubt should the decision to accept or reject Asthana have been taken.

It is speculated that in the tradition of the CBI being the

handmaiden of the government, an attempt was made to keep Asthana as an 'acting director' for a while (since he was perceived to be the 'blue-eyed boy of the powers that be'), and then have him appointed as director through the high-ranking three-member committee. Not being able to do so and in some ways being forced to appoint Verma, whose credentials in terms of playing footsie with the government were not very clear, the decision was taken to keep Asthana as the number two and entrust him with sensitive cases. According to some less-than-charitable interpretations, there was also a school of thought which believed that Asthana could be relied upon to keep an eye on the director. Thus, ab initio, the course which was set out was suspect in its 'intentions'.[6]

Second, even if one were to believe that Asthana was appointed with the best of intentions, the government should have stepped in at the first sign of disquiet and ensured that he was either moved out or provided a sinecure where he could mark his time until the superannuation of the incumbent director. He could have then tried his luck for the top job. It is a well-known fact that, administratively, the CBI is under the DoPT, of which the PM is the minister in charge. Even though the Supreme Court may have ordained that the CBI will be under the superintendence of the CVC, ultimate control is exercised by the Prime Minister's Office (PMO). Hence, the intervention from that level should have come much before the rot began to spread. Either the potential for it becoming a conflagration was underestimated or it was believed that it would play itself out. Both aspects were belied, resulting in huge embarrassment for the government.

---

[6] Manoj Joshi; 'View: It's time to reform the CBI'; *The Economic Times*; 24 October 2018; https://economictimes.indiatimes.com/news/politics-and-nation/view-its-time-to-reform-the-cbi/articleshow/66338206.cms Accessed on 8 June 2019.

Third, the CBI is not new to political intervention or its actual lack of autonomy. These factors have coexisted for decades, and successive generations of directors have perfected the art of managing to live with them. Increasingly, there is a decline in the professional capability of officers being appointed to the agency with a preference for 'loyal' officers. This has become a dangerous trend, resulting in prosecutions proving to be increasingly faulty. As a result, acquittals are the order of the day. The most recent instance was of seventeen accused being let off by the CBI special trial court in the high-profile 2G spectrum allocation case.

Fourth, it is a sad reflection on the competence and independence of an agency when the Supreme Court orders that an investigation by an incumbent central vigilance commissioner be supervised by a retired judge. It somehow smacks of lack of trust in the agency. What is the status of a retired judge to be able to oversee the investigation being conducted by a central vigilance commissioner, a statutory appointee? Of course, there have been instances of court-supervised investigations, but those have been supervised by an active bench—an acceptable situation. Such oversight by a retired judge definitely does not augur well for the CVC. It undermines the dignity of an institution and should have evoked a request for reconsideration by the incumbent commissioner.

DECLINE IN CREDIBILITY

This decline in the institution's credibility, however, seems to have commenced in the aftermath of the declaration of emergency in June 1975. As happened with several other institutions then, the CBI was also 'captured' by giving the then director an extension of tenure and hence getting him in alignment with the PMO.

It was under the directions of the PMO that cases were booked and intimidatory tactics commenced against persons who raised their voice against the establishment. A major landmark in the politicization of the CBI was during the tenure of Indira Gandhi as PM. It was found that under the direct instructions of D. Sen, the then director of the CBI, the houses of four officers of the industry ministry who were collecting material for answering a question in Parliament on the functioning of Maruti, were raided by sleuths of the agency. The Parliament, after the Shah Commission inquiry, found the director guilty of obstructing the officials in performing their duties and sentenced him to a prison term along with the PM and her private secretary, R.K. Dhawan.[7]

Soon after the Emergency, a new feature began to take root in the CBI. It involved first choosing the person to be targeted for harassment and then booking cases to launch investigations against them. It was the first time that a home minister, Charan Singh, 'directed' the CBI to book a case against Indira Gandhi in the Jeeps scandal and have her arrested. This is against the established practice of the CBI, which commences investigation and in the course of that investigation conducts searches, interrogations and arrests. The trend of targeting opponents through the CBI appears to have commenced in that period.

In several cases investigated by the CBI, its quality of investigation has been found wanting. In the case of irregular allotment of the 2G spectrum involving A. Raja and sixteen others, who had been charge-sheeted by the CBI, each of the accused was acquitted by the court purely for the lack of clinching evidence. In para 1,817 of the judgement[8] the trial court made

---

[7] Madhave Godbole; 'Why a Revamping of the CBI Is Necessary'; *The Wire*; 27 September 2018; https://thewire.in/law/why-a-revamping-of-the-cbi-is-necessary
Accessed on 8 June 2019.

[8] 'Waited for seven years; couldn't find concrete evidence: CBI Judge in 2G case verdict'; *Outlook*; 21 December 2017; https://www.outlookindia.com/

the following scathing observations while acquitting the accused:

> There is no evidence in the records produced before the Court indicating any criminality in the acts allegedly committed by the accused persons relating to fixation of cut-off date, manipulation of first-come first-served policy, allocation of spectrum to dual technology applicants, ignoring ineligibility of STPL and Unitech group companies, non-revision of entry fee and transfer of ₹200 crore to Kalaignar TV (P) limited as illegal gratification. The charge sheet of the instant case is based mainly on misreading, selective reading, non-reading and out of context reading of the official record. Further; it is based on some oral statements made by the witnesses during investigation, which the witnesses have not owned up in the witness box. Lastly, if statements were made orally by the witnesses, the same were contrary to the official record and thus, not acceptable in law. The end result of the above discussion is that, I have absolutely no hesitation in holding that the prosecution has miserably failed to prove any charge against any of the accused, made in its well-choreographed charge sheet. I may add that many facts recorded in the charge sheet are factually incorrect.[9]

In the Aarushi murder case, the CBI charged the parents of the murdered child with the twin murder of their daughter

---

newsscroll/waited-for-seven-years-coudnt-find-concrete-evidence-cbi-judge-in-2g-case-verdict/1215005
Accessed on 8 June 2019.

[9]"Full text of special court's judgment in 2G spectrum scam case: 'Huge scam seen by everyone where there was none'; *Firstpost*; 22 December 2017; https://www.firstpost.com/india/full-text-of-special-courts-judgment-in-2g-spectrum-scam-case-huge-scam-seen-by-everyone-where-there-was-none-4270757.html
Accessed on 18 July 2019.

and domestic help. The Allahabad High Court was scathing in its comments on the quality of investigation and observed that the theory of the agency was an 'impossible hypothesis' which was 'patently absurd'. The Court went on to acquit the parents, maintaining that the prosecution had 'miserably failed' to establish that they had destroyed material evidence. This was also a very severe indictment of the investigative capabilities of the agency, particularly in a case in which there was no possibility of any kind of political pressure.

The case of the longest duration has been the Bofors case, which deals with the acquisition of howitzers from a Swedish company. In this case, too, the Delhi High Court quashed all the charges against the Hinduja brothers, whom the agency had arraigned for being conduits and recipients of kickbacks. Even in the three-decade-old fodder scam of Bihar (now Jharkhand), none other than the apex court had remarked that the CBI had 'failed to live up to its reputation' and that there was 'intolerable lethargy' in filing the appeal.[10]

In the investigation and trial that followed the Bhopal gas tragedy of 1984, the CBI was publicly seen as ineffective. Former CBI joint director B.R. Lall, investigating the case, maintained that he was asked to remain soft on the extradition of Union Carbide chief executive officer (CEO) Warren Anderson and drop the charges (which included culpable homicide).[11] This statement made by a then serving officer brings out the rot that had begun to set into the organization.

---

[10] Krishnadas Rajagopal; 'Fodder scam: SC pulls up CBI for delay in filing appeal'; *The Hindu*; 8 May 2017; https://www.thehindu.com/news/national/fodder-scam-sc-pulls-up-cbi-for-delay-in-filing-appeal/article18410680.ece Accessed on 8 June 2019.

[11] 'Was told to go soft on Warren Anderson: Former CBI official'; *NDTV*; 8 June 2010; https://www.ndtv.com/india-news/was-told-to-go-soft-on-warren-anderson-former-cbi-official-420245 Accessed on 8 June 2019.

In another significant instance of the agency being hauled up for lax investigation, the Himachal Pradesh High Court sought the personal appearance of the CBI director over the tardy pace of investigation into the murder and gang rape of a sixteen-year-old girl in the Kotkhai area of Shimla district in July 2017. The Court was compelled to observe: 'To our utter dismay, we find the instant progress report with regard to the investigation of the crime to be unsatisfactory. Perhaps the investigating agency is clueless with regard to the persons involved in the heinous crime.'[12]

WITHDRAWAL OF GENERAL CONSENT

The Supreme Court and high courts have, from time to time, directed the CBI to investigate cases in different states. However, Section 6 of the DSPE Act prohibits the CBI from operating outside Delhi without permission from state governments. Thus, in strict legal terms, if a state refuses permission to the CBI to operate within its limits, the agency cannot even conduct raids there unless it gets permission from a court.

The recent infighting in the CBI has provided some of the state governments, which are not well disposed towards the BJP-led government, scope to withdraw the general consent given to the agency, authorizing it to operate in their state.[13] The first to do so was Andhra Pradesh (under former Chief Minister N. Chandrababu Naidu), followed by West Bengal. Now there are

---

[12]Saurabh Chauhan; 'Kotkhai rape-murder: HC directs CBI to file fresh status report on April 25'; *Hindustan Times*; 30 March 2018; https://www.hindustantimes.com/india-news/kotkhai-rape-and-murder-hc-directs-cbi-to-file-fresh-status-report-on-april-25/story-1FTjRl1NZaF3kSCitYTFWK.html Accessed on 8 June 2019.

[13]'Can states ban the CBI from investigating?'; *The Times of India*; 17 November 2018; https://timesofindia.indiatimes.com/india/can-states-ban-cbi-from-investigating/articleshow/66663465.cms Accessed on 8 June 2019.

news reports suggesting that Punjab may consider similar action.

The withdrawal of general consent by the Andhra Pradesh government may well change the rules of engagement of the CBI in relation to the officials, leaders and people of that state. Whilst officially the Andhra government would have us believe that the infighting within the CBI has led to erosion of confidence in the agency, the fact remains that the family of then CM Naidu appears to have had many 'run-ins' with the CBI. Whether these were politically motivated or otherwise, the following instances have lent grist to the grapevine: Sana, the person at the centre of the sparring between the present director and special director, is apparently known to be a Naidu insider.

There was another PIL in the Andhra Pradesh High Court seeking a CBI probe into the allegedly corrupt dealings of Nara Lokesh, the son of the former chief minister and himself a minister. Yet another PIL sought a CBI probe into ₹21,000 crore worth of fake MoUs being allegedly signed by the former CM and his son.[14] Each of these points to the 'politicization' of the CBI.

RESTORING CREDIBILITY

The challenge before the government is to restore the credibility of the organization. Peripheral attempts and tinkering on the sidelines will not cure the CBI of the deep-rooted malaise that afflicts it. The real problem for the agency lies in its charter of duties as it continues to function under the archaic DSPE Act of 1946. It is not protected by any special legislation as its functions are based merely on a government resolution that draws its

---

[14]Prabhash K. Dutta; 'Fear or politics? Why Chandrababu Naidu blocked CBI's entry into Andhra Pradesh'; *India Today*; 16 November 2018; https://www.indiatoday.in/india/story/fear-or-politics-why-chandrababu-naidu-blocked-cbi-s-entry-in-andhra-pradesh-1390070-2018-11-16 Accessed on 8 June 2019.

powers from the aforementioned Act. For the complex web of investigations that it is called upon to undertake, the powers vested in it under this Act fall woefully short of its need. Both the CVC Act, 2003, and the Lokpal Act, 2013, deal partly with the powers and functions of the CBI, including providing some much-needed safeguards. But till date, the CBI does not have an Act of its own, although the need for a comprehensive Act has been felt for a long time.

The Estimates Committee of Parliament had recommended that the CBI be given statutory status and have legal powers to investigate cases with interstate ramifications. The parliamentary standing committees in 2007 and again in 2008 had recommended that a separate Act be promulgated for the CBI 'in tune with the requirements of the time to ensure credibility and impartiality'. In 2008, the committee felt that 'the need of the hour is to strengthen the CBI in terms of legal mandate, infrastructure and resources.'[15] However, it appears that successive governments have preferred to keep the parrot 'caged'.

The need for an independent statute for the CBI also arises from the fact that the provisions of the DSPE Act mandate to the central government, under Section 4 of the Act, the power of superintendence over the CBI. Invariably, in cases being investigated by the agency, the government seems entitled to seek the details of any ongoing investigation. It was possibly this loophole that the government was exploiting when, despite the fact that it was a Supreme Court-supervised investigation in the coal mine allocation case, the Home Ministry and the PMO both tried to introduce their own perspectives into the draft affidavit that the CBI was preparing for submission to the Court.

---

[15]'Left-Right-Centre: Is CBI the handmaiden of the government?'; *The Hindu*; 14 July 2017; https://www.thehindu.com/opinion/op-ed/is-cbi-the-handmaiden-of-the-government/article19272931.ece Accessed on 8 June 2019.

The Supreme Court verdict which provided for superintendence by the CVC over the CBI in the Vineet Narain case left this lacuna intact. The judgement stated: 'While the government shall remain answerable for the CBI's functioning, to introduce visible objectivity in the mechanism for overviewing the CBI's functioning, the CVC shall be entrusted with the responsibility of superintendence over the CBI's functioning.' The Court went on to add, '[The government] shall take all necessary measures to ensure that the CBI functions effectively and efficiently and is viewed as a non-partisan agency'.

These words clearly indicate that the primary responsibility for the effective functioning of the CBI falls upon the government. The Court has handed over the superintendence, in part, to the CVC but how independent is the CVC itself? It is a statutory body which is under the administrative control of the DoPT and hence, for all practical purposes, remains, if not answerable, yet accountable to that department.

The CVC is ill-equipped to deal with the CBI. Apart from conducting stock-taking of the pending cases and such other theoretical checks, there is nothing much that the CVC can do by way of effective 'superintendence' of the CBI. Invariably, the commissioner is also a former bureaucrat, handpicked by the government and in some ways owing allegiance to it and thus prone to pressure himself.

However, vesting the CVC with the 'superintendence' of the DSPE (and thus the CBI) in relation to investigation under the Prevention of Corruption Act, 1988, was only one part of the mandate. For the remaining areas, the Act left the superintendence to the government. So, this superintendence is shared today between the CVC and the government, such that while the answerability for the CBI's functioning is with the government, the power of 'superintendence' in corruption cases lies with the CVC.

In the midst of all this, another element has arisen. It is

the tendency of the Supreme Court to conduct investigation supervised by it, as highlighted most recently in the ongoing examination of the Rafale fighter jet purchase from France. This investigation is on a petition jointly filed by Yashwant Sinha and Arun Shourie, former ministers, and lawyer-activist Prashant Bhushan, seeking a CBI inquiry into the entire process leading to the purchase of thirty-six Rafale fighter jets in fly-away condition. The central government has provided all the details, including the purchase price of the aircraft (in a sealed cover).

In the course of the hearing, the attorney general is reported to have said that the Court is not judicially competent to decide what aircraft and weapons should be bought, as it is a matter for experts. In fact, in a most unusual move, the CJI appears to have asked for senior Air Force officers to appear in court and answer questions. The logic was that the Court was dealing with requirements of the Air Force and would like to hear from its officers regarding the jets to be acquired, and not from civilian officials of the Ministry of Defence (MoD).

This action of the Court has attracted diverse comments, but the principal theme emerging is that the purchase of defence aircraft is a prerogative of the elected executive, and unless a case of corruption or irregularity is made out and investigated, the Court should not be interfering at this stage. This indeed is the opinion among informed, disinterested persons around the country, as the apex court interfering at this stage of a defence procurement exercise is certainly transgressing into the mandate of the government. In ordinary circumstances, such a complaint would need to be investigated by the agency to establish whether a prima facie case is made out. That does not appear to have happened. Any order of the 'last court of appeal in the land' at this stage would be akin to putting the cart before the horse—any comment by the Court will prejudice investigation or trial by any other court.

TIME TO UNCAGE THE PARROT

Accountability institutions that form the foundational pillars of any democracy seem to be losing their structural strength. That is probably the reason an otherwise decisive government did not see or, if it saw, did not act on early warning signs. There could even be a possibility of misdemeanour being ignored. The CBI seems to be becoming a 'handmaiden' to investigate, if not intimidate. The onus is now squarely on the government to cut its losses, and, wielding the hammer, set about ensuring that it is not held guilty of allowing the credibility of these institutions to hit rock-bottom during its tenure.

Considering that the agency seems to be the final port of call for any major act of crime or corruption, there is an urgent need to arm it with a distinct mandate of keeping an 'arm's-length' relationship with the government. This should be genuine and not undertaken merely for visibility purposes. The specific statute must ensure that the agency does not report to the government and is made accountable to the Parliament like the ECI. However, it needs to be recognized that the CBI is a police organization and, if left independent, may have the propensity to turn 'rogue'. Hence, its functioning must be oversighted by a high-level committee comprising the PM, the leader of the Opposition in the Lok Sabha, the CJI and the Lokpal. Such a body must monitor the functioning on a quarterly basis to ensure autonomy and maintain the professional integrity of the agency.

After about four decades since being originally mooted, the Lokpal and the Act constituting it have seen the light of day. The time has come for the Lokpal to be given constitutional status of the sort the CAG and ECI enjoy. It can then be made the administrative head of these two bodies, such that the CVC operates as the administrative arm and the CBI becomes the investigative arm. This would ensure that interference from the government is obviated as the Lokpal would be undertaking the superintendence of the CBI and, itself being a constitutional appointee, be devoid of control or possibility of 'meddling' of the type that was seen and adversely commented upon by the Supreme Court in the coal mine case.

The officers of the CAG are distanced from governmental control and hence can be relied upon to be objective in their functioning. A similar setup would provide insulation from political or administrative interference by the political executive. The reports of the Lokpal could go directly to the Parliament in very much the same manner in which the reports of the CAG are placed in the legislature. The political executive has no say in the preparation of those reports. This framework would ensure that the CBI is seen, and operates, as a professional body with no extraneous influence of any kind. Such a decision would greatly enhance the credibility of the government as well.

The CBI does not have a very encouraging track record of successful prosecution, especially in high-profile cases. The role of prosecutors in the organization needs overhauling. Often, the director of prosecution plays a secondary role and gets swamped by the same political allegiances that bedevil the director of the organization, especially when the director gets the appointment after lobbying and hence ab initio starts with an 'I owe you' tag.

The US has witnessed powerful and prominent attorneys like Preet Bharara, thereby balancing the investigative and prosecuting powers of the agency. In the Indian system, with prosecutors kowtowing to investigators, the system of checks and balances within the organization disappears. A case of credibility of the prosecutor is that of Robert Mueller, who headed the US Federal Bureau of Investigation (FBI) from 2001 to 2013, and is now the special prosecutor looking into the alleged Russian interference in the US presidential elections. The media has widely reported that despite President Donald Trump's unhappiness with the investigation, he has been unable to fire him. This speaks highly of the stature and thus credibility of the prosecution process.

It needs to be recognized that, regardless of the structure that the government or the Parliament creates for the CBI, it can only be as efficient or apolitical as the people who operate it. The destinies of institutions are shaped by the people who populate them and define their powers. Thus, the CBI's dependence on the home ministry for its staffing or the law ministry for its lawyers in itself undermines the efficiency of the agency. The creation of a dedicated cadre of officers, similar to those functioning under the CAG who are not prone to any political overtones and are protected in their functioning, must be considered. IPS officers on deputation face the spectre of returning to their states and being prone to political vendetta. There is the unfortunate case of a UP-cadre IPS officer who retired as CBI director. He found to his horror that for spurious reasons, the approval of his pension documents had been withheld by Mayawati, the then chief minister, because he had investigated cases against her!

These are only some indicative solutions to the malaise that plagues the CBI. The superstructure of the organization needs to be strengthened such that officers who do not become the stature of the agency cannot harm the citadel, as appears to have happened. The cancer that has set into the organization needs to be exorcised by a huge scalpel. The overhaul has to be all-pervading. It has to be done by a government that has the political will and strength of conviction to be able to 'uncage the parrot' and permit it to justify itself as a major pillar to ensure probity, accountability and impeccable integrity, thereby contributing to good governance in the country.

7

THE CIVIL SERVICES

Has the Steel Frame Sagged?

The Indian civil services inherit their legacy from the nineteenth-century (1858) Imperial Civil Service (ICS) of the British Empire. This service was responsible for the efficient administration of the Empire in British India, whose jurisdiction extended into Burma (now Myanmar), and what is now Pakistan and Bangladesh. Originally, almost all the members of the service were British nationals. In 1922, the British government administration permitted the entrance examination for the civil service to be taken from India too. Conducting the examination only in the UK had permitted only select Indians with the financial capability for travel to take the exam. Being able to take it in India tilted the balance in favour of a dominant number of Indians entering the service.

The British had laid great emphasis on an independent, efficient and accountable civil service. British PM David Lloyd George, while speaking in the UK Parliament in 1922, had referred to the Indian Civil Service as the 'steel frame'. He stated:

> If you take the steel frame out, the fabric will collapse....
> There is one institution we will not cripple, there is one institution we will not deprive of its functions or of its

privileges, and that is that institution which built up the British Raj—the British Civil Service in India.[1]

This statement clearly demonstrates the importance the administration attached to a permanent civil service that would implement the policy decisions of the elected government.

In its original architecture, the ICS mirrored the Civil Service of Whitehall or the Westminster model, wherein a cadre of permanent civil servants advised and facilitated Cabinet members in policy formulation and implementation. However, this cadre comprised a very small number of selected officers who supervised the administration of the entire country. In 1931, the ICS comprised 1,032 officials out of the overall strength of roughly one million persons who administered undivided India, with its then population of about 350 million. The superior nature of the service was also recognized by the fact that the ICS officers were handsomely compensated. In 1935, a secretary from the ICS drew ₹6,666. At the time, the US secretary of the treasury is reported to have earned only half as much.[2]

A NEW GENERATION OF CIVIL SERVANTS

Independent India's first home minister, Sardar Vallabhbhai Patel, also recognized the importance of having a uniform administrative structure and wanted to institutionalize an All-India Service under the control of the central government. This initiative was strongly opposed by the chief ministers of the states, since they felt that a central government-controlled service would substantially erode their authority. They favoured the State

---

[1] Kuldeep Mathur; *Recasting Public Administration in India: Reform, Rhetoric, and Neoliberalism*; Oxford University Press (2018)
[2] Anirudh Krishna, *Continuity and Change: The Indian Administrative Service 30 Years Ago and Today*, Commonwealth and Comparative Politics, 48(4):433-444 (November 2010)

Civil Services over the All-India Service. The home minister's proposal, however, managed to prevail over a rather reluctant Constituent Assembly, and the political leadership decided to retain the basic structure of the ICS, renaming it the Indian Administrative Service (IAS). It was felt that Indian leaders were not familiar with alternative models and, considering the strife prevailing within the country after the Partition, it would be wise to continue with a tried-and-tested setup, which could be customized at a later date.

This certainly proved to be correct, as even strident Indian nationalists who had serious misgivings about retaining the basic fabric of the ICS were appreciative of the stellar role played by the service during the testing times post-Partition and acknowledged that the service had been impartial, high-minded, conscientious and incorruptible.

Another category of services created was the Central Services. Whilst the former category served the central and state governments and in fact acted as a bridge between the two, the latter was confined to regulation by only the central government. In common parlance, unless not specifically intended, the reference to 'civil service' has come to mean the IAS, whose members serve in the regional as well as the central government. The civil service has continued to be mandated with powers to collect revenue and enforce law and order, thereby being a strong institution for undertaking social structure projects and ensuring planned economic development.

The three All-India Services—the Administrative Service, the Police Service and the Forest Service—have been instrumental in ensuring consistency, uniformity and integrity across India. This was recognized by the government and Sardar Patel, in particular. In fact, speaking to IAS probationers on 21 April 1947, Patel stated:

> A civil servant cannot afford to and must not take part in politics. Nor must he involve himself in any communal

wrangles. To depart from the path of rectitude in either of these respects is to debase public service and to lower its dignity...Unhappily, India today cannot boast of an incorruptible service, but I hope that you, who are now starting as it were, a new generation of civil servants will not be misled by black sheep in the fold, but would render your services without fear or favour and without any expectation of extraneous rewards.³

Today, 21 April is marked as Civil Services Day.

THE NEED FOR URGENT REFORM

However, with the passage of time, cracks have been observed in the quality of the 'steel frame'. Critics of the service feel it has become insensitive and unresponsive to the needs of citizens for whose welfare the administration functions. The officers are also seen to be functioning from their 'ivory towers' without really appreciating grass-roots issues. In fact, some even feel that the bureaucracy has become the single dominating entity resisting change for bringing about a flexible and people-oriented administration.

It is widely believed that while the Indian economy has grown rapidly in recent years, the country's governance setup and bureaucratic quality have declined. Sustainable economic development requires good governance. The quality of administration ensures fulfilment of the stated objectives of any elected government in terms of inclusive development and targeted delivery of specialized schemes, such as guaranteed rural

---

³Office of the Registrar General & Census Commissioner, India; Ministry of Home Affairs, Government of India; Census Reports 1931; http://censusindia.gov.in/Census_And_You/old_report/Census_1931n.aspx Accessed on 16 June 2019.

employment, assured primary education programmes and rural health missions.

The bureaucracy, particularly the IAS, performs a very critical role in ensuring that the fruits of development indeed reach the people. However, it is perceived that the IAS is hamstrung by political interference, outdated personnel procedures and a mixed record on policy implementation, and hence is in need of urgent reform. State governments with a very narrow agenda, often dictated by caste and regional considerations, have repeatedly tried to erode the objective character of the civil service. They abuse their authority through transfers and inconsequential assignments meted out to officers seen to be upright and not acquiescent with their politically motivated demands. This has not only politicized the essence of the service, but has damaged its morale—rendering it submissive to these requirements.

It is recognized that the civilian administration has become far more complex now than in the last century. Considering the fact that bureaucrats do not function in a vacuum and are subject to political interference and regional pressures, their objectivity in functioning has come up for adverse scrutiny at times. This factor, coupled with the deep-seated suspicion that career advancement does not take place only on merit, has created serious motivational issues. The service is often perceived as lacking in competence and professionalism, harbouring political bias and suffering declining independence—and, of course, concerns around malfeasance and probity abound.

There is also a need to make the performance appraisal system more objective. Successive administrations have tended to introduce supposedly objective and hence more complex and fine-tuned structures, but end up succumbing to playing 'favourites' at the last-mile stage. There is, of course, the issue of unattractive compensation. Whilst this is not too dominating, yet there needs to be a much more differentiated system of compensation for the higher bureaucracy than the present system of compensating middle rungs adequately without providing attractive increases as one rises in the hierarchy.

There are several reasons attributable for the decline in the quality and efficacy of the civil service:

i. Short tenures in posting;
ii. Increasing political interference;
iii. Declining quality of incumbents;
iv. Inadequate monetary compensation to attract the best talent;
v. Lack of specialization in a complex administrative environment;
vi. Relatively greater attraction for political alignment and hence malfeasance;
vii. Attraction for forging alliances at the regional level and inadequate incentive to serve at the Union government level; and
viii. Opaque system of performance appraisal.

Whilst several other factors could be cited for the perceived decline in quality of the bureaucracy, most of them would be subsumed by the factors mentioned, so an analysis is in order.

DEEPER ANALYSIS

It has to be recognized that with the increasing advent of regional parties and coalition governments coming to power in the past three decades, the political narrative has become focused towards narrow political and regional considerations. Local political leaders prefer to have officers who prioritize their dictates above the objective demands of the situation. An increasingly intransigent political executive has thus attempted to select officers who do their bidding. Those who do not conform are sidelined and handed inconsequential assignments. Such punishment or threat of constant transfers and short tenures is often utilized to pressure officers into submission.

Quality educational services are of primary concern for officers with schoolgoing children. Keeping them constantly on the move or inflicting short tenures results in officers moving their families in quick succession, and hence rapidly changing schools, which adversely impacts their children's education. The other option is to keep their families in the state headquarters and move from one assignment to another alone. The latter situation has attracted the sobriquet of 'suitcase officers', who seize every opportunity to rush to where their families live and hence pay inadequate attention to their assignment—which in field postings requires more or less 24x7 attention.

This 'technique' of harassing officers by constantly keeping them on the move has been effectively deployed by governments in Bihar, UP and Haryana. The most widely known example of using the threat of frequent transfer to ensure acquiescence by officers and, in the absence of such submissive tendencies, to punish them by frequent transfers is that of Ashok Khemka. An officer of the 1991 batch of the Haryana cadre, Khemka has been transferred fifty-two times in his career of about twenty-seven years, ostensibly because he exposed endemic corruption in various state departments.[4] While this is indeed an extreme case, politically motivated transfers are done in the garb of public interest.

An analysis done by *The Times of India*[5] of the

---

[4]Jagyaseni Biswas; '52 transfers in 27 years: Is IAS officer Ashok Khemka paying a price for honesty?'; 7 March 2019; https://www.moneycontrol.com/news/india/52-transfers-in-27-years-is-ias-officer-ashok-khemka-paying-a-price-for-honesty-3615511.html
Accessed on 5 July 2019.
[5]'All you want to know about IAS transfers'; *The Times of India*; 8 January

executive record (ER) sheets of 2,139 IAS officers currently in service reveals that frequent transfers are common among all cadres and levels. The study reveals that about two-thirds of the officers have had average tenures of eighteen months or less. The fifteenth report of the second Administrative Reforms Commission (ARC) has highlighted appointments to the highest level of administration that have lacked transparency and objectivity. The report further observed that transfers often coincided with a change in the political regime. This leads to instability of administration and lack of faith in the system among the people, and adds to the cost of administration.

The malady does not manifest itself in state governments alone. In a recent study published by *The Economic Times*,[6] it is reported that major departments in the Government of India, such as Chemicals and Petrochemicals, Fertilizers, School Education, Rural Development, Urban Development, Posts, North Eastern Region, Minority Affairs and Renewable Energy, have seen five secretaries since 2014 (under the present NDA government). Departments such as Coal, Economic Affairs, Higher Education, Minority Affairs, Micro, Small and Medium Enterprises, and Textiles have seen four secretaries. These frequent changes (tenures ranging from barely nine months to a year) point to the fact that an officer is shifted even before he can settle down in such complex departments. Often, the reasons for the shift are unknown. The officer certainly does not know, so even if there is

---

2014; https://timesofindia.indiatimes.com/all-you-want-to-know-about-ias-transfers/photostory/28561372.cms
Accessed on 16 June 2019.

[6]Chaitanya Kalbag; 'Gujarat Assembly Elections: Why there is so much more at stake for PM Narendra Modi this time'; *The Economic Times*; 14 December 2017; https://economictimes.indiatimes.com/news/politics-and-nation/why-there-is-so-much-more-at-stake-than-gujarat/articleshow/62060549.cms?from=mdr
Accessed on 16 June 2019.

a need for corrective action, it is not taken.

Increasing political interference has been a phenomenon observed across all states and cadres. Ostensibly on the principle of participation of elected representatives in ensuring responsive administration, small-time politicians have begun to interfere in administration. The lamentable aspect of such interference is the threat of frequent transfers and inconsequential assignments if their demands are not met. It is most unfortunate that electoral politics has now come to be associated with money. This has established a cozy business-politician nexus, where the 'business' is often of the illegal variety. Any strong and objective action taken by the administration immediately attracts the wrath of the local, small-time politician who is often in cahoots with illegal business interests.

A recent example of this is an episode that played out in the Noida district of UP, where an intrepid junior lady officer took on the illegal sand-mining mafia. Her unrelenting action against them attracted the wrath of the state's then young chief minister, who had seized power on the promise of providing good governance. Durga Shakti Nagpal, a 2009-batch UP cadre officer, was posted as the sub-divisional magistrate (SDM) in Noida, where she received information of large-scale illegal removal of sand from riverbeds after nightfall. She enforced police patrolling and registered sixty-six FIRs and arrested 104 persons associated with the crime, besides confiscating eighty-one vehicles.

This attracted the attention of the local politicians who provided 'protection' to the illegal business operations. They could not get her transferred as she had acquired immense public support by her actions. They thus devised other means, and at the behest of the local functionaries of the SP (then the party in power in UP), the officer was suspended ostensibly because she had ordered the demolition of a wall constructed illegally near a mosque, which led to communal tension. The chief minister, often seen as a beacon of hope for good governance in the state, demonstrated his vulnerability to the business-politician nexus. He bowed to the pressure to 'teach the officer a lesson' and thereby sent a signal to other such intrepid officers who might dare to take on politicians. Despite Noida being a stone's throw from New Delhi, Sonia Gandhi herself writing to the PM to intervene in the matter, PILs being filed in court and every right-thinking senior politician/officer supporting Nagpal's cause, no remedy emerged in her favour.

This was a typical case of political interference, often designed to further local political interests, which are nefarious in their objective and are carried out ostensibly in 'public interest'.

There is a similar case in Kerala. T.V. Anupama, a 2010-batch IAS officer, was posted as the district collector (DC) of Alappuzha in August 2017. She soon submitted two reports of illegal encroachment and conversion of land use related to government land by a resort, which happened to be owned by Thomas Chandy, the then transport minister in the ruling coalition state government. The minister denied the encroachment. Nothing would have happened but for the Communist Party of India (CPI) faction in the ruling coalition deciding not to participate in Cabinet meetings until Chandy resigned. This forced the minister to finally resign in November 2017. The officer, of course, was subsequently transferred to Thrissur district.

In the early 1970s, I was an SDM in the same Thrissur district, which had a few Jacobite Syrian churches. The Jacobite Syrian community had split into two factions: one owing allegiance to the Catholicos and the other to the Patriarch of Antioch. The two factions developed disputes over the ownership and worshipping rights of the churches. Thus, under a provision of the Code of Criminal Procedure (CrPC), the churches had been taken over by the SDM in that district, as also in other districts where such disputes had arisen. Every Sunday, these disputed churches were opened for two hours in the morning for one faction and two hours in the afternoon for the other faction, to enable worship.

However, some miscreants belonging to one faction destroyed property of a church located in a small town called Chelekara. Since the miscreants were identified by the police, as a penalty, they were debarred from entering the church. This faction had access to the chief minister, who also belonged to the same district. They approached him, seeking that he direct me to reverse my order. The Chief Minister did not speak to me, but issued directions to the district magistrate (DM) to instruct me.

I, however, did not immediately withdraw the order as it would be succumbing to undue political influence. Such intransigence from a young officer was not viewed kindly and the following week I was shunted from the SDM's post and made the project officer of the small farmers' development agency! This rather harsh action was taken by a chief minister who was otherwise known to be very good to officials and completely backed their actions. It was an early lesson in my career.

Much has been said about the declining quality of human capital that the civil services are now either endowed with or attract. As regards recruitment, the First (1966) and Second (2005) ARCs have recommended various changes. Regarding recruitment, the Second Commission recommended significantly lowering the permissible age of entry into the service. Earlier, aspirants were required to be in the age group of twenty-one to twenty-four years to take the civil services examination. Now the upper age limit has been relaxed to thirty-two years for general candidates and thirty-seven for reserved candidates. The number of attempts is limited to six for general candidates and nine for Other Backward Classes (OBCs) while being unlimited for Scheduled Castes and Scheduled Tribes (SCs and STs). The following are very compelling arguments for lowering the age for recruitment:

- At the time of recruitment, it is expected that officers will be moulded and trained in service ideology, a culture of integrity and dedication, and to be apolitical in their conduct. At twenty-two/twenty-three years this is feasible. However, at thirty-three or thirty-eight years of age, when new entrants join the training establishment, they are hardly amenable to any moulding. At this age, opinions, political ideologies and attitude to life usually have already been formed. Also, the successful aspirants would not have remained idle prior to joining the civil services. They would have worked in other jobs and would carry that baggage too on recruitment into the civil services. Hence, attempting to train or mould them at that age would be futile.
- Irrespective of the age of entry, retirement for all has to be at sixty years. A short career span of twenty-seven or twenty-two years would not enable officers to reach the pinnacle of the service, as the normal aspiration would be. As a consequence, service aspirations would take a back seat and derail motivation to perform in the best traditions of the service, thereby making the officer vulnerable to enticement of different kinds. Hence, political affiliations, caste convergences, regional interests and, above all, integrity issues, come to the fore. Such enticements are the bane of professionalism and objectivity in the civil services.

In view of these predilections, any framework designed to bring about reform in the civil services must be premised on 'catching the aspirants young' so that they can be adequately moulded and made to imbibe the traditions and qualities of an objective civil servant.

The compensation receivable by government servants has always been an issue that attracts a great deal of attention. The pay package of a secretary to the government compares very adversely with any corporate executive exercising even a minuscule percentage of the responsibility that the former bears. The secretary draws a salary of ₹30 lakh per annum. The chairman of the largest public-sector bank draws a similar amount. However, the median salary of a CEO in a mid-sized corporate would amount to about ₹3 crore while the CEO of a mid-sized private bank would draw a salary of about ₹5 crore. Despite the fact that salary hikes recommended by Pay Commissions merely cover inflation, the award is greeted with alarm since it is seen to be leading to huge revenue deficits in central and state budgets and bringing about inflationary tendencies.

A significant feature of the governmental salary structure is that the differential between the top-most echelons of government as compared to the lowest rung suffers from a compression factor. This implies that over the years, the differential has narrowed, with promotions to higher echelons not being matched by commensurate or pro rata increases in salary. Such compression introduced situations wherein promotions, after progressive rates of income tax, often led to salary declines in their real value. This factor has had a demoralizing influence. It may not be fair to generalize that lower pay scales lead to greater lure for malfeasance among all civil servants. However, its influence cannot be denied. At the same time, with the private sector offering a plethora of opportunities, with compensation for an average-level executive being significantly higher than that of a secretary to the government, the attraction of the service has begun to lose its sheen. The result has been that the best and brightest, who would have earlier opted for the civil services, do not see it as a major career opportunity any more.

The decline in terms of professionalism and human capital in an increasingly competitive environment is an issue that needs to be addressed too. An adequately equipped service in terms of professionalism and specialization would improve the quality of governance it provides. In a complex administrative environment, the capability of a generalist service to deliver has come up for adverse observations. Domain knowledge has not only become increasingly necessary, but lack of it is rendering officers incapable of adding any quality to governance. Frequent rotation in postings among diverse sectors leaves them bereft of any in-depth domain knowledge.

Modern-day administration has necessitated the need for a certain degree of specialization among civil servants. Thus, there is a need for bureaucrats to specialize in financial management, public health, town and city planning, sports administration and the education sector. Officers could be encouraged to specialize in these sectors after gaining basic knowledge and experience in general administration so as to grasp the complexities of implementation at the ground level. The government would also be better advised to utilize the services of these 'generalist-turned-specialist bureaucrats' in their respective areas of specialization.

Inclination towards political alignment, often leading to malfeasance, has been an issue of concern regarding the civil services. The IAS has huge public and political exposure. Officers interact with the political executive or even local political elements in their day-to-day functioning. The 'if you cannot resist them, join them' syndrome has caused irreparable harm. Such tendencies have led to objectivity and apolitical decision-making falling by the wayside.

There have also been many occasions when politicians have successfully divided the bureaucracy along caste and regional lines. The most illustrative cases of breaking the back of upright officers emerge from Bihar. In the words of Manish K. Jha and Pushpendra in *Governing Caste and Managing Conflicts, Bihar, 1990–2011*:

> To make the bureaucracy defunct, ineffective and vulnerable to demands and whims of the elected leaders of backward castes, it was necessary to centralise power,

humiliate the bureaucracy in public gaze, punish it by frequent transfer and postings, and frequently overrule its decisions. For the first time, in post-Independence Bihar, the fear of the administration and police started waning from the minds of the lower-caste people. All sorts of symbolism were used. One powerful symbol used to be pictures of Lalu Prasad often in newspapers where he would keep his feet on the centre table on the lawn of his residence and bureaucrats would either stand or sit in front facing his feet. Stories abound about how he would speak in rustic language with his officers that would amount to hurt and humiliation in any 'civilised' parliamentary culture. He would visit poor people and introduce himself as 'Raja' (king) of the state and would advise people to be fearless of their 'sevaks' (servants)—the bureaucrats. The 15 years of Lalu-Rabri regime witnessed the lowest number of police firings and lathi-charges on the masses. He would prevail over rules as well as rationality to ensure support to his caste members and other OBCs even when they acted against the law. *Ultimately, the administration lost the power to resist and bowed to the will of politicians* [italicised emphasis mine].[7]

Such predilections among politicians in recent times have caused untold harm to the apolitical nature and professional integrity of the civil services. It is as a consequence of such constant and sustained efforts that endemic political interference has led to officers relatively vulnerable in terms of moral fibre falling prey to rent-seeking tendencies. Once they do so, they feel trapped to comply with the questionable demands of politicians for fear of

---

[7]Manish K. Jha and Pushpendra; *Governing Caste and Managing Conflicts Bihar, 1990–2011*; http://www.mcrg.ac.in/PP48.pdf
Accessed on 16 June 2019.

reprisal. As a consequence, political alignments appear the easier career option.

IAS officers are retained on the cadre strength of state governments. The Centre does not have a cadre of its own. According to convention, 25 per cent of the officers of each cadre are required to be on deputation to the central government. Officers who have displayed outstanding performance in the state are chosen to serve in the Union government. Thus, officers coming to the Centre are handpicked from the states and are uniformly meritorious. There is thus a challenge to perform well while serving in the central government, as one is pitted against the best in the country. In the states, one is in a cozy and familiar environment, whereas the Centre is an ocean where one has to survive by dint of performance.

This poses a challenge that officers posted in their home states who have developed a comfortable relationship with the political executive there opt not to undergo. These officers have, very early in their careers, decided to just be passengers, move upwards along with routine time-based batch promotions, not show any initiative or dynamism and just enjoy the perks of office. They forge their political alignments and choose the comfort of the home cadre. This category of officers adds to the deadwood and cannot be relied upon to undertake onerous responsibility.

A major feature determining the upward mobility of officers is the process of empanelment. An officer has to undergo scrutiny for being empanelled for appointment as a joint secretary, additional secretary or secretary to the Government of India. This empanelment process is obviously undertaken according to certain well-conceived parameters. The unfortunate part is that no officer is aware of these parameters. Every year that empanelment takes place, there are surprising omissions—officers considered to be outstanding by their peers and cadre mates and certain choices for empanelment are excluded. Similarly, there are surprise inclusions—officers perceived by peers and cadres alike to be mere fellow travellers or complicit in issues unbecoming of an officer make the grade. The critical issue is that an officer never gets to know the reason for his omission. As such, he does not know how he can improve himself.

Further, these parameters keep changing. In addition to the routine appraisal on the basis of Annual Appraisal Reports of officers, an eminent persons' group is set up to provide inputs on the officers in the zone of consideration. These inputs are at best 'hearsay' evidence, which can and does mar careers. At times, a 360-degree appraisal process is instituted and this appears to be routinely overriding the annual performance appraisals. On certain occasions, two batches are taken up for empanelment together, leading to large-scale omissions and hence avoidable heartburn. Thus, the incentive for advancement via the empanelment process has limited credibility, as at times it works to the detriment of officers who have had the courage to stand up to politicians and hence get targeted.

TIME TO CHANGE GEAR

These issues that plague the civil services indicate that piecemeal and peripheral attempts at tinkering will not bring about any perceptible reform in officers' capability to deliver objectively. Irrespective of the form of government, viz. a monarchy, theocracy, communist regime, dictatorship or parliamentary democracy, there is a permanent bureaucracy that functions below the dominant regime for implementation of government policies. Across all geographies and regimes in the world today, civilian administration has had to keep pace with the altered models of governance.

Recognizing the need for an overhaul of our bureaucratic practices, two ARCs were appointed in 1966 and 2005. They submitted very far-reaching recommendations, which addressed every aspect of the malady that afflicts the bureaucracy, and provided pointers for the overhaul. However, their recommendations have been largely left untouched or, if implemented, flouted more than followed. The most glaring example has been the recommendation that certain key appointments have a fixed tenure. This has been merrily flouted by 'under-adherence' as well as 'over-adherence' to it!

We had the remarkable case of the then cabinet secretary being shown the door when UPA-I came to power in 2004 and a new cabinet secretary being appointed regardless of the non-completion of the incumbent's tenure. The fact that no explanation was even remotely attempted to be offered is besides the point. On the other hand, as against the prescribed two-year tenure for a cabinet secretary, the replacement was given four years!

Administration at the state level has become distinct from that at the Union-government level. At both levels, professional skills and capabilities are varied. At the state level, the requirement is timely delivery of quality services such as education, health, rural development and municipal administration; the need at the Union-government level is more for conceptualizing and architecturing schemes that are innovative and better targeted, and seek to empower the people more than they seek to entitle. In a study conducted by professors John-Paul Ferguson and Sharique Hasan in Stanford University,[8] utilizing the records of 3,000 IAS officers to examine the impact of specialization, it was seen that there was a positive and statistically significant relationship between accumulated experience and post-empanelment job offers. Officers with an above-average level of specialization were 43 per cent more likely to be empanelled as joint secretaries.

---

[8]John-Paul Ferguson and Sharique Hasan; 'Specialization and Career Dynamics Evidence from the Indian Administrative Service'; *Administrative Science Quarterly* 58(2):233-256 (June 2013)

The unique requirement of an IAS officer is that he is called upon to function at the district, state and Union-government levels, where the job requirements at each level are very distinct. There is also substantial variation between regions. The skill sets and sensitivities required in the Northeastern states are very different from the southern states or J&K. Whilst their initial skills and academic discipline may serve them well in the early years, there are demonstrated successes among officers who have acquired expertise later in their careers for sectors for which they display aptitude or inclination. Often, officers are subject to advanced generalist training in varied sectors to afford them all-round exposure, thereby making them misfits in specialized sectors at higher levels, leading to a square-peg-in-a-round-hole syndrome.

While it is not expected that the IAS officer will have to be an IT expert, a structural engineer or a medical specialist, yet certain basic specialization in his field of choice or aptitude after about fifteen years of service should be mandated as a necessary condition for upward mobility. Officers are routinely deputed for Phase IV and Phase V training, which is roughly at the joint secretary or additional secretary levels. At this stage, training of the officer's field of specialization/interest such as medical administration, physical infrastructure development, education, public finance, etc., should be insisted upon instead of a routine 'one size fits all' kind of training. This training should be attuned towards their domain expertise, aptitude and potential as seen in their performance on previous assignments. Further, it should be made imperative for the administration to post only such skilled officers in departments to overcome the round-peg-in-a-square-hole syndrome.

Thus, it would certainly enhance the human capital value of an officer if his initial academic qualification is in the medical sciences for him to attempt higher specialization in medical administration or health sectors. Similarly, with the large numbers of engineering graduates that qualify for the service every year, it would again be useful to permit them higher administrative training in physical infrastructure sectors, such as power, roads, ports/airports or urban planning. It is when officers with an initial engineering/medical degree with no later upgradation of their skills in those sectors begin to dabble in those sectors that it creates avoidable conflict with the domain experts. Hence, there is need for continuous domain specialization or upgradation of skills as officers move up the hierarchy.

It needs to be recognized that irrespective of the agency that devises the schemes, the implementation has to be at the state level. Hence, it is essential to orient the training of the state-level bureaucracy more towards timely implementation, leakage-free execution and transparent administration. Their approach will have to be tethered to the efficacy of the scheme's objectives being realized. They will have to be attuned to field orientation so that they oversee implementation. Thus they will have to be moulded as 'field level officers' and not 'ivory tower' policy planners.

OUT-OF-THE-BOX THINKING

On the other hand, the officials at the central level have to be more oriented towards conceptualizing schemes, studying efficiently devised projects in other parts of the world and customizing them to Indian requirements. PM Narendra Modi has been exhorting officers to think 'out of the box' and 'innovatively'. However, the existing bureaucracy, accustomed to thinking in a particular mould, may not be able to change gear overnight and start scripting innovative projects. It would be more advisable to attract experienced technocrats who have conceived similar projects in other countries and involve them in innovating projects. There are several such professionals in the power, roads, ports, airports, petroleum and renewable energy sectors who, if given the opportunity, would be willing to set apart three to five years of their professional careers to benefit the country.

Such lateral and technocratic expertise can be attached to major infrastructure ministries. Thus, a group of experts could be engaged in the power ministry, the petroleum ministry, the national highways, the energy department and so on. A centralized agency like NITI Aayog, despite revamping, may not be able to deliver to expectation. Perhaps it is time to engage that concept at a ministry level where a concentrated and focused application of professional skills could be more effective.

We have had remarkable instances of a secretary moving from the industries department to the defence ministry and then, within the year, being moved to the finance ministry with no previous experience of finance administration. There were also bizarre instances of two senior Tamil Nadu cadre officers posted in important central government departments being repatriated to the state ostensibly for being posted in critical posts and, once in the state, being posted in defunct public-sector corporations. There have also been examples of officers being posted as secretaries in the health and education ministries of the Government of India with no previous exposure to these departments at the state or central level.

As mentioned earlier, a major contributor to the lack of motivation is the enhanced age at which certain aspirants join the service due to the prevailing upper age limit for recruitment. At thirty-three years on recruitment, the system of seniority-cum-merit for career advancement leaves very little scope for officers to reach the highest echelons of the bureaucracy by the time they retire. Such career constraints, which are evident at the time of joining itself, lead to officers falling easy prey to political attractions and hence losing objectivity.

There is also the factor of uncertainty of tenure, which, despite a landmark judgement of the Supreme Court, is flouted regularly by the central and state governments without providing any explanation for not adhering to the guidelines. In 2013, the Supreme Court directed the central and state governments to establish civil service boards to manage the tenure, transfer and posting of All-India Services officers. Unfortunately, the order has been ignored at both levels, thereby leaving the officers at the mercy of the party in power. This high-level advisory board needs to be institutionalized. The reasons for transfer must be recorded. This will serve as a defence mechanism against politicians using transfer as a tool to punish officers who act independently.

The growth of regional parties and their disproportionately high weightage in coalition politics has raised the stakes and hence the importance of politicians. To perpetuate and strengthen their hold on the administrative process, politicians seek to subvert the formal administrative machinery. The politician attempts to ensure that even routine decisions are pushed up to his level and not taken at the bureaucratic level. A politician will invariably take politically motivated decisions which may not strictly conform to the law of the land. Unless this is resisted and effectively pointed out by the bureaucracy, good governance will become a casualty.

A basic malady afflicting the service is that all officers, irrespective of their track record in administration, necessarily rise to the highest grade of pay before they retire. This does not give any incentive to perform better. There is also no compulsory weeding out of proven non-performers at any intermediate level of service. The government needs to institute a transparent system of review, maybe at about fifty and fifty-five years of age, for officers to be compulsorily retired if deemed unfit for further service. There has been some initiative by the present government for removing officers after a review post their attaining the age of fifty. In fact, in an earlier study of about 1,000 IAS officers, only two were declared unfit and were processed for removal from service.[9] A clutch of Revenue Service officers has recently been weeded out after a review. This is a good move, which will send an effective signal to other officers. An attempt should be made to institutionalize an objective mechanism for this.

The Second ARC had recommended the strengthening of accountability mechanisms by instituting a system of two intensive reviews at the fourteen- and twenty-year marks to determine the continuance of officers in service. It was also recommended that a Civil Service Reform Bill be introduced to ensure a minimum tenure for senior posts and establish safeguards against arbitrary dismissals.

It cannot be said that the IAS or the Indian bureaucracy is inept and inefficient and has been unable to provide good governance for sustained economic development. Where permitted to function independently and with adequate autonomy, it has delivered admirably. An example of its capability is its repeated conduct of elections on such a massive scale and without any glitch. The dominant factor in its ability to deliver is that it should be granted the independence to function on its own merit and capability and not have extraneous influences on its functioning.

For economic development to be sustained over the long term, it has to be supported with a good governance system. There is thus a need to make the bureaucracy much more effective, independent and efficient. A thorough overhaul of the recruitment norms, training and re-skilling, and indemnification from political interference to ensure objectivity, will have to be contemplated urgently for administration to encourage and support rapid economic growth.

---

[9]Subhomoy Bhattacharjee; 'Only 2 of 1,089 IAS officers inept: DoPT'; *Business Standard*; 22 April 2016; https://www.business-standard.com/article/economy-policy/only-2-of-1-089-ias-officers-inept-dopt-116042200066_1.html Accessed on 16 June 2019.

8

THE CENTRAL VIGILANCE COMMISSION

Teeth Must Replace Dentures

In 1991, India embarked on widespread transformative economic-policy reforms that encompassed the entire landscape of the political economy, including trade and globalization, the financial sector, IT and agriculture. The initiative also sought to adopt a far more market-friendly and accessible government setup. This resulted in the dismantling of the centrally planned and highly interventionist policy regime that India had originally embraced. The mission was to reduce government involvement in economic decision-making, to ensure macroeconomic stabilization and to open up to international trade and capital flows.

The reforms stabilized the economy. This transformation helped the economy grow to about six times its size then, and knock on the doors of double-digit growth. India debunked the myth of the Hindu rate of growth and set the course for taking its rightful place among the leading economies of the world. This has helped India engage with the world on an entirely different plane.

However, for development to be sustainable in the long term, it has to be premised on an edifice of good governance. Recognizing this fact, the nation began to script a new culture, seeking greater transparency and probity in administration. But it was not a smooth process, as the central government had to interact with regional governments where political focus was usually on issues that were limited to the political economy of that region. The reforms also had to go through a succession of coalition governments, where regional parties sometimes exercised influence disproportionate to their representation in the government. It led to allegations of a culture often referred to as 'crony capitalism' wherein economic favours were handed out by politicians. However, due to heightened political awareness and a public which had become more discerning and demanding, such cronyism had a short-term reign. One of the lessons from this political experience was the need to strengthen our accountability institutions, particularly those exercising greater vigilance and transparency over the administration.

THE CVC IS BORN

But the need for creating a permanent setup to deal with and prevent corruption in public institutions had already been felt in the early days of Independent India. A debate in the Parliament in 1962 on the issue of corruption in administration led Lal Bahadur Shastri, the then minister of home affairs, to set up a committee under the chairmanship of K. Santhanam, MP, to review the existing instruments for checking corruption in the central services and to advise practical steps to make anti-corruption measures more effective.[1]

The committee identified four major causes of corruption:

---

[1] Speech of the president at the inauguration of the seminar on the occasion of Golden Jubilee Celebrations of Central Vigilance Commission; Press Information Bureau; Government of India; President's Secretariat; 11 February 2014; http://pib.nic.in/newsite/PrintRelease.aspx?relid=103447 Accessed on 8 June 2019.

i. Administrative delays;
ii. Governments taking upon themselves more than they could manage by way of regulatory functions;
iii. Scope for personal discretions in the exercise of powers vested in different categories of government servants; and
iv. Cumbersome procedures in dealing with various matters which were of importance to citizens in their day-to-day affairs.

It was felt that there was a conspicuous absence of dynamic integration between vigilance units in various ministries and the administrative vigilance division of the department of personnel. The committee conceptualized an apex body for exercising general superintendence and control over vigilance administration. The vision was to create a body having the technical expertise to deal with matters related to engineering works, constructions and the like. They recommended that the body undertake an inquiry into the transactions of suspected public servants or into allegations of improper conduct or practices. Accordingly, the central government established the CVC in February 1964.

CHURNING VIS-A-VIS THE APPOINTMENT

The CVC is headed by the central vigilance commissioner, to be appointed by the president of India, by warrant, under his hand and seal. But in 2010, the CVC underwent a process of churning in the appointment of a central vigilance commissioner. Under the CVC Act, the appointment by the president is done on the basis of the recommendation of a committee consisting of the PM, the home minister and the leader of the Opposition in the Lok Sabha. Since the incumbent was due to demit office on 6 September 2010, the committee met on 3 September to finalize the appointment of the new central vigilance commissioner.

Of this three-member panel, the PM and the home minister preferred P.J. Thomas, who was then secretary in the Ministry of Telecommunications. But the leader of the Opposition, the third member of the committee, objected to this name on the grounds that Thomas was named as an accused in the charge sheet of the palmolein oil import case in Kerala (1991), when he was food secretary in the government of Kerala.

However, the objection was not sustained and the committee decided to recommend the appointment of Thomas. The recommendation was approved by the president and Thomas was sworn in as the new central vigilance commissioner on 7 September. Very soon thereafter, the appointment was questioned and a PIL filed in the Supreme Court by, amongst others, a former central vigilance commissioner.

The main contention in the PIL was that Thomas could not be considered a person of 'impeccable integrity' as he was charge-sheeted in a case that was subjudice and in which he had merely secured bail. It was also contended that there was a 'conflict of interest' in his case as he was serving as telecom secretary and there was an allegation that he was apparently involved in the cover-up of the 2G spectrum allocation scam. The Court took serious note of the allegations in the PIL, since it had been raised against a person who would be supervising the functioning of the CBI, and he himself appeared to be an accused before it.

While delivering its verdict[2] quashing the appointment of

---

[2]'Supreme Court quashes appointment of PJ Thomas as Central Vigilance Commissioner'; *The Economic Times*; 3 March 2011; https://economictimes.indiatimes.com/news/politics-and-nation/supreme-court-quashes-appointment-of-pj-thomas-as-central-vigilance-commissioner/articleshow/7617430.cms Accessed on 8 June 2019.

Thomas, the Supreme Court was extremely critical of the decision of the high-powered panel that appointed him to the post, since it had been done despite strong dissent from the leader of the Opposition. The apex court stated that the appointment of Thomas was against the 'institutional integrity' that the CVC stands for. The Court felt that the panel's choice amounted to 'official arbitrariness' and stated that the panel's recommendation was not an 'informed decision'.

The bench severely criticized the committee for not considering the relevant material, including the pending criminal case against Thomas and the recommendations of the DoPT between 2000 and 2004 for initiating disciplinary proceedings against him. Despite stout defence by the government, the Court set aside the appointment—terming it *non est* (did not exist). The Court was clear that it did not discount the appointee's personal integrity but only his suitability for the job. The Court also rejected the contention that the appointment of the central vigilance commissioner cannot be brought under judicial review.

Thus, Thomas had to step down barely six months after his appointment. This landmark judgement sent a clear signal to the government that appointments to statutory bodies must be considered carefully from all angles to ensure that institutional competence and integrity are not compromised by the appointment of persons whose suitability is questionable.

I have known Thomas as a colleague in the Kerala cadre for well over forty-five years. His integrity is impeccable. In this entire imbroglio, he became a victim of long-drawn court procedures and governmental apathy in expediting the palmolein case, which has dragged on for about twenty-five years with no legal conclusion in sight yet. That notwithstanding, the case is being quoted to emphasize the significance that people and courts attach to this critical institution of public accountability.

EXPANDING ITS REMIT

In 1991, a routine arrest of certain militants linked to the Hizbul Mujahideen in Kashmir led to the discovery of a link with four hawala (money-laundering) brokers. The payment of bribes to several high-ranking politicians and bureaucrats from a funding source linked to suspected terrorists was unearthed. All suspects were prosecuted, leading to the resignation of six serving ministers in the then government and also the leader of the Opposition in Lok Sabha.

The prosecution was supported by a PIL filed by a spirited person, Vineet Narain (this is popularly known as the Vineet Narain case).[3] Despite widespread publicity and shock at the involvement of such senior functionaries as the accused, all the court cases eventually collapsed as the diaries in which the initials of the recipients were recorded were judged by the Supreme Court to be inadequate evidence.

This led to huge public outrage against the investigating and prosecuting agencies. Members of the public were dismayed by the failure of the CBI. It was widely felt that the investigations were conducted with the apparent intent to protect certain implicated individuals, who were extremely influential in government and political circles.

The Court, while commenting on the shoddy investigation, decreed that the CBI had failed in its responsibility to investigate allegations of public corruption. It laid down guidelines to ensure the independence and autonomy of the CBI and ordered that the agency be placed under the supervision of the CVC,

---

[3] Rahul Pathak; 'Top Indian politicians named in Jain Hawala scandal'; *India Today*; 31 March 1994; https://www.indiatoday.in/magazine/special-report/story/19940331-top-indian-politicians-named-in-jain-hawala-scandal-808967-1994-03-31 Accessed on 8 June 2019.

an independent governmental agency intended to be free of executive control or interference.

The Court stated:

> While the Government shall remain answerable for the CBI's functioning, to introduce visible objectivity in the mechanism for overviewing the CBI's functioning, the CVC shall be entrusted with the responsibility of superintendence over the CBI's functioning. The CBI shall report to the CVC about cases taken up by it for investigation; progress of investigations; cases in which charge-sheets are filed, and their progress. The CVC shall review the progress of all cases moved by the CBI for sanction of prosecution of public servants which are pending with the competent authorities, especially those in which sanction has been delayed or refused.[4]

This directive freed the CBI, albeit theoretically, of supervision by the central government, thought to be partly responsible for the inertia that contributed to the CBI's previous lack of urgency with respect to the investigation of high-ranking officials. The CVC was made responsible for ensuring that allegations of corruption against public officials were thoroughly investigated, regardless of the identity of the accused and without interference from the government.

The Supreme Court also ruled that the director of the CBI would be appointed on the recommendation of a committee headed by the central vigilance commissioner, with the home secretary and the secretary in the department of personnel as members. The committee was to also seek the opinion of the incumbent

---

[4]Supreme Court Judgement: Vineet Narain case; http://www.cvc.nic.in/sites/default/files/vm17ch1/Vineet%20Narain%20Vs%20UOI%20_SC%20Judgement_1993.pdf
Accessed on 8 June 2019.

director of the CBI before forwarding its recommendation to the appointments committee of the Cabinet.

Despite this direction, the nature and degree of actual control that the CVC exercises on the CBI is not clearly specified. While the verdict of the Supreme Court is indeed quite unequivocal, a parliamentary committee felt that the superintendence should be such that it 'does not amount to interference in the agency's functioning'. The government, in fact, has been criticized for treating the CBI 'as its handmaiden'. It is unfortunate that whilst every party when in the Opposition has criticized the ruling party for misusing the CBI and has sought that it be freed from the executive control of the government, on coming to power, it has failed to do so.

While passing its decree in the case, the Supreme Court directed that statutory status be conferred upon the CVC. Thereafter, the central government promulgated an ordinance on 25 August 1998 to comply with the Court's directions. Later, the CVC Act was passed by both Houses of Parliament in 2003 and came into force with effect from 11 September 2003.

MAJOR INITIATIVES

The CVC has been entrusted with the task of exercising superintendence over vigilance administration and implementing government policies against corruption. Over the years, the CVC has acquired experience in overseeing vigilance administration of various organizations and has stressed preventive, punitive and participative measures to mitigate corruption levels.

Each ministry/department/organization has a vigilance wing headed by a chief vigilance officer (CVO). CVOs are functionally independent and are appointed after prior consultation with the CVC. The CVC also undertakes verification of antecedents of public servants prior to consideration for higher appointments at a board level in central public sector undertakings, banks and the like, and statutory appointments under the central government.

The CVC has conducted fairly effective campaigns to popularize the efficacy of preventive vigilance. Preventive vigilance involves adopting a package of measures to improve systems and procedures to reduce and eliminate corruption. These include simplifying rules and regulations; ensuring transparency and accountability; reducing discretion and public interface; and leveraging technology for e-procurements and e-payments, use of websites for dissemination of information and creating awareness and use of CCTV in places of public dealing.

A major initiative of the CVC has been disseminating the need for instilling values and morals at an early age in the upbringing of every child. In 2012, it introduced the value education kit with a view to creating a moral curriculum in schools that emphasizes the values of honesty and integrity. This kit consists of a value education handbook for teachers and a CD with songs, along with activity cards for students from nursery to Class XII. The Central Board for Secondary Education (CBSE) has made the process more inclusive by ensuring that value education is an essential part of curricular and co-curricular activities.

COMBATING CORRUPTION AND ITS RELATED DIMENSIONS

The basic law to address corruption is the Prevention of Corruption Act, 1988. With increasing multidimensional and technological growth, the mode and manner of corruption have also undergone a sea change. Though existing laws are adequate to deal with corruption, they need more teeth and scope to counter the changing scenario. For example, the Act catered only to passive bribery, i.e., bribe-taking. Internationally, however, both the bribe-giver and bribe-taker—whether a natural person, legal person or entity or their representative or agent—are equally liable in matters of bribery and are treated on the same footing. In order to address, inter alia, the supply side, i.e., active bribery, the government passed the Prevention of Corruption (Amendment) Act, 2018. This has ensured that gratification is not limited to pecuniary gratification and covers attachment and forfeiture of property and makes giving a bribe a specific offence.

There are diverging views on whether bribe-giving under all circumstances must be penalized. Some have argued that a coerced bribe-giver must be distinguished from a collusive bribe-giver. According to the statement of objects and reasons of the Bill, the amendments to the Act were introduced to bring it in line with the UN Convention against Corruption, though certain variations remain.

The Act has also mandated that trials be conducted on a day-to-day basis and completed in two years. In cases where the trial is not completed in two years, the onus is on the special judge to record reasons for not having done so. This is a very significant limitation, as, in a study conducted by a three-member committee set up by the CVC, it was highlighted that on an average, it takes more than eight years to finalize a major vigilance case from the date of occurrence of irregularity. The fast-tracking of trials in criminal cases of corruption and stringent penalties would certainly act as a deterrent since, at present, cases are known to drag on indefinitely.

SINGLE DIRECTIVE, MULTIPLE OPINIONS

While delivering its verdict in the Vineet Narain case, the Supreme Court had struck down the validity of a directive issued by the central government (commonly referred to as 'the single directive') that required the CBI to seek the approval of the central government before pursuing investigation against bureaucrats of the level of joint secretary and above. The Court maintained that it violated the independence of the investigative process.

However, the CVC Act, 2003, reinstated this requirement. This directive was again struck down by a Supreme Court constitution bench verdict of 6 May 2014, on the grounds that it violated the right to equality guaranteed by the Constitution. The Prevention of Corruption (Amendment)Act, 2018, passed by the Parliament, now reintroduces the requirement of prior sanction for prosecution of public officials and former officials who are serving or have served the Union or state governments.

The issue of seeking prior permission before investigation has elicited disagreement from the Court. Members of the public have also been critical of this provision being reintroduced by the government. It is alleged that 'such is the power of babudom and its hold over netas that it has managed to bring this immunity clause back for the third time'.[5]

Whilst it might be true that some corrupt people may be shielded, or may have been shielded, under the section, yet the propensity for misuse by launching trumped-up charge sheets or investigations against officials not willing to succumb to pressure without this proviso has been huge. A case in point is that of the officers in the coal ministry who are being prosecuted for having supposedly 'abetted' the irregular allotment of coal mine blocks. The then coal minister and the then PM, who took the decision of allotment, have escaped prosecution.[6]

---

[5]Yogendra Yadav; 'Time to blow the whistle'; *The Hindu*; 12 December 2016; https://www.thehindu.com/opinion/lead/Time-to-blow-the-whistle/article16793830.ece
Accessed on 8 June 2019.

[6]"Coal scam: As PM, not possible to go through all files, Manmohan tells CBI'; *The Indian Express*; 1 October 2015; https://indianexpress.com/article/india/india-others/coal-scam-many-other-issues-to-worry-as-pm-manmohan-singh-to-cbi/
Accessed on 8 June 2019.

Another instance is that of the secretary, additional secretary, joint secretary and director in the Ministry of Finance being charge-sheeted, ostensibly for having recommended the Aircel Maxis FDI.

Such is the unfairness of the system that members of the political executive, on whose verbal directions some irregularities may have been committed, escape the law, whereas low-level functionaries who merely process files are held as perpetrators.

It could be argued that these are mere investigations and if the officer is not guilty, he need not be apprehensive. However, experience indicates that investigations take years and even if the officer is exonerated, the harassment he faces at the hands of the investigation agencies is enough to break his morale and ruin his career. If the fear of the 'three Cs' (viz. the CAG, CVC and CBI) is a deterrent to decision-making, doing away with this clause would bring decision-making to a grinding halt.

DOES VIGILANCE DELAY DECISION-MAKING?

There has been considerable debate on the extent of the CVC's contribution towards good governance and public accountability. A common complaint of the executive is that the CVC's overhang often acts as a negative and demoralizing influence on officials serving in government and public corporations. It is alleged that the fear of vigilance overreach delays decision-making, as it usually focuses more on the procedure than the result. It is also alleged that government officials are not able to take important commercial decisions having a bearing on attracting investments and ensuring economic development largely because, in hindsight, any decision can be criticized on the grounds that it favours one party or another. It is felt that often the CVC does not have the capacity to appreciate commercial decisions taken in public-sector banks or state trading bodies and penalizes officials for acts done after a substantial passage of time.

Another deleterious effect of the CVC intervening in any irregularity is that once a case is registered by it, it drags on for years, thereby stymieing the career progression of the implicated officer. The Annual Report of the Commission for 2017 indicates that at the end of 2016, the number of complaints pending inquiry and reports from central vigilance officers in other organizations was 596, of which 344 had been pending for over three years. The CVC also does not have any investigative agency of its own and has to rely upon the CBI or the Enforcement Directorate (ED) to assist it.

There is a further process of the CVC for granting 'vigilance clearance' to officers due to be appointed to higher echelons. This often takes a very long time and can become a stumbling block in facilitating early appointment. Such delays are noticed in appointments to senior positions in public-sector banks. In a selection made recently by the Banks Board Bureau (BBB) for the appointment of managing directors in the State Bank of India (SBI), it was learnt that the CVC was unable to give vigilance clearance to three of the four persons in the panel selected. This uncertainty dragged on for more than six months, leaving one of the four positions of managing director vacant.

This is a highly undesirable situation; a position left vacant in the largest bank of the country is bound to have a debilitating effect on the functioning of the bank. The government, the CBI and the CVC should have worked towards an early resolution of the issue. Letting the issue drag, as we resort to correspondence among official agencies, has been the bane of timely decision-making in the public sector, thereby being a serious hurdle to good governance.

WHISTLE-BLOWERS' RESOLUTION

Satyendra Dubey was a project engineer working with the National Highways Authority of India (NHAI). Known to be sincere and dedicated, he had, in 2003, exposed several cases of flouting of rules leading to corrupt practices in projects being undertaken by the NHAI. Dubey's letters to the higher-ups at NHAI regarding financial discrepancies and poor implementation of the road-building contracts, while he was posted in Koderma, Jharkhand, enraged his superiors, resulting in his transfer to Gaya, Bihar. This transfer ensured that the issues raised by him remained uninvestigated.

Frustrated by the unresponsive attitude of the NHAI towards wrongdoing in the Golden Quadrilateral (GQ) project, which had been launched by the then PM, Dubey wrote a letter to the PMO in November 2003, detailing the modus operandi of the corrupt practices and pointing to the kingpins of the racket. He also requested that his identity be kept confidential, since he was aware of the propensity of the group involved in these irregularities to harm him if they got to know that he had filed a complaint. The letter claimed the involvement of major international companies that had cornered the GQ project through huge payoffs and outsourced projects to local contractors at bargains, pocketing heavy margins.

Dubey's request for maintaining anonymity was not heeded by the PMO, which, as a matter of routine, forwarded his letter to the concerned departments. It is alleged that in the course of the letter travelling to many offices, it fell into those very hands whom Dubey had implicated in the complaint. They are alleged to have hatched a plot to eliminate him. He was gunned down near his home while returning on a cycle rickshaw from a wedding. In a trial by a special CBI court, three persons were sentenced to life imprisonment in connection with the murder. After the conviction, Dubey's family maintained it was disappointed with the verdict as those who were actually guilty of the murder—the higher-ups—had gone scot-free.

In response to a PIL in connection with Dubey's murder, the Supreme Court directed the central government to devise a suitable mechanism to act on complaints from whistle-blowers till such time as suitable legislation was enacted. Thereafter, the central government, through the Public Interest Disclosure and Protection of Informers (PIDPI) Resolution dated 21 April 2004, made provisions for action on complaints from whistle-blowers. This resolution is popularly known as the whistle-blowers' resolution and it designated the CVC as the agency to receive and act on complaints or disclosure of any allegation of corruption or misuse of office from whistleblowers.

PROMOTING ETHICAL VALUES, TRANSPARENCY AND PROBITY

The CVC, as an institution to improve probity and ensure transparency and accountability in government-functioning, is essential. While transparency is advisable in all organizations, whether commercial or government, accountability becomes important largely because government officials perform duties on behalf of the public or the persons who elect them. To that extent, their obligation to ensure a more transparent and accountable system is greater. To be empowered to perform a robust vigilance function, it is essential that the CVC be given greater autonomy and the nature of its 'superintendence' over the CBI be more clearly defined.

The inefficacy of the CVC in the entire saga of CBI infighting has been laid bare. In the course of the selection meeting considering the appointment of Rakesh Asthana as special director of the CBI, the incumbent director raised a doubt about his integrity. Why did the CVC not get this investigated before recommending the appointment? Was the central vigilance commissioner free to take an independent decision is the issue in question. As long as the CVC remains an organization that continues to function as an adjunct of the department of personnel in the government, it will remain vulnerable to interference.

The CVC as a standalone institution under the administrative control of the department of personnel and administrative reforms may not be able to perform its mandated duty to perfection and with objectivity. Now that the Lokpal has been chosen, it appears to be a more credible institution that complainants can go to for redressal of their grievances. The Lokpal will take over the work of sanctioning prosecution, besides exercising its power to order preliminary inquiries and full-fledged investigations by any agency, including the CBI.

This will debilitate the CVC further. Hence, there is a need to quickly reappraise its role and make it function as the administrative arm of the Lokpal rather than the government having to duplicate the structure. Having a multitude of institutions will create problems of duplication and coordination, thereby delaying the administrative process still further. With the CVC working under the Lokpal, well-groomed and streamlined machinery will be available to lend direction to the efforts of the Lokpal rather than setting up another institution and having its officers trained ab initio.

The Parliamentary Standing Committee on Personnel, Public Grievances, Law and Justice, has also recommended integrating the CVC and the anti-corruption wing of the CBI to work directly under the command and control of the Lokpal to deal with corruption cases, citing overlapping of functions. The committee felt that the CVC and the CBI should form two silos of the newly created institution of the Lokpal, and the functions of the Lokpal and the CVC should be clearly specified. The Lokpal, in turn, should utilize these organizations for conduct of inquiry, investigation and prosecution.

Vigilance should not be viewed as a negative activity. The CVC, or even the Lokpal, should be an agency to promote and disseminate the need for ethical values, transparency and hence probity in government-functioning. It should be recognized as a vehicle to carry forward a campaign for inculcating these values in all government departments and activities. Unless the country moves upwards in the ranking of nations for display of ethics and probity in administration, sustainable progress, foreign investment and movement of capital will pass India by.

9

RIGHT TO INFORMATION
Balancing Power and Accountability

It is said 'knowledge is power' and hence the right to information is empowering. It is the edifice on which a robust democratic society can be built and was the inspiration behind India getting its RTI Act in 2005. The crux of the dispensation being granted in the passing of the Act is conveyed in its preamble:

> And whereas Democracy requires an informed citizenry and transparency of information which are vital to its functioning and also to contain corruption and to hold Governments and their instrumentalities accountable to the governed. And whereas revelation of information in actual practice is likely to conflict with other public interests including efficient operations of the Governments, optimum use of limited fiscal resources and the preservation of confidentiality of sensitive information; and whereas it is necessary to harmonize these conflicting interests while preserving the paramountcy of the democratic ideal; now, therefore, it is expedient to provide for furnishing certain information to citizens who desire to have it.[1]

---

[1] The Right to Information Act 2005; *The Gazette of India*; Ministry of Law and Justice; https://rti.gov.in/rti-act.pdf
Accessed on 30 June 2019.

The RTI Act was approved by the Parliament in May 2005 and came into force in October that year. It replaced the Freedom of Information Act, 2002, which never came into force. Under the RTI Act, all Indian citizens have the right to seek information not only from the central and state governments, but also from public authorities, including local bodies, namely the rural and urban panchayats. The Act covers all constitutional and statutory public authorities controlled or substantially funded by the government. Its legislative intent is to empower the citizen, to promote transparency and accountability in the working of every public agency, reduce the gap between the information provider and the information seeker, qualitatively upgrade efficiency in administration of public offices, mitigate corruption and promote good governance.

TOWARDS A TRANSPARENT AND OPEN GOVERNMENT

In the initial years post-Independence, the working of the government, essentially being a legacy of the colonial regime, continued to be shrouded in secrecy. Issues pertaining to the government were often seen to be in conflict with the provisions of the Official Secrets Act, 1923. This Act was promulgated by the British to shroud government matters in secrecy and confidentiality. The law provides a framework for dealing with espionage, sedition and other assaults on the unity and integrity of the nation. This law, as a legacy of the British administration, had inculcated the culture of secrecy in India. The tendency of secrecy has been further ingrained into the governmental system by the Civil Service Conduct Rules, 1964, which prohibit the communication of an official document to anyone without authorization.

However, efforts started quite early to make the system more transparent, and definite steps were taken to facilitate the process. The setting up of the First ARC in January 1966 was a significant move by the then government in this direction. The ARC, inter alia, recommended in 1969 that the Official Secrets Act be repealed. But this recommendation was rejected by the government, taking refuge in the argument that it was the only law to deal with cases of espionage, and wrongful possession and communication of sensitive information detrimental to the security of the State. The ARC had also recommended that the Departmental Security Instructions be amended, and 'ordinarily, only such information should be given a security classification which would qualify for exemption from disclosure under the RTI Act'. But the government continued to maintain that it was not possible to classify documents on the basis of various sections of the RTI Act.[2]

Perhaps one of the more definitive nudges towards persuading the government to make its functioning transparent and open was through the Supreme Court verdict in the Bennett Coleman case in 1972. While deciding on the issue of equal right for all to get access to adequate quantities of imported newsprint, the right to information was held by the Court to be included in the right to freedom of speech and expression granted by Article 19(1)(a) of the Constitution.

The right to information was also supported by the judiciary in another case, one which seemingly greatly influenced the course of democracy in India. In 1971, socialist leader Raj Narain contested and lost the mid-term poll against Indira Gandhi from the Rae Bareli parliamentary constituency. He, however, filed a case in Allahabad High Court against her, alleging that she had unfairly used the state administrative machinery to advance her electoral interests. In the course of the proceedings, Narain sought

---

[2]http://www.hillagric.ac.in/others/ARC-Reports/pdf/Administrative ReformsCommission-1stReport.pdf Entry 13. Classification of Info. Para 4.1.8. Accessed on 1 July 2019.

to examine the contents of the Blue Book, which prescribes the security protocol for the PM. The State claimed that this was a privileged document and could not be brought into the public domain. Disagreeing with the State, in a landmark verdict, the High Court held that if a document of evidentiary value was required in court under the provisions of the Indian Evidence Act, 1872, a court may order such document to be disclosed in court proceedings, even if official permission was not obtained to release it. This, the Court maintained, could be done if the public interest served by the disclosure clearly outweighed that of secrecy.[3]

In 1989–90, there was a change of government at the Centre. The National Front government, which came to power, called for more open governance. This was around the time when civil society was also becoming active in demanding the right to information. At the grass-roots level, efforts were made by the MKSS, a non-party people's movement in Rajasthan. An important step that the MKSS took in 1993 was to hold an indefinite dharna in five Rajasthan tehsils, demanding the right to inspect bills, vouchers and muster rolls of village development works.[4] Anna Hazare's *maun vrat* has also been effective in focusing attention on the need for RTI as a weapon to fight corruption. An organization called Bhrashtachar Virodhi Jan Andolan (People's Movement against Corruption) was created by him in 1991 to launch a campaign to introduce RTI in Maharashtra. Parivartan was co-founded by Arvind Kejriwal towards the end of 1999, which laid emphasis on assisting citizens in matters related to income tax, food and ration, and electricity in parts of Delhi.

---

[3] State of UP Vs Raj Narain & Ors on 24 January, 1975; https://indiankanoon.org/doc/438670/
Accessed on 29 June 2019.
[4] Aruna Roy; *The RTI Story: Power to the People*; Roli Books (2018)

WHEN HOPES WERE RAISED

There is an interesting episode during the Atal Bihari Vajpayee government which illustrates the desire gaining currency to make the functioning of government more 'open' and its coming up against mindset issues. In 1998, Ram Jethmalani, the minister of urban affairs and employment, was the chief guest at a national seminar on 'Safer Cities'. During his address, he informed the audience that his ministry's functioning would be made transparent as he would be proposing changes to enable access to information to be made easier and immediate.[5]

On returning to his office on 10 October (a Saturday), he dictated an office note outlining the procedure for granting access to government records, upon being sought by the public. He did this on a holiday to pre-empt opposition from his party colleagues in the government. As a preamble to the order that he was proposing to issue, he set out the declared national agenda of his party, viz. the assurance of a stable, transparent and efficient government. This was RTI in its most rudimentary form. He, however, had not realized that there was a bureaucracy that he would have to contend with!

On seeing the minister's instructions, the secretary in the department drew attention to certain issues that he thought the minister should consider. He noted:

1. There was a Freedom of Information Bill on the anvil. Would it not be better to await the passage of the Bill?
2. Though the Official Secrets Act, 1923, may not figure in the Ministry of Urban Affairs and Employment, yet it would be advisable to get a clearance from the Home Ministry, for they alone had the power and jurisdiction to define 'official secrets'.

---

[5]Prashant Sharma; *Democracy and Transparency in the Indian State: The Making of the Right to Information Act*; Routledge (2015)

3. The guidelines by which the minister was seeking to enforce a fundamental right violated Rule 9 of the All-India Services (Conduct) Rules. The rule reads: 'Unauthorised communication of information which prohibits a government servant from communicating information directly or indirectly to any person including another government servant except in accordance with a general or special order authorising such communication.'
4. By virtue of rules 11 and 12 of the Allocation of Business Rules, it may be necessary to consult the DoPT before such measures were introduced.

The secretary went on to compliment the minister for providing a number of safeguards in the nature of exceptions from the new norm, viz. Cabinet notes, vigilance inquiries and Budget proposals. However, he pointed out that the minister had missed out a whole range of information, which, if disclosed, would be suicidal for the government, and highlighted a few areas where furnishing information would make governance impossible.

Free access would inhibit junior officers from expressing their views fearlessly in matters concerning influential persons. The secretary suggested a proviso to the order stating that the issue could be left to a nodal officer, who could decide whether the access to information sought would adversely affect the department or the government, and if it did, the access should be refused, and if he/she was in doubt, it should be referred to the higher instance in the bureaucracy, which should not be below the rank of a joint secretary.

Jethmalani responded to the secretary's note on 16 October, indicating that he was of the view that the opinion of the home ministry was not necessary for running his ministry, and that the officers should stop referring to the Official Secrets Act at the slightest pretext. Thereafter, he quoted extensively from a judgement of the Supreme Court in *SP Gupta Vs Union of India*. He even summarized the principles laid down in the judgement, which mentioned that exposure to public scrutiny was one of the surest means of achieving a clean government and that the people had the right to know every act and everything that had been done publicly. He drew upon the judgement to emphasize that no democratic government could survive without accountability. After setting down the principle, he dismissed the objections raised on the basis of the conduct of business rules. He objected to the matter being referred to the cabinet secretariat and agreed merely to a copy of his note being sent to it.

No sooner had the note reached the cabinet secretary, than he replied, informing the ministry that the Freedom of Information Bill was under consideration by a group of ministers, and therefore it was necessary to study the implications of the instructions regarding access to information issued by the minister of urban affairs. It was also conveyed that the PM had directed not to give effect to the order issued by the minister. This was on 20 October 1998.

RTI had prevailed for all of ten days.

A LANDMARK IN DEMOCRACY

After the UPA government came to power in May 2004, a draft Bill was prepared and discussed in the standing committee of the Parliament, which maintained that in keeping with the spirit of maximum disclosure and minimum exemption, currently exempted matters such as security, sovereignty, integrity of the country, relations with foreign countries and Cabinet papers should not be standard exceptions. The standing committee suggested in its report that the essence of the Bill lay in the effectiveness of the mechanism to access information. It therefore recommended that the status of the Information Commission, to be set up under the Act, be elevated to that of the ECI. The Bill was passed by both Houses of Parliament and received presidential assent in June 2005, with some provisions being made effective in October 2005.

The Act covers the three pillars of democracy, viz., legislature, executive and judiciary. In the executive, it covers the central and state governments, all local self-governing bodies, bodies that are either owned or substantially financed by the government, and even NGOs that are substantially financed by the government. Its coverage extends to institutions that are directly or indirectly financed by funds provided by the appropriate government. Its enactment has ensured that RTI is a fundamental right for the public and that the right has become legally enforceable.

There is certain 'exempted information', which has been built into the Act for very valid reasons. These are issues that concern the sovereignty, integrity, security interests of the country, relations with foreign states and information received in confidence from a foreign government. It also exempts information that impedes the process of investigation by government agencies, Cabinet papers, personal information leading to invasion of privacy, infringement of copyright, intelligence and security agencies. Thus, the coverage is fairly widespread, with the exemptions being functionally relevant to the cause of the nation or a private individual.

CIC: THE FULCRUM OF THE NEW DISPENSATION

The Central Information Commission (CIC) is the fulcrum of the new dispensation that has brought the RTI into play. It functions as an independent appellate mechanism and oversees the implementation of the RTI Act. We shall, therefore, look into the conceptual evolution of the CIC. In the RTI Act, the two-tier appellate mechanism was retained, with the first appeal within the department to be disposed of within thirty days while there was no time limit imposed on the disposal of the second appeal, which was with the CIC.

The significance of the CIC can be understood in its proper perspective by discussing important orders and relevant provisions in the Act.

It has often been observed that public authorities resort to Section 8 of the RTI Act, which deals with exemptions from disclosure of information. The Department of Biotechnology of the Government of India had, under Section 8(1)(d), denied access to information to Greenpeace, a global environmental NGO, about the ill effects of transgenic food crops that were being field-tested across the country. The relevant provision of the section states that public authorities have no obligation to provide 'information including commercially confidential, trade secrets or intellectual property, the disclosure of which would harm the competitive position of a third party, unless the competent authority is satisfied that larger public interest warrants the disclosure of such information'. Greenpeace appealed against this denial to the CIC.

The CIC, however, took a different view from that taken by the government. It took cognizance of the provision of Section 4(1)(d) of the RTI Act, which states that every public authority shall provide reasons for its administrative or quasi-judicial decisions to affected persons. The CIC observed that the government should proactively put out all relevant data. It drew attention to Section 4 of the RTI Act, which stipulates that public authorities must provide as much information as possible *suo motu* at regular intervals.[6]

In this significant decision, the RTI Act was also made applicable to notes (internal memos) on files, apart from letters

---

[6]Manoj Mitta; 'CIC orders govt to divulge toxicity of GM foods'; *The Times of India*; 14 April 2007; https://timesofindia.indiatimes.com/india/CIC-orders-govt-to-divulge-toxicity-of-GM-foods/articleshow/1907423.cms Accessed on 30 June 2019.

and other documents available, as correspondence in these files. The decision, however, did not go down well with government functionaries and they continued to evade such disclosure. It was only after a penalty was imposed on a joint-secretary-level officer by the CIC for not providing information that the government relented. The case related to information about the procedures involved for selecting national gazetted holidays of the central government. The RTI applicant had sought the notings on file, based on which the decision to declare national and gazetted holidays was taken. These had been disallowed on the grounds that there was no obligation to disclose any information which would prejudicially affect the sovereignty and integrity of India.

The government defence was that it was a decision of the Central government to declare a closed holiday on Dr Ambedkar's birthday from 1990 with the due approval of the competent authority. It was contended by the government that the decision to declare a holiday was taken according to the guidelines prescribed and displayed on the website of the Ministry of Personnel, Public Grievances and Pensions and did not include file notings. The CIC, after hearing the parties, concluded that it was a clear case of refusal of information, since the website had fallaciously shown file notings to be exempted information on the said website.

The CIC in its order expressed strong displeasure and described as appalling that the nodal ministry for the RTI had sought to emasculate the mandate given under Section 19(7) of the RTI Act, which makes the decision of the CIC legally binding. The CIC further commented that instead of doing what a public authority was expected to do under the law, the department of personnel had created an extraordinary situation which constituted an assault on the rule of law, the cornerstone of our legal system.

Strong words, indeed!

This issue of making available notings on files and seeking

cover under Section 8 of the Act was finally put to rest recently by the Delhi High Court in its order of 12 February 2018. An RTI applicant had filed an application on 6 November 2010 seeking the certified copy of a report sent by the then governor of Karnataka to the Union home ministry related to the political situation in Karnataka and reasons for imposing President's Rule in the state. He had sought to know what action had been taken by the government on the report and also sought the file notings related to the action. These details were denied to him by the government, citing Section 8 of the Act.

After seeking permission from the CIC, where his appeal was pending, he approached the Delhi High Court, which ruled:

> ...[That] the information sought for by the petitioner is exempt from disclosure under Section 8(1)(e) of the Act, cannot be sustained. The contention that notings made by a junior officer for use by his superiors is third party information, which requires compliance of section 11 of the Act, is unmerited. Any noting made in the official records of the Government/public authority is information belonging to the concerned Government/public authority. The question whether the information relates to a third party is to be determined by the nature of the information and not its source. The Government is not a natural person and all information contained in the official records of the Government/public authority is generated by individuals (whether employed with the Government or not) or other entities. Thus, the reasoning, that the notings or information generated by an employee during the course of his employment is his information and thus has to be treated as relating to a third party, is flawed.[7]

---

[7] In the High Court of Delhi at New Delhi; W.P.(C) 7845/2013; *Paras Nath Singh Versus Union of India*; https://dtf.in/wp-content/files/Delhi_HC_Judgement_dated_12.02.2018_-_Paras_Nath_Singh_Vs_Union_of_India.pdf

The Court further held that Section 8 of the Act provided for exemption from disclosure of certain information and none of the provisions of Section 8 provided for blanket exemption that entitled the respondent to withhold all file notings.

POLITICAL PARTIES: UNITED IN DEFIANCE

In yet another significant order, the CIC resolved the question of whether the RTI Act was applicable to political parties.[8] The CIC received two complaints: one pertaining to disclosure of the accounts and the second pertaining to the funding of political parties. Political parties contested the applicability of the RTI to them as they maintained that they were neither public authorities nor publicly funded. The CIC, however, held that political parties were public authorities under Section 2(h) of the RTI Act when the criterion of indirect substantial financing by the central government was applied.

This reasoning of the CIC was premised on the fact that political parties were allotted large tracts of land in prime areas of Delhi either free or at concessional rates. The rent charged from them for the land did not reflect the true value of these properties, which, according to the CIC, amounted to indirect financing. This concessional rent, when added to the income tax exemption enjoyed by them, amounted to substantial financing. The CIC further took note of the government indirectly subsidizing political parties by allotment of government houses at concessional rates to them. The rent that was being charged from the political parties did not reflect the true rental value of

---

Accessed on 30 June 2019.
[8]Utkarsh Anand; 'Political parties can't be under RTI Act: Centre tells SC'; *The Indian Express*; 25 August 2015; https://indianexpress.com/article/india/india-others/political-parties-cant-be-under-rti-act-centre-tells-sc/ Accessed on 30 June 2019.

these properties either.

This arrangement, the CIC held, contributed to the indirect financing of political parties by the central government. The CIC in its order also mentioned that political parties were beneficiaries of free air time on All India Radio and although these amounts may be small, they still benefited the kitty of each party. It felt that political parties constituted an important segment of society and were responsible for its growth and development. Further, the ruling party draws up its development programmes on the basis of its political agenda, which affects the lives of citizens directly or indirectly. It is therefore necessary that they be accountable to the public at large. Political parties are important institutions and can play a critical role in heralding transparency in public life; they perform public functions, which define governance parameters and the socio-economic development of the country. All this, the CIC held, justified their inclusion as public authorities under the RTI Act.

Political parties, however, ignored the CIC order—leading to the filing of a PIL in the Supreme Court. In response to the PIL, the government took a totally contrarian view to that of the CIC. It stated that bringing political parties within the jurisdiction of the RTI Act would adversely affect the internal working of the parties, which had not been envisaged by the Parliament when enacting the law. It would also result in political rivals filing RTI applications with malicious intent, which would adversely affect their political functioning. The government held that political parties could not be termed public authorities because they were neither formed under the Constitution nor by any act of Parliament. It was also contended that provisions under the Representation of People Act, 1951, and the Income Tax Act, 1961, already imposed a liability on political parties to make sufficient disclosures about their income and expenditure.

It is significant that the government did not rest with filing the affidavit in the Court. To nullify the conclusion of the CIC, which it believed to be erroneous, a Bill was introduced in the Lok Sabha in 2013 to amend the RTI Act so as to specifically exclude political parties from the definition of public authority. The Bill, however, lapsed with the dissolution of the Lok Sabha in 2014.[9]

It needs to be emphasized that, as agents of introducing probity and transparency in public life, and to set a model for citizens to emulate, political parties must volunteer to be included in the RTI domain to curb the belief that political funding is not a source of unaccounted-for money in circulation. They have to steward the movement for introducing openness in public life and introduce a model for probity and accountability.

MOCKERY OF THE LAW

A former CJI, the late Sarosh Homi Kapadia, had opined that the law pertaining to RTI was comprehensive and had contributed to transparency in the government but was being misused to ask irrelevant questions, thus seriously impeding the working of judges. He cited as instances questions that were asked to him, which included why he had attended the Nani Palkhivala Memorial lecture, what time he had left for the event, whether he had eaten lunch or had had tea, and the name of the lawyer who had invited him to the function.[10]

---

[9]Shobha S.V., Shibani Ghosh, Sowmya Sivakumar and Nishikanta Mohapatra; 'Right to Information: For Inclusion and Empowerment'; RTI Fellows report; https://rti.gov.in/rti_fellowship_report_2011.pdf
Accessed on 30 June 2019.

[10]Dhananjay Mahapatra; 'Right to Information good law, but being misused: CJI S.H. Kapadia'; *The Times of India*; 13 April 2012; https://timesofindia.indiatimes.com/india/Right-to-Information-good-law-but-being-misused-CJI-S-H-Kapadia/articleshow/12642471.cms
Accessed on 30 June 2019.

Certainly, this is total misuse of the RTI facility afforded to citizens and makes a mockery of a very important provision in the law which is supportive of democracy and good, transparent governance.

There have been many instances of misuse. We have so-called RTI activists who seem to take pride in asking interminable questions of the government or public bodies, with no perceptible objective being fulfilled after receiving the answers. I refer to an RTI posed to me in 2007 while I was serving in the finance ministry. The questions were:

1. How many cars does the Punjab National Bank own?
2. Where are these cars located and who are the officers authorized to use them?
3. How many cases of misuse of bank cars have been reported and what is the action taken by the bank management on these complaints?

When these questions were asked, the bank must have had about 5,000 branches. Did the effort and human resources required to collect this data even marginally serve public purpose in making the information available in the public domain? Even if the answers were provided, they would have probably been buried in some corner of a newspaper.

RTI is a facility afforded by law to citizens for fulfilling significant public benefit by reducing the opacity of decision-making by public authorities. It cannot be reduced to ridicule of government time, effort and money expended in collecting information which, when brought into the public domain, is of no significance to society.

Thus, every member of the public must judiciously exercise the right, which has been provided to him by the legislature, and not fritter away the facility such that public bodies begin to treat every question with disdain and thus defeat the purpose for which the facility has been provided. It is only to discourage such frivolous queries, which put an avoidable burden on government functionaries, that the Supreme Court observed in August 2011: 'The nation does not want a scenario where 75 per cent of the staff of public authorities spends 75 per cent of their time in collecting and furnishing information to applicants instead of discharging their regular duties.'[11]

The public needs to make a distinction between a populist approach and a realist query to introduce accountability in government decision-making and thereby appreciate the practical challenges confronting its implementation. It has been repeatedly clarified that the CIC cannot be used as an agency to settle personal scores and can adjudicate only on issues of public interest. The Supreme Court held that 'the Information Commission does not decide a dispute between two or more parties concerning their legal rights other than their right to get information in possession of a public authority.'[12]

ATTACKS ON THE RISE

There can be no doubt that there is some misuse of the law. However, based on personal perceptions and surveys, it would be difficult to conclude that the Act is being grossly misused. The tragic incidents of deaths of people over RTI-related matters are pointers to the fact that inconvenient information was sought under the RTI Act, which could have been the cause of these

---

[11]'Act under siege'; *The Telegraph*; 1 June 2016; https://www.telegraphindia.com/opinion/act-under-siege/cid/1449956
Accessed on 30 June 2019.

[12]Nikhil Dey, Bhupender Yadav and Bimal Julka; 'Has the Right to Information Act been weakened?'; *The Hindu*; 27 July 2018; https://www.thehindu.com/opinion/op-ed/has-the-right-to-information-act-been-weakened/article24523104.ece
Accessed on 18 July 2019.

extreme incidents. The deaths of activists mostly resulted from queries on the corruption in rural development projects, namely Mahatma Gandhi National Rural Employment Guarantee Act (MGNREGA), the Swajaldhara scheme, private house/shop construction on public land, illegal mining cases, and so on.

Reports of the Commonwealth Human Rights Initiative (CHRI) point to around 251 cases directly related to RTI where people were attacked, murdered and physically harassed. At least fifty-one murders and five suicides have taken place between 2005 and 2016. Maharashtra topped the list, with ten alleged murders and at least two suicides, followed by Gujarat, with eight alleged murders and one suicide. Next was UP, with six alleged murders and one suicide. In addition, there have been at least 130 instances of attacks, including attempts to murder RTI users, during this period.[13] Such violent incidents indicate that the information seeker was treading on ground involving substantial wrongdoing and hence was becoming inconvenient for the delinquents. These are instances that require alacrity of action and very significant oversight by government functionaries. Not delving deeper into the issues raised by these people, who became targets, will serve as encouragement for wrongdoers, thereby defeating the very purpose for which this fundamental right has been afforded to citizens.

RISING PENDENCY: KILLING THE LANDMARK ACT

In terms of simplicity of the appellant structure, the Indian transparency law compares fairly well with other countries.

---

[13] Anahita Mukherji; 'Maharashtra tops country in attacks, murder of RTI activists'; *The Times of India*; 22 December 2013; https://timesofindia.indiatimes.com/india/Maharashtra-tops-country-in-attacks-murder-of-RTI-activists/articleshow/27743408.cms
Accessed on 30 June 2019.

However, despite this simplicity, the applications for information pending for disposal are the most numerous in the world among the countries for which comparative data has been collated in a World Bank study.

There could be two reasons for such high pendency. The first is the lack of adequate machinery available for quick disposal of such a large number of applications in a country as diverse as India, with the existence of institutions that are not always the best examples of transparency. The second reason could be a large number of applications requiring careful consideration at the appellate levels, as there is a natural tendency on the part of the public authorities in general to take umbrage and deny information.

Alluding to the issue of pendency, Shailesh Gandhi, a former central information commissioner and an active proponent of RTI, stated that rising pendency was killing the landmark Act. 'When I was in the CIC, we decided that we would dispose of a minimum of 3,200 cases per year. I myself was doing 5,000 cases a year and 6,000 in my last year. Yet this norm is being flouted, and Information Commissioners are working less and less, and pendency is piling up,' he said.[14] There have been reports of highest pendency from Maharashtra, with Pune alone struggling with more than 5,000 cases. These will have to be tackled with a certain amount of urgency or else the public will begin to lose trust in the system.

There is, however, no denying the fact that the transparency law has opened a new horizon for citizens to participate more actively in governance. In the process, it is possible the system has generated frivolous requests, but at the same time, it has raised some substantial queries on governance and public accountability.

---

[14]Rukmini S.; 'With no CIC, RTI appeals pile up'; The Hindu (ITALS); 25 November 2014; https://www.thehindu.com/news/national/with-no-cic-rti-appeals-pile-up/article6630810.ece
Accessed on 16 July 2019.

The RTI movement, as it has emerged, came from a strong feeling amongst a section of society that more vibrancy had to be brought into the country's democratic governance system so as to draw it closer to citizens' aspirations.

PROPOSED AMENDMENTS

The central government had proposed certain amendments to the RTI Act in April 2017 and tasked the CIC with facilitating these amendments. The proposals involved giving the chief information commissioner the sole power to assign a case involving an appeal or a complaint to a single information commissioner, as against assigning it to a bench. Such a proposal was seen as going counter to the very spirit of the Act, which requires the chief information commissioner to be assisted by the information commissioners in assigning cases. The existing provision enjoins a collective responsibility, whereas a single authority assigning could be seen to be doing so under duress of the government or any other agency.

Another rather controversial change proposed was of a complaint being deemed withdrawn in the event of the complainant's death. This proposal had evoked serious objections from the public, as about seventy persons who had filed RTI complaints had died. Thus, implementing the proposal could have endangered the lives of complainants. However, the CIC, after deliberating on the proposed amendments, advised the government against introducing them, as they were flawed. This advice reaffirmed faith in its independence as the government dropped the proposal for amendments.[15]

---

[15]Dilsher Dhillon; 'India's government has decided against amending the Right to Information Act'; *Business Insider*; 1 June 2018; https://www.businessinsider.in/indias-government-has-decided-against-amending-the-right-to-information-act/articleshow/64415067.cms Accessed on 30 June 2019.

A COLLABORATIVE EFFORT

Public functionaries have to rid themselves of the colonial mindset, which associates secrecy with every government process and transaction. Concerns have been expressed in some quarters that the disclosure of information inhibits free and open expression of opinion by government officials during the decision-making process. If the officials have approached the issues with objectivity and followed rules, then this argument holds no water. The benefits of disclosure of information far outweigh the inconveniences experienced by the decision-makers in the government. There is a need to sensitize public functionaries on the right to information and educate them about its real intent.

One beneficial step would be to institute a mechanism where citizens could question the working of their representatives and the governance institutions that deliver services. The World Bank study referred to earlier states that the maximum number of applications in India originate from a few departments/institutions, such as the Department of Posts, Employees' Provident Fund Organisation (EPFO), Bharat Sanchar Nigam Limited (BSNL), Delhi Police and SBI. These are essentially service departments/institutions or those concerned with the core of the governance system such as law and order, and citizens' expectations of them are high.

The Act is being used by civil-society organizations and the media to bring about positive change in the levels of corruption and accountability. Issues like the public distribution system, pensions, road repairs, electricity connections and telecom complaints have been dealt with by people through RTI. It has hugely emboldened honest officers, who feel empowered as decisions are now open to civil society and media scrutiny, which acts as a deterrent for any extraneous pressure.

Citizen groups need to channel their efforts in the direction of the efficacy of the RTI Act on the substantive issues of providing information and enforcing the provisions of the Act. They would hugely benefit society by enhancing the awareness of applicants and respondents through periodic seminars and workshops.

The legislature has done the people a great service by providing a law for the right to information, as such a law is a fundamental prerequisite for any participative democracy that can boast of transparency and accountability. The law is fundamental and equitable in the sense that it is equally applicable to the gram panchayat, the PMO or the Supreme Court, thereby giving the common man the power to hold his government and other pillars of a vibrant democracy accountable for all acts and decisions. Since its inception in 2005, it has made an impact on all public bodies and every discourse on government by ensuring that officials are conscious of public oversight. It strengthens democracy and promotes good governance by enhancing the citizen's ability to participate in the process.

Sincere and objective application of this law requires a collaborative effort between a government with the requisite political will and an active civil society possessing acknowledgement of its role. It requires better education of the people and a commitment from all to uphold the rule of law. The law imposes equal responsibility on the public authority and on the RTI user to ensure that their approach is judicious and well considered. The Act has sufficient safeguards built into it to protect the interests of both parties. We need to recalibrate our thinking in favour of the public as well as our style of functioning in public bodies. While the former cannot afford to be frivolous or far too generous in its use of RTI, the latter cannot seek perennial refuge under different clauses to shirk responsibility. It has to be recognized that a vibrant democracy requires an informed and concerned citizenry as much as a government which is sensitive and sympathetically forthcoming towards its citizens.

10

SPORTS ADMINISTRATION

The Priest Becomes More Important than the Deity

As I waited at Delhi's Indira Gandhi International Airport to board a flight on 30 January 2017, a journalist called to say she had just heard in the Supreme Court that a committee of administrators (CoA) had been appointed to manage the administration of the BCCI, and that I was to be its chairman. This came as a surprise as TV channels had been stating that another name was under consideration for the appointment. The journalist assured me I was the final choice and sought my comments. My first reaction was that I was deeply interested in cricket and followed it closely. I mentioned that I would be like a 'night watchman', who comes to the crease to bat overnight for only a limited time, to soon make way for the seasoned and established batsmen. I also said that I would like to ensure early implementation of the reforms recommended by the Lodha Committee, have elections conducted in the BCCI and make way for the democratically elected committee to run the affairs of the board according to its newly mandated constitution.

Little did I imagine then that I would have to serve as the longest 'playing' night watchman, not because I was a good batsman and the opposing team could not get me out, but because the team sought to be displaced by the Court would refuse to leave the ground despite having been given out! It was highly intriguing that cricket and other sports administrators were so unwilling to quit even after spending decades in the administration of the game. Before I learnt the reasons for their reluctance first-hand, I gleaned a lot from a well-researched article on this very aspect of sports administration.

In his incisive story in the 22 July 2013 edition of *India Today*, Kunal Pradhan analysed why sports administrators refuse to retire despite being in the job for decades and regardless of facing adverse media attention and, quite often, critical judicial pronouncements.[1] He cited three examples. The first was that of BJP leader V.K. Malhotra, eighty-six, who was president of the Archery Association of India (AAI) for forty years, until the body was de-recognized by the sports ministry for age and tenure violations. The next was Congress leader Suresh Kalmadi, seventy-four, who was 'life president' of the Athletics Federation of India (AFI) and president of the Indian Olympic Association (IOA) for fifteen years. The third instance was that of V.K. Verma, who headed the Badminton Association of India (BAI) for fourteen years, until he had to step aside over his role in the Commonwealth Games organizing committee. Similar cases in other sports bodies have compelled the government to take steps to cleanse Indian sport and instil transparency and accountability into sports bodies. Since these bodies are not State institutions and are registered along different regulations, the government went about drafting guidelines for regulating them.

This was in the form of the National Sports Development

---

[1]Kunal Pradhan; 'Tainted sports administrators refuse to retire. Here's why'; *India Today*, 22 July 2013; https://www.indiatoday.in/magazine/sport/story/20130722-suresh-kalmadi-lalit-bhanot-indian-olympic-association-abhay-singh-chautala-764702-1999-11-30
Accessed on 4 June 2019.

Code of India (NSDCI), introduced in 2011.[2] However, vested interests among senior politicians, who have been presiding over these sports bodies themselves, have ensured that this Bill has not been passed in Parliament. It is being repeatedly torpedoed only to ensure that so-called sports administrators, who have captured these associations purely by virtue of their ability to muster votes, continue with their stranglehold over them indefinitely.

Pradhan mentions that the IOA was suspended by the International Olympic Committee (IOC) in December 2012, citing, inter alia, lack of basic principles of ethics and violation of good governance norms laid down in the Olympic Charter. The major transgression was that the IOA wanted a member to be allowed to hold an executive post for twenty consecutive years, until the age of seventy. The Olympic Charter, however, permits the president a maximum tenure of eight years, in two terms of four years each. What was further seen as preposterous was that IOA officials were seeking to propose that an outgoing president be made an honorary chairman of a sports federation during his four-year 'cooling-off' period. The then IOA joint secretary sought to justify this proposition with the most ingenious argument ever: 'There are not too many selfless, good people in Indian sports administration.'[3] Fortunately, better sense prevailed and this proposal was given the go-by.

Yet another example is of the AAI, which was de-recognized in 2012 by the government for violating the age and tenure

---

[2]Government of India; National Sports Development Code of India, 2011; Ministry of Youth Affairs and Sports; Department of Sports; https://yas.nic.in/sites/default/files/File918.compressed.pdf
Accessed on 4 June 2019.

[3]Kunal Pradhan; 'Tainted sports administrators refuse to retire. Here's why'; *India Today*; 22 July 2013; https://www.indiatoday.in/magazine/sport/story/20130722-suresh-kalmadi-lalit-bhanot-indian-olympic-association-abhay-singh-chautala-764702-1999-11-30
Accessed on 4 June 2019.

guidelines laid down in the sports code. The association even fell foul of the judiciary. There was a direction from the Delhi High Court not to grant recognition to the AAI unless it held elections as per the Sports Code. The AAI incurred this disqualification upon the election of Malhotra as the president, since he had served for more than three consecutive terms and had attained the age of seventy. At the time of his election in 2011, Malhotra was eighty-one years old and sought to be president for his tenth tenure.[4] It was rather ironical that the AAI had lost its recognition because Malhotra had refused to step down despite having been president for four decades.

It is indeed remarkable that a sports administrator is so indispensable that the national body becomes secondary to the individual and the body would rather be disqualified than have its ten-time president resign. The quality which brings about such indispensability in a particular person remains to be uncovered by any outside observer. The AAI could ultimately move to regain recognition only after Malhotra put in his resignation in order to join the All India Council of Sports (AICS), which was being revived after twelve years. Incidentally, when the AICS went into closure, Malhotra was its chairman.

Pradhan cites the example of yet another sports administrator, Lalit Bhanot, who was the general secretary of the AFI until he was removed for alleged involvement in irregularities in the 2010 Commonwealth Games. He had by then notched up a tenure of twenty-five years in the AFI.

These examples have been highlighted merely to draw attention to the state of sports administration in the country. Against this background, I have attempted in this chapter a

---

[4]'V.K. Malhotra quits AAI after 40 years'; *The Times of India*; 16 October 2015; https://timesofindia.indiatimes.com/sports/more-sports/others/VK-Malhotra-quits-AAI-after-40-years/articleshow/49404756.cms Accessed on 4 June 2019.

detailed examination of the governance structure and similar instances of indispensability of individuals in the richest sports body of the country, the BCCI. I will also examine why the Supreme Court had to spend so much of its precious time on the governance setup of the BCCI.

INDIA'S TRYST WITH CRICKET

The BCCI website[5] provides a very interesting insight into the development of cricket in India. It mentions that the first-ever record of cricket being played in the country is by sailors from a British ship, which had docked off the coast of Kutch sometime in 1721. The sailors were seen playing cricket for exercise and recreation. The Calcutta Cricket Club (later the Calcutta Cricket and Football Club, or CCFC), established in 1792, appears to be the first recognized club for the sport in the country. The club is reputed to be the second-oldest cricket club in the world, after the Marylebone Cricket Club of the UK, which was established in 1787.

The Parsees were the first Indian civilian community to take to cricket. They set up the Young Zoroastrian Club in Bombay in 1850, and were followed by the Hindus, who formed the Hindu Gymkhana (Bombay Hindu Union Cricket Club) in 1866. Cricket was also gaining in popularity in other cities around the same time. It was in 1884 that a team from Sri Lanka played a match in Calcutta (now Kolkata). That was the country's first shot at international cricket. And 1911 witnessed the first-ever tour of England by an 'all-India' team sponsored and captained by the Maharaja of Patiala.

A meeting in Delhi on 21 November 1927, attended by around forty-five delegates comprising cricket representatives from Sind,

---

[5] www.bcci/tv/about-bcci-html
Accessed on 4 June 2019.

Punjab, Patiala, Delhi, the United Provinces, Rajputana, Alwar, Bhopal, Gwalior, Baroda, Kathiawar and Central India, reached a consensus that a board for cricket control was essential to manage, develop and control the game in the country. Subsequently, a meeting held at the Bombay Gymkhana on 10 December ended with the unanimous decision to form a 'provisional' board to represent cricket in India. The BCCI was finally established in 1928.

ENTER THE BCCI

Since its inception, the BCCI has organized and regulated cricket in India. The body is registered under the Tamil Nadu Societies Registration Act, 1975, and constituted along democratic lines. The state associations elect their representatives to the general body of the BCCI, which then elects the office-bearers.

The BCCI is a member of the International Cricket Council (ICC), which is the global governing body of cricket. The ICC was housed in the Marylebone Cricket Club at the Lord's ground in London. However, around 2003, the revenues of the ICC began to show buoyancy and since the UK government was not willing to provide tax exemption, it set up base in Dubai, a more tax-friendly location, in August 2005. While the need of the hour was to bring the commercial and administrative wings together in a tax-friendly location, the move to Dubai signalled the rise of a new cricketing power centre in the South Asian region. The shift was largely driven by the initiatives of N.K.P. Salve and Jagmohan Dalmiya, thereby evidencing the declining hold of the UK and Australia on world cricket.

There has been considerable debate over the nature and character of the BCCI. In the *Zee Telefilms Vs Union of India* case,[6] the government took the stand that the BCCI was a 'state' since it was in de facto control as the national apex body of cricket in the country. It buttressed its argument with the fact that the team that the BCCI selected represented India as its official team. Hence, the government maintained that the BCCI had a public function to perform and was accountable to the government and the public at large. The BCCI, however, replying to the writ petition filed against it in the matter pertaining to the grant of exclusive television rights for cricket matches, argued that it was not a 'state' within the meaning of Article 12 of the Constitution and was a mere private, autonomous entity with no public mandate or governmental control. The BCCI took this line of argument despite the fact that it considered itself the 'single national governing body for all forms of cricket in India'. In its verdict, the Supreme Court rejected the contention that the BCCI came within the scope of the definition of 'state' as defined in the Constitution. The Court declared that it was essentially an autonomous, non-statutory body with no declared monopoly over the game of cricket, no public function to discharge, and since it received no significant financial assistance from the government, it could have no oversight by the government. This happens to be the last word on the nature of the institution.

ACTION ON AND OFF THE FIELD

At the turn of the millennium, the BCCI continued to be a staid and conservative body dedicated to conventional formats of the game such as Test cricket in the international arena, and the Ranji and Duleep trophy tournaments within the country. These were

---

[6]Zee Telefilms Ltd. and Anr. Vs Union of India (UOI) and Ors.; AIR2005SC2677, 2005(1) SCALE666, (2005)4SCC649; http://www.nja.nic.in/P-950_Reading_Material_5-NOV-15/3.%20Zee_Telefilms_Ltd.pdf Accessed on 4 June 2019.

the times when newer formats of the game were being tested and, with increasing media focus, were ushering in an era of greater commercial activity.

However, comfortable in its time warp, the BCCI was not willing to accept proposals from a private person who had no exposure to the cricketing community of India, to launch a 'festival of entertainment beyond just cricket' along the lines of the NBA basketball league in the US. That person was Lalit Modi. The BCCI felt that such ideas should come from state associations and not from private individuals. It was only after the Indian Cricket League (ICL) was launched by the Essel Group and the BCCI did not recognize it that thinking veered around to organizing another similar tournament.

It was from here that Lalit Modi took over and began to guide the Indian Premier League (IPL) with a massive media push and with the setting up of ten clubs (or franchises), which were bought by high-profile businesspersons and Bollywood personalities. Title sponsors and media rights were roped in and IPL 2008 was launched with remarkable revelry and fanfare. In fact, such was the brand value of the tournament that at the inaugural ceremony of the third IPL season at the DY Patil Sports Stadium in Mumbai, Lalit Modi and other personalities landed at the venue in helicopters.

With players' auctions and media rights in addition to these high-profile personalities, big money had moved into IPL. However, somewhere along the journey of the IPL, glamour, big money and ambition led to adventurism! That it could portend big trouble was not properly envisaged. Things became so heady for some that caution and the need to maintain propriety were ignored. Cricket-related activity and betting on games seemed to have become the order of the day and allegations of spot-fixing led to arrests of players and supporters of some franchises. Issues snowballed with PILs cases being filed, and soon the Supreme Court had to step in.

To derive a better perspective of how the issues grew further complicated, it is important to focus on the pattern of governance of the BCCI. The general body comprises a nominee from each recognized state cricket association.[7] The erstwhile[8] organizational structure of the BCCI comprised a president, five vice-presidents (one for each zone), a secretary, a joint secretary and a treasurer, as elected office-bearers. They constituted the governing council, which was the apex decision-making body of the BCCI, and were elected from among the general-body members. The administrative structure below the governing council comprised full-time staff, at the level of general managers and below. There was, however, no full-time CEO or chief financial officer (CFO), in the organization until 2016.

According to the present constitution, approved by the Supreme Court on 9 August 2018, the BCCI shall have a nine-member apex council, of whom five shall be elected office-bearers, elected by the full members (representing different states) of the BCCI in its annual general meeting, with one more being elected by the full members from among their representatives. The five elected office-bearers shall hold the posts of president, vice-president, secretary, joint secretary and treasurer. There shall then be a nominee of the CAG and two former players (one male and one female) nominated by the players' association.

The problems in the BCCI came to the fore when allegations of spot-fixing surfaced during the 2013 season of the IPL. Three players—S. Sreesanth, Ankeet Chavan and Ajit Chandila—were arrested on allegations of fraud and cheating, and manipulating their performances in the matches on the dictates of bookies. The police also arrested Gurunath Meiyappan, who happened to be

---

[7] Not all states had been given the status of full membership earlier.
[8] Since 9 August 2018, the Supreme Court has directed the implementation of a new BCCI constitution.

closely associated with the Chennai Super Kings (CSK) franchise.[9] It was also alleged that Raj Kundra, the co-owner of another franchise, the Rajasthan Royals, was betting on the IPL games.

To probe these complaints, the IPL governing council set up a three-member panel. However, it was later learnt that the probe panel had been constituted without the knowledge of the governing council members. Soon PILs were filed in the Supreme Court alleging corruption and mismanagement. The Court subsequently constituted a three-member panel to look into the allegations of corruption in the IPL. The panel, headed by retired judge Justice Mukul Mudgal, after detailed investigation found Meiyappan and Kundra to be involved in betting. The panel also drew attention to the issue of conflict of interest of N. Srinivasan, the father-in-law of Meiyappan, since he was then BCCI president, a factor that had been raised by several persons during the inquiry. But the panel refrained from pronouncing any opinion, since the matter was not in its terms of reference. The panel, however, did observe that since the issue had been repeatedly stressed before it, its members deemed it appropriate to bring the matter to the notice of the Supreme Court.

COA TAKES SHAPE

In January 2015, the apex court appointed another three-member panel, headed by a former CJI, Justice R.M. Lodha, to make suitable recommendations to ensure reforms in the practices and procedures of the BCCI and suggest amendments to its memorandum of association, rules and regulations. The Lodha Committee, after very intensive interactions with various

---

[9]'Gurunath Meiyappan arrested in IPL betting case'; *The Hindu BusinessLine*; 25 May 2013; https://www.thehindubusinessline.com/news/gurunath-meiyappan-arrested-in-ipl-betting-case/article20617648.ece1
Accessed on 4 June 2019.

stakeholders, submitted its recommendations in January 2016, suggesting a major overhaul in the constitution of the BCCI. The Court accepted these recommendations and directed the BCCI to adopt the new constitution by convening an annual general meeting. The Court was proceeding in the belief that the BCCI discharged 'public functions' and hence there was a need for it to be transparent and accountable. The Court intervention had also met with a great deal of public approval, since the general perception was that the institution was closely held and managed by only a select few.

Elected office-bearers in the BCCI raised objections similar to the ones raised by the office-bearers of the IOA to the NSDCI, particularly with respect to the age cap of seventy years and the limitation on tenure with a 'cooling off' between tenures. The media and other 'BCCI watchers' felt that those who had established their stranglehold over the BCCI and state associations for decades were obviously not willing to let go and hence kept objecting to the reform suggestions. Soon, the intransigence of the elected functionaries came to such a pass that the court had to order the imposition of the new constitution suggested by the Lodha Committee. Even this verdict of the Court was ignored and members continued to resist, inter alia, the 'one state one vote'[10], the age cap and the 'cooling off' clauses. Despite various directions of the Court in October, November and December 2016, the intransigence persisted.

On 2 January 2017, finding that the BCCI members had still not complied with its verdict, the Court ordered the removal of the then president, Anurag Thakur, and secretary, Ajay Shirke. It ordered the formation of a four-member CoA to 'supervise the

---

[10]Maharashtra (Mumbai, Vidarbha and Maharashtra) and Gujarat (Baroda, Rajkot and Gujarat) have historically had three member associations each. These have existed for decades, thereby permitting each of these states three votes in the BCCI annual general meeting.

administration of the BCCI through its CEO and ensure that the directions contained in this court judgement dated 18 July 2016 are fulfilled'. The Court went on to observe that 'upon the CoA, as nominated by this court assuming charge, the existing office bearers shall function subject to the supervision and control of the CoA. The CoA will have the power to issue all appropriate directions to facilitate due supervision and control'. In a further order on 30 January, which named the four-member committee, the Court stated, 'The CEO of the BCCI shall report to the CoA and the administrators shall supervise the management of BCCI.'[11]

In its consultations with various stakeholders, the Lodha panel had discovered that the BCCI did not have a full-time professional CEO to manage its administration. In fact, as per the Memorandum of Associations (MoA), it was the part-time, elected, honorary secretary who functioned as the administrative head of the institution. The panel was convinced that there was a need to separate the governance and management functions of the BCCI and have a CEO look after the management functions.

THE TRUE VILLAIN

So what ails the administration of the BCCI? Why has the BCCI been in the news for all the wrong reasons over the past few years? Were the state associations, which are the constituent bodies of the BCCI, well administered? To answer these questions and to be able to appreciate why so many cases had been filed in different courts and why the Supreme Court had to devote its time to the BCCI, we need to examine the functioning and failures of its governance structure.

The government and the BCCI may have argued that the

---

[11]In the Supreme Court of India; Civil Appellate Jurisdiction; Civil Appeal No. 4235 of 2014; https://www.sci.gov.in/jonew/judis/44446.pdf Accessed on 5 July 2019.

BCCI was not a 'state' in the strict sense of the word. However, it cannot be denied that a cricket team selected by the BCCI is recognized as the team representing the country. It is also a fact that the BCCI collects revenue and utilizes the resources so collected to build cricketing infrastructure and conduct tournaments, in which states are formally represented. Any credible institution professing to do so must ensure a full-time management setup with good financial accountability and transparent systems of administration. The BCCI prided itself on having a management system presided over by the most experienced cricket administrators in the land.

However, when the challenge of big money, star power, 24x7 national-media focus and its own internal conflict of interest transgressions arose, the soft underbelly of the BCCI was revealed. There was no transparency in its administration and its governance structure revealed that amendments to its rules and regulations were made at short notice, perhaps to pave the way for its functionaries to undertake commercial ventures. It had no code of ethical conduct for its office-bearers, no ombudsman to delineate the fault lines and, above all, offered a structure which acquiesced to the power dynamics of the electoral ecosystem.

However, the redeeming factor was that the common man had begun to seek accountability and use the weapon of the PIL. This compelled the country's richest sports body, despite all its influential connections, to have its 'autonomy' invaded and its woefully inadequate accountability and management practices revealed.

Somewhere along the way, the elected office-bearers appeared to have lost sight of the interest of cricket and begun to pursue their own interpretation of what the game should be. This brought about a great degree of discomfiture among players, cricket lovers and cricket administrators. Families made it a tradition to have their representatives occupy, if not usurp, positions in state associations. There were instances of office-bearers occupying positions for a dozen years and more. Naturally, a person occupying a post for ten or fifteen years would have a morphing of his own interest as the national interest. Or at least believe that his interpretation was the ultimate. Personal interests developed.

The most glaring example was that of the controversial amendment to the BCCI constitution's clause 6.2.4, which allowed board officials to have a commercial interest in the IPL and the Champions League T20. The Supreme Court in its judgement pertaining to the 2013 IPL corruption case had declared this amendment 'void and ineffective, unsustainable and impermissible in law', as it was said to have 'authorized' the 'creation and continuance' of a conflict of interest situation. The two-man bench of Chief Justice T.S. Thakur and Justice F.M.I. Kalifulla said the amendment of the rule was the 'true villain' in the situation at hand and had perpetuated the conflict. The rule had been amended in September 2008, six months after the Chennai franchise was sold to India Cements, which was owned by the then BCCI secretary, N. Srinivasan.[12]

A SOLID FOUNDATION OF CORPORATE GOVERNANCE

Instances of self-perpetuation and morphing of personal interest into that of the institution clearly point to the failure of the governance structure to provide good governance practices and the lack of a professional administrative system to ensure accountability and transparency. Irrespective of the legal definition of these bodies, it is undeniable that they will henceforth be held accountable for the actions they take. Thus,

---

[12]'Court strikes down controversial BCCI clause'; ESPNcricinfo; 22 January 2015; http://www.espncricinfo.com/india/content/story/823061.html Accessed on 4 June 2019.

it is only essential that good governance practices, with built-in integrity and ethical codes, be adopted at the earliest. This is exactly what the Lodha Committee had sought to do.

The committee recommended a two-tier structure. At the apex level is the board of governance (called the apex council), which shall have all the powers of the general body to provide strategic guidance to the institution. It is the agency empowered to take all the policy-level decisions and exercise superintendence over the CEO and all the committees, in the discharge of the duties assigned to them. Thus, it becomes the principal decision-making body as selected by the general body.

At the administrative/management level are the full-time professional managers, with the CEO heading the team. It needs to be emphasized that to ensure good corporate governance, the CEO has to be a full-time professional who has adequate exposure to cricket, experience in managing a large organization and familiarity with legal and regulatory responsibilities. Only then can accountability and transparency be established. This is the edifice on which the NSDCI 2011 has been premised. It was devised after a thorough study of sports bodies around the world and had factored in all the essential features to ensure good corporate governance.

Good corporate governance also stipulates that directors of the board should not occupy positions for unlimited periods. It is for this reason that the Lodha package of reforms had prescribed a 'cooling off' between any two tenures at any position in the BCCI apex council.[13] It is only natural that a person getting an

---

[13] The 2013 Companies Act limits the tenure of office of an independent director to a maximum of two tenures, with a cooling-off period of three years between the two tenures. During the cooling-off period of three years, he should not be appointed in or be associated with the company in any other capacity, either directly or indirectly [proviso to section 149(11) of 2013 Act].

uninterrupted tenure as an office-bearer would develop crony interests and rigidity in ideas, thereby leading to lack of objectivity. Boards in other countries, such as the England and Wales Cricket Board and Cricket Australia, have a two-tier structure. A board of governance occupies the first tier, while a full-time professional executive setup is at the second tier.

In fact, Cricket Australia revamped its board a few years back and cut down the strength from fourteen members to nine on the grounds that fourteen was ineffective and large. It was felt that vested interests had developed, which had become evident in their subjective decision-making. This had led to poor practices by the management, and no transparency and accountability. There was no succession-planning and long-term vision for the development of men's and women's cricket. This led to a decline in the performance of the national team and much acrimony between the players' association and the board. The revamped board has introduced a new means of governing cricket in Australia with accountability, transparency and objectivity.

Ironically, much has been said by those who have been associated over long periods with the BCCI. They insist that continuity over a few years is essential for building relationships in different boards and developing familiarity with ICC practices, persons and issues. This argument has been advanced to thwart the norm for cooling off. However, besides the fact that it does not take much time for anyone to familiarize themselves with issues and practices, voting and consensus are not based on individual relationships. Voting on issues in the ICC is determined by the country's self-interest.

It is significant that it took Vikram Limaye (one of the members of the CoA) barely five days after being appointed to the CoA to understand the new financial model of the ICC and devise an alternative format which offered a win-win formula to participating countries. This alternative could not be tested in the ICC Board meeting as Limaye was not the authorized representative of the BCCI to the ICC Board and the authorized representative (the then acting secretary) was committed to reiterating a revenue-sharing model devised in 2014. This model never got operationalized, as it had been reversed by a vote of 9:1. The 2014 model, which had been premised on the 'big three'[14] formula, was expected to net the BCCI $570 million but had not been operationalized so that no revenues as per that formulation ever accrued to India. It is reported that Srinivasan had got that model approved when he was the ICC president, but the moment he moved out, the model got reversed in favour of more equitable distribution.[15] As per the revised formula devised under the chairmanship of Shashank Manohar, India's share had been determined at $295 million.

The CoA soon realized that chasing the 2014 formula was like chasing a mirage. It made good media coverage to talk of BCCI domination over the ICC and that experienced administrators could recover lost ground, but it was soon realized that we needed to cut our losses and seek the best that the BCCI could receive under the new formula. The CoA was successful in negotiating an enhancement from $295 million to $405 million.[16] India thus continues to get the lion's share at 22.8 per cent of the gross

---

[14] Daniel Brettig; 'New ICC finance model breaks up Big Three'; ESPNcricinfo; 27 April 2017; http://www.espncricinfo.com/story/_/id/19253630/new-icc-finance-model-breaks-big-three Accessed on 4 June 2019.

[15] Ibid

[16] K. Shriniwas Rao; 'ICC "hikes" India's revenue share; bilateral structure could undergo sea change'; *The Times of India*; 23 June 2017; https://timesofindia.indiatimes.com/sports/cricket/news/icc-hikes-indias-revenue-share-bilateral-structure-could-undergo-sea-change/articleshow/59279864.cms
Accessed on 4 June 2019.

revenue of the ICC. England is a far second at 7.8 per cent with $139 million (as shown in the table below).

THE ICC'S NEW REVENUE-SHARING FORMULA
• India: **$405 million** (22.8%)
• England: **$139 million** (7.8%)
• Australia, Pakistan, West Indies, New Zealand, Sri Lanka and Bangladesh: **$128 million** each (7.2%)
• Zimbabwe: **$94 million**
• ICC's Associate Members: **$240 million**
• Full Members: More than **86%**
• ICC's Associate Members: **14%**

Thus, in an attempt to ensure a stellar reputation for a body which, in years to come, will have to, under stakeholder pressure, become more transparent and accountable, the elected apex council must usher in good governance norms, setting ethical standards by example and ensuring that there is no conflict of interest and misuse of insider information. Mihir Bose, an experienced journalist and first sports editor of the BBC, in a comprehensive book on Indian cricket, sums up the administration of cricket in the country in the following words:

> As I write, BCCI is still to be reincarnated in the way the Lodha Committee has laid down. When it is, the officials must show a maturity the old officials did not. Not the old hubris of which the old men who ran the BCCI had an excess, but awareness that India and Indian cricket have come a long way. India's status as a super power of cricket also imposes certain obligations and responsibilities that extend beyond India to the wider cricketing world. India cannot and should not behave like a colonial despot as the

old board often did. And never more than when they had forced through a deal at the ICC, helped by England and Australia, to create a monopoly not different to the one England and Australia had in the days of white supremacy. In this case India had to retreat but it illustrated the lack of farsighted leadership that has always been a problem in Indian cricket.[17]

ENSURING INTEGRITY OF ADMINISTRATION

Good governance dictates that at the professional and full-time employee level, a good corporate culture is introduced. There is need to divide administration into three parts: cricketing activities, finance and administration, including logistics and procurement. The first category is best left to former reputed cricketers such as the cricket advisory committee for selection of a head coach. It comprises illustrious players such as Sachin Tendulkar, Sourav Ganguly and V.V.S. Laxman. This committee should also nominate selectors and not leave it to the general body to nominate selectors and that, too, on an annual basis. There have been allegations of members of the general body appointing selectors from their 'coterie' and thereby influencing decisions during team selection.

Professionals working in the second and third category referred to above must introduce procurement procedures, pre-and post-audit mechanisms and ensure non-interference from outside. There is a role for an ombudsman and an ethics officer to ensure the integrity of the administration. I do not propose to go into the details of what needs to be done. The Court has already done so. We merely need to implement it and ensure that the institution does not slide back and become captive to vested interests.

---

[17]Mihir Bose; *The Nine Waves; The Extraordinary Story of Indian Cricket*; Aleph Book Company (May 2019)

TOWARDS A STRICTER CODE OF CONDUCT

Cricket is known as a gentleman's game and players are the ambassadors of that game. Young and old alike consider them to be role models in many ways. Hence, cricketers need to be conscious and sensitized to the fact that they should conduct themselves in a very correct fashion while in public and follow a code of conduct. They cannot feel that they are either privileged or entitled. Discipline and conduct off the ground as much as on it are important not only for the team or the BCCI, but for all cricket lovers who repose so much love, trust and admiration in their cricketing icons. Hence, the kind of utterances that were made by the duo of Hardik Pandya and K.L. Rahul on the popular television show *Koffee with Karan* are most regretful. The BCCI has launched a roadmap to sensitize young and upcoming cricketers about their conduct and utterances in public places. It is hoped this will mould young minds in the right direction.

OLD ORDER CHANGETH, YIELDING PLACE TO THE NEW

The events over the past five years have put the BCCI in critical public glare. Observation has turned to amazement in the last three years as, despite the Supreme Court ordering that the BCCI and the state associations adopt the constitution approved by it, the elected members refuse to accept the verdict on some ground or the other. Why is it that only a certain group of people must control the administration of the BCCI or its member associations, despite having been at the helm for decades? Discounting the 'expertise of seasoned cricket administrators', the Supreme Court observed while delivering its verdict on 9 August 2018:

> A considerable amount of fire has been directed against the provision for a cooling off period. The position of an office

bearer in the state associations and in the BCCI is not a matter of 'service' in the conventional sense. Office bearers should not construe their position as employees with a vested right to a particular tenure of service. Undoubtedly, the submission that individuals must continue for a period which enables them to develop experience in the administration of the game cannot be discounted. Equally, it is a matter of concern that vested interests and conflicts of interest develop around power centres which have unbridled authority. Dispersal of authority is a necessary safeguard to ensure against the perpetuation of power centres. Individuals who administer the game of cricket must realise that the game is perched far above their personal interests. Important as experience in administration is, it is far-fetched to assume—and far more difficult for the court to accept—that experience rests on the shoulders of a closed group of a few individuals. In fact, opportunities to a wide body of talent encourage a dispersal of experience and democratisation of authority.[18]

Is there no other talent available in the country that can provide fresh and innovative thinking to a body that runs cricket? A tsunami of allegations of fixing, betting and conflict of interest issues necessitated the Supreme Court's stepping in. Sports administrators will have to accept the reality that the world of sport, like every other activity in the country, is now under 24x7 public scrutiny, with the citizen seeking transparency and accountability from them. They shall henceforth survive in the same fishbowl in which the corporate, political or government functionaries live. They have to either accept this reality and ensure that good governance premised on an edifice of probity,

---

[18]Board of Control for Cricket in India Vs Cricket Association of Bihar & Ors.; Civil Appeal No. 4235 of 2014

professionalism and transparency is ushered in, or face being discredited by the sports-loving public.

The administration of the BCCI is no different from the model followed by any corporate institution. The core values underlying both are the same. The onus is on administrators to ensure that the game is delivered to the cricket lover in the country in its unadulterated and pure form, without any self-appointed experienced cricket administrator adding his two-bit to it. It is the wiser among them who will see the writing on the wall and accept the reality. It will be the ill-advised and reckless, sanguine in their misguided self-belief of being the 'gifted ones', who will step into the uncharted territory of acute vigilantism to which sports bodies will henceforth be subject.

A true lover of the game is one who recognizes that the time has come to pass on the mantle of administration to new and fresh minds while he himself sits back and fulfils the role of a mentor. This is as true in corporate governance as it is in sports governance. Hence, those who truly love the game will be doing it a great favour by facilitating the baton's passing on. They have had their time in the sun. They have achieved and delivered much. It is now for them to prove the truism that 'the old order changeth, yielding place to the new', and thereby walk away into the sunset with a halo still around them.

Cricket in India is not a mere game or passion—it is a religion. Cricketers are treated akin to gods. The BCCI is the link between the cricketers and the cricket lovers of India. Thus, if cricketers are deities and the public devotees, the BCCI naturally dons the role of the pujari or the priest. The question that is going to be haunting the BCCI is: is the pujari more important than the deity?

11

TEMPLE ADMINISTRATION

More than Divine Intervention

Some ten years ago, the Shree Padmanabhaswamy (or Lord Vishnu) temple suddenly broke into national news. The reason was the reported discovery of unimaginable wealth in its vaults. The otherwise sleepy, laid-back and easy-going atmosphere within the temple precincts was suddenly jolted into prominence in the national media.

I have lived in Thiruvananthapuram for about a decade and have visited the temple several times for darshan and also when accompanying visitors from the north who wished to worship there. None of us living in the capital city of the state had in our wildest dreams imagined that Lord Padmanabhaswamy held such immense wealth in His vaults. In fact, it is rather surprising that hardly anyone among us even knew of these vaults. What the world had seen, if it had indeed even noticed, were a few rooms with locks sealed in the age-old tradition of being covered with cloth and sealed with lac. What the Lord had protected for centuries behind those ordinary padlocks, after the value of His possessions became common knowledge, is costing the Kerala government ₹330 million (annually) through a company of police stationed there solely for the safekeeping of this treasure.

What treasures do the vaults contain? The Supreme Court had ordered their opening and preparation of an inventory but also placed a gag order on the seven-member observer team, stating that they could reveal the contents only to the Court. However, in July 2011, when the vaults were opened, bits and pieces of information floated out and were netted by an exceedingly anxious and expectant media. Among the reported contents of five of the six vaults (one remains unopened) are: a three-and-a-half-foot-tall solid, pure-gold idol of Mahavishnu, studded with hundreds of diamonds and rubies and other precious stones,[1] an 18-foot-long pure-gold chain, a gold sheaf weighing 500 kg, a 36-kg golden veil, 1,200 'Sarappalli' gold-coin chains that are encrusted with precious stones, and several sacks filled with gold artefacts, necklaces, diamonds, rubies, sapphires, emeralds, gemstones, and objects made of other precious metals.[2] There was also ceremonial attire for adorning the deity, a sixteen-part gold anki weighing almost 30 kg and a pure-gold throne studded with hundreds of diamonds and other precious stones, meant for the 18-foot-long reclining deity.[3] According to varying reports, at least three, if not more, solid gold crowns were also found, studded with diamonds and other precious stones.[4] Some

---

[1] 'Golden idol of Vishnu found at Sree Padmanabhaswamy temple'; *The Hindu*; 3 July 2011; https://www.thehindu.com/news/national/kerala/golden-idol-of-vishnu-found-at-sree-padmanabhaswamy-temple/article2154027.ece
Accessed on 1 July 2019.

[2] Mahadevan; 'Padmanabhaswamy temple throws up a treasure trove'; *The Hindu*; 1 July 2011; https://www.thehindu.com/news/national/kerala/Padmanabhaswamy-temple-throws-up-a-treasure-trove/article13725209.ece
Accessed on 1 July 2019.

[3] Prakash; Kerala's 'Padmanabha temple treasure worth over ₹60k crore'; *India Today*; 3 July 2011; https://www.indiatoday.in/india/south/story/kerala-padmanabha-temple-treasure-136720-2011-07-03
Accessed on 1 July 2019.

[4] Temples of Kerala—Sri Padmanabhaswamy Temple; https://temples.newkerala.com/Temples-of-India/Temples-of—Kerala-Sri-Padmanabhaswamy-Temple.html

media reports also mention hundreds of pure gold chairs and thousands of gold pots and jars among the articles in Vault A and its antechambers.[5]

With this kind of wealth reportedly found in it, it is no surprise that the temple has attracted so much attention. It has also raised a number of legal issues and controversies, which are incessantly discussed in courts, the media and government corridors. It is, therefore, necessary to look at the issues around the temple in three parts: the historical significance of the temple, the mystique surrounding its vaults and the treasure contained in them, and the administrative structure governing the temple management.

UNDERSTANDING THE LEGACY

Thiruvananthapuram, as the very name suggests, is the abode of Lord Anantha, the serpent on whose coiled body Sree Padmanabha reclines. It is thus only natural that the capital city of Kerala, once the seat of the Travancore royal family, secures its identity as the home of Anantha or Adi Sesha. Lord Padmanabha Swamy is the presiding deity of the royal family and is also worshipped by Hindus residing in the city and outside. There is no written evidence of when this temple was established, but historians and scholars assert that the shrine finds reference in Tamil literature of the Sangam period between 500 BC and AD 300.[6]

Accessed on 1 July 2019.
Aswathi Thirunal Gouri Lakshmi Bayi; *Sree Padmanabhaswamy Temple*; Bharatiya Vidya Bhavan (2013).
[5]Jake Halpern; 'The Secret of the Temple'; *The New Yorker*; 23 April 2012; https://www.newyorker.com/magazine/2012/04/30/the-secret-of-the-temple Accessed on 1 July 2019.
[6]Temples of Kerala-Sri Padmanabhaswamy Temple; https://temples.newkerala.com/Temples-of-India/Temples-of—Kerala-Sri-Padmanabhaswamy-Temple.html
Accessed on 1 July 2019.

In the sanctum sanctorum, the serpent provides the bed for the reclining Lord Padmanabha, who is depicted in eternal yogic sleep. Its five hoods facing inwards, signifying contemplation, also provide protection to the Lord. While the Lord reclines in His yogic sleep, His right hand is placed over a Shiva lingam. The two consorts of Vishnu—Sridevi, the goddess of prosperity, and Bhudevi, the goddess of the earth—are by his side. Brahma emerges on a lotus which emanates from the navel of the Lord. The deity is covered with katusarkarayogam, a special Ayurvedic mix, which forms a plaster that keeps it clean.[7]

To obtain darshan and perform worship, one has to ascend the Ottakkal Mandapam. The deity, which is about eighteen feet in length, is visible through three separate doors—Thirumukhom, Thiruudal and Thrippadam. As the names of the three entrances indicate, the visage of the reclining Lord and the Shiva lingam underneath His hand are seen through the first door. The body of the Lord, Sridevi, Bhudevi, Brahma, the gold Abhishekamoorthy and the Ulsavamoorthy are visible though the second door. The Lord's feet are visible through the third door.

The devotees have to strictly follow the traditional dress code, which, for males, is the white mundu or dhoti, leaving the torso bare. Women are required to wear saris. The major festival in this temple is Lakshadeepam (one lakh lamps), held once every six years. The last edition was in January 2014.

THE TRAVANCORE ROYAL FAMILY

In the first half of the eighteenth century, in line with matrilineal customs, Anizham Thirunal Marthanda Varma succeeded

---

[7]Temples of Kerala-Sri Padmanabhaswamy Temple; https://temples.newkerala.com/Temples-of-India/Temples-of—Kerala-Sri-Padmanabhaswamy-Temple.html
Accessed on 1 July 2019.

his uncle, Rama Varma, as king at the age of twenty-three. Till then, the temple and its properties were controlled by Thiruvananthapuram Sabha and later by Ettara Yogam (council of eight and a half) with the assistance of the Ettuveetil Pillamar (Lords of Eight Houses). Marthanda Varma curtailed the 700-year-old stranglehold of the Ettuveetil Pillamar and his interfering cousins, following the discovery of conspiracies the lords were involved in against the royal house of Travancore. The last major renovation of the temple commenced immediately after his accession to the musnud. The idol was reconsecrated in 1731 with 12,000 shaligrams (black marble representations of Vishnu) brought from the Gandaki river north of Varanasi.

On 17 January 1750, Anizham Thirunal Marthanda Varma surrendered the kingdom of Travancore to Sree Padmanabha Swamy and pledged that he and his descendants would be vassals or agents of the deity, who would serve the kingdom as Padmanabha Dasa (slave). Since then, the name of every Travancore king is preceded by the title 'Sree Padmanabha Dasa'. In fact, the present members of the royal family insist, 'A servant has the right to leave the master; if I don't like to work with you, I walk out and I say goodbye, but a slave has no option of independent action. He is forever bound to his master's feet. So, we prefer that.'[8]

The temple continued to remain under the direct control of the rulers of Travancore. The system of the Travancore king running it continued during the period of the last ruler, Sri Chithira Thirunal Balarama Varma, from 1931 to 1949, when the Instrument of Accession was signed, integrating the princely states of Travancore and Cochin (now Kochi) into one, and bringing Travancore-Cochin as a Part B state under the Constitution. Even after the end of the dynasty, the former rulers

---

[8]Jake Halpern; 'The Secret of the Temple'; *The New Yorker*; 23 April 2012; https://www.newyorker.com/magazine/2012/04/30/the-secret-of-the-temple Accessed on 1 July 2019.

continued as trustees of the temple and enjoyed certain privileges in its administration. The Sree Padmanabhaswamy Temple Trust, a public religious trust with the sole objective of meeting the expenses of the temple connected with the daily puja, festivals, repairs, maintenance and so on was set up by the maharaja ahead of the Privy Purse abolition. This trust had the maharaja as the chairman and four others as members.

The royal family continued to manage the trust and hence the wealth of the temple, without any outside oversight. Over a period of time, distrust among temple employees and devotees led to the filing of a lawsuit. In 2007, advocate Ananda Padmanabhan filed a lawsuit on behalf of two devotees against the temple administration for mismanaging the temple and pleaded that the government appoint new trustees to manage the deity's wealth. The claim in the lawsuit was that there was a huge amount of wealth stored in vaults belonging to the temple and this was being misappropriated. In the lawsuit, certain other persons also impleaded themselves, particularly K. Padmanabha Das, a former temple employee who claimed to be an eyewitness to the removal of treasure from the temple premises. The lawsuit was allowed by a Trivandrum lower court, which ordered the government to take over the temple and its possessions.

However, the royal family contested the verdict in the Kerala High Court on the grounds that for centuries their family had traditionally presided over the temple administration and protected its possessions. By then, T.P. Sundararajan, a police officer-turned-lawyer claiming to be a public-spirited person who felt that all was not well with the temple, also joined Padmanabha. Focused on the temple, he had even set up a law firm and named it Temple Law Firm.

Earlier, in 1991, the Kerala High Court, by a common judgement on a writ petition filed by the successor of the last ruler, had held that the petitioner, Uthradom Thirunal Marthanda

Varma, the then maharaja, or any successor of his family, could not claim control or management of the temple under Section 18(2) of the Travancore-Cochin Hindu Religious Institutions Act, 1950, after the death of the last ruler. The Court thus maintained that the petitioner, who was the then maharaja, did not automatically step into the shoes of the last ruler and therefore could not claim management rights over the temple under the provisions of the Act. Disposing of the appeal filed by the royal family, the High Court issued a direction to the state government to immediately take steps to constitute a body corporate or trust or other legal authority to take over control of the temple, its assets and management, and to run it in accordance with the traditions hitherto followed.

Aggrieved by this judgement of the Kerala High Court, the maharaja and the then executive officer of the temple filed two special leave petitions (SLPs) before the Supreme Court. In May 2011, after hearing all the arguments and the concerns expressed about the presence of six vaults in the temple precincts, the apex court constituted a five-member expert committee to advise on the inventory, conservation and security of the articles in the vaults. Before deciding on the stewardship of the temple, the Supreme Court ordered that a team of observers, two of whom were former judges of the Kerala High Court, would inspect the vaults (only two of which had been opened) and take stock of the valuables contained in them. In view of security issues, the Court had directed the commissioners not to reveal the contents to the public and merely make a record, which would be shared only with the Court.

INSIDE THE TRILLION-DOLLAR VAULTS

There is a great deal of folklore and superstition associated with the temple vaults. On the doors of Vault A is the embossed image of a cobra. Folklore maintains that the cobra is the guardian of the deity and whenever there is any threat to the temple, a swarm of snakes will emerge to ward off the intruders. It is also said that Vault B has not been opened for centuries and even the commission headed by former High Court judge Justice C.S. Rajan could not open it, as it had three doors and they could get past only the two outer ones. Superstition also has it that anyone attempting to open this vault is doomed to suffer severe maladies and ill luck.

Whilst it is believed that a huge cache of gold, precious stones and antiques of unimaginably high value were found in the vaults that could be opened, in obedience to the gag order of the Supreme Court, the value and quantum of the treasures were never made public. However, Jake Halpern, a 'reporter-at-large' with *The New Yorker*, wrote that he met Justice Rajan after a considerable length of time and enquired about the nature of the wealth that had been found in the vaults. Justice Rajan decided to reveal the details to him despite the gag order, on the grounds that time had elapsed and also that his work with the Court was over. It is best I reproduce the narration of the description that Justice Rajan gave to the reporter in his own words:

> Upon entering the temple, Rajan and the others headed toward the sanctum sanctorum, where the main idol reclines. The idol is a likeness of Padmanabha—a slumbering god who is one of Vishnu's many incarnations—and it contains twelve thousand and eight sacred stones that were collected centuries ago from the Gandaki River, in Nepal, and carried to Trivandrum by elephant. The observers passed through the sanctum sanctorum and visited an adjacent storage area, where they came to the six vaults, including A and B, which had metal-grille doors that looked as if they had not been opened in a very long time.

The doors to Vaults A and B required multiple keys, which had been entrusted to Varma and the temple's current executive, V.K. Harikumar. ...One of the observers was a fifty-nine-year-old attorney named M. Balagovindan, who was Sundararajan's personal lawyer and a trusted friend. Balagovindan also spoke with me, and he recalled his first glimpse of the treasure: 'When they removed the granite stone, it was almost perfectly dark, except for a small amount of light coming in through the doorway behind us. As I looked into the darkened vault, what I saw looked like stars glittering in a night sky when there is no moon. Diamonds and gems were sparkling, reflecting what little light there was. Much of the wealth had originally been stored in wooden boxes, but, with time, the boxes had cracked and turned to dust. And so the gems and gold were just sitting in piles on the dusty floor. It was amazing.'

According to Rajan, the observers instructed temple employees to haul everything from Vault A upstairs, for inspection. It took fifteen men all day. Rajan said that beholding the treasure was a 'divine moment.' There were countless gold rings, bangles, and lockets, many encrusted with gems. And there were gold chains, each studded with jewels and eighteen feet long—the length of the main idol. Rajan told me that coin experts estimated that the vault held approximately a hundred thousand gold coins, spanning centuries of trade: Roman, Napoleonic, Mughal, Dutch. He also described seeing a set of solid-gold body armour, known as an angi, built to adorn the main idol.

The vault also contained loose diamonds, rubies, emeralds, and other precious stones. According to Balagovindan, the most impressive gems were the large diamonds, some of which were a hundred and ten carats—'the size of a large thumb,' as he put it. The archaeologists and gemmologists estimated that a small solid-gold idol of Vishnu, encrusted with hundreds of gems, was worth thirty million dollars... So far, no one has formally calculated the value of the treasure found in Vault A. But Harikumar, the temple's executive—who has now seen the hoard on at least two occasions—has estimated that it is worth at least twenty billion dollars.[9]

As fate would have it, about a fortnight after the vaults were opened, Sundararajan developed fever. Though the fever was not very high or severe, he proclaimed that he had only a few hours left. The next morning, he seemed to wake up fine but soon collapsed and died. It was widely reported in the media that Sundararajan had succumbed to 'the curse of the cobra'.

Meanwhile, Vault B was still posing difficulties in opening. Its third and innermost door had three latches. One of these latches was jammed, preventing the court observers from opening it. However, before any further attempts could be made to force open the door, the royal family made one more attempt before the Supreme Court not to open the vault, since they felt that it would compromise the spiritual integrity of the temple. Meanwhile, an astrologer had even conducted a devaprasnam (an astrological ritual performed in the temples of Kerala to primarily determine 'divine opinion' regarding the functioning of the temple). The finding of the devaprasnam was that the deity was not pleased with the wealth in the vaults being displaced. It was felt that these valuables were not mere wealth but were also divine. The devaprasnam aside, on the request of the royal family, the Court mandated that Vault B not be opened for the time being. The Court has continued to delay its decision and till now has

---

[9]Jake Halpern; 'The Secret of the Temple'; *The New Yorker*; 23 April 2012; https://www.newyorker.com/magazine/2012/04/30/the-secret-of-the-temple Accessed on 1 July 2019.

not ordered the opening of the vault. Hence, the vault remains unopened and an inventory of its contents has not been made.

INSTANCES OF MISMANAGEMENT

The expert committee referred to earlier had by 2012 submitted four reports stating that the inventory of the artefacts contained in the vaults was nearing completion. In its hearing held on 23 August 2012, the Court felt that for better appreciation of the issues involved and the controversy being generated, there was need for an amicus curiae to be appointed to assist the Court. Gopal Subramaniam, senior advocate and former solicitor general of India, was approved for the role by the Court.

Subramaniam filed a 577-page report alleging malpractices in the administration of the temple. According to him, the authorities had failed to perform their ethical duties by opening many bank accounts and trusts, and had not filed income tax returns for the past ten years. He alleged that Vault B was opened despite a previous ruling of the Supreme Court prohibiting it. The report states,

> The large amount of gold and silver, the discovery of which was a shock, is a singular instance of mismanagement. The presence of a gold plating machine is also yet another unexplained circumstance. This discovery raises a doubt of the organized extraction by persons belonging to the highest echelons. There appears to be resistance on the part of the entire State apparatus in effectively addressing the said issues. The lack of adequate investigation by the police is a telling sign that although Thiruvananthapuram is a city in the state of Kerala, parallelism based on monarchic rule appears to predominate the social psyche.[10]

---

[10]'Amicus Curiae seeks audit of temple wealth'; *The Hindu*; 19 April 2014;

The amicus curiae also sought a detailed audit of the temple accounts on the grounds that revenues were not being deposited into the temple coffers and proper registers were not being maintained. The Court, on his recommendation, ordered the appointment of a former CAG (myself) to do a special audit of the temple accounts.

GRACE AND HUMILITY REIGN SUPREME

On being entrusted with the task of conducting the audit, I sought a meeting with the royal family. The family is respected among the people and is known for its culture, learning and encouragement of the state's art and culture. The family is popularly known outside Kerala through the world-famous painter and portraitist Raja Ravi Varma. My wife, Geeta, and K.S. Premachandra Kurup, a retired IAS officer, who was the secretary to the Supreme Court-appointed commission, and I called on the royal family. They were represented by the present maharaja, Moolam Thirunal Rama Varma, and his wife, Dr Girija Rama Varma. Moolam Thirunal, as he is popularly known, is an entrepreneur and the managing director of Aspinwall Ltd. Also present were Princess Aswathi Thirunal Gouri Lakshmi Bayi, her son, Aditya Varma, and Princess Pooyam Thirunal Gauri Parvathi Devi.

The family was a picture of grace and humility. They were exceedingly courteous and gave us a background of the temple history and mythology surrounding it. Princess Lakshmi Bayi is a scholar, writer and poet. She presented me with her book on the temple, a magnum opus on the history of the land and how it is interwoven with that of the temple. Meeting the family was a privilege.

---

https://www.thehindu.com/news/national/kerala/amicus-curiae-seeks-audit-of-temple-wealth/article5927269.ece
Accessed on 1 July 2019.

INADEQUACIES IN THE TEMPLE ADMINISTRATION

The special audit commenced in June 2014 with an audit team comprising a retired IAS officer, a retired deputy accountant general and five former senior audit officers from the office of the accountant general, Kerala. It was not an easy process, as the temple did not have a well-defined administrative structure and neither did it follow well-defined financial or accounting procedures. The entire arrangement was ad hoc, with sundry persons being entrusted with specific tasks from time to time. None of these persons were qualified in any of the areas critical to temple management, such as inventory management, accounting procedures, cash management, bank transactions, security and safekeeping issues, and so on. With respect to the period prior to 2008–09, complete records and relevant documents were not available and hence a thorough audit could not be conducted.

I proceed to describe some of the inadequacies that were noticed during the audit,[11] which point to ineffective management and lack of a transparent and accountable system in the temple administration, which has led to allegations of pilferage of the treasure accumulated over centuries. All kinds of wild allegations have been made about people who could have been complicit in the pilferage. In the absence of any concrete information, it will not only be unfair but very unwise to make assertions. Hence, what is being described are issues that came to light from pure perusal of records.

Opening of Vault B

Vault B is the most intriguing of the six vaults in the temple, with so much mystique surrounding it. Whilst the other five have been opened, it is often claimed that this vault has been left unopened

---

[11]Special audit of the SPST and its properties and SPSTT; Special audit authority; March 2016. Part II.

for centuries. The superstition surrounding it says its opening will cause suffering and large-scale distress, with ill omen befalling the person who opens it. Notwithstanding these superstitions and contrary to common belief, an inspection of the mahazar register revealed that Vault B had been opened at least seven times between July 1990 and December 2002. There is, however, vehement and authoritative denial of this. Such issues add to the mystique.

This fact of the records showing Vault B was opened was mentioned in our audit findings. The observation got into the public domain after the audit report was submitted to the Supreme Court. Members of the royal family must have read about it. Subsequently, a news item appeared in *Malayala Manorama*, a Kerala daily, quoting Princess Lakshmi Bayi as clarifying that the report was referring to the outer door of Kallara (vault) B, which was opened in 2011 by the Supreme Court-appointed observers.[12]

It is speculated that this vault is the largest and because it is guarded by serpents, may contain treasures far beyond what the others contain. The fact remains that there are claims and denials regarding the opening of this vault. Permission has been sought from the Court to open it, but no direction has been forthcoming. Its contents and the superstition surrounding it continue to fuel wild imaginings.

Purification of Gold

The temple did not have a system of ascertaining the weight and purity of gold and silver articles before handing them over to jewellers for melting and purification for ornamentation works. For example, the weight of the gold taken out from the cellars for melting, according to the weight recorded by the gold work contractors in a particular transaction, was 887 kg. On melting

---

[12] *Malayala Manorama*; 13 August 2014

and purification of the gold, the pure gold returned was only 624 kg. The loss in the process was 263 kg, which was nearly 30 per cent, indicating that there is no benchmark for the percentage of loss that should be permitted in the purification process. What was returned by the jewellers after purification was accepted, on trust, as accurate. This obviously led to speculation and allegations.

In another transaction, it was revealed in the audit that 14.629 kg of 24-carat gold rakes and 1.938 kg of pure gold (since converted into pure gold) were issued to the contractor between June and December 2010 for gold ornamentation works in respect of Ashtadikpalakars (guardians of the eight directions) on the roof of the Ottakkal mandapam (a single-stone platform). All this gold and semi-finished work has not been received back from the contractor, despite the passage of about ten years.

Ornamental Precious Metal Utensils

Each category of articles made of precious metals was assigned a separate serial number. Gold pots bearing numbers from 1 to 1000 were used for festivals during the period up to July 2002. Thereafter, the pots that were taken out bore numbers from 1001. The fact that the number borne by one of the pots taken out on 1 April 2011 was 1988 was indicative of the reality that there were at least 1,988 pots in the cellars. After melting 822 gold pots for meeting the requirement of gold for ornamentation works, there should have been at least 1,166 gold pots in stock. However, the numbers assigned to the gold pots were from 12-4-1 to 12-4-397, which indicates that there were only 397 gold pots. There was thus a shortage of 769 gold pots with an aggregate weight of 776 kg.

There was another instance of 32.86 kg of gold articles and 570.34 kg of silver lying unaccounted for in the treasurer's room. Retention of gold and silver articles for years, without due issuance and acceptance records, in the custody of the treasurer without being insured, apart from the risk involved, gives rise to the possibility of theft/mismanagement. It is certainly not prudent inventory management.

Unauthorized Opening and Photographing of Contents

It was revealed in the course of audit that, perhaps to create a permanent record of the items available in the vaults, the then trustee decided to make an album of the valuables. The C and D vaults were opened and 1,022 articles were photographed (including 397 pots) in August 2007. However, the whereabouts of the album and the photographs are not known. The temple authorities disowned any knowledge or possession of these photographs, negatives or album. They are not even aware of the agency that did the photography or who met the cost of such photography. At the same time, certain photographs, purportedly pertaining to the temple, are available on the Internet.

There are many stories about attempts to clandestinely sell some of the artefacts. There may be no truth in them. There is no needle-pointing at any particular person in connection with these purported attempts but these facts emerging from the audit lend grist to the rumour mills.

Properties of the Temple and Trust

There is no proper consolidated record of the properties owned by the temple, or which of its properties have been leased. Even where records are available, they are not accurate. The audit team found that the temple authorities were not even aware of encroachment on their property. A spot verification revealed that the area in the temple's possession was much less than the 5.72 acres it was supposed to possess as per records. Secondly, even for property owned by it and leased out, there were no lease/rent agreement. The temple was thus not in a position to enforce any lease or rent agreements. No realization of rent or enhancements could be effected from small shops and buildings in the temple perimeter due to lack of lease/rent agreements. The amount of rent arrears from twenty-six occupants alone was ₹19.25 lakh per annum. These occupants seemed to be defaulters from 2008 onwards, but even this was not verifiable.

Thirdly, an amount of ₹31,998.68, fixed in 1970–71, was receivable by the temple as an allowance from the state government. The government of Tamil Nadu had enhanced this allowance tenfold in 2008 (for properties owned by the temple in what is the state of Tamil Nadu now) but no attempt had been made by the temple administration to get it enhanced by the government of Kerala.

These are some of the issues that seem to have beset the temple and its administration over the years, thereby leading to the conclusion that its management is lax and that it has consequently suffered severe loss of revenue, valuables and real estate.

CORRECTIVE MEASURES

A temple administration, inasmuch as any other administrative structure, must be easy and effective in operation, ensure the integrity of the systems and be premised on an edifice that provides functional efficiency. This particular variety of administration deviates from the conventional corporate structure in that it has to factor in a sizeable chunk of the temple priests and other functionaries who may not have any exposure to any kind of administrative principles and would be guided entirely by religious practices and procedures they hold sacrosanct.

These are the very issues that had been examined and addressed in far more complex and larger bodies, which have to cater to many more devotees, more properties and inaccessibility of shrines. I am referring to the Shri Mata Vaishno Devi Shrine

Board in Jammu, the Tirumala Tirupati Devasthanams (TTD) in Andhra Pradesh, the Sabarimala shrine in Kerala, and the Kedarnath and Badrinath shrines in Uttarakhand. Each has undergone a reform process in its administrative structure such that it is able to ensure that devotees get all facilities for a comfortable darshan, the amenities are modern and pilgrim-friendly, and there is no leakage in the accounting of the offerings to the temple by devotees.

It is, therefore, important to examine the inadequacies seen in the administration of the Shree Padmanabhaswamy temple so as to recommend certain correctives that need to be introduced. They are categorized under five heads in order to address the appropriate activity.

Administrative structure

The administrative structure as existing in the temple is loosely defined. It seemed to have been created on an ad hoc basis, depending on needs as they arose from time to time. It also seemed to have been set up depending upon the reliability or loyalty of the person entrusted to perform a specific task or manage a section of the administration.

It will be most appropriate to provide a two-tier administrative setup to ensure efficient management of the temple administration, which has been tried and tested in similar temples such as the Guruvayur Devaswom and the TTD. The first tier is at the apex level: a managing committee comprising independent, senior and experienced persons having a credible image to ensure that objective and transparent systems are put in place. This administrative committee could be chaired by a retired civil servant of chief secretary rank or a retired chief executive of a large corporate body professing Hindu religious belief. It could have representatives of the royal family, the Kerala government, the thantri (priest) of the temple and two independent prominent citizens. This apex body would comprise people working on a part-time basis, who would take all policy decisions and provide guidance and supervision to the full-time executives. This committee would be serviced by the executive officer of the temple, who should be a senior officer of the government well versed in all aspects of administration.

There should then be a hierarchy of professional managers—headed by an executive officer who is assisted by persons knowledgeable about the professional and religious aspects of the temple administration. They would be from the fields of finance, internal audit, security, civil and electrical maintenance, and stores, vigilance, treasury and data entry specialists. Further, streamlined systems for purchase, maintenance works, vigilance, auction and sales of articles donated to the temple need to be put in place. There is also the need for a well-structured audit system to provide the oversight essential for the credibility of any public body.

Accounting

Good accounting is the backbone of any efficient administration, but the temple suffered from a complete absence of any well-defined accounting structure. In an establishment of the kind that is required for the temple administration, one does not have to reinvent the wheel. Considering the need for efficient and accurate accounting of all transactions in the temple, a very scientific, professional and computer-based simple accounting manual can be devised. This manual would provide for the rigour that needs to be maintained in counting the donations in the hundi (donation box), payment of bills, petty payments and bank reconciliation, physical verification of assets, and accounting for stock of gold, silver and other precious materials, and other valuables.

Gold and silver purification process

A very normal tradition in temples is for devotees to donate gold and silver items. Usually, devotees put their donations anonymously into the hundi. In the case of gold and silver articles, the purity of the donation is not uniform. Quite often, some of these items are damaged and cannot be retained in their current form. In some cases, devotees specifically donate chains, crowns, headgear and the like to adorn the deity. These are used during special occasions.

It is these loose items that need to be handled with care. A norm devised at the Guruvayur Devaswom was to hand over all the gold articles to the government mint for purification and conversion into Guruvayur (Sri Krishna) lockets of five and ten grams to be sold to devotees. This has become a very popular attraction and since the purification and locket-making is done in the government mint, there is no scope for leakage or any suspicion. This is a model that can be followed in the Padmanabhaswamy temple too.

Amenities for Devotees

The temple had always attracted swarms of devotees from the state and local areas. Now that it has come into the limelight for various reasons, including the treasure trove, it is attracting pilgrims and tourists from far-off places as well. However, the facilities available for devotees in and around the temple are woefully inadequate and in a state of disrepair. Male devotees are required to wear dhotis before they enter the temple. For those who do not have dhotis, these are available on sale. However, there is no cloakroom for devotees to change. Even basic toilet facilities are not available. The temple administration needs to create modern cloakroom/freshening-up facilities for men and women. Even guestrooms could be created in the buildings owned by the trust, as available in the Guruvayur temple, where the facilities cater to pilgrims of every income level.

Preservation and Display of Temple Treasure

The temple possesses a huge amount of gold, precious stones, jewellery and antiques. This treasure trove has aroused immense interest among tourists and devotees for its huge value. Some of these artefacts and antiques are centuries old but are not available for public viewing. It is only appropriate that the Lord's possessions are made available to His devotees to see and appreciate. Keeping them locked up in vaults is of no value to either the deity or His ardent devotees. It would be of great attraction if these priceless items are housed in a small, secure and modern museum. Ordinarily, non-Hindus are not permitted to enter the temple premises, but the museum can easily be located on the perimeter, thereby facilitating direct entry from the road for tourists.

An innovative self-financing scheme for the small museum would ensure minimal expense to the temple trust. Charities and donations from devotees could constitute the initial capital investment with a bridging amount, if required, from a financing institution. An annual annuity from the temple budget could repay the loan. The museum would have an appropriately priced ticket, the collection from which would be substantial.

DUAL ACCOUNTABILITY

Social activists and reformers have been at the forefront of movements to ensure that the State remains aloof from the management and administration of temples in the country. The Supreme Court has, however, continuously adjudicated on religious freedom and rights of citizens. Writs have been filed in the Supreme Court to do away with the Hindu Religious and Charitable Endowments Act, 1959, as being unconstitutional and arguing that temples should not be in the clutches of government. There is no doubt in the reasoning that the government, with its manifold other responsibilities, should stay away from the management of temples. However, reforms of the kind that were seen when the Shri Mata Vaishno Devi Shrine Board was formed to take away the administration from the clutches of certain private groups have been a boon for devotees. There is thus a strong case for temple administration to be entrusted to well-regulated and systematically created structures that are independent of the government and managed by a body of experienced professionals.

Such management structures are important, as devotees repose blind faith in deities. They seek to worship their gods not merely to seek favours, but more often for peace of mind. When the devotee comes to worship, quite often to places like Sabarimala or Vaishno Devi, they reach the shrine after an arduous journey. It is the responsibility of those who manage the temple administration to facilitate the darshan. Temple administrations, as much as any corporate body, municipality or government, have a responsibility to ensure that temples are well managed, the premises are kept clean and hygienic, and pilgrims are provided unfettered access to the deity. Any lack of such administration is as much doing injustice to the deity as to the devotee. The other responsibility is to prudently deploy the contribution, in cash or kind, made by the devotee. Not doing so is another failing of the temple authorities.

The temple administration has dual accountability: to the deity and to the devotee. It is required to ensure a transparent, accountable and well-governed administration, in which all principles of efficient management apply. In the case of the Sree Padmanabhaswamy temple, the Lord has protected His treasures, obviously gifted to Him by His ardent admirers, for centuries without putting any burden on others. Now that His treasures have been uncovered, the temple administration has the onerous responsibility of carrying His legacy forward.

12

CASE STUDY

ADARSH COOPERATIVE HOUSING SOCIETY

A Case of the Fence Eating the Crop

A 102-metre-tall, thirty-one-storey building containing about hundred apartments, stands in the Backbay Reclamation area of Colaba, an upmarket locality in south Mumbai, in a Coastal Regulation Zone (CRZ). Permission for housing schemes in CRZ areas is granted only by the Ministry of Environment, Forest and Climate Change (MoEFCC), Government of India. The construction of the building was completed in 2010 but it remains unoccupied. It would be a matter of great surprise as to how such a large building, in such a prominent part of Mumbai, remains unoccupied. The surprise would be greater if one were to discover the names of the high-profile owners of apartments in the building.

To unravel this mystery, one would have to go into the processes (read machinations) resorted to in order to bring about the construction. It is essential to study this case, as it is an outrageous instance of how the very people who are mandated to implement laws to regulate irregular activity fail to do so. Such case studies are landmarks in the process of evolution of good governance and throw light on the fact that the most stringent of laws and regulations are destined to fail when those authorized to apply them neglect them or even collude to ignore them for personal gain and aggrandizement. Further, these delinquents draw courage from their experience that public memory and media attention have a very limited span and, with the passage of time, they will manage to get away with the spoils.

In this particular case, every authority mandated to work for public good, whether selected or elected, colluded in the face of lure for personal profit. A chief minister, who would have taken an oath to serve the people, a chief secretary, who would have sworn by probity and objectivity, and chiefs of the Army and Navy, who are under pledge to place the interests of those they command before their personal interests. Each of these authorities failed miserably and let down those very people whose interests they were to protect.

THE PLOT TAKES SHAPE

Any case study on good governance would need to analyse how this came about—a huge building was constructed in a tony locality in violation of building norms, and no one noticed it while construction was on! We thus need to go into the history of the approval process and evaluate how all the agencies that should have regulated the construction are now claiming that no such permission/approval was ever given by them.

The trail begins with an innocuous letter written on 7 February 2000 by Ramachandra Sonelal Thakur, a sub-divisional officer in the Defence Estates Office (DEO), Mumbai. Though a serving government official, he had written that letter in his capacity as the chief promoter of the Adarsh Cooperative Housing Society (the society had not been registered, it had only been proposed when he wrote the letter) to the chief minister of Maharashtra.

The society was seeking the transfer of about 4,000 sq m of land for the construction of residential accommodation. In the letter, he refers to discussions the society seems to have had with the chief minister. He states that the proposed plot of land is under the occupation of the Army authorities and 'we have negotiated with the local military authorities who have expressed their willingness to allow the society to go ahead with the project if certain amount of accommodation was also provided for army welfare i.e. for girls' hostel for female children of army officers serving in far-flung remote and field areas.'[1]

Upon receipt of the letter, the chief minister sought a report from the revenue department on the proposal (the revenue department is the custodian of all government land in the state). That department thereupon referred the letter from the chief minister's office to the district collector (DC). The DC carried out an inspection of the land. In his report, he said that the land was enclosed by a boundary wall by Army authorities and was under their occupation. He informed the government that he had requested the Army authorities for clarification on the status of the land.

The Army's Maharashtra, Gujarat & Goa (MG&G) area headquarters informed the DC that the land fell 'outside the defence boundary and…necessary action at your end may be taken as deemed fit for the welfare of service personnel/ex-servicemen/their widows'.[2]

On 29 March 2000, the revenue department sought the 'no

---

[1] Report Of The Inquiry Committee Constituted In Pursuance Of Bombay High Court Order Dated 29th April 2016 In WP 452/12 (On The Role Of Defence Officers In The Adarsh Cooperative Housing Society Case); Government of India; Ministry of Defence; https://mod.gov.in/sites/default/files/report24.pdf Accessed on 16 June 2019.
[2] Ibid

objection' of the area headquarters for making this 4,000-sq-m land available for construction purposes, since the land was under their occupation. The area headquarters, displaying remarkable alacrity, on the very next day, wrote to its lower formation (known as the sub-area) and the Defence Estates Officer (DEO), Mumbai, seeking a report by 1 April on the status of the land. Displaying singular haste once again, and without waiting till 1 April, the DEO confirmed on the same day that the land in question 'fell outside the defence boundary and belonged to the government of Maharashtra'. The area headquarters then conveyed this information to the state government on 5 April, and requested the state government to proceed on its own.

It needs to be emphasized at this point that such speedy action in government departments is indeed rare. The reply from the Army evokes surprise on various counts. First, the promptness with which it replied—within six days of receiving the initial letter. Secondly, no authority is ever willing to give up ownership or occupancy of land in its possession. This is a universal phenomenon. Thirdly, a site inspection by the collector had shown that the land in question had been 'walled in' by the military. Yet, they were willing to forgo it.

Nevertheless, let us for the present accept that the promptness displayed by them was a result of their genuine interest in the welfare of serving or retired personnel and their families. Did things indeed progress as projected or were there deviations? In this regard, it is important to examine the role of the Maharashtra government.

WHEN RULES ARE MADE TO BE BENT

The request of the society did indeed evoke unusually rapid responses from every desk its proposals passed through within the state government. The DC's report on 12 May had mentioned that the land in question, though in the possession of the Army, was earmarked for widening of the existing road by the Mumbai Metropolitan Region Development Authority (MMRDA) and hence its approval would have to be taken if it were to be allotted to the society. The society seemed to have discussed this issue with the then minister of revenue (Ashok Chavan at that time, who later became the chief minister), as they wrote to him on 2 June, referring to a meeting with him.

In the same letter, the society stated that it would be willing to leave an area of about ten to fifteen feet for widening of the road. It clarified that though the area was in the vicinity of the military area, there was no proposal from the military to widen the road. To bolster its case, it added the standard phrase which seemed to have become the sole driving factor speeding up the society's request, viz. 'to accommodate and reward our heroes of Kargil operation who bravely fought at Kargil to protect our Motherland'.[3]

The specific request to the revenue minister was to allot this particular piece of land, which, though in the possession of the military authorities, they did not have any proposal to utilize for road-widening. This proposal of the society was accepted in principle by the revenue department and after following due procedure of calling for objections and so on, the Urban Development Department (UDD) approved a modification to the MMRDA development plan. It also agreed to waive 60.97 m from the width of the road leading to the south Colaba harbour link and decrease the width of the adjacent Captain Prakash Pethe

---

[3] Report Of The Inquiry Committee Constituted In Pursuance Of Bombay High Court Order Dated 29th April 2016 In WP 452/12 (On The Role Of Defence Officers In The Adarsh Cooperative Housing Society Case); Government of India; Ministry of Defence; https://mod.gov.in/sites/default/files/report24.pdf
Accessed on 16 June 2019.

Marg from 60.97 m to 18.4 m. The waived area was added to the residential zone. Thus, the width of a public road was drastically reduced to provide more residential land!

This was in contrast to the stand taken by the MMRDA earlier, as the audit report of the CAG found, in a request made by the Zila Sainik Board in Mumbai for allotment of the same land for construction of a rest house.[4] That request had twice been turned down by the Maharashtra government on the grounds that the land was required for the widening of the same road!

This is a classic case of a master plan being amended so that a stretch of land earmarked for road-widening is converted into residential land to facilitate the housing project of a society.

In his report, the DC had also suggested that the membership of the society first be approved by the government. The list of members, as initially submitted by the society to the collector, comprised twenty persons. However, there was pressure to include additional members. In view of the DC's suggestion, the issue of membership of the society was discussed with the then revenue minister, wherein it was proposed that 40 per cent of the membership of the society should comprise civilians. Thus, of the total at that time (forty), nineteen members could be civilians, whereas thirty-one would be from the armed forces.

This decision was promptly accepted by the society, in writing, on the very day of the meeting and the membership was fixed at nineteen civilians and thirty-one defence personnel. It was only then, apparently, that the government proceeded to examine the earlier mentioned proposal for grant of additional land from the adjacent plot for residential purposes.

By January 2003, when the revenue and forest departments of the Maharashtra government issued a letter of intent to the society regarding the allotment of additional land and conversion

---

[4]Report of the CAG on Adarsh Cooperative Housing Society, Mumbai

of it to residential land, the membership of the society had swelled to seventy-one.

Clearly, a society that started with only defence personnel as members soon not only took on an increasing number of civilian members, but the number of civilians had surpassed the defence members within two years. By the time the building was nearing completion, the defence members numbered half the civilians. This contrasts with the earlier decision that civilians were to be only 40 per cent of the total membership.

At the rate at which the membership of the society was increasing, members soon realized that it was not possible to accommodate all of them within the available area and the permissible floor space index (FSI). Hence, they applied to the UDD for an increase in the FSI. The modus operandi adopted was to seek addition of the FSI of the adjacent vacant plot, which was under the occupation of the Brihanmumbai Electricity Supply & Transport Undertaking (B.E.S.T.), a public-sector company. This request was made on 12 July 2004. Two days later, a meeting was convened by the minister of urban development to examine the feasibility of this request. In the meeting, the then principal secretary of the UDD pointed out that the additional FSI sought by the society from the adjacent plot of land was not feasible, unless that plot was de-reserved.

Meanwhile, the Adarsh Cooperative Housing Society was formally registered on 28 September 2004, and the plot of land that had been originally sought was handed over to them in October. It was then that the activity for de-reservation of the adjacent plot, which was under the possession of B.E.S.T., gained momentum. In October, B.E.S.T. indicated in writing that the plot was needed by it for providing access to the bus depot and hence it would not recommend its de-reservation. The minister of urban development convened another meeting in December that year to discuss this issue. But B.E.S.T. continued to raise its objection.

Yet another meeting was convened by the minister on 5 January 2005. In this meeting, the principal secretary of the UDD stated that the plot of land in B.E.S.T possession was government land and if B.E.S.T., a public commercial undertaking, wanted it as an access for their depot, it would have to bear the cost of the land at the prevailing market rate. This was clearly an arm-twisting tactic, since payment of market rate would have imposed a very heavy financial burden on B.E.S.T.

On 11 January 2005, the PSU left the decision to the government, requesting that their interests be protected in permitting the existing access. Sadly, this faith of B.E.S.T. in the government was belied, and on 5 August the government allowed the additional FSI of the land under B.E.S.T. possession to be transferred to the society. The CAG audit report records that the son of the principal secretary of the UDD had by then been enrolled as a member of the society!

Interestingly, while approving the plan of the society building in September 2005 and January 2008, the MMRDA had deducted 15 per cent FSI for recreational ground. The society had sought release of this FSI in June 2006, but this was rejected by the government. The society began to repeatedly approach the government for release of this FSI also by quoting instances in the Backbay Reclamation area where recreational ground was not deducted from individual plots.

Finally, in July 2009, the then chief minister approved this long-standing proposal not to deduct the area of the recreational ground from the FSI granted to the society. The CAG audit report (p.20) points out that by May 2009, the name of the collector, Mumbai city, who was dealing with the case, was also added to the membership list of the society.

ENVIRONMENTAL CLEARANCE: NO MAJOR HURDLE!

It is alleged that the building was constructed in violation of the Environment (Protection) Act of 1986 and the CRZ regulations on the following counts:

1. The building does not have the prior permission required under the CRZ notification, 1991, of the GoI, and
2. It uses higher than permitted FSI of 1.77, as against the permissible FSI of 1.33 applicable for that area.

The land in question was located in the CRZ notified by the Government of India in 1991. Any construction in such a zone, as per an amendment to this order in 2002, required the clearance of the MoEFCC. The clearance was sought by the state government from the Government of India, claiming that it proposed to allot this plot for 'construction of welfare and housing facility to serving and ex-servicemen of defence services'. This letter was issued by the UDD of the state without the knowledge of the environment department or the Maharashtra Coastal Zone Management Authority (MCZMA). Besides, the letter was factually incorrect, since the state government had not yet decided to allot the plot to the society (the letter of intent was issued only in January 2003). It was also not true that the allotment was for serving and ex-service personnel.

The MoEFCC, usually a very zealous protector of its turf, wrote back on 11 March 2003, stating that the plot in question fell within the CRZ 2, for which the central government had already delegated powers to the state government (MCZMA) for regulating construction activity in that zone. Within four days of receipt of this very conveniently worded letter from the Government of India, the state UDD promptly wrote, on 15 March, to the municipal corporation, stating that 'the ministry of environment has communicated their "no objection" to allow the said residential development since it falls within the CRZ 2 area, which satisfies the norms of notification of 1991, and amendments made in 2002. Now, there appears, therefore, no objection to allow the residential development to the Adarsh Cooperative Housing Society on the land included in the residential zone as per the notifications sanctioned by the government.' This again was an assertion which was not true, since the central government had merely pointed to its falling in the CRZ 2, the powers to regulate which had been delegated to the state government (through the MCZMA). The proposal, in fact, was never placed before the MCZMA.

The lax reply from the Government of India and the misleading interpretation of the letter by P.V. Deshmukh of the UDD helped the society overcome the rather rigid processes of environmental clearance. Again, purely coincidentally (I presume), Deshmukh had also been enrolled as a member of the society!

SHAMELESS TALE OF BLATANT VIOLATIONS

But there were more hurdles that had to be crossed. As per a notification under the CRZ, any building to be constructed in that area must be subject to the existing local town and country planning regulations. The regulation prevalent was the Development Control Rules, 1967 (DCR, 1967). These rules did not permit 'the construction of any building in that zone to a height which was more than one-and-a-half times the sum of the width of the streets on which it abuts and the width of the open space between the street and the building as measured from the level of the centre of the street in front'. The sum total of the interpretation of this regulation for the proposed building was that its height could not exceed 45.6 metres. This regulation had to be read with the DCR, 1991, which did not impose any height restriction but decreased the FSI from 3.5 to 1.33.

However, the reduction of FSI had already been circumvented by the society. It was rather odd that the society and the government were consistently interpreting both the restrictions in favour of the society and allowing it to circumvent both, viz. the DCR, 1967, and the DCR, 1991, by using the FSI of the neighbouring plot.

Around this time, independent of this proposal, the government of Maharashtra set up a High Rise Committee, chaired by a retired chief justice of the Tamil Nadu High Court, to scrutinize the approvals granted for all buildings proposed of a height exceeding 70 m. Adarsh Society had put up a proposal for constructing a building of twenty-seven floors (stilt+two-level podium+twenty-seven floors) with a height of 97.6 m. This proposal was accepted by the committee, as the MMRDA had recommended that the marginal open spaces and parking proposal were in accordance with the DCR, 1991. The chief engineer issued a No Objection Certificate (NOC) to the society on 1 September 2007.

The society commenced its construction. It was not content with the approval given for twenty-seven floors and went ahead and constructed twenty-eight floors, to a height of 100.7 m. How it derived the confidence that it would indeed get approval for the additional floor it was constructing from the High Rise Committee is inexplicable. It probably had influential backers. The society maintained that whilst the NOC was issued for a height of 97.6 m on 1 September, the structural design that had been submitted to the committee was for a height of 103.4 m. They thus argued that there was no need for the plan to be placed before the committee again.

The deputy chief engineer of the municipal corporation recommended 'that whilst the total approved plan is for stilt+two-level podium+27 upper floors up to a height of 97.60 metres, the height up to the top of the elevator machine room is 102.80 metres and height up to the top of overhead tank is 104.60 metres and the high rise committee has granted approval to a height of 97.60 metres up to the terrace floor level as per the approved plan. As such there is no necessity to obtain fresh NOC from the high-rise committee.'[5]

One can hardly make sense of this recommendation, let alone appreciate its technical logic. However, the municipal commissioner saw wisdom in this argument of the deputy chief engineer, and approved the proposal of the society. Of course, purely coincidentally again, the son of the municipal commissioner became a member of the society and hence the allottee of an apartment. The membership of the society had by then grown to 100.

The eventual position that emerged was that the NOC granted was up to the twenty-seventh floor, including the machine room and overhead tank, with a height of 104.45 metres. After construction of the twenty-eighth floor, the total height of the building had become 107.55 metres and yet it was felt by the very authorities mandated to check such rampant violation that another reference to the High Rise Committee was not necessary.

YET ANOTHER SAGA OF UNSCRUPULOUS GREED

The society also went about circumventing the income eligibility conditions. The society was to allot 650-sq-ft apartments to persons with an income limit not exceeding ₹12,500 per month. No income limit had, however, been prescribed for apartments with a carpet area of 1,076 sq ft. Most conveniently, the society had decided to construct apartments of that size. Initially, the society had submitted a list of twenty members, which later became forty-one. This list was sent by the government to the collector for verification of eligibility. The collector, in his

---

[5]Report of the CAG on Adarsh Cooperative Housing Society, Mumbai

communication dated 18 March 2004, had stated that out of the forty-one members only nineteen were eligible.

Meanwhile, news of the society taking shape and the building being planned was spreading. Since the building was located in a very prominent and upmarket area, more people were keen to seek membership. But the income limit prescribed for eligibility of members was becoming a constraint. On the persuasion of some influential members, the government was prevailed upon, in February 2005, to relax the income limit, as well as to waive the requirement of domicile, in respect of retired state government employees and serving and retired armed forces personnel from Maharashtra. In May 2003, due to the obvious attractiveness of possessing a unit in this apartment building, a member of the Maharashtra legislative council approached the government seeking a relaxation of this income limit for ex-servicemen, ostensibly as a 'good gesture to our brave soldiers'. The relaxation was granted, and thus enabled many serving and retired officers to become members.

The society continued to be persuaded by various authorities to take on additional members. In June 2009, the state government issued an order permitting two generals, who were former chiefs of army staff, to become members of the society. It may be recalled that in its first communication, the chief promoter of the society had sought land for, among other persons, a hostel for daughters of officers serving in far-flung places. No such accommodation was provided. But more surprisingly, the defence authorities did not seem to miss the absence of any such provision either.

Another huge concession provided to the society was that the government of Maharashtra, on 9 July 2004, had accorded sanction for transfer of the land to the society by levying a minimum total charge of ₹10.19 crore for the plot. This implied a share of barely ₹10 lakh per member—for land in Colaba! This rate was a mere 10 per cent of the prevailing market rate in that area.

The modus operandi clearly had become one of providing membership to any official who was raising an objection to the various approvals that the society was seeking. It was also additionally taking influential persons as members, who would help open doors of higher authorities to get clearances. The society and the proposed building had clearly become the cynosure of all eyes.

THE LAW FINALLY CATCHES UP

The machinations associated with the functioning of the society did not escape public attention. There were allegations in the media every day, followed by demands in the legislative assembly for a commission of inquiry. The National Alliance of People's Movements led by Medha Patkar started a major campaign demanding a commission of inquiry to probe the alleged wrongdoings of the society and the substantial concessions given by the government. The movement alleged quid pro quo in all clearances granted to the Adarsh Cooperative Housing Society.

As a consequence of growing public pressure, in January 2011, the government was compelled to institute a two-member commission of inquiry under the chairmanship of a retired judge, Justice J.A. Patil, to examine the alleged irregularities related to the society. It was to examine various aspects such as the ownership of the land on which the building had come up, whether it was reserved for Kargil war widows, whether the adjacent road was narrowed down, the relaxation in height restriction, if any, whether there was any violation of CRZ notifications and whether public servants had been on the wrong side of the law. The panel was to submit its report within three months.

Meanwhile, the heat had caught up with former revenue minister Chavan, who had by then become chief minister. It was found that his relatives, including his mother-in-law, owned three flats and it was Chavan who had given the nod to the society as revenue minister and even approved the sale of 40 per cent flats to civilians.[6] Several RTI queries also revealed that a number of bureaucrats who facilitated approvals at every stage got flats registered in the names of their children—a glaring example of quid pro quo. Chavan was forced to resign as chief minister on 9 November 2010. In 2011, the CBI registered an FIR against Chavan and thirteen others for criminal conspiracy and under various sections of the Prevention of Corruption Act (PCA) and filed a charge sheet against them in July 2012.[7] In a later decision in 2017, the High Court dismissed the governor's sanction to prosecute Chavan.

The commission of inquiry, which was to have submitted its report in three months, finally did so in 2013, after having been granted eight extensions of its original tenure. In its findings, the commission reported that the land belonged to the government of Maharashtra and not the Ministry of Defence (MoD) and that the land or membership of the society was not in effect reserved for either housing for defence personnel or Kargil war heroes. Its salient findings were:

1. At present the list of members stands at 103, out of which only 37 members belong to the army and out of that too, only 3 members are related to the Kargil war.
2. The following concessions were found to have been inappropriately given to the Society:
    - The categorisation of the plot was modified from Transit Camp/Parade Ground to residential.

---

[6]'Ashok Chavan got three flats for in-laws for clearing Adarsh'; *The Indian Express*; 23 July 2012; http://archive.indianexpress.com/news/-ashok-chavan-got-three-flats-for-inlaws-for-clearing-adarsh-/978088/ Accessed on 16 June 2019.

[7]Ibid

- A road of width 60 metres was reduced to 19 metres to provide land to the society.
- FSI of the adjoining bus depot was irregularly given to the Adarsh Society.
- 15 per cent of the area was permitted to be used for commercial purpose rather than residential.
- The income ceiling of ₹12,500 per month was waived for all, to facilitate entry of members who were otherwise ineligible.
- Construction started without obtaining environmental clearance.
- Occupation certificate was awarded even before the building was fully ready.[8]

The commission revealed in its findings that there were twenty-two benami (fictitious or proxy) transactions benefiting beneficiaries who could, by no stretch of imagination, ever dream of owning an apartment in Mumbai. The startling list of beneficiaries includes a driver from Nagpur who had never visited Mumbai and a roadside vegetable vendor. Among other beneficiaries, the commission indicted four former chief ministers, one former chief secretary (whose son had been allotted an apartment), and several other additional chief secretaries and secretaries. After recording its finding, the closing comments of the commission are highly revealing in their castigation:

> Adarsh is not a saga of ideal cooperation but it is a shameless tale of blatant violations of statutory provisions, rules and regulations. It reflects greed, nepotism and

---

[8]'Adarsh Corruption Society: : Tale of a Scam'; JAL—Serving and Preserving Humanity; 17 February 2011; http://socialactivistjal.blogspot.com/2011/02/adarsh-corruption-society-tale-of-scam.html Accessed on 18 July 2019.

favouritism on the part of some people who were, in one way or the other, associated with the Adarsh CHS. It is a sad story of unscrupulous greed of some persons closely connected with the said society. It is found that some persons not being satisfied with allotment of a single flat in the said society, have tried and succeeded in securing flats for their nears and dears. For this purpose, they went even to the extent of making benami transactions in violation of the provisions of the Benami Transactions (Prohibition) Act, 1988. That such an episode should take place in the progressive state of Maharashtra is a matter of deep regret.[9]

In 2010, after a spate of media reports about alleged wrongdoings in the Adarsh Society, there was a flurry of activity, including a PIL filed in the Bombay High Court questioning the height clearance given in a sensitive area. The matter was also taken up by the CBI and notices were issued by the MoEFCC, leading to multiple cases being filed in the High Court. A criminal case was filed in a special CBI court. The government of Maharashtra and the civic administration revoked the occupation certificate granted in September 2010 as well as the water and electricity supplies to the building. No member had begun to reside in the building yet.

In January 2011, the MoEFCC had passed an order to raze the building within three months as it was 'unauthorized', since it violated coastal zone regulations. The society members approached the High Court, challenging that order, and sought a stay on the demolition order, which was granted till the Court took a final view. Finally, in April 2016, the High Court pronounced its order

---

[9]Justice J.A. Patil Commission Final Report Adarsh Scam; https://www.scribd.com/document/249714320/Justice-J-A-Patil-Commission-Final-Report-Adarsh-Scam
Accessed on 16 June 2019.

directing the demolition of the thirty-one-storey structure. The Court also directed that the state initiate criminal proceedings against officers involved and restore the land to the Maharashtra government. The MoD was directed to initiate a departmental inquiry against its officers for not taking action earlier. Meanwhile, the society sought a three-month stay on the demolition order so that they could appeal in the Supreme Court. This stay was granted.

The scene of action then shifted to the Supreme Court. The apex court in July 2016 directed the centre to take possession of the building. As of now, the building is in the possession of the central government and the CBI inquiry is on.

WHY ADARSH IS A LIVING EXAMPLE

It is said that the *Mahabharata* included all kinds of characters who could possibly exist in the world—good, bad and ugly. The Adarsh saga is similar but with the difference that the 'good' turned 'bad' the moment opportunity beckoned. It encompasses every kind of irregularity: nepotism, greed and display of qualities highly unbecoming of persons in positions of authority. There is clear evidence of ignoring the norm for personal aggrandizement and benefit. The commission constituted by the Maharashtra government found evidence of quid pro quo on the part of chief ministers, chief secretaries, principal secretaries, municipal commissioners, diplomats, district magistrates, senior armed forces officers and the like. There are twenty-two instances of benami transactions; twenty-five of the 102 applicants were found to be ineligible. It is also a truly remarkable case of egalitarianism, when two former chiefs of the armed forces are owners of apartments alongside a driver, a vegetable vendor and a peon.

The other factor which turned out to be highly questionable was the manner in which chiefs of the Army and the Navy, who are expected to be role models and lead from the front and for whom the welfare of the people they command is supposed to be foremost, stooped to snatch apartments which were ostensibly meant for 'Kargil war widows'. This was a naked display of greed, which should not go unpunished, as its effect on the morale of the armed forces is deeply distressing.

It is most unfortunate that, of the officers indicted by the MoD inquiry, only a handful of middle-ranking officers are undergoing criminal prosecution. This is the vulnerability of the system. To ensure that probity and integrity prevail in the government and the armed forces, an example needs to be set by prosecuting the most senior among the delinquents—whether in the political executive, the civilian bureaucracy or the armed forces. The government would be failing in its duty to check corruption if the highest in the land go unpunished and lowly officials are made scapegoats for a plot conceptualized, navigated and realized by the personal greed of those that these officials have to look up to. What is happening now is a travesty of justice—the Army chief goes scot-free while his underlings are prosecuted; the chief minister gets away while middle-level politicos are prosecuted; and the chief secretary goes unpunished while small-time deputy commissioners are prosecuted. Good governance prevails when the norms, regulations and laws of the land are applied equally at all levels.

These lessons cannot be ignored. It would be criminal not to devise safeguards against similar skulduggery in future. The penalty should be exemplary, as those very persons mandated to safeguard government property or holding authority misused it for personal aggrandizement. Allotment of a finite national resource should be done in a transparent manner. It is not enough for a government department to profess transparency; such transparency should be visible in all its actions. It is the burden that a government official carries the moment he takes up that assignment. Hence, when the process for such actions commences, viz. change in classification of land allotted, the concerned authority must publicly display the intent through the media. These days government departments have websites. They must clearly declare the intent of the administration. Next, the list of beneficiaries must be prominently displayed for anyone having an objection to raise it. Lastly, the penalty for the wrongdoer should be swift, exemplary and demonstrative.

There has been substantial debate on whether the building should be demolished or retained. It is undeniable that the building stands in a prohibited area. However, considerable quantities of resources such as cement, steel, bricks and other fixtures like electrical and plumbing fittings have been used in the structure. These are resources that the nation can hardly afford to lose. At the same time, while sentiments dictate its demolition, the cost of demolition will be huge. How can the wrongdoers be compelled to bear the cost of demolition when the highest among them are not even being prosecuted? And why should the State bear the cost of demolition? I would strongly advocate its retention because there is always a shortage of accommodation in the government. The building should be confiscated by the State and handed over to the armed forces for allotment to its personnel. This will marginally mitigate the shortage.

We need also to be cognizant of the opportunity cost of the construction. All the material and resources used, the cost of investigation and appointment of the commission have been a terrible drain of government time and material resources. They should not be wasted. The same resources could have been put to some legitimate use elsewhere. Hence, demolishing the building would be a double whammy.

I would also argue for the greater 'moral or psychological' pressure that the retention of the building would bring to bear since it would serve as a standing testimony of the folly committed. Let them see it every day, as a living monument to the fiend within them and the malfeasance and devilry that egged them on to commit a misdeed that has brought so much ignominy upon them. Adarsh, the wicked joke that they tried to play on people in the name of Kargil widows and girls' hostel for soldiers serving in far-flung areas, should make them die a million moral deaths. Razing the building would be like erasing their misdeeds.

In a globally networked world, where capital, labour and enterprise move irrespective of geographical frontiers, the distinguishing factor is always how well the State is administered. Foreign investors, businessmen and enterprise gravitate to domains where fair play, rule of law and equality of opportunity prevail. Development and economic growth need to be nurtured by good governance, both in corporate structures as well as in the government. It is only with good governance that long-term sustainability of such economic growth can be ensured. It also ensures the build-up of trust between a government and its people. Discriminatory application of the laws of the land between the influential and rich and the deprived and poor leads to the erosion of this trust and a breakdown in the desire to be 'law-abiding' in the common man. Good governance ensures the sustainability and equal distribution of the fruits of economic development.

Good governance is the exercise of power and authority by the institutions of the State as mandated by the Constitution for channelizing resources towards the welfare and economic development of citizens. Accountability of public functionaries is an integral part of any good governance architecture and it extends far beyond mere compliance with legal obligations and maintenance of probity on their part. The test of accountability is the efficient delivery of public services and their outreach to the citizen at the end of the delivery channel. Accountability, in its broadest sense today, is recognized as inclusive of equity and justice, fairness and transparency, participation and empowerment. It is crucial for the government and its functionaries to display such transparency and accountability as they act on behalf of the citizens and it is on them that the common man has bestowed the right to represent him and act on his behalf.

To betray this trust is criminal.

EPILOGUE

Towards Robust and Participative Governance

The nation awaited the dawn of 23 May 2019 with, veritably, bated breath. The counting of votes cast in general election 2019 was scheduled for that day. And, as that memorable day progressed, it left in its wake a vast swathe of varied responses to the political developments. Those responses brought to my mind Charles Dickens's haunting lines in *A Tale of Two Cities*:

> It was the age of wisdom, it was the age of foolishness, it was the epoch of belief, it was the epoch of incredulity, it was the season of Light, it was the season of Darkness, it was the spring of hope, it was the winter of despair, we had everything before us, we had nothing before us....

The mood encapsulated by Dickens is an astonishingly apt description of the week following the declaration of the results of the general election. No words by this author could reflect the temper of those days better, no matter from which side of the political divide one viewed the events that unfolded.

In the run-up to the election, much was said and discussed about India's institutions. The ECI was under relentless onslaught; the CAG was being attacked; the Supreme Court got its share of veiled barbs; and the bureaucracy and civil service were facing the usual blitzkrieg that accompanies an election. Persons and agencies vented their ire against institutions for 'not delivering to their dictates'.

There is nothing unusual in this trend. It is the new normal. It has become the done thing to attack institutions simply for performing their duty!

But it goes to the credit of these robust institutions that they have managed to survive the onslaught. It needs to be recognized by politicians, as well as citizens, that governance is best served by allowing institutions the autonomy and independence mandated for them. It also needs to be recognized by the political executive that these institutions have been created by them, and the autonomy vested in them is by the legislature itself.

The tendency of any government that comes to power is to appoint its so-called 'confidants' to head the institutions, in the anticipation that they will toe the government's line. However, the experience has been that once in the chair, the appointees have invariably maintained the sanctity of the institution, displaying the professional integrity required of them. In fact, repeated attempts to cramp their functioning have met with a push-back. One such attempt was narrated in the foregoing pages, describing the attempt to dilute certain aspects of the CIC.

The institutional autonomy of prominent organizations is espoused by every political outfit which is not in government. However, once they get voted to power, this issue is promptly relegated to cold storage! But, considering that these institutions form the bedrock of good governance and thus have a direct bearing on the accountability that a citizen can hold their government to, their autonomy derives special significance.

It has been argued in the chapters on the CBI and the RBI that the effectiveness of the institutions depends on the maturity, acumen and competence of the occupants of their highest posts.

This has been amply borne out by the changes effected in the top echelons of the respective organizations. With all the turmoil that the CBI was going through, after the appointment of the new director (January 2019), calm has prevailed and business has gone on with no more media 'scoops' (which had become a daily phenomenon). The same calm was seen after the appointment of the new governor of the RBI (December 2018), which had been subject to repeated 'breaking news' alerts of news channels, with reams of newsprint devoted to opinions of experts crawling out of every nook and cranny, on the much-hyped differences with the government over policy formulation.

In fact, in a press conference on 6 June 2019, to explain the quarterly policy stance, the RBI governor stressed that the monetary policy committee (comprising government and bank officials) had unanimously arrived at all the decisions. The very same officials had been reportedly at loggerheads ahead of the meeting scheduled on 14 December 2018! These examples underline the fact that it is not the structure of the institution that needs to be faulted but the personnel fleshing out that structure.

Much mud-slinging has taken place over the integrity and objectivity of the ECI. The EVMs were maligned by various 'bandhans' and political outfits. There was much acrimony over the counting of votes, with delegations suddenly realizing that VVPAT votes needed to be counted before the EVM votes. The drama continued until the day prior to counting and seemed to have infiltrated the ECI too.

Thankfully, the ECI maintained its equanimity and continued with the pre-determined procedure and carried out the mandatory random matching of EVM and VVPAT counts of five per assembly segment as directed by the Supreme Court, post the counting of EVM votes. The results were remarkable. Not a single mismatch between the EVM and VVPAT counts—over 20,000 counts. The humble EVM had acquitted itself. The ECI had yet again proven itself to be the custodian of democratic freedom and processes in this vast country, where nearly 900 million votes had been cast, with about 1.2 million election officials performing their duty with commitment to their mandate.

Is it, then, fair to blame the institutions? They will deliver. They have delivered. We need merely to give them the freedom to deliver. In the final analysis, it needs to be recognized that in a parliamentary democracy, since ultimate accountability is that of the Parliament and the elected representatives, the political executive is indeed supreme and possesses the ultimate power over regulatory institutions.

A final word, about the greatest gift we Indians have— the gift of democracy. It is a system of the people, by the people and for the people. And it is we the people who vote our representatives to the Parliament. It is these representatives that we need to hold accountable, even if it be once in five years, for the trust reposed in them. It thus follows as a natural corollary that accountability rests with an elected government. Since the Parliament has created institutions and has granted them autonomy, there needs to be an obligation for transparency and full disclosure from them in return. There needs to be a national debate on the functioning of these institutions to ascertain whether they can withstand public scrutiny, with stringent standards of transparency and objectivity. Whilst functional autonomy is a sine qua non for the quality of governance, robust checks and balances must be built into the institutional architecture. In an age of technological dynamism, processes and systems can easily be built to ensure that the institutions are held to account for the functions they are mandated to perform. Without such checks, whether it is the Parliament, the executive, constitutional institutions or even the Supreme Court, these institutions will fall prey to the corroding influence of unbridled power.

ACKNOWLEDGEMENTS

As I settle down with my laptop to acknowledge the debt owed to all the persons who have helped in my journey to analyse the working of the robust public institutions of India, I realize the twists and turns that this journey has taken. This manuscript should have been completed a year back. However, in recording the capacity of the institutions to so effectively meet with the onslaught rendered unto them, from inside and outside, I kept trying to play catch up in being contemporary with the goings-on. By the time I could incorporate the resilience of the Election Commission over the pressures exerted on it in the course of the Gujarat Rajya Sabha elections, the Supreme Court was facing a crisis of sorts from within and by its own.

No sooner was the chapter on that updated, the CBI began to provide drama of its own. Things were moving at such a rapid pace that even catch-up was proving difficult. Then there was the episode of the governor of the Reserve Bank suddenly resigning. Soon the heat and dust of the elections to the Parliament commenced.

The delay notwithstanding, it has been a fascinating experience. Public institutions of India that we take for granted without giving a thought to the challenges they face are indeed an edifice we need to be proud of. In being proud of them, there is also a reciprocal duty that we have to perform. It is the moral and bounden duty of every citizen to take an oath to 'preserve, protect and strengthen' these institutions. They are as much for 'we the people' as democracy is 'of the people, by the people and for the people'. If democracy has to sustain economic development and if economic development has to ensure the welfare of the people on a sustainable basis, each one of these institutions must prosper and contribute to good governance.

The idea for this project came to me from the Institute of South Asian Studies (ISAS) which has encouraged me, in the winter of my career, to think freely, think constructively and record for posterity the results of such introspection. The lead was taken by Mr Gopinath Pillai, the 'young' octogenarian chairman of the institute, who has been a pillar of strength. The former director, Subrata Mitra, was very encouraging. C. Raja Mohan, the director, has been very supportive of the project from the time I discussed it with him. My colleagues in the institute, who guided and lent me their expert opinion, have been part of this treatise. Dr S. Narayan, Dr D. Subba Rao, Dr Amitendu Palit, Dr Ronojoy Sen, Hernaikh Singh, Sithara and so many younger colleagues have been useful sounding boards. To each one of them, named and not named, I owe a debt of gratitude. Dr Partha Pratim Mitra, my colleague from my finance ministry days, provided very useful inputs. Thanks, Partha, you are doing a great service in the skilling and employability space.

My publishers, Rupa Publications, led by the young and capable Kapish Mehra, kept exhorting me. Yamini Chowdhury, the senior commissioning editor, a quintessential headmistress, persevered with me, seeing this work to completion. Thank you, Kapish, you have been a great source of encouragement and I suspect you will not let me rest even after this book. And to you, Yamini, thank you! You did succeed in getting work out of a rapidly ageing guy. My thanks also to my friend, Vasundhara Raj Baigra, Yana Banerjee-Bey, and each one in the Rupa family who have the onerous task of editing what I write. And the even more onerous task of selling what I write. Dr Asim Chowdhury helped me with a great deal of primary research. Thank you, Asim.

Last but not the least, I owe immense gratitude to my wife, Geeta, who harboured the suspicion that my laptop was probably getting greater affection from me. Though I secretly felt that my being busy at my desk greatly helped her hone her skills at golf, which she did not play too often—only eight days a week! Our children, residing in different parts of the globe, wonder why I give so much of time and importance to my post-retirement career! I suspect they whisper to each other that the old man is going bonkers in believing he will become an author of repute!

Finally, I have taken the risk of airing my opinions very freely in the book. Our Constitution provides us that freedom of speech, thought and expression. I hope I have not stretched that liberty too much. I take sole responsibility for the views expressed. I request the readers to take it in the spirit of yet another voice in the cacophony that goes around. With this request, and advance apology in case I have been remiss anywhere, I commend this book to you. For you to read and ruminate over its contents and consider if our institutions are under any kind of threat and whether you are doing your bit to preserve them.

INDEX

Aam Aadmi Party (AAP), 63
Accountability institution, 4, 117
Adarsh Cooperative Housing Society, 250, 257
    case study on, 245
    environmental clearance, 252–253
Adityanath, Yogi, 51
Administrative Reforms Commission (ARC), 146
Aircel Maxis FDI, 173
All India Council of Sports (AICS), 203
Allahabad High Court, 35, 36, 130, 181
All-India Service, 140
    administrative, 141
    forest, 141
    police, 141
All-India Services (Conduct) Rules, 184
Allotment of spectrum, 41
Ambedkar, B.R., 3
An Undocumented Wonder, 56, 65
Andhra Pradesh High Court, 132
Annual Appraisal Reports of officers, 155
Annual Report of the Commission, 174
Anti-Defection Act, 1985, 69
Apex council, 214
Archery Association of India (AAI), 201
Army authorities, 246
Army's Maharashtra, Gujarat & Goa (MG&G), 246
Association of Unified Telecom Service Providers of India, 102
A Tale of Two Cities, 267

Athletics Federation of India (AFI), 201
Auction process, 40
Audit
    compliance, 100
    financial, 100
    performance, 100, 101
Audit Act of (1971), 109
Audit and Accounts Department, 100

Badminton Association of India (BAI), 201
Bahujan Samaj Party (BSP), 67
Ballot box, 71
Bank for International Settlements (BIS), 90
Bank of England, 78
Bank of Japan, 78
Banks Board Bureau (BBB), 174
BCCI case, 43
BCCI secretary, 213
Bharat Sanchar Nigam Limited (BSNL), 198
Bharatiya Janata Party (BJP), 51
Blue Book, 182
Bombay Hindu Union Cricket Club, 204
Brihanmumbai Electricity Supply & Transport Undertaking (B.E.S.T.), 250
British administration, 180
British Broadcasting Corporation (BBC), 64

CAG's argument, 40
CAG audit report, 18, 251
Calcutta Cricket Club, 204
Calcutta Football Club, 204
Carbide chief executive officer (CEO), 130
Central Board for Secondary Education (CBSE), 170
Central Bureau of Investigation (CBI), 51, 120
  2G spectrum allocation case, 127
  Aarushi murder case, 129
  Bofors case, 130
  fodder scam, 130
  Hyderabad-based businessman, 124
  politicization of, 128
Central Information Commission (CIC), 186–190
Central Services, 141
Central vigilance commissioner, 123
  Act (2003), 133, 169, 172
Chennai Super Kings (CSK), 209
Chidambaram, P., 82
Chief Election Commissioner, 54, 57, 58
Chief financial officer (CFO), 208
Chief vigilance officer (CVO), 169
Chief Justice of India, 24, 25
  method of appointment of, 26
Civil Service Conduct Rules (1964), 180
Civil Service Reform Bill, 161
Civil Services Day, 142
Coal blocks
  captive, 40
  government allotment, 39–42
Coal India Limited (CIL), 40
Coal mine allocations, 121
Coal mine blocks, 41
Coalition governments, 144
Coastal Regulation Zone (CRZ), 244
Code of Criminal Procedure (CrPC), 148
Colaba harbour link, 248
Collegium system, 29–31
  functioning, 30
Committee of administrators (CoA), 200
Committee on Public Undertakings (COPU), 111
Commonwealth Games, 201
Commonwealth Human Rights Initiative (CHRI), 195
Communist Party of India (CPI), 148
Compliance audit, 100
Compressed natural gas (CNG), 41
Comptroller and Auditor General, 100
  origin, 96–98
  pillars of good governance, 98–103
  social accountability gains, 103–105
Constituent Assembly, 2, 3, 55
Constitution, 4, 25, 49
  Article 324 of, 51
  fundamental rights, 34
  protection of fundamental rights, 31–33
Council of States, 25

Decision-making process, 50
Declaration of emergency, 33–36
Defence Estates Office (DEO), 245
Delhi High Court, 29, 103, 130, 189, 203
Delhi Special Police Establishment (DSPE) Act, 1946, 121
Democracy, 41, 179
  landmark, 185–186
  quality and vibrancy, 22
Democratic republic, 2, 4
Department of Economic Affairs (DEA), 83
Department of Posts, 198
Department of Telecommunications (DoT), 38
Departmental Security Instructions, 181
Desai, Morarji, 81
Development Control Rules (1967), 253
Dhawan, R.K., 128
Director general of fire services, 125
Do What I Do, 86
DoPT, 166
DPC Act (1971), 10, 97, 102, 131, 109
DSPE Act, 131
DY Patil Sports Stadium, 207

Index • 275

Economic editors' conference, 107
Economic-policy reforms, 162
Election campaign, 1
Election commission, 51, 56, 60
   firm, objective and transparent, 69–73
   manifestos, 61
   observer, 69
   one nation, one election, 68–69
   petition, 59
   powers, 59
   press conference, 51
   symbols, 61
   three-member body, 58
   without fear or favour, 73–74
Electronic voting machines (EVMs), 52, 64, 269
Employees, Provident Fund Organisation (EPFO), 198
Enforcement Directorate (ED), 174
Essel Group, 207
Estimates Committee, 17
Executive record (ER) sheets, 146

Federal Bureau of Investigation (FBI), 137
Financial audit, 100
Financial committees
   Committee on Public Undertakings (COPU), 17
   Estimates Committee, 17
   Public Accounts Committee (PAC), 17
Financial Sector Legislative Reforms Commission (FSLRC), 84
First Information Reports (FIRs), 49
First-come-first-served (FCFS), 38
Foreign direct investment (FDI), 82
Freedom of Information Act, 2002, 180
Freedom of Information Bill, 183
Fundamental rights, 31

Gandhi, Indira, 44, 76, 81, 128, 181
Gandhi, Rajiv, 79, 121
Golden Quadrilateral (GQ) project, 175
Government Accounting Office (GAO), 99

Government of India Act of (1919), 2, 97
Government of India Act of (1935), 2
2G Services
   allotment procedure, 39
   spectrum allocation for, 38–39

Habeas Corpus case, 34
Haryana High Court, 44
Hawala (money-laundering) brokers, 167
Himachal Pradesh High Court, 131

ICC Board, 216
Imperial Civil Service (ICS), 139, 141
Income Tax Act, 1961, 191
Income tax authorities, 66
India Today, 201
Indian Administrative Service (IAS), 141
Indian bureaucracy, 161
Indian civil services, 139
Indian Cricket League (ICL), 207
Indian economy, 142
Indian Evidence Act, 1872, 182
Indian Olympic Association (IOA), 201
Indian Premier League (IPL), 207
Indira Gandhi International Airport, 200
Information technology (IT), 118
Interministerial screening committee, 39
International Atomic Energy Agency (IAEA), 115
International Cricket Council (ICC), 205
International Monetary Fund (IMF), 76.
International Olympic Committee (IOC), 202

Judicial appointments, 27
Justice
   Bhagwati, P.N., 34
   Dinakaran, P.D., 30
   Kalifulla, F.M.I. 213
   Khanna, H.R., 34
   Lodha, R.M, 209
   Rajan, C.S., 229
   Shah, A.P., 29
   Thakur T.S., 213
   Verma, J.S., 27

Kalaignar TV (P) limited, 129
Kalam, A.P.J. Abdul, 43
Kargil operation, 248
Kerala High Court, 227
Khan, Azam, 51
Kingdom of Travancore, 226
Koffee with Karan, 219
Krishnamachari (TTK), T.T., 80

Law Commission, 29, 69
Legal process, 38
Lodha Committee, 200, 210, 214
Lok Prahari, 66
Lokpal, 136, 177
Lokpal Act (2013), 133

Madras High Court, 30
Maharashtra Coastal Zone Management Authority (MCZMA), 252
Mahatma Gandhi National Rural Employment Guarantee Act (MGNREGA), 195
Maintenance of Internal Security Act (MISA), 34
Malhotra, V.K., 201
Marylebone Cricket Club, 205
Ministry of Defence (MoD), 135, 258
Ministry of Environment, Forest and Climate Change (MoEFCC), 244
Ministry of Finance, 79, 173
Ministry of Home Affairs (MHA), 51
Ministry of Personnel, Public Grievances and Pensions, 188
Model Code of Conduct (MCC), 61
Model Code violations, 72
Modi, Narendra, 1, 8, 52, 158
Moily, Veerappa, 106
Mukherjee, Pranab, 107
Mumbai Metropolitan Region Development Authority (MMRDA), 248, 249

National Judicial Appointments Commission (NJAC) Bill 2014, 27, 28
NDA government, 27

NJAC system, 31
Nani Palkhivala Memorial lecture, 192
National Alliance of People's Movements, 257
National auditor, 99
National Highways Authority of India (NHAI), 175
National Sports Development Code of India (NSDCI), 201–202
NITI Aayog, 159
No Objection Certificate (NOC), 254
Noddy books', 104
Non-banking financial companies (NBFCs), 85
None of the Above (NOTA) option, 53
Non-performing asset (NPA), 89

OBC quota, 62
Official Secrets Act (1923), 181, 184
Old boys' club, 30
Olympic Charter, 202
Opposition
  leader, 19
  parties, 20
  role, 19
Other Backward Classes (OBCs), 149

Panchayati Raj Institutions, 109
Parliament, 5, 12, 19, 23, 25
  efficacy, 22
  Lokpal, 22
  Members of the Parliament Local Area Development Scheme, 22–23
  privileges, 23
Parliamentary democracy, 109
Parliamentary Standing Committee, 177
Participatory process, 27
Patel, Ahmed, 71
Patel, Sardar Vallabhbhai, 140
Patkar, Medha, 257
Pawar, Sharad, 106
Performance audit, 100, 101
Permissible floor space index (FSI), 250
Planning Commission, 110
PM-led committee, 125

Policymaking, 38
Polling stations, 52
Prasad, Rajendra, 4
Prevention of Corruption Act (PCA), 258
Primary education programmes, 143
Prime Minister's Office (PMO), 126
PRS Legislative Research secretariat, 17
Public Accounts Committee (PAC), 17
Public auditors, 112
Public Grievances, Law and Justice, 68
Public Interest Disclosure and Protection of Informers (PIDPI) Resolution, 176
Public Interest Petitions (PILs), 28, 113, 212
Public-private partnership (PPP), 109
Punjab High Court, 44

Quality educational services, 145
Quraishi, S.Y., 56

Radhakrishnan, S., 99
Rafale fighter jet, 135
Rajasthan Pradesh Congress Committee, 65
Ramnath Goenka Memorial Lecture 2018, 50
Rangarajan, C., 78
Ranji and Duleep trophy tournaments, 206
Reddy, Y.V., 81
Regional parties, 144
Regulations of Audit & Accounts, 102
Representation of People Act, 1951, 191
Reserve Bank of India Governor, 75–91
    Jha, L.K., 81
    Patel, Urjit 91
    Rajan, Raghuram, 86
    Rangarajan, C., 78
    Reddy, Y.V., 81
    Subbarao, D., 83
Revenue Service officers, 161
Rights
    civil, 37
    fundamental, 37
    political, 37
Right to Information, 179
    Act, 110, 179, 180, 186, 190, 192, 194, 197
    activists, 193
    collaborative effort, 198
    proposed amendments, 197
    related matters, 194
    transparent and open government, 180
Rules Committee, 15
Rural health missions, 143
Rural panchayats, 180

Samajwadi Party (SP), 60
Scheduled Castes, (SCs), 149
Scheduled Tribes (STs), 149
Second Administrative Commission, 106
Securities and Exchange Board of India (SEBI), 85
Seshan, T.N., 58
Shah, Amit, 52
Shastri, Lal Bahadur, 163
Shekhar, Chandra, 77
Shourie, Arun, 135
Shri Mata Vaishno Devi Shrine Board, 238–239
Sikkim High Court, 30
Singh, Manmohan, 44, 105
Singh, V.P., 77
Sinha, Sachidananda, 2
Sinha, Yashwant, 135
Social-sector schemes, 104
    primary education, 104
    rural employment, 104
    rural health, 104
Special leave petitions (SLPs), 228
Sports administration
    integrity of administration, 218
    stricter code of conduct, 219
Sports Code, 203
Sree Padmanabhaswamy Temple Trust, 227
Srinivasan, N., 213
Standing Committee of Parliament on Personnel, 68

State Bank of India (SBI), 67, 174
Subbarao, D., 83
Sub-divisional magistrate (SDM), 147
Supreme Audit Institutions (SAIs), 99
Supreme Court, 25, 28, 30, 31, 36, 40, 43, 50, 51, 59, 60, 113, 116, 121, 126, 134, 160, 168, 171, 176, 194, 199, 206
  bedrock for good governance, 24
  court halls, 26
  design of the building, 26
  history of, 25
  interpretations of Article 21, 36
  judgement, 29
  judges of, 26
Swajaldhara scheme, 195

Tamil Nadu High Court, 254
Tamil Nadu Societies Registration Act, 1975, 205
Temple administration
  corrective measures, 238–243
  inadequacies in, 234–238
  legacy, 224–225
The Economic Times, 146
The Hindu Business Line, 24
The Prevention of Corruption (Amendment) Act, 2018, 172
The Times of India, 145
Tirumala Tirupati Devasthanams (TTD), 239

Travancore Royal Family, 225

UN Convention against Corruption, 171
Unified Access Services Licences (UASL), 106
Union of India, 103
Unitech group companies, 129
UPA government, 101, 185
Urban Development Department (UDD), 248
Urban panchayats, 180

Vajpayee, Atal Bihari, 183
Verdicts of the high courts, 25
Voter verifiable paper audit trail (VVPAT) machines, 52

Westminster model, 140
Whistle-blowers' resolution, 176
Who Moved My Interest Rate, 83
World Bank, 76, 78
World Intellectual Property Organization (WIPO), 115
Writ petition, 34

Yadav, Akhilesh 60
Yadav, Lalu Prasad, 71
Yadav, Mulayam Singh, 60

Zila Sainik Board, 249